PRAISE FOR

ONE DAY YOU'LL BURN

"A brilliant first novel. Joseph Schneider's contemporary writing evokes some of Hollywood's most classic crime stories, from *Chinatown* to *LA Confidential*."

—Dick Wolf, creator of *Law & Order*

"*One Day You'll Burn* is much more than just an intriguing Hollywood mystery, it's a captivating character study of a unique academic/historian-turned-police-detective who can't keep his deep intelligence from bubbling out—often to his own embarrassment and the reader's delight. Joseph Schneider has created a very appealing character whom readers will definitely want to see more of."

—Kenneth Johnson, bestselling author of *The Man of Legends*

"Schneider redefines the detective genre while giving us a history lesson of Hollywood, the town of dreams it was, and the nightmare it has become."

—Jim Hayman, executive producing director of *Judging Amy*

"An auspicious and engaging debut. Mr. Schneider conjures up an original protagonist in LAPD Homicide Detective Tully Jarsdel—and prestidigitates a thoroughly thrilling narrative ride through the mean streets and glittering boulevards of Los Angeles. The reader looks forward to many more Jarsdel mysteries in the coming years."

—Eric Overmyer, TV writer and producer

"*One Day You'll Burn* knocked me out. It's a riveting, richly-layered detective novel that satisfies and surprises on every single page. Joseph Schneider is a major new talent in the world of crime fiction."

—Lou Berney, Edgar Award–winning
author of *The Long and Faraway Gone*

"Tully Jarsdel joins the gumshoe greats in this whip-smart riff on sunbaked LA noir."

—David Stenn, TV writer and producer

ONE DAY YOU'LL BURN

A NOVEL

JOSEPH SCHNEIDER

Poisoned Pen
PRESS

Published by Poisoned Pen Press, an imprint of Sourcebooks
P.O. Box 4410, Naperville, Illinois 60567–4410
(630) 961-3900
sourcebooks.com

Library of Congress Cataloging-in-Publication data is on file with the publisher.

Printed and bound in the United States of America.
SB 10 9 8 7 6 5 4 3 2 1

For my folks, Diane Frolov and Andrew Schneider,
my first and greatest teachers.

1

Hollywood was at its worst in early morning. The gray light hit in all the wrong places, deepening the cracks in the facades and making the black, fossilized stains of chewing gum dotting the sidewalk stand out like leeches. Dawn made Hollywood into an after-hours club at closing time—the party over, the revelers departed or collapsed where they stood, the magic gone.

As the first pale hues spread across the desert sky, a coyote ventured down from Griffith Park. The wildfires that had torn through the hills that summer had scattered the rabbits and scrawny deer she depended on for food, and the coyote had been reduced to competing with raccoons over the contents of trash bins. But she wasn't strong enough to fight them—had already lost an eye—so now she was across Los Feliz and passing Pink Elephant Liquors, suddenly alive to the scent of meat, picking up speed, down Western Avenue and then left onto the boulevard, faster, until her instincts took over fully and sent her streaking along the sidewalk toward her claim.

A block east, Dustin Sparks—whom *Fangoria* magazine had once called the "Godfather of Gore"—stared in amazement at the human-shaped thing lying at his feet. Back in '87, he'd worked on a movie about a gym that had been built over an old prison graveyard.

When the local power plant melted down, the radiation cloud woke up the corpses, which broke through the gym's floor and began attacking the members. An aerobics instructor had tried hiding in the sauna, but the murderous dead had jammed the door and cranked the heat up all the way, roasting her in her spandex suit. It was a stupid idea—no way a sauna could get that hot—but he'd been happy to build the dummy of the burned woman. It hadn't been a tough job, technically speaking; he'd begun with a wire frame, wrapped it in foam, then covered the whole thing in strips of latex. Over the barbecue paint job, Sparks had finished with a coat of glossy sealant, which left it all with a wet, organic look.

What lay in front of him now so closely resembled that long-ago prop that, at first, he thought his brain must have finally started to misfire. It was only a matter of time, he knew, considering how many years he'd spent frying it. His arm began throbbing again—invisible, hot bands of iron cinching into his flesh. He gripped the limb, trying to massage the scrambled nerves back into dormancy, and glanced up at the sound of someone approaching.

But it wasn't a person. A coyote—eyes wide, tongue lolling—flashed across the cement and clamped its jaws onto the leg of the Halloween dummy. Sparks stumbled back, but the animal didn't seem to notice him.

At least I know I'm not seeing things, he thought. *Coyotes don't eat hallucinations.*

As Sparks watched, the coyote whipped its head from side to side until it separated a fist-sized chunk from the thigh, then lifted its nose skyward and snapped it down. It lunged forward again, burying its snout into the wound it had made, and repeated the process, trembling with what Sparks could only suppose was primal ecstasy.

The thing on the ground wasn't a dummy. It was too real—the way it lay, the proportions, the viscera, the detail. The smell, which was of roasted meat, not of rubber and paint. Sparks understood these things, but dimly.

Coyotes don't eat hallucinations, he thought again, *but they also don't eat Halloween props.*

The animal licked its chops and looked around. It noticed Sparks, lowered its head, and growled. Sparks backed away, stepping off the sidewalk and turning his ankle in the gutter. The pain was bright and urgent, but there was enough adrenaline kicking into his system to keep his attention on the ragged predator. Holding his palms out in a placating gesture, he shuffled in the direction of his apartment. He realized he was staring into the coyote's eyes and dropped his gaze. *You aren't supposed to look in their eyes, right? Or are you? Do they respect you more if you do?* He couldn't remember, just kept moving.

The coyote waited until Sparks was halfway down the block before returning to its meal. Sparks broke into a limping run, casting anxious glances over his shoulder until he turned onto his street.

———

The arrival of lights and siren scared off the coyote, and the responding officers, both veterans, had gaped thunderstruck at the remains for a full minute before radioing detectives and blocking off the scene. Paramedics arrived, even though the body was unquestionably that—a body—along with a truck from Fire Station 82, which was just down the street. They were soon joined by more police units and parking enforcement officers, and together, they extended and reinforced the barricade, which now stretched from Western to Harvard. The resulting snarl of traffic pressed against the surge of rush hour commuters filing onto the nearby 101 on-ramp. Like a clog in an artery, the crime scene caused other vital systems to fail. Los Feliz, Sunset, and even Santa Monica Boulevard began to slow. Franklin was at a dead stop in both directions, and Hollywood was a sea of stopped cars from La Brea to Hillhurst.

The corpse lay at the base of a pagoda in Thailand Plaza, a restaurant-market complex west of Little Armenia. The pagoda was tiled in mirrored glass and housed the statue of a deity. The serene, gilded god sat on a throne under an elaborate canopy. It was a local landmark and a sacred site for Thai immigrants, who decorated it daily with garlands of fresh flowers. A rickety table at the foot of the pagoda allowed devotees to leave offerings—mostly food and incense. And at some point in the dark, early morning hours, someone had violently upturned the table and dumped the body of the murdered man.

By the time Tully Jarsdel arrived, he had to navigate between vans from KTLA, FOX, and ABC7. Word of the homicide had reached local anchors, and anyone enjoying the morning news with a cup of coffee would get a rare treat to start their day.

Lieutenant Gavin met him at the perimeter, briefed him on what little they knew, and told him his partner was already on scene. "Been here a half hour already."

"Sorry," said Jarsdel. "Traffic from my direction was—"

Gavin waved him away. Jarsdel signed the perimeter log and stepped under the tape. He didn't need to ask where the body was. Against a backdrop of dingy sidewalk and the sun-faded peach walls of Thailand Plaza, the privacy tent was a stark white anomaly of clean, ordered lines, as conspicuous as an alien craft. Jarsdel headed toward it and the body inside, his heart rate kicking up. It was always that way with him—like those dreams where you're helplessly drawn toward a door you don't want to open.

He stopped, distracted by the sound of shouting. An argument had broken out in front of the barricade where Serrano met Hollywood Boulevard. A man with a camera had tried to duck under the tape, and a patrol officer was threatening him with arrest. Jarsdel recognized the cop as Will Haarmann. He'd recently transferred from Valley Bureau, where he'd been picked as the face of a *Los Angeles* magazine article titled "Yes, We Have the Hottest Cops in America." Jarsdel wouldn't have known about the piece or about Haarmann, except for some anonymous station comedian who'd cut it out and left it on his desk. It'd been accompanied by a Post-it reading *Tough break—maybe next time!*

Jarsdel watched, fascinated, as the man became more combative.

He shouted something to Haarmann about rights of the press, then stepped forward, lifting his camera to take a picture of the officer. Haarmann put his hand out to stop him, and the civilian swatted it aside. The cop went on autopilot then, quickly spinning the man around and bracing him against the squad car. The camera, which looked expensive, sailed a few feet and smashed into the curb with the sound of a champagne glass breaking. Within seconds, the citizen was shoved into the back seat of the car, his loud protests snuffed by the door closing behind him.

Jarsdel thought Haarmann had made a mistake. He hadn't used excessive force, but anyone with a phone could've caught the whole thing, and petty shit like that could antagonize potential witnesses. He made a mental note to avoid working with Haarmann on any sensitive assignments, then reluctantly crossed the last dozen yards to the tent.

The first thing he noticed was the smell. It wasn't the sour-sweet uppercut of putrefaction, nor was it the sickening copper of congealing blood. The smell emanating from the tent was so unusual under the circumstances that Jarsdel thought for a moment his mind was playing tricks on him.

He hadn't yet had breakfast, and the unmistakable odor of cooked meat gave his stomach a twinge. He pushed open the tent flaps and stepped inside.

———

It didn't look like any body he'd seen before, and in his five years on the force, Jarsdel had lost count of how many times he'd looked upon death.

The corpse was naked. Even its hair was gone, with only a few patches of ash to mark where it had once been. Heat had contorted the body so that it was more or less in a fetal position, what pathologists called the "pugilistic attitude"—elbows flexed, knees bent toward the chest, genitals tucked between the thighs. Patrol had radioed that they'd chased off a coyote, but to Jarsdel, it looked more like a shark had been at work. The right leg was ravaged.

Though the body lay on its side, the head was twisted upward, giving the investigators a clear view of the face, something Jarsdel found at once horrifying yet irresistible to look upon.

The lips had been cooked to nearly nothing, stretching back to expose a set of yellowed teeth, and gave the impression that the man was grinning up at them. The eyes were gone, either having popped in the heat or dried up like raisins and disappeared into the ocular cavities.

Jarsdel wanted to bend down so he could touch it and saw that Ipgreve, the medical examiner, had been smart enough to bring a gardener's pad to cushion his knees.

"Can I borrow that a sec?"

"Sure," said the ME, straightening up.

Jarsdel knelt and ran a gloved hand lightly along the cadaver's thigh. "Still warm. Like a cooked turkey."

"Yup."

"Evenly, though. No charring. Like it was baked slow in an oven."

Jarsdel wiped a sleeve across his forehead. It was getting hot inside the privacy tent, due in no small part to the hundred-fifty-pound slab of cooked human they were sharing the cramped space with. He shook his head as if to clear it. "What are we even looking at here?"

"It gets weirder," Ipgreve said. "Check out his fingers."

Jarsdel did. The hands were curled into fists, but the fingernails he could see were badly damaged—split or melted, others missing entirely. He could tell by their odd cant that a few of the fingers were broken. The victim had tried desperately to claw and beat his way out of whatever had held him prisoner.

The ME squatted beside Jarsdel. "And c'mere. Take a closer look at his face. See?"

Jarsdel had been trying his best not to—thought he might be seeing those gaping black eye sockets and that lipless, grinning mouth in his dreams. Steeling himself, he forced his attention to where Ipgreve was pointing. The burns had turned most of the cadaver's flesh a deep chestnut brown, but the skin on the forehead was splotchy with bruising.

"What do you make of it?" Jarsdel asked. "Knocked unconscious before...before whatever happened to him?"

"No, I don't think so. I'll show you why." Ipgreve lifted the cadaver's head. "If he'd been struck from the front, then we'd also likely have contrecoup bruising on the back or sides of his head, where he fell. But thanks to all the hair being burned off, we can see it's clean. No bruises." Ipgreve gently lowered the head back down. Using a pen, he indicated the discolorations. "We've got several major blows—at least four, probably five. We might even have a skull fracture with this one here. I think these injuries were sustained as he struggled to escape. Either that, or..."

"What?"

The ME made a face. "Might've done it on purpose—tried to knock himself out. Had to've hurt like hell, going out that way."

"Then that's your finding? He was baked alive?"

"You know it's too early for me to say conclusively, but considering the nature and extent of the perimortem trauma, I'd put it at the top of my list." Ipgreve shook his head, marveling at the thing in front of them. "Can't wait to get this guy on my table."

"I admire your enthusiasm."

"You have any idea just how odd this is?" Ipgreve went on. "Yes, it was an oven, but not an ordinary oven. Something big enough to hold a man, but with no element or open flame. The heat was immense but indirect. Not even a rack, else we'd have grill marks on the body. Rules out anything you'd have in a restaurant, even an industrial baking facility. And it's gonna play hell on your timeline. Won't see any of the usual determining factors, like putrefaction or rigor, and obviously, he won't cool like a normal body." As he spoke, Ipgreve inserted a probe below the sternum. He removed it, then fed a thermometer into the hole. The digital readout blinked.

"I'd say our fella here was exposed to temperatures in excess of four hundred fifty degrees. While it won't be any help with time of death, a liver spike'll at least give you an idea of when he got here."

The thermometer beeped, and Jarsdel leaned closer for a better look.

"138.3," said Ipgreve, writing down the temperature. "What'd it get down to last night? Upper fifties? So..." He made some calculations.

Jarsdel knew whatever Ipgreve came up with would be very rough. Time of death using body temperature was usually calculated by an algorithm based on Newton's law of cooling, and ideally incorporated two measurements taken hours apart. The fact that this body was outside, in an unstable temperature, further complicated the estimate.

"What time's it? Almost nine? Then he hasn't been here more than about three hours, give or take." Ipgreve concluded. "If it were much longer, he'd be at more like 120, maybe 110. Air temp has only risen to 66 degrees, which is still on the chilly side, and you also gotta figure the sidewalk would've acted as an effective cooling agent. But the body's still warm. This guy's bigger, of course, but what you said about it being like a turkey wasn't far off. Just imagine taking your bird out of the oven on Thanksgiving and putting it on the patio. Won't stay hot for long."

That wasn't good news. Jarsdel had checked: Thai Pavilion, the restaurant located above the market in Thailand Plaza, closed at midnight, with the last employees leaving around one thirty. That meant that not only would no one at the restaurant have seen anything, but foot traffic would've been practically nonexistent when the body had been dumped that morning.

Ipgreve was right—calculating a timeline would be next to impossible. There was no telling how long the body had been kept in its original location before being moved. They'd have to link it with a name before they'd be able to reconstruct the victim's final hours, and getting an ID was going to be tough. They couldn't exactly put a picture of him on television, and considering the damage to the hands, fingerprints would likely be useless. Forensic dentistry could confirm a victim's identity, but it didn't do any good unless you already had someone in mind. Their best bet was to coordinate with Missing Persons, then arrange for DNA matching once a likely subject emerged.

Jarsdel found his gaze drifting back to the body. He tried to imagine who the man had been and how he'd come to deserve—according to someone's peculiar logic—this particularly gruesome end.

"Gonna go look for my partner." Jarsdel stepped outside. The fresh air felt good. So did being away from that grinning thing in the tent.

He spotted Morales on the other side of the pagoda, conferring with an FSD tech. The man was his partner but also his superior, a fifteen-year veteran with the LAPD—six of those in homicide. He was squat, dark-skinned, with a broad face and almond eyes. His coarse black hair was swept back into a stiff, unmoving helmet with what Jarsdel supposed must have been handfuls of styling gel. When he walked—which he avoided doing as much as possible—he did so stiffly, like a retired athlete who'd amassed a catalogue of injuries.

Morales saw Jarsdel approaching. "Hey, Prof."

Jarsdel smiled without humor. "Morales."

"You know Carl? He's doing our sketch."

Jarsdel shook hands with the FSD tech, who went back to drawing on a tablet with a stylus. The tablet was a recent innovation. Crime scene sketches had always been done by hand, maybe with the aid of a compass to get the scale right. But technicians with the Forensic Science Division used software like ScenePD or Crime Zone, allowing them to create crisp and accurate diagrams of even the most complex scenes in a matter of minutes. And while all officers were trained in sketching a crime scene, the FSD's work was usually more impressive to a jury. Its members were considered impartial specialists, with no particular stake in the direction an investigation went. That made it harder for defense attorneys to cast them as bad guys out to get their clients.

Jarsdel moved closer and looked over Carl's shoulder as he drew. "I know we've got lots of reference pictures, but I want as much detail on the altar as you can get."

Morales looked dubious. "This pagoda thing? You think it's important?"

"I think it's the most startling aspect of the case."

"Startling, huh? Shit, Professor. You oughta take a look at the body, you want startling."

"I already have."

"But this is what gets your attention."

"The body was posed right in front of it. I doubt that was arbitrary."

Morales grunted and studied the pagoda more closely. The head that sprouted from the golden statue's neck featured four faces. "What do you think, Buddha? You an integral part of this investigation?"

Jarsdel glanced up from the tablet. "That's not Buddha. He's Phra Phrom, the Thai representation of Brahma."

"Who cares?"

"It's not a minor distinction. Brahma's a Hindu god, much older than the Buddha. Different cosmology and way of worship. If leaving the body here has any significance, it lies in the killer's understanding of who this god is."

"So what, like, people used to sacrifice to this guy?"

Jarsdel frowned. "No, not at all. That's what's so strange. Brahma's the god of creation, a force of good, of benevolence. He's never associated with harm or destruction."

"So maybe it's just a coincidence the body being here, and your theory's bullshit."

"Possible."

"Besides, I thought your specialty was dead white guys."

"My bachelor's was in political science. Had to take classes in cultural literacy." Morales rolled his eyes, but Jarsdel pretended he didn't notice. "It was a deeply cynical and profane thing to do, dumping the body here."

"Not to mention killing the guy in the first place, though, right?" Jarsdel looked around. "How are we doing on surveillance cameras?"

Morales pointed to the Thai market, which would normally be open by now. "Just one, but it's trained at an angle on the door. Wouldn'ta captured anything near the altar. Might be able to get something off a traffic camera, but it's a real long shot. Closest one is three blocks east, so unless the body was strapped to the roof of the car on its way over here, I don't know what we'd be looking for."

Carl, the FSD tech, turned his tablet so Jarsdel could get another look at it. "What do you think?" He rotated the image and zoomed in and out on various points of interest. He'd rendered the image without the privacy tent, of course, and had placed the body exactly as it lay at the foot of the altar.

Jarsdel nodded his approval. "Good. Send it to me."

Another FSD man approached the detectives. "I think we're done. Got a few cigarette butts, a flattened Coke can, some chewing gum. Scene's pretty clean. The pagoda's covered with prints, but it's a public street. Anyone could've left them. I'm ready to release the scene if you are."

Ipgreve emerged from the tent, peeling off his gloves. "We gotta get him indoors," he said. "You almost done?"

Morales turned to Jarsdel. "Well, Prof? We good here?"

"Why are you asking me?"

"Want you to take lead for now."

"Why?"

Morales paused, studying his partner. "Chain of command, rookie. Sounds like you got some specialized knowledge to offer on this case. Put some of that schooling to work." Morales gave him a saccharine smile. "Look on the bright side. When we find the asshole, you can be the one to make the report to the LT. Maybe even get another chevron on your jacket."

Jarsdel knew the inverse of the statement was equally true: that if they didn't find the asshole, he'd be the one having to justify their investigative strategy to Lieutenant Gavin. And Gavin didn't like him any more than Morales did.

A news copter had joined them, beating the air overhead and forcing those on the ground to shout to be heard. Jarsdel looked from his partner to the mass of people pressed against the barricade, then past them, to the crush of traffic struggling up Western. A street vendor was taking advantage of the captive potential customers, moving up and down the rows of cars with bags of cotton candy. Haarmann's prisoner was bucking back and forth in the patrol car. Seeing Jarsdel looking at him, the man stopped, shouted something, and stuck out his tongue. It was a child's gesture and felt strange and ugly coming from a grown man.

"You home, Professor?" asked Morales.

Jarsdel gave a slight nod, looking once more at the statue of Brahma, likely the only witness to the identity of the murderer. He'd sat the night in vigil, in quiet contemplation, tranquil as a frozen lake even while confronted with the astounding savagery visited upon one of his children. Jarsdel felt a sudden sense of shame on behalf of his species, who'd been given so much and repaid it all with blood and steel.

But look, he thought at the statue. *I care. I'm here, and I'll make it right. Just give us a little longer to push back the darkness.*

2

They watched as the ME slipped paper bags over the corpse's hands, preserving any potential physical evidence, and secured them at the wrists with rubber bands. "I'll try to raise his prints back at the lab, but don't hold your breath. He's pretty badly burned."

"You're tellin' me," said Morales. "Smells just like carnitas. I'll never be able to eat that shit again, goddamn it." He shook his head. "Just a week from my pension, and I get a case like this."

Ipgreve looked surprised. "You're pulling the pin? I thought you were sticking till mandatory retirement."

"It's a joke, man. You know, every cop movie ever."

"Oh. I get it."

"Can you get to him today?" Jarsdel asked, nodding at the body.

"Oh, for sure," said the ME. "I'll have to move some guys around, but I wanna hear what this one's gotta say." Ipgreve waved away a fat blowfly, which flew neatly into the John Doe's left eye socket.

A thought occurred to Jarsdel—at this time yesterday, whoever that was lying there had been up and walking around, alive, thinking about his lunch or his job or his girlfriend. Now he had a bluebottle dancing around in his skull.

Morales grimaced and bent to massage his leg.

"Knees again, huh?" said Ipgreve. "Pressure change with the

weather, probably. Those can be a bitch. You want something for that?"

"No. Thanks."

"Sure? Just because all my patients are dead doesn't mean I'm not a real doctor. I can write you a scrip."

"I'm fine."

Several more flies joined the cadaver as it was zipped into the body bag. Coroner's assistants began taking apart the privacy tent, and the John Doe was lifted onto a stretcher. As it was loaded into the back of a van bound for the LA morgue, the crowd gathered at the police barricade fell briefly silent.

Jarsdel checked his notes. "I want to talk to the caller, the special effects guy. Dustin Sparks."

"It's your show, man. Do what you think is best," said Morales.

"You wouldn't start there?"

"I'm following your lead, Prof."

Jarsdel sighed. "He's got an apartment on Winona. That's only a couple blocks away. Be easier to walk it in this traffic." He regretted the words as soon as they were out. "Sorry, I mean, we can—"

"You wanna walk, we can walk," Morales said.

The two men signed out at the crime scene log and headed east, brushing off a reporter from KCAL9 who'd camped out on the Harvard side of the barricade. They walked in silence, passing a junior market, an Armenian bakery, and a florist with a *going out of business* sign in the window.

Finally, Jarsdel spoke up. "Look, I want to be partners on this. You want me to take lead, that's fine, but it's important we work together. If you have better ideas than I do, I hope you'll share them with me."

Morales feigned puzzlement. "You mean it's possible I might have a better idea than you? Even without a PhD? That doesn't seem like—how'd you put it?—*a minor distinction*."

The walk was already taking its toll. Morales had developed a limp, and patches of sweat dampened his dress shirt.

"Hey," said Jarsdel. "I was reading the new book about the Bell

Gardens Butcher. I didn't know it was your idea to use low-angle sun photography to find the burial sites. That was clever."

"I have my moments."

"You know, that's one of the ways they find Roman walls. Or where they used to be, I mean. The earth is so compacted in those areas that even though the stones may be gone now, you can see the impressions they made. Take a picture in the morning and compare it to one taken at dusk, and they just pop out of the landscape."

Morales didn't respond. They turned on Winona and soon located the apartment building, a shabby, three-story box painted a fecal shade of tan. A metalwork sign bolted to the facade identified the complex as the Winona Chalet. There was no buzzer or directory, just a locked iron gate protecting the meager courtyard from trespassers. Jarsdel referred again to his notes, found Sparks's number, and dialed it on his cell. The voice that answered was wary.

"Yeah, who's this?"

"Mr. Sparks, this is Detective Jarsdel, LAPD. We're hoping you wouldn't mind coming downstairs and answering a few questions."

"If you're another reporter, I'm going to be supremely pissed off."

"No, sir, not reporters. My partner and I are here at the gate. We'd like to talk to you if we can."

Sparks hesitated. "Fine, whatever," he said and hung up.

Jarsdel and Morales waited only about a minute, but the strained silence made it seem longer. Morales had wrapped his stubby fingers around one of the gate's rods, taking some of the pressure off his legs, and was staring fixedly at the building's double glass doors. Jarsdel considered whether it might be time to request a transfer to a different partner, then dismissed the idea. Few other things would be more harmful to his career, especially considering a mere eleven months had passed since he'd been promoted to the Detective Bureau. If he complained he couldn't get along with Morales, he'd be branded a whiner, and no one would want to work with him.

The man who emerged from the building didn't look at all the way Jarsdel imagined he would. According to the 911 operator, Dustin

Sparks had been out for a jog when he'd come across the body, but this man was sallow and heavyset, wearing a faded Iron Maiden T-shirt, black cargo shorts, and unlaced combat boots. A greasy comb-over of dyed-black hair was doing its best to cover his bald crown.

"I need to see some ID," Sparks said as he approached.

Jarsdel and Morales held out their badges. Sparks scrutinized them. "Not sure I'm buying it. How do I know what those things are supposed to look like?"

Morales drew his jacket aside, letting Sparks see his .45 Kimber Classic. That seemed to convince him.

"I take it you've been having problems with the press," said Jarsdel.

"Uh, yeah, that's one way to put it. I don't know how you guys run your investigations or whatever, but now I've got reporters calling me every five seconds."

"I'm very sorry about that. High-profile cases like this tend to spring leaks. That's why it's so important for us to get to you before anyone else does and to advise you not to discuss what you saw with the media."

"Free country, though, right? 'Specially if they're paying."

"That's up to you, yes. But there may be aspects about what you witnessed that could help us catch the perpetrator. If we can withhold that information from the public, we'd have something we could use to identify a suspect."

"You keep calling me a witness," said Sparks, dragging his fingers through his hair. "But it's not like I actually saw anything happen. I probably wasn't even the first person to see the body—just unlucky enough to be the one to call it in to you guys."

"Mr. Sparks, would you mind if we continued this conversation in your apartment?"

"Why? We're fine here."

Jarsdel glanced at Morales, who looked amused, and turned back to Sparks. "It's kind of an awkward way to conduct an interview—you on one side of the gate, us on the other."

"I told you, there's nothing to interview about. I saw the body, I called you guys."

Jarsdel produced his notepad. "You mentioned to the 911 operator that you work as a special effects technician and that's how you were able to determine the body wasn't just some sort of Halloween dummy, is that right?"

"Yeah."

Jarsdel made a note. "And you were out taking a jog?"

"Yeah. So?"

Jarsdel made another note, this time deliberately writing for longer than the answer seemed to deserve. "About what time did you leave your apartment this morning?"

Sparks shifted from foot to foot. "Uh, I don't know. I don't usually check the clock before I go out to exercise."

"So you exercise regularly?"

"Sometimes."

"How many days a week you go jogging?"

"I don't know. Three or four."

"Always around the same time?"

"Usually just after I wake up."

"Good, so what time do you wake up?"

"I don't know. Different times, depending on the day."

Jarsdel watched him closely. The man's affect was flat; he stared straight ahead at the detectives, unblinking, and didn't use his hands or arms while he spoke. His answers, too, had no life in them, no animation in the eyes as the memories were recalled.

"On days you don't exercise, what time do you wake up?"

"I have no idea. Eight. Probably eight."

"But the 911 call came in at just after six, so today, you'd have had to leave pretty early, correct?"

Sparks shrugged, and Jarsdel made more notes.

"Describe your route."

"My route?"

"Your jogging route."

"My jogging route," Sparks repeated, as if the words were strange and new.

"In other words, did you come upon the body along the first or second half of your route?"

"On my way back."

"In your call, you mentioned a coyote. Was it already there, or—"

"No, it showed up right then, right as I was standing there."

"And about how long had you been out before you saw the body?"

"I don't know. Ten, fifteen minutes."

Jarsdel paused, fixing Sparks with a look of weary skepticism. He had no reason to single out that particular answer for scrutiny; his aim was to give the man a long, uncomfortable gap he'd be compelled to fill with more words. Words were bindings, sure as a set of irons, but ones provided by the subjects themselves. Jarsdel sometimes even imagined them springing from the speakers' mouths and wrapping around their bodies. The point was to get as many words said as possible. Truth or lies didn't matter—just get them said and get the story locked down. The more words, the tighter and more numerous the bonds.

Sparks was uneasy. "What? I mean I'm not totally sure about the time. It was early."

"Did you approach the body from the east or west?"

"I'm not good with those kinds of things."

"Did you see the body while going toward Thailand Plaza from the direction of Winona or coming the other way, from Western Avenue?"

"Oh. From Western."

"From the north or south side of the street?"

"I just told you, I'm not—"

"Did you see the body from across the street, then go over to take a closer look, or were you already on the same side of the street the body was on?"

"Oh. Same side of the street."

"North side," murmured Jarsdel, making another note. "And what were you wearing at the time?"

"Wearing? Why do you care?"

"In case we get a witness who identifies you as having been standing near the body, we want to be able to rule you out as a suspect."

"Okay, I was wearing this, what I'm wearing now."

"You go jogging in combat boots?"

"I...uh...changed my shoes."

"But the rest is exactly what you had on?"

"Yeah."

"You didn't take a shower when you got home?"

"No, man, it's like I said—I been trying to keep away from reporters all morning. Haven't had two seconds to myself."

Jarsdel made more notes.

"Are we almost done?" asked Sparks.

"Almost. Out of curiosity, have I seen any movies you've worked on?"

Sparks sighed. "I don't know, have you?"

"I meant can you name a few for me?"

"All the stuff I do these days is straight to streaming. Nothing you've heard of. Promise."

Jarsdel smiled. "Okay. Let's get back to your route. I'm still confused—you leave here, then what? Take me through it."

Sparks turned to Morales. "Christ, I thought you guys just wanted to ask a couple questions. How much longer's this gonna take?"

Morales didn't answer, and Jarsdel jumped back in. "Where do you usually go?"

"I don't know, man. I just go. I don't think about it. Why is this important?"

"You don't remember which way you went this morning? How about when you came out this gate? Did you make a right or a left?"

"A right."

"A right. And when you got to Hollywood Boulevard—a right or a left?"

"Another right."

"Another right," Jarsdel repeated. "And for how long? When did you turn off?"

"I don't know."

"Because otherwise, you would've seen the body much sooner. You would've run into it on the first half of your run, not on the second half, right?"

"I guess."

"So?"

"So *what*, man?"

"What was your next move? Where did you go so you didn't see the body until you were heading back? Side streets? Help me out."

"You're twisting my words around."

Jarsdel creased his brow. "I'm sorry. How am I doing that?"

"Look, I'm not a thousand percent positive exactly when I saw the body, okay? Maybe I saw it on the first half and then called it in on my way back."

"You saw a dead body and decided to finish your jog before calling it in?"

"Maybe. I don't know."

Morales spoke for the first time. "It's not what my partner would call 'a minor distinction.'"

"Jesus." Sparks rubbed his face with both hands, shaking his head.

Jarsdel leaned closer and spoke in a low, almost soothing voice. "Is it maybe possible you weren't out jogging?"

Sparks continued shaking his head, then, shoulders slumped, stopped to look up at his apartment building. Jarsdel was pretty sure he was hoping he could somehow teleport back inside or wind back the clock to before he'd decided to venture out that morning.

"I don't wanna talk anymore."

"Listen," said Jarsdel in the same coaxing tone. "We're homicide detectives. Long as your morning errands didn't include killing someone, it's of no interest to us whatsoever."

"This is none of my business anymore," said Sparks. "I did my part."

"I'll tell you something," Morales said. "You'd be doing a good thing, helping us find out who did this. I honestly don't care what you got going on. What is it? Girls? Narcotics?" Sparks flinched a little, and Morales pressed on. "Okay, so let's say you got a habit. You're out on a buy, you see something. Why you're there doesn't matter. What matters is you're there, and you can help us. Obviously you care, or you wouldn't have called it in. That gives you some major points with me. That other shit? Forget it. Let's talk about what you saw."

Jarsdel gave the last little push. "There's no way you're gonna get in trouble talking to us. We're after people who commit murder. You talk to us, and you become one of the good guys."

Sparks nodded, his eyes focused on a spot somewhere between the two detectives. "I got problems. Got cut rigging this chainsaw effect a few years ago..." He let them see his right forearm, where a network of pink scars dimpled the pale flesh. "A fucking chainsaw. Guys were supposed to take the teeth out of it, right? Stupid, so goddamned stupid. So now I'm addicted to Oxy." He shrugged. "If I don't take 'em, I can't use the arm at all. Gotta use the arm to work, you know? That's my situation. Anyway, I'm in real bad pain early this morning. Wakes me up, covered in sweat. I call my guy, and he meets me over by the Metro station."

Jarsdel scribbled furiously. "Corner of Hollywood and Western?"

"That's the one."

"And what time are you talking about here?"

"I'd say about five, maybe quarter after."

Jarsdel and Morales exchanged a look. That fit with their timeline. "You don't believe me?" asked Sparks.

"No, that's not it at all," said Jarsdel. "What'd you see?"

"I'm headed back toward the apartment, and this van pulls up 'bout a hundred feet away. Tires screeching and everything. Scared the hell out of me—thought they gotta either be cops or some dudes after my Oxy, so I duck into a doorway to hide. But I don't hear any shouting or even talking or anything, and then there's this racket, like they're moving something, so I peek out to take a look. I see a guy jump back into the van and take off."

"Would you be able to identify him?"

"No way. Split second."

"Was he white? Black?"

"White, I think." He added, before Jarsdel could ask, "Wearing dark clothes. Didn't get a good look at his face, but he was a young guy. You could tell by the way he moved."

"Any facial hair?"

"I'm telling you I barely saw him."

"He drive away in your direction?"

"No. Pulled a U-turn."

"Can you describe the van?"

"Either white or cream-colored, I couldn't tell."

"Any idea on the make or the year?"

"I don't know a whole lot about cars, but I can tell you it was a Dodge Ram. Had the chrome ram's head thing on the hood."

"Anything else? Dents or scrapes? Maybe a cracked window?"

"Not that I saw."

"Just a plain white van? No logos or anything?"

"Nope."

"What about a license plate? You get any of it?"

"No."

Jarsdel put away his notepad. "Why'd you wait so long to report it?"

"I don't know," said Sparks. "Guess I didn't want to get busted for the whole Oxy thing. Told myself I'd call if no one else did. Then it's getting up to six o'clock, and I still don't hear any sirens. Couldn't believe it. Dead guy right in the middle of the sidewalk. And then I'm thinking about that coyote and all the damage it's doing, and I figured I should let you guys know." He shook his head at the memory. "I'll never forget that shit. I mean, I've got a strong stomach, but whatever those guys did to him..." His eyes widened in alarm. "Hey, wait a second. What if someone comes after me now I talked to you?"

"You don't have to worry about that," said Jarsdel. "Your identity will be kept confidential."

"Confidential? What about all those reporters?"

"All anyone knows is you're the one who called it in. Everything you've just said stays between us."

Despite Jarsdel's assurances, Sparks grew pale. He leaned on the gate with both hands. "I'm so fucking stupid. So stupid. I'm a dead man."

"Mr. Sparks," said Morales. "You're completely safe, okay? We've never had any of our witnesses harassed in any way."

Jarsdel knew that wasn't true, but he also saw the necessity of calming Sparks down. They might want to talk to him again, maybe even subpoena him. "You have my word," said Jarsdel. "Your name will be kept out of it."

Sparks wasn't mollified. "Can I go?"

"Yes, sir. And thank you." He handed Sparks his card. "If you think of anything else, no matter how small, please get in touch. You've been a huge help."

Sparks waved his hand as if clearing away a foul smell, then slouched back into the building.

"Okay, Prof," said Morales. "What's next?"

"That was good, right?" said Jarsdel. "I mean, the way we played off each other. It felt pretty natural."

"Uh-huh." Morales's lips twitched. "What's next?"

"I guess maybe have the red-light camera on Wilton checked for any traffic infractions this morning between four and seven. Follow up on anything resembling a van."

"What if he didn't run the light? Then what?"

"Some of those cameras are also equipped with radar. Woulda got him if he was speeding."

"Not bad," said Morales. "But it won't work."

"Why not?"

"Disconnected." He smiled at Jarsdel's confusion. "You don't keep up with local politics much, do you? Traffic cameras being phased out. Cost more to run than they bring in. They'll hang on to the carpool and HOV cameras, but that red-light shit? Just decoration before somebody takes 'em down."

"Are you sure? I talked to a West Hollywood sheriff's deputy a couple weeks ago, and he said—"

"Yeah, that's WeHo. WeHo's not in our jurisdiction. I'm talking about the contract between LAPD and the camera company, and that expired six weeks ago. They still got a few operational in Santa Monica and Beverly Hills and WeHo, but who cares? Doesn't do us any good."

Jarsdel considered for a moment. "What about Caltrans cameras? You know, the ones where you can watch the live feeds to see how backed up the freeways are?"

But Morales was already shaking his head. "They don't record anything, just give real-time info on traffic conditions and accidents."

Jarsdel felt himself growing frustrated. "Okay, any time you want to put an idea out there, feel free."

Morales shrugged. "What can we do? Nothing to canvass—just a bunch of businesses, and they were all closed. We got a witness, but all he can tell us is he saw a van with maybe a white dude in it. We won't know anything new till Ipgreve gets back to us on the autopsy. You oughta chill out, Professor." Morales turned and began heading back down Winona.

Jarsdel caught up with him easily. "I really wish you'd stop calling me that."

"You do, huh?"

"Yes, I do."

"Not up to me, man. S'what everybody calls you. Even Gavin."

Jarsdel hadn't known that, and the news stung. If even his commanding officer didn't take him seriously, probably no one else did either. He considered defending himself to Morales, pointing out that he'd gone through the same academy, had the same training, endured the same grueling years of patrol duty before passing the detective's exam—that who he'd been before getting his badge didn't matter and said nothing about his worth as a police officer.

But even in his head, it sounded ridiculous. Of course it mattered, especially to those who'd given over their lives—and, with guys like Morales, literally their limbs—to the force. Jarsdel knew that the more he insisted he be accepted, the more he'd sound like a poseur, a dilettante. The best thing to do was work hard and close cases.

And that's exactly why Morales wants you to take lead on this, he thought. *Because it's a loser, and he knows it.*

Jarsdel hoped that wasn't true, but even if it was, he also had a feeling that the case's very strangeness might be the key to its own unraveling. He saw his investigations as huge, tangled knots of fiber. Most other cops he knew used the jigsaw puzzle analogy, working at accumulating evidence piece by piece until a picture emerged. But for Jarsdel, it was the opposite. He wasn't interested in collecting but in eliminating, tugging here and there until he found the golden thread, the one that—when painstakingly teased from the rest—could unwind everything. Jarsdel believed this approach produced the cleanest results, freeing the investigator from the sway of preconceptions and biases, the dizzying noise that could obscure clear thinking as sure as if it had presence and weight.

They turned right onto Hollywood, following Sparks's earlier route, and made their way back toward the police barricade. Traffic cops were doing their best to funnel cars onto side streets, but the 1920s-era grids couldn't accommodate the onslaught of twenty-first-century traffic. Jarsdel's head began to ache from the miasma of car exhaust, the din of braying horns, and the ever-present, ear-rattling pulse of the news helicopters.

There was no stillness in the city. It was a constant, churning stew of action and reaction, as if the people's drives and passions were in a way linked to the volatile, unquiet land itself. The land that, carried along the scar of the San Andreas fault, moved inexorably north-ward up the continental plate, its passage marked by cataclysmic bursts of seismic energy. There was no changing its violent destiny. It was already shaped and mapped out by the tremendous forces at work below the surface. Los Angeles would one day become an

Alaskan suburb, appearing off the coast of Anchorage in about seventy-five million years. Not that long, geologically speaking.

But none of that mattered to Jarsdel. He understood impermanence, understood it better than most people ever could, holding in his mind the histories of entire civilizations from Mesopotamia to Byzantium—was an expert, so to speak, on the triumph of entropy, corruption, and rot. He also believed impermanence was a psychological trap, a facile excuse not to care. And he also knew that, despite the insistence of cynics and doomsayers, things were getting better. Jarsdel had nearly the whole of recorded human history to draw on and could prove that somehow, incredibly and despite impermanence, the consciousness of his species was evolving. As the gross world was buffeted and rent by whim or disaster, a collective inner world of love and compassion was growing. Its architecture was incomplete, but it was being sustained and augmented moment by moment, year by year. Victories could not be measured by mere physical structures. Even the most vaunted—the Acropolis, Chichen Itza—would one day be worn down to little more than sand castles. No, victories could only be measured by the human heart, whose capacity was boundless. The poor, tortured body that had mobilized hundreds and gridlocked thousands more represented a last gasp, a recidivist spasm in an old and dying way of life.

As he ducked into his car, he caught another glimpse of Brahma and smiled. There was some stillness in the city after all. *I'm here to make it right*, he thought, repeating his promise. *To be among those who renew the world.*

3

LAPD's Hollywood Division was headquartered in a station just south of Sunset, about two miles from the morning's crime scene. It was a drab, tired-looking building, an exemplar of mid-1960s civic architecture, but not without its peculiar charms. The squad room, otherwise as functional and joyless as that of any big-city police department, proudly displayed a few movie posters along with its forest of bulletins and official placards. And instead of a fountain or memorial wall as a tribute to fallen officers, the station had its own Walk of Fame—the names of the dead captured in a row of coral terrazzo stars laid into the cement out front.

Still, despite its unassuming appearance, Hollywood Station was indispensable to the neighborhood. From the slopes of Mount Olympus, an enclave of multimillion-dollar homes, to the tattoo parlors and S&M dungeons of Melrose, it served as the responsible adult in the room, a stern but fair referee in the endless, often fatal contact sport of urban survival. There was no such thing as a typical call in Hollywood. Officers might begin a shift by taking a complaint from an entertainment lawyer whose wine cellar had been burgled and finish the day with a trio of MS-13 gangsters who, upon discovering a homeless man who'd castrated himself, proceeded to kick him to death in a fit of disgust.

The division operated within the jurisdiction of the vast West Bureau, whose boundaries stretched all the way to the Pacific Ocean and included nearly a million souls. Tully Jarsdel owed his early promotion not to his superiors at Hollywood Station but to the head of West Bureau, Deputy Chief Cynthia Comsky.

As a rookie, Comsky had worked a foot patrol in Hollywood during the bad years, the eighties and early nineties, when murder rates spiked to levels unseen in Los Angeles since it had been a frontier oil town. She'd served as assistant watch commander during the riots, keeping a clear head amid the madness, and her deployment strategies had been instrumental in stemming the tide of destruction. She rose to patrol captain by 2000 and division commander by 2005. By that time, homicides were on the decline, falling eventually to record lows.

But the slowdown in violent crime had unforeseen consequences for the division. Hollywood Homicide, which had for decades been among the city's most effective arms of law enforcement, was dissolved, the eight seasoned detectives reassigned. Most were absorbed by Olympic Division, where West Bureau's murder investigations were consolidated. The rest transferred downtown to the elite Robbery-Homicide Division—RHD—which was assigned the city's highest-profile cases.

The ceasefire didn't last. Crimes against persons were back up again—not to the dizzying heights they had reached during the bad years, but enough to make the police commission and the city council take notice. It had been Deputy Chief Comsky's idea to revive Hollywood Homicide, but as with any decent sequel, she proposed a neat little twist.

Comsky envisioned the new Hollywood Homicide—known as "HH2" around the station—as a proving ground for the highest-scoring rookies in the department. These green but undeniably brilliant detectives possessed a specialized education that, she felt sure, could be used to catch killers. Lucky candidates would be offered a once-in-a-lifetime promotion—swept to the front of the line, seniority be damned, straight to Homicide. There, they'd be paired with veteran murder cops who'd mentor and guide them in the art of field investigation.

The city council had gone for the idea but with conditions. First, the proposed homicide squad would have four members, not eight. Second, Lieutenant Bruce Gavin would be appointed as HH2's immediate supervisor. Gavin was a council favorite, a man who thrived amid the triplicate forms and waxed linoleum halls of bureaucracy. His new role appeared to some as a conflict of interest: make Comsky's team shine, maintaining a stellar closure rate and sending the message that committing murder in Hollywood was a losing proposition. That would in turn knock local stats back down to where they'd been a decade earlier. However, low numbers also meant the division's homicide desk would likely again be rendered obsolete.

But Jarsdel knew it was a win-win for Gavin. If stats fell, he'd earn the gratitude of both the city council and Comsky herself, who was all but guaranteed to become the next chief of the LAPD. Getting on her good side would bump him up the ladder, probably to division commander. And if HH2 failed and stats remained high, well, the whole thing was Comsky's idea, not his. He'd still be the council's man, and they'd all agree he had done his best.

Comsky's project had been a gamble, but so far, it was paying off. Jarsdel's counterpart at HH2 was Detective Kay Barnhardt, who, before she put on a uniform, had been a practicing clinical psychologist. Gavin had matched Barnhardt with Detective Abe Rutenberg, who'd initially taken the pairing as an insult, forcing his new partner to endure weeks of tired psychotherapy jokes. But several closed cases later, Rutenberg freely acknowledged that Barnhardt's insights had helped put away the bad guys. HH2 on the whole, in fact, had made arrests in nearly seventy percent of its cases. Of those that'd gone to trial, all had resulted in convictions.

Gavin embraced the team's success, took credit for it, in fact, despite it being what he claimed was a departmental albatross, a Barnumesque gimmick that would have hobbled the career of a lesser man than he. Gavin had said as much during a long and ill-advised screed over a round of drinks at the Bigfoot Lodge. Everything about HH2 stank, from its doctoral detectives to its conspicuous formation just ahead of a mayoral race that would open a spot at the top of the LAPD. And though he'd never say it to her face, he thought Comsky was using a temporary spike in homicides to put on nothing more than a big show. Jarsdel and Barnhardt weren't real cops, just actors sent in to soften the image of the police, making it more palatable for Hollywood intellectuals and leftist political donors. He would've almost admired the audacity of Comsky's charade if he hadn't had to participate in it.

And who was this Jarsdel guy, anyway? Who gave a shit about his scores on the detective's exam? He didn't look right. Didn't look the way a cop should. He was tall enough, sure—six foot two, maybe even six three—but unimpressive, lanky and soft. And he had those round, wire-rimmed glasses and that schoolboy haircut and those rose-pink cheeks, like he'd just had his first kiss. What murder suspect would ever take him seriously?

"And you know what the worst part of all this is?" Here he'd stabbed a meaty finger into the tabletop and glared across at his cop buddies. "To be back in fucking Hollywood. Back in the shit. I was with you guys in the PAB, don't forget that. You know how many years it took me to get there? Eighth floor. Could throw a rock out my window and hit city hall. And *you*"—he had pointed at Media Relations Commander Sam Schirru—"you greasy little asshole, you're in my old office now, right? Well, don't get too comfy. I'll be back before you know it. Fuck it, no—keep the office. I'll take the floor above you."

The PAB—Police Administration Building—was LAPD's gleaming downtown headquarters at 100 West First Street. Tall, imposing, and flush with funding, it ranked with the likes of London's Curtis Green Building and Hong Kong's 1 Arsenal Street as one of the world's great metropolitan police stations—a monument to order and sanity. Under the chief of police's direct supervision, both sworn and civilian personnel went about their work with quiet, humorless efficiency. You wouldn't find any movie posters or Walk of Fame stars at the PAB.

As HH2's supervisor, Gavin ran his detectives with all the inspirational flair of a claims adjuster. Every decision was carefully weighed and assessed until two unspoken rules emerged into practice—anything that approached the bounds of academy doctrine was heresy, and it was better to make no moves at all than risk making a wrong one. Gavin was making it clear he was simply Comsky's representative. If the unit tanked or fell into scandal, it wouldn't be because Lieutenant Bruce Gavin had gotten creative.

Now, as Gavin sat across from Jarsdel and Morales, he leaned back in his chair—the only souvenir from his office at the PAB—and held up a hand.

"Stop, stop."

"Sir?" asked Jarsdel.

"Go back and tell me that last part again."

"I was just saying that our witness doesn't think he'll be able to make a positive ID."

"No, before that."

"That Mr. Sparks is addicted to Oxy?"

Gavin nodded. "There you go. That's all you need that matters. ID or no ID, he's an addict. You wouldn't need a Century City hotshot attorney to blow apart his testimony, so he's effectively off the table. Forget it. What else?"

"We'll check with auto theft for any Dodge vans reported stolen, but that's all we have for now."

Gavin pinched the bridge of his nose. "So a guy was cooked, then dumped right in the middle of Hollywood Boulevard, and all you've got is one unreliable witness who, in the end, may not have seen anything at all. Ever think of that? Could've just been trying to get rid of you."

Jarsdel glanced at Morales, but finding no help there, he faced his lieutenant. "Dr. Ipgreve said he could squeeze our DB in this afternoon. We'll know more then."

"Okay, that's a big no-no, Detective. We don't say 'DB' anymore. *Big* no-no. You wanna talk like a cop from TV, then be a cop on TV. But if a grieving family or the media gets hold of you calling a dead body a DB, they're going to think you're insensitive. And if they think you're insensitive, then the whole LAPD's insensitive. Like it or not, you represent us out there. So it's 'victim' or 'decedent.' *Jesus.*"

"I apologize, sir."

"And unless there's a note inside the guy's stomach telling us who did it, I can't imagine there'll be anything of evidentiary value. Guy's practically a mummy. DNA'll be compromised, and any material we may get off the body could just as easily have come from the street." He turned to Morales. "What do you think?"

Morales shrugged. "Pretty much the waiting game. Best bet is sit on Missing Persons, see what comes in. Guy hasn't been dead long, so anyone who might miss him is probably just starting to get worried. I'm thinking we either get something in the next couple days or we get nothing at all."

Gavin nodded and pointed at Jarsdel. "Twice-daily progress reports until it's solved. We don't know who the victim is, but the nature of the homicide has spooked a lot of people. I also want you to investigate possible ties to organized crime. I'm sure there's a Thai mafia or something, so let's look into how they kill their victims. I can get you a translator if you need one."

Jarsdel opened his mouth to speak, then hesitated.

"Spit it out," said Gavin.

"There is a Thai mafia," said Jarsdel. "The Chao Pho—but they have no appreciable presence in the United States."

"Jesus Christ," Gavin murmured.

"Encyclopedia Brown over here," said Morales.

"Look," said Gavin, "until you come up with something better, I'd love for you to explain who besides the mob is gonna take the trouble to do something like this. It takes time, manpower, privacy."

"I agree," said Jarsdel.

"I'm touched."

"But I've never heard of anyone doing this before. Not even the bosses back in Thailand."

"That's not really gonna be the thing, though, right? I mean, just because you haven't *heard* of something doesn't mean we all—*boom*—slam on our brakes and wait for you to enlighten us." He turned to Morales. "Anything you need from me?"

"Nope. We're good."

"That's what I like to hear."

They walked out of Gavin's office. "Makin' friends all over the place," said Morales.

Jarsdel ignored him and went to his desk, where he unclipped his phone and brought up the new Sparks audio file. Like many detectives, Jarsdel recorded all his field interviews. His preferred method was a wireless microphone clipped to his tie. The mic, when paired with his phone, could be activated discretely and without spooking the subject. In every cop movie or TV show, the police always asked permission to record a conversation, so Jarsdel had been surprised when, as a cadet, he learned that hardly happened in real life. The law was clear—a citizen had no expectation of privacy from a police officer; anyone could be recorded, whether or not they knew it was happening.

Jarsdel emailed the file to himself and opened it on his computer. He created a new folder on his desktop, naming it "Brahma John Doe," and dropped in the track. Then, plugging in a set of earbuds, Jarsdel listened to the interview again. It was only about four minutes long, and he realized that Morales and Gavin were right. There was hardly anything on it that could help. A white van. One man, no description.

He decided to follow up anyway, doing a quick search for any Dodge Ram vans reported stolen in LA County in the last few weeks. He came up with two, but neither were white, and one had already been recovered. The other served as a bus for transporting elderly congregants to Christ the Light in Rampart. It was described as purple, with the church's name stenciled on both the driver's and passenger's sides. Jarsdel supposed the thieves could have repainted the van, but then he noticed the year of manufacture was listed as 1986. A check of Dodge models revealed that the ram's head logo wasn't introduced until the '90s, and Dustin Sparks had made special mention of having seen it in his statement. That ruled out the church van definitively, and Jarsdel was back to where he started.

He checked his email's inbox and found a zip file from FSD. He clicked on it and found himself staring at a thumbnail mosaic of hundreds of that morning's crime scene photos. He began taking a virtual tour of the scene, first studying the pagoda, then moving on to the body itself—the brutalized husk of a man, the profane offering at the feet of the divine. Without the noise of the street and the helicopters above, it was easier to focus, but that didn't make the answers come any more readily.

His phone rang, and he picked it up. "Jarsdel, Homicide."

"Detective, this is Ken Peyser."

"Oh. Yes, Councilman. What can I do for you?"

"I'm here with Mr. Chakrii Parnpradub, president of the Thai Association of Southern California. Mr. Parnpradub is understandably concerned about what happened this morning, and I've assured him you're taking every available measure to keep the community safe."

Jarsdel wasn't sure what to say. Was that a question? "Of course," he said.

"Do we know the ethnicity of the victim?"

"Not yet, but we'll have more information this afternoon."

"I don't think I need to impress upon you the seriousness of the situation. Several of my constituents view the crime as an attack against Thai culture—the desecration of the, you know, the statue thing. If the victim also turns out to be Thai, we could be talking about a hate crime."

"A hate crime?"

"Well, it certainly begs the question, doesn't it?" asked Peyser. "A guy's burned alive and—"

"Right, yes. We'll explore all possible angles."

"That sounds like a line, Detective."

"A line?"

"Like something you'd tell the press."

Jarsdel imagined Peyser grandstanding on the other end of the phone, eager to prove his relationship to the Thai community extended beyond the occasional order of pad see ew. Finally, Jarsdel said, "I'm not trying to be evasive. But we're in the earliest stages, and I don't have anything concrete yet."

"I trust you'll keep me informed."

"Yes, sir."

"Good. Talk soon."

A shout went up from the direction of the station's holding area, and three uniformed officers charged through the office, hands braced against their sidearms. They disappeared around the corner, and there was more shouting.

"Watch him! Watch him!" cried one of the officers.

"Stop resisting!" yelled another. There was the sound of bodies scrabbling against one another and the urgent squeak of shoe rubber on linoleum. Underneath it all, someone was growling in the deep baritone of an idling chainsaw.

"Do not even *try* to fucking bite me."

"Get his head! Get his head!"

The growling grew strained and desperate, a sound closer to panic than rage.

Jarsdel glanced across at Morales, whose desk pressed up against his own. The detective was on the phone, a finger jammed in his other ear to block out the noise. Besides that, he showed no sign of being bothered by the scuffle. Even after years of law-enforcement experience, Jarsdel still couldn't help his heart hammering, couldn't help the steely finger of adrenaline in his guts whenever violence erupted. The most he could do was pretend he was unaffected, cool. He did so now, fixing his expression into something he hoped resembled boredom as Morales hung up.

"No adult males reported missing within the last forty-eight hours," he said to Jarsdel. "Last one to disappear was Ghost Rider, and that was five days ago."

"What? Ghost what?"

"Ghost Rider. You know, one of those street performers dressed up like a superhero. Wears a motorcycle jacket, head is just a skull. You had a ten-year-old, you'd know who he is. Anyway, it's like I told the LT. We're gonna have to wait."

One of the officers ordered the rest to stand clear. "Get back! I'm gonna hit him!"

There was a pop, then a ticking sound, like the igniter on a gas stove but faster. A man howled.

"You with me, Prof?" asked Morales.

"Yeah, I'm just thinking," said Jarsdel. "What about getting a forensic artist to come up with a rendering—recreate what he would've looked like before he died?"

"Good luck getting that approved. You're talking a couple thousand bucks, easy. Unless your vic is someone special, there's no way Gavin'll spring for it."

Jarsdel was baffled. "If we knew who the victim was, I wouldn't need a composite."

Morales shrugged. "Catch-22, I guess."

A groan came from the corridor. "Gimme your arm! Gimme your fucking arm now!"

"I'm gonna hit him again! Stand clear!"

More rapid ticking, then a new voice wailing, "Oh Jesus! Jesus, Jesus, Jesus, I'm sorry...I'm *sorry!*"

"Gimme your arm!"

"I will, oh Jesus, I will. I'm *sorry.*" There followed a series of pathetic, hitching sobs.

"He's done. Get him up," someone said.

The sobs continued. "Oh *gawd*, I'm sorry. I'm sorry..."

"Pick up your feet."

"I'm *sorry.*"

"Fuck it. Here we go."

The man continued to cry, but the sound grew fainter as he was dragged away. A door latched shut, cutting off his voice entirely. They had dumped him in a cell for noncompliant arrestees. By the time he sobered up, he'd be facing a whole new set of charges on top of what he'd already been brought in for.

"Look," said Morales. "You want my advice? You're overthinking this. You've had this case, what, three, four hours, and you want it solved? Typical rookie bullshit. This ain't TV. Things don't happen that fast."

Jarsdel pointed at his phone. "That was Councilman Peyser."

Morales flicked a dismissive hand. "So what? He knows what's up. Just gotta put on a show for the voters."

Jarsdel looked up as two officers emerged from the hallway, faces red from exertion. He noticed one of them was missing the Taser from his belt. "Motherfucker," he said. "Now I gotta fill out all that shit."

Morales grunted in sympathy. Any use of force was meticulously documented. Even the Taser would be examined, a microchip inside the grip analyzed to reveal exactly how many jolts the officer had administered. He'd have to explain, if called upon in court, why he'd felt it necessary to shock the prisoner a second time. Like all LAPD, Jarsdel had been tased in the academy. It didn't merely hurt; pain was something you could deal with, something you could tough out. For Jarsdel, it had seemed as if an invisible, godlike hand had thrown him to the ground and held him there. It was a terrifying, helpless feeling, and it always amazed him when suspects could tolerate more than one hit before surrendering.

"He misused 'begs the question,'" said Jarsdel.

Morales blinked. "Huh?"

"Councilman Peyser. He said the body being burned alive 'begged the question' as to whether it was a hate crime. That's incorrect."

"What—"

"Begging the question is a very specific logical fallacy, a type of circular reasoning. *Petitio principii* is the Latin name for it. Burning alive may *raise* the question of it being a hate crime, but it doesn't *beg* the question. I love it when people try to sound smarter than they really are."

Morales looked at him in astonishment. Jarsdel's phone rang again. It was Ipgreve.

"Your John Doe just got more interesting," he said. "Get here soon as you can."

Jarsdel passed the news to Morales, who stood, checking his watch. "Lunch rush traffic by now. Be nuts gettin' over there. Might as well grab something to eat first. Just don't go Rain Man on me anymore."

4

Jarsdel could still taste the carne asada burrito he'd picked up at a lunch truck on Riverside. It had been delicious—perfect, even. But now, in the autopsy suite of the LA County morgue, the lingering flavor of beef and onions mingled with the smell of industrial chemicals and the deeper, creeping funk of death. The inside of his mouth tasted sour, corrupt.

Not for the first time, Jarsdel thought how the room resembled a hotel kitchen. Giant stainless-steel sinks lined one wall, and stacks of cutting boards rested on the counters between them. Ladles and tongs drip-dried in a hanging basket, and assorted knives glinted from a magnetic rack. The similarities ended there, however. Kitchens didn't usually feature a large rectangle on the floor demarcated with bright yellow tape reading *Splash Zone*, nor were there dangling garden tools—shears and limb cutters—for cracking the stubborn vault of the human chest. Two long, glass vases sat in a cubby, both full to the brim with what looked like river rock, though Jarsdel knew they were actually gallstones. On the wall near the sinks was a drain-cleaning log, and he thought the citizenry would be surprised to learn that all the runoff from autopsies went into the same system as their mouthwash and shaving scum.

The suite's surreality was heightened by the giant mosquito

zappers humming away in the corners—a defense against surprise hatchings of fly larvae, which could lie dormant in a human corpse as long as it remained in the refrigerator. Once it warmed up, so did the maggots. On Jarsdel's last visit, the entire department had been in the midst of a week-long siege, and the autopsy had taken place to the accompaniment of sizzles and snaps as the flies met their end.

But today, it was quiet. The few flies that had joined the cadaver in its body bag had flung themselves into the zappers as soon as they'd been released, and the usual banter between the ME and his assistant was muted and subdued. The body before them represented a totality of misery and suffering rarely seen, even by veteran witnesses of horror like Ipgreve.

Before Jarsdel and Morales had arrived, the medical examiner had already performed the rudiments of the external investigation—photographing, x-raying, and weighing the cadaver. He'd also made the requisite Y-shaped incision along the body's trunk and removed the chest plate, which now rested on a separate table.

Jarsdel and Morales slipped on masks and goggles as Ipgreve reached a gloved hand into the incision. He pulled back the skin, revealing the internal organs. Jarsdel's face twisted in revulsion, and he noticed that even Morales looked queasy.

What should have been a healthy, glistening pink had been cooked to a muddy reddish brown. Pockets of congealed blood—as black as chocolate syrup—sat between the organs. The intestines had ruptured in the heat, and what Jarsdel supposed was fecal matter could be seen amid the mass of ravaged tissue.

Ipgreve dabbed a finger in a pool of blood and rubbed it against his thumb. "I've seen every kind of burn victim you can imagine. Nothing like this. Consistent, even heat for an hour, maybe more, in an enclosed chamber of some kind. Total body third-degree burns resulting in profound loss of blood protein and water content leading to hypovolemic cardiovascular collapse. So yes, he was literally baked to death. Weighed in at 156, but I'd bet he'd've been in the neighborhood of fifteen or twenty pounds heavier before he went into the oven."

Morales nodded. "That'll help with missing persons. Any idea on race?"

"Caucasian. Skin would be even darker than it is now if he were Latino or African American, and measurements of the skull and maxilla rule out an Asian background."

Jarsdel felt some relief; at least he could call up Ken Peyser and put a stop to the hate crime theory. "Dr. Ipgreve," he said. "You mentioned on the phone there was something we needed to see?"

The medical examiner moved around to the cadaver's right and gently lifted its hand. Metal rods were clamped to the fingers, making them splay out as if in greeting. "We had to attach the straighteners very carefully. Pull too hard and the fingers'll pop right off like drumsticks. As I suspected, we weren't able to get any prints, but..."

He slowly turned the hand palm up. There was a snapping sound somewhere in the shoulder, and the skin split open, but everyone's attention was on the hand.

Stuck to the cadaver's open palm was a small red disc. Jarsdel didn't recognize it at first, then made out the familiar image of an eagle, wings spread wide. A quarter, painted red.

"I don't get it," said Morales.

"Someone went through the trouble of gluing this to the guy's hand," said Ipgreve. "Did a pretty thorough job of it too. If I tried taking it off, the rest of his palm would come with it. Have to get some solvent so we can get the coin off to the lab."

"Does it tell us anything?" asked Jarsdel.

"Only that whoever did it glued it on before he was cooked."

"Yeah," said Morales. "And we also know they wanted us to find it. No chance the coin could get lost if it's superglued on. Prof, any ideas what it means?"

Jarsdel shot Morales an irritated look, but he'd bent to get a better look at the coin. "No."

"Never lived in an apartment, huh?" said Morales with a smile.

"I'm over at Park La Brea."

Morales snorted. "That ain't a real apartment."

"What's your point, Morales?"

"On-site managers get free laundry. Landlords give 'em these red coins so they don't get mixed up with the profit."

"Hadn't thought of that," said Ipgreve. "When I was a kid in Jersey, some people painted quarters red in protest when they raised the toll from fifteen cents to twenty-five. Paint's too fresh, though, and your explanation makes more sense."

Jarsdel wondered how either theory made any sense but decided not to say anything. His gaze strayed to a standing autopsy scale that'd probably been in use for decades. Someone had affixed several statistics to the dial's wide face. *Largest Liver 1600 grams*, read one. *Spleen Queen 1560 grams*, read another. Jarsdel's favorite came with a date, *1-2-09*, and read *King of Hearts 1260 grams*. It seemed in LA, there was always a last-minute chance at celebrity.

———

Ipgreve followed them as they left the autopsy suite. The three men peeled off their masks and gloves and dropped their goggles on a tray to be sterilized. They stood by a squat, waist-high air filter—dubbed R2-D2 by the staff—one of several in the building whose job it was to combat the smell of decomposition. The result was a kind of stalemate. The air wasn't foul exactly, but it wasn't pleasant either.

Ipgreve raised his voice over the lusty whoosh of R2-D2. "So like I said, we'll get the coin off to the lab, see if we can learn anything about the paint or the glue. We'll check to see if the killer put a nice thumbprint right in the middle of the coin when he glued it on, but you know as well as I do that's unlikely."

"And you're sure we can't get the vic's fingerprints?" said Morales.

The ME grunted. "You're welcome to give it a try if you want. I don't know—there's maybe one thing I can do. If it works, I'll give you a call. In the meantime, I'll try getting a DNA sample that's not complete mush. Maybe we got lucky and the center of his heart didn't get up to more than about 110."

"So just to clarify," said Jarsdel, referencing his notes, "we should be checking Missing Persons for a white male, approximately five foot eight and somewhere between 171 and 176 pounds."

"I can't get you an exact number on the weight because we don't know how long he was in the oven. Height's even tougher, considering what the heat did to his muscles. But yeah, I'd say five foot eight is safest."

Jarsdel put away his notebook. "Doesn't exactly stand out in a crowd, does he? Three fillings, and the X-rays say he had a broken right arm somewhere in his past. But no tattoos, no major surgery or obvious infirmities. Then again, he could've been completely blind, and we wouldn't know."

"You find any likely candidates, send me the dentals. Until then..." Ipgreve shrugged.

"It's his first time taking lead," said Morales. "He wants answers, and he wants them now."

Jarsdel braced himself for a chuckle from Ipgreve, but the ME didn't even smile. "I don't blame him," he said, nodding his head in the direction of the autopsy suite. "That's probably the cruelest thing I've ever seen one human being do to another. I'll sleep better myself when you catch him."

5

C ities are unnatural things, Jarsdel thought.

The traffic on Third Street was punishing, the kind of soul-rending slog Angelenos learn to endure as a simple fact of life. In traffic like this, Jarsdel couldn't help thinking of Çatalhöyük, one of the first fledgling efforts of humankind to live in a city. It had been a mess—dwellings piled one upon the other, not a single road or sidewalk. In order to get anywhere, you had to walk on your neighbors' roofs. To Jarsdel, it was absolute proof that cities weren't in our DNA but were rather an artificial construct we had to condition ourselves to accept.

The thought didn't bring him much comfort as he crept toward Highland Avenue, where he saw the light was out. At the best of times, the intersection of Third and Highland was a battle of wills. With the light out and the drivers left to fend for themselves, it was miraculous no one had been killed. Jarsdel waited his turn and finally crossed, noting it had taken him thirty minutes to go as many yards.

By the time he pulled into Park La Brea, the sun hung low and heavy in the sky, casting long shadows across the grounds. Despite Morales's assertion otherwise, Park La Brea was indeed an apartment complex—a massive, 160-acre enclosed lot of newer high-rise towers surrounded by clusters of '40s-era townhouses. It was in one of these, on Maryland Drive, that Jarsdel lived. The walls were plastered-over cinder block, practically earthquake-proof. The Park La Brea townhouses had even shrugged off the Northridge quake of '94, which had caused tens of billions in damage across the city. The trade-off was that the rooms were stifling in the summer and freezing in the winter. You could turn on the air or heating, of course, but the systems were so old and loud that you risked missing a phone call or sleeping right through your alarm.

There was no reserved parking, but Jarsdel got lucky and snagged a spot only a few doors down from his own. The heat hugged him tightly as soon as he stepped from the car, but it was a relief to be on his feet again after the drive from the coroner's.

The loneliness didn't fully descend until he was inside his apartment. He'd done everything he could to guard against it, had thought that by surrounding himself with the things that pleased him, he'd be happy. Framed vintage travel posters of Dubrovnik and Rio shared the walls with a prized plein air painting of Big Sur and an advertisement for *Caesar's Soldiers*, a History Channel special he'd been featured on as an expert. His overflowing bookshelves groaned under an equally unusual assortment. *The Irish Pub Cookbook* and *Sexual Homicide: Patterns and Motives* were crammed on either side of a rare, six-volume edition of Edward Gibbon's *The History of the Decline and Fall of the Roman Empire*. Curio cabinets and built-in nooks celebrated every corner of Jarsdel's restless mind—high school fencing trophies, an ancient phallus pendant, a deck of cards from Revolutionary France where the usual court cards had been replaced by Liberty, Equality, and Fraternity. A leaded shillelagh war club. A chunk of three-thousand-year-old amphora. A mummified cat from the Valley of the Kings. It was Jarsdel's sanctuary, carefully engineered so that no matter where he looked, he'd see some reflection of himself.

And none of it helped. He should have known it wouldn't. He'd read the Stoics, all of whom agreed solace couldn't be found in mere objects. Jarsdel had hoped that maybe, just on that one point, they'd been wrong. Instead, he found himself caught in the perverse cycle of the addict: the more he grew to depend on his sanctuary, the less it fulfilled him. And yet the thought of cleaning the place out terrified him. It would be easier to saw off a limb.

The silence in his apartment was dense and unsettling, somehow made worse by the day's feverish, sickly heat. Jarsdel turned on the AC to take care of the heat and put on a Sonny Chillingworth album to fend off the silence. But when the air kicked on, he could barely make out the sweet melody of Chillingworth's slack-key guitar and so opted for music instead of comfort.

He turned off the police GPS alert on his phone, poured himself a glass of wine, and stepped onto the small, screened-in patio. It was a degree or two cooler outside, enough for him to think. He opened his laptop and sat down, shedding his gun and handcuffs as he did so. A moment later, Jarsdel was staring at the morning's crime scene photos again, hoping that something new would jump out at him now that he knew about the red quarter. Nothing did, and he soon decided he'd looked at that ruined body enough for one day. He snapped the computer closed and took a long swallow of wine.

It was seven o'clock. Outside the complex and only a few blocks away was the Farmers Market and adjacent outdoor mall, the Grove. Jarsdel ate at the market almost daily, and not just because he was a dreadful cook. He went there because every night, even on a Thursday like today, the place would be thronged with tourists. Crowded.

Safe.

At home, there was too much space for his mind to spin out, to ruminate on all he'd left behind when he joined the force. Few people can so easily pick out the single most critical decision of their lives. Jarsdel could, and his abandoned career—and the alternate life it represented—seemed to exist somewhere beside him at all times, like an apparition.

In that other life, he wasn't living alone at Park La Brea. In that other life, his dads still spoke of him with pride in their voices, still had him and his fiancée over for dinner on Fridays, dinners that would conclude with him and Baba—a professor of ancient history—cracking a few beers and guffawing their way through *Walker, Texas Ranger* reruns. Meanwhile, his other father—simply Dad—would hole up in the study with Maureen, both of them able to chat for hours about their shared discipline, English literature.

What a team the four of them made. Enough IQ points in one room to start their own space program, Dad had joked.

Jarsdel finished his wine and went back inside, locked his weapon in a fingerprint-access floor safe, and set off for the Farmers Market. The department preferred that he be armed even when he was off duty, but he didn't like the way the gun felt against his body when he wasn't on the job. It separated him, made him something other, and he had a hard enough time feeling like he belonged as it was. The kind of camaraderie he craved in the Farmers Market crowd was impersonal, but it was still camaraderie.

He crossed Third Street with two dozen French teenagers who'd just been let off their tour bus and followed them into the main marketplace, where they scattered for the shops and stalls.

Jarsdel began to relax as he headed for the food stands, making up his mind as he went that he was in the mood for beef bulgogi, and LA Korea made his favorite in the city. The staff there knew him well enough that as soon as they spotted him in line, they began heaping up a plate with seasoned bean sprouts and cucumber salad. By the time his entree was ready, Jarsdel had bought a pint of Chimay from 326 Beer & Wine. He managed to grab a small table just as it was being vacated and ate and drank amid the soothing din of a hundred conversations.

There were others like him too—sad, single regulars he saw night after night. The heavy, thirtysomething woman with the tips of her blond hair dyed a snow-cone purple who always ordered clam chowder in a sourdough bread bowl. The pinch-faced man with the goatee and the tam-o'-shanter who ate while reading the newspaper and who'd every now and then shake his head and blurt out "Unbelievable" or "Jesus," as if he wanted someone to ask him what was going on. And the pretty young writer, sadly a decade too young for Jarsdel, who'd stake out a table early in the evening and hammer away on her laptop, never ordering any food, oblivious to the angry glances she'd earn from diners desperate for a seat.

Jarsdel loved his compatriots; together, they made a kind of club—Team Loneliness, perhaps—and in their own silent way, they gave each other strength. They might be lonely, but at least it was a group effort.

The seasoned Korean steak went perfectly with the strong, heady ale. He drank it quickly, then ordered another. By the time he'd finished his meal, Jarsdel was cresting the wave of a gentle buzz. He looked again at the writer. She'd brought out a book and was holding it in one hand, glancing back and forth between the open page and her computer screen. When she set it down, Jarsdel could see it was a copy of *Common Errors in English Usage*. At least she was serious about her work, he thought.

Maybe she only *looked* young.

Maybe he could talk to her.

But it seemed that would break an unspoken code. Membership in Team Loneliness was supposed to be anonymous.

But why? Why did it have to be?

He considered, then stood and approached her table.

"*Audentes fortuna iuvat.*"

The woman raised her eyes to his. Her hair had been dyed a dark, pomegranate red, lips painted to match. She wore a maroon tank with spaghetti straps, and Jarsdel could see a dusting of freckles across her shoulders, under her face powder too. A light silk scarf was tied around her neck, giving her a Parisian look.

"Excuse me?" she asked.

"It's Latin. An old saying from Virgil."

"Oh. Okay." She turned back to her laptop.

Jarsdel felt a hot sting of embarrassment and went back to his table without another word. Once there, he kept his eyes down and nudged around a clot of rice with his fork. He could hear his pulse in his ears, something that only happened in moments of profound shame, and was about to leave when he heard the scraping of a chair against concrete.

"Sorry, hi."

Jarsdel looked up from his plate to see the girl sitting across from him, arms folded. She'd packed up her computer, which now jutted from a knitted shoulder bag along with *Common Errors*. Jarsdel was amazed to see she was smiling.

"I was in the zone," she said. "Wasn't trying to be mean."

"No, that's fine," said Jarsdel. "I shouldn't have interrupted."

"You're allowed." She held out her hand. "Becca."

"Tully." They shook, and he was startled at how cold her hand was. It must have shown on his face, because the girl made a sound somewhere between a sigh and a laugh.

"I know. I have Raynaud's. Once it starts getting cold, I have to wear gloves, or my hands start turning blue."

"Oh, that sounds painful."

"It sucks."

He couldn't think of anything else to say on the subject, so he pointed to her book. "Pretty much got that memorized. I love stuff like that—you know, like is it 'chomping at the bit' or 'champing at the bit'? Or why is 'twelve p.m.' incorrect? Fascinating stuff."

Becca nodded. "It's 'champing at the bit.' And it can't be post meridiem if it's exactly meridiem. 'Noon' is preferred."

Jarsdel grinned. He didn't think he was handsome when he grinned, the way his top lip thinned out and made him look toothy, but he couldn't help it.

She smiled back at him. "You're a teacher or something, right?"

"Not too long ago. Really that obvious?"

"Well, you did get pretty excited over grammar. For some reason, I don't think it would make most of the guys in here quite so giddy. And the glasses help."

"They do," Jarsdel agreed. "You know, when I was younger, even when I didn't need glasses, I still wore clear lenses just so people would take me a little more seriously."

"Boys are so cute when they're insecure." Something new appeared in Becca's smile, something that caused a warm, familiar stirring in Jarsdel's blood.

"Well, if that were true, I would've been on the cover of *Tiger Beat.*" She laughed at that. *This is going great,* Jarsdel thought. He suddenly felt very free, very easy in his own skin. Any anxieties he'd had a few moments ago were fading if not gone altogether. It was remarkable how tenaciously high-school jitters could hang on to you if you let them. *I was a pasty, awkward kid, yes, and everyone thought I'd become a teacher, which I did. But now I'm a sworn police officer, a homicide detective in the LA-goddamned-PD, and I put real murderers into real prisons. A month ago, I arrested a man who'd grabbed his girlfriend's colicky one-year-old by the ankles and swung him headfirst into a kitchen countertop. Wonder what the wedgie squad at Poly would think of that?*

"I see you here a lot," he said. "And I have to say, I'm curious. Can I ask what you're working on?" It was a harmless enough question, but Jarsdel would ruminate on the scene over the next few days and eventually decide this was the precise moment he'd swerved the conversation down the road to catastrophe.

Becca hesitated. "It's hard to describe."

"It's okay. You just seem very dedicated, and—"

"No, I'm actually glad you asked. If you can't describe your work to people, you don't have much of a chance of getting it seen."

"Makes sense."

"Well, it's basically a play about Los Angeles, but I never actually come right out and say it. It's more like an alternate-universe version of LA. It's a fantasy piece, but I've always thought, like, if you want to comment on something, you can do it much better through fantasy or augmented reality."

Jarsdel thought about that. "You mean like how *Animal Farm* is an—"

"*Animal Farm*! Exactly. Or how *Frankenstein* is cautioning us to be careful in our pursuit of knowledge and science. I mean, she wrote that in 1818, and nobody listens, and the next century, we've got A-bombs."

"Hmm," said Jarsdel, "it's interesting you mention that. You know, that's actually a very common misinterpretation."

"What do you mean?"

"The idea that Shelley's warning us of the dangers of science run amok. It feels right, but it's facile—really more of a backward projection of our own notions. And I think probably also a confusion between the book and the 1931 film. In that one, there's certainly the theme of 'don't tamper in God's domain.' But that was shot just a little after World War I, so it makes sense that there's a sense of anxiety about what science is up to. But Shelley's writing in a time where the concept of science as this runaway train simply isn't on the radar. There's no—"

"But that's what I mean," Becca said. "She predicted all that. She knew even then where it was all leading."

Jarsdel shifted in his seat. "That's...uh...I'm sorry. That's just not what she was talking about. *Frankenstein* is about what a god or a demiurge owes its creation—what responsibilities it has to the life it summons and ultimately whether it has the right to create life at all. The monster is built and animated, but he had no choice in the matter, and now he suffers. It's Miltonic. Just look at the epigraph from the 1818 edition. It's right from *Paradise Lost*: 'Did I request thee, Maker, from my clay / To mould me man?' The science aspect of the book is actually quite vague, no more than a device for telling the story."

Becca's smile flattened into a taught line. "Okay, I'm pretty sure I know what I'm talking about. I have a master's in ethics and applied philosophy, and that was my thesis."

Jarsdel was amazed. "Your thesis was on the ethics of science in *Frankenstein*?"

"In popular literature, but yes, I spent a whole chapter on *Frankenstein*."

"And your professor signed off on that?"

Becca gave her head a quick little shake, as if she couldn't believe what she was hearing. A strand of hair snagged in the corner of her mouth, and she flicked it away. "What are you saying exactly?"

"I'm sorry," said Jarsdel. "I guess I think the problem with a lot of advanced degrees these days is that the professors don't really push their students. The college cashes its tuition check, and the whole process gets kind of rubber-stamped along the way." He hurried to amend his statement. "I'm not saying that's what happened here. Not at all. I..."

Becca looked at him, stunned.

"Let me clarify," Jarsdel went on. "One of the reasons I quit teaching is that I actually got calls and emails from parents. And I'm talking about college kids here. Parents complaining that their kids are under stress, that they really didn't deserve whatever grade they got, and so on. Now of course, I'm not obligated to respond to these idiots. In fact, FERPA makes it illegal for me to comment on a student's academic standing. But what do you suppose happens? Those same parents then contact my department head, and before I know it, I'm getting *the talk*—ease up on this and that, reconsider my rubric—which is all basically just a way of telling me to lower my standards so everyone can be a winner."

He tried to stop himself but was astonished to find that he couldn't. His harangue had taken on a life of its own. "We've actually gotten to the point that parents are bailing their adult children out of schoolwork. It's crazy. And I think in general, there's this culture of entitlement that's poisoned academics, and not just at the under-graduate level. People figure they paid for a degree, and that ought to take them ninety percent of the way there, and that's why we end up with these bloodless, jejune theses that contribute nothing to the overall conversation, to the progress of analytical thought."

By that time, Jarsdel had buried himself so deeply that there was no coming back. All the same, that last sentence was the concrete cap on the gravesite, the one whose marker might have read *Tully & Becca, 7:54 to 8:01 p.m.*

She stood and gathered her things. Jarsdel, equally disgusted and amazed by his performance, watched her do this with mute resignation. Becca slung the knitted bag over her shoulder and left the food court but not without framing a middle finger in the center of her departing back.

Jarsdel nodded. It had been well-deserved.

———

He wandered the marketplace, stopping to buy a postcard of Douglas Fairbanks and Mary Pickford, then again at Littlejohn's for a pound of English toffee. He considered walking around the Grove. Its nightclubs, movie theater, and restaurants always attracted huge crowds, and Jarsdel could lose himself in them for a while. But after the mellow cool of the Farmers Market, Jarsdel decided the Grove's newer, slicker vibe wasn't what he was looking for. He also felt he'd polluted his sanctuary, violated the trust of Team Loneliness, and was no longer welcome.

He went back across Third and let himself into the Park La Brea complex. When he made it to his apartment, the pleasant drunk he'd been building was beginning to wear off. He still had plenty of wine left and poured another glass before corking the bottle and putting it in the fridge. He opened the patio door for some air and ended the evening with a documentary about the Battle of Verdun.

It was interesting enough to keep Jarsdel up another hour, but his body's demands for rest soon won out. The last image he glimpsed before slipping into sleep was of a nameless French soldier, one of the first men to fall before the modern flamethrower. The photo was over a century old, the sepia film striped with scratches, and a blackened Adrian helmet lay near the body. But otherwise it was *him*, his John Doe, and its expression of pure, agonized terror followed Jarsdel into his dreams, where even the dead could scream.

6

J arsdel was having an early lunch at his desk when Ipgreve called.

"Tried the last trick I could think of to get those prints from the John Doe," said the medical examiner. "Cut the skin off the hands and basically put 'em on like gloves."

Jarsdel had a bite of Greek salad halfway to his mouth. A greasy slice of gyro meat quivered on the end of his fork.

"Thought with some structure back in them, we might be able to roll some decent prints," Ipgreve went on. "Forget about it. Collagen's completely cooked out. Skin just fell apart."

Jarsdel put down his fork. "Okay," he said, "what about the DNA?"

"Internal organs are too badly damaged to get a reliable sample, but it doesn't matter. Sometimes you'll get a car fire, and those can burn hot enough to make a guy basically into charcoal, but I can still snag a DNA profile. Pretty neat, really. Just takes a little more work, which is why I didn't go for it right away. You dig some pulp out from one of the molars. Even in extreme temperatures, the molars preserve the genetic markers."

"What's our timeline on results?"

"Three weeks at the least," said Ipgreve.

"And there's no way to speed that up, I'm assuming."

"Not unless you got a degree in biochemistry."

Jarsdel thanked Ipgreve and hung up. He gave his food one last look but decided he wasn't hungry anymore and pushed it into the trash. Probably for the best. He didn't think he'd exercised once since he had become a detective.

He looked across at Morales, who was poring over his day planner. Jarsdel opened his mouth to speak, but the other man cut him off.

"No. No missing-persons reports fitting our guy."

"No adult white male of average height?"

"Not lately. Only white dude gone missing is another costumed character. The Riddler this time, but he was over six feet, too tall to be *Señor Caliente*."

"You sure that's the only one?" said Jarsdel. "Did you call?"

Morales sighed and looked up. "Jesus Christ, Prof. Sergeant Ramsdell's gonna let us know if anyone remotely like our guy gets called in. Hasn't even been twenty-four hours. Relax." He went back to looking at his day planner. "Gotta fucking testify this afternoon. Twice. And I get a nice two-hour break in between to hang around the goddamn courthouse."

The cases Morales had to testify for had been in the works for over a year, before they'd partnered. One was a fatal stabbing in a nightclub at Hollywood and Edgemont, and the other was a strong-arm robbery outside a liquor store on Western. The victim had survived but had been beaten so badly by the pair of assailants that the DA was going for attempted murder.

Jarsdel didn't mind testifying. After spending so many years lecturing college students, he secretly missed the opportunity to speak in public. He was good at it, comfortable and confident on the stand, and the city prosecutors loved him. When he'd been promoted to detective, he had received a congratulatory note from the district attorney herself. It was, in many ways, his favorite part of the job, but he decided not to share that with Morales.

He checked the time and saw it was almost noon. He rose from his chair. "You coming?"

Morales grunted and pushed himself up, grimacing as his weight settled onto his legs. They crossed the squad room and stopped outside the largest office in the station. The blinds were lowered but not drawn, and Jarsdel could see three men in animated conversation. One was Lieutenant Gavin, and Jarsdel recognized the man to his right as Councilman Ken Peyser. Behind the desk sat Captain Lowell Sturdivant, the division's commanding officer. He was a tall man and wore a tight, silver crew cut. His hands were large, the knuckles hairy, marble-sized knobs, but the fingers that branched from them were oddly elegant, even delicate. He glanced through the window and, noticing Morales and Jarsdel, waved them in.

Peyser stood and shook the two detectives' hands. "Have a seat," he said, as if it were his office.

"We've just been catching Ken up on things," said Sturdivant once everyone was seated. "Anything new to share?"

"No luck on the prints," said Jarsdel. "But Dr. Ipgreve should have a DNA profile for us in about three weeks."

Peyser sighed and shook his head. "I've got some very freaked-out citizens in my district."

"I thought we had that contained," said Gavin. "Victim's a white male, so we rule out any racial motives."

"People aren't stupid," said Peyser with the authority of someone laying out a great truth. "They know we're holding something back."

"Of course we're holding something back," said Sturdivant. "I'm not going to get in front of four million Angelenos and tell them our victim was cooked alive."

"But if it gets out ahead of us, we're in real trouble," said Peyser. "I say we put out a public appeal, give as many details as we can spare."

"Such as?" said Gavin.

"Manner of death," began Peyser, then put up a hand when he saw Sturdivant about to argue. "Not everything. Just enough to get the gore hounds to stop sniffing around. Otherwise, it begs the question as to why we're being so guarded."

Morales snorted, then rubbed his nose. The men stopped to look at him. "Allergies," he said. "Sorry."

Peyser went on. "We say the guy died from exposure to heat and was then moved. Nothing about an oven or anything, because even between us, that's still speculation. We don't even need to say it's necessarily murder."

"Oh, come on, Ken," said Sturdivant.

"Well, who knows? Could've been an insurance scam gone wrong. Survivors panicked and dumped the body. My point is we still don't know what we're dealing with. We're speaking to the public openly and honestly and saying hey, we need your help. Aboveboard's the way to go on this."

Sturdivant turned to Jarsdel. "If we engage the public, what can we hold back?"

"Not very much, sir," said Jarsdel. "I suppose the way the body was posed, with its head at the base of the statue. And of course the killer would have to be able to explain—to the satisfaction of our ME—how the body ended up the way it did."

"The coin," said Morales.

"Right. The coin," agreed Jarsdel.

"What coin?" asked Peyser.

"The body was found with a quarter glued to its right palm."

"Glued?"

Jarsdel nodded. "1996. Painted red. It's probably our best piece of evidence, even though there isn't much it can tell us. No prints, and the glue was badly damaged by the solvent when we finally got it off. Lab thinks it's just common superglue anyway—no method of tracing it. Same deal with the paint."

"Okay," said Gavin. "So we make an official statement. But I want it cleared with Chief Comsky first. HH2 is her baby, and I'm not about to do anything to piss her off."

"That's fair," said Sturdivant. "Ken? Anything else?"

"No. I really appreciate you guys working with me on this. It'll ease a lot of people's minds if they feel they're being kept in the loop."

Sturdivant raised his strange, willowy hands. "That's it, then. Detective Jarsdel, could you hang back a minute?" He waited until the others left and the two of them were alone.

"How's it coming?" asked the captain.

"Pretty good, I think. Sir."

"Pretty good, huh? Big responsibility, this case."

"Yes, sir."

Sturdivant plucked a letter opener from a desk caddy and began turning it over in his hands. "I don't think it's any secret what Lieutenant Gavin thinks of HH2. He's a hell of a cop but old-fashioned. Lot like me, actually. I'd be lying if I said I thought the division needed a new homicide squad, let alone one with such a wonky makeup. You really have a PhD in history?"

"No, sir. I was in the last year of my program when I left."

"You find your background helps you in your police work?"

"I don't mind writing reports."

Jarsdel's attempt at humor went unnoticed. Sturdivant set the point of the letter opener on a yellow legal pad and began slowly twisting the blade. The paper dimpled beneath the steady pressure. "Don't get me wrong. I actually put a lot of stock in test takers. Shows a man's willing to apply himself. Discipline and a passion for the job. You want an example, look no further than our late Chief Parker. But there's a lot more to police work than academics."

"Yes, sir."

"I understand you nearly washed out behind the wheel."

Jarsdel wasn't expecting this. Sturdivant was referring to the police academy's grueling Emergency Vehicle Operations course, which, it was true, had nearly cost Jarsdel his badge. A recruit could ace firearms, law, tactics, and everything else but still fail out if his driving scores were poor. Jarsdel had been only one flattened road cone shy of being dismissed from the program.

"It wasn't my strongest subject."

Sturdivant grunted, continuing to twist the letter opener. "I don't have my measure of you yet, Detective. I don't know if you're a liability or an asset. I don't know if you're just playing cop or if you're some kind of rare talent who came late to the job. I'll put it another way—this case will either do a lot of good for you or a lot of bad for you. All depends on how it goes. That make sense?"

"Yes, Captain."

"So I'm offering you a way out."

"Sir?"

Sturdivant glanced down at the letter opener, which had by now punched through several pages of the legal pad. He stopped turning the blade, set it back in the desk caddy and, frowning, rubbed his thumb over the wound in the paper. "I know Morales wants you to lead, but I very much doubt that it's in your best interest at this stage of your career. A word from me and I can override him. Gavin too. Keep you out of the limelight a little longer."

"I see," said Jarsdel.

"I'm not sure you do. You've never had to face a hostile media, never had to explain to a panicked city and a grieving family why a case is stalled. And I'll tell you something you probably already know. Lot of people would like to see you fail and HH2 right along with you. You represent a worrying trend in this department. Think of how it looks to guys like your partner. Just a few years in patrol and you get bumped to a rank it took him twice as long to make. And why? Because you're smarter on paper. You blowing this case would go a long way toward convincing Chief Comsky she'd made a mistake, that there's no substitute for the kind of cop smarts you only get from time on the street."

"Everyone knows I'm lead. If I back off now, it'll look just as bad."

"Not so," said Sturdivant. "I'll say it was a command decision, nothing against you personally. Just that we wanted a seasoned detective calling the shots."

Jarsdel was suddenly very conscious of his glasses. He took them off, slipped them into his pocket, and tried to stand a little taller. "No thank you, sir. I think I'll see it through if that's okay."

Sturdivant nodded as if he'd expected this answer. "Well then," he said, "I'll be curious to see what happens. Very curious."

"Is there anything else, sir?"

The old cop smiled. "Nope. Good luck out there. You'll need it on this one."

7

Waiting for the DNA to come back was like being adrift on a windless sea. There was no action, no momentum, and each passing day brought with it a greater certainty that nothing would change.

In the meantime, Jarsdel and Morales turned their attention to a cold case—the bizarre serial poisoning of local dogs. In late 2005, an unseen killer had begun tossing deadly meatballs into yards around Los Angeles. Owners would find their beloved companions either dead or close to it—convulsing, eyes rolled back to the whites, foam oozing from their mouths. Inspection of the dogs' stomach contents revealed that the killing agent in all cases was water hemlock, a pretty and extremely poisonous plant common throughout the state. So far, eleven animals had been murdered.

The killer was methodical and disciplined, allowing as many as two years to pass between attacks. He—or she—was also highly selective in the choice of victims—not in the dogs themselves, which ranged from Chihuahuas to Rottweilers, but in the owners, who were all attractive couples in their twenties. The most remarkable aspect of the case, however, was the killer's eerie timing. Without exception, the dogs were killed on the couples' wedding day.

Using LAPD's COMPSTAT system, the crimes had been

computer mapped to check for any common variables. But so far, nothing substantive could be deduced. None of the couples lived near one another. Some were wealthy, but most weren't. No two shared the same social circles, fields of employment, wedding locales, caterers, or DJs.

The detective who'd first spotted the link between the cases— Rick Jackson, a Robbery-Homicide pro who'd since retired—came up with what many considered the best theory: the couples were being targeted at dog parks. Three of them ran their dogs at Runyon Canyon, four at Griffith Park, two in Silver Lake, and two in Long Beach. The theory held that someone was pretending to befriend the couples and, in the process, finding out when they were to be married. The killer would then simply follow them home, make note of where they lived, and come back on their wedding day.

The problem was what to do with that information. The poisonings took place so far apart that a stakeout or decoy strategy was impractical. For that same reason, publicizing the case would be equally ineffective. Too much time elapsed between the killings for any concerted public effort to pay off, and the ensuing panic would cause more harm than good. Furthermore, dog parks were social places, and the couples could never clearly recall whom they'd told about their upcoming nuptials. To date, not a single useful description of the culprit had emerged.

The only thing investigators could depend on was that the killer must, ironically, also be a dog owner. Otherwise, it would be impossible for whomever it was to approach the young couples without arousing suspicion. But again, what to do with that information? All they could really do was wait, hoping the alert they'd sent to vets and animal hospitals across LA County would yield a fresher crime scene the next time a dog was poisoned.

The case had slogged through the system for fifteen years, passing from detective to detective until finally landing at the desk of Oscar Morales. And when he moved to Hollywood Station, the case had followed. Now Tully Jarsdel had been added to its long list of custodians. At first, he'd questioned why Homicide was handling it, correctly assuming they didn't usually get involved in animal murders.

"Officially," Morales had said, "any serial out there targeting pets is probably on his way to doing people. It's the same kind of crazy. Unofficially, one of the victims—you know, one of the dogs— belonged to Chief Ballard's niece. You believe that? Of all the people in LA, this fuckin' wacko pisses off the chief of goddamn detectives. So we'll get him."

But so far, they hadn't. What they did have was a catchy nickname for their boogeyman, inherited from previous investigators, and one for which Sturdivant had threatened suspension if it were ever leaked to the media: the Dog Catcher.

And now Jarsdel and Morales were parked on North Catalina Street in the Hollywood Hills. A break between the houses revealed a stunning view of the city, the day so bright and clear it looked like a matte painting.

Jarsdel turned to Morales to ask him a question and noticed the other man's belt and pants were undone. "What are you doing?"

"Huh?"

"What's with the pants?"

"Always do that when I'm in the car. So I don't stretch out the waist. More comfortable."

"Oh."

"Was there something you wanted to do here, or you just gonna keep staring at my briefs?"

"Sorry." Jarsdel looked out the window. "That the place?" he asked, pointing to a home done in the Spanish-Moroccan style so popular in the 1920s.

"Yeah," said Morales.

"You can't see into the yard at all." It was an obvious statement, and Morales didn't acknowledge it. The house was protected by a high, white stuccoed wall, and the only way in was through a heavy wooden door. A doorbell intercom was affixed to its right.

The home belonged to the last couple the Dog Catcher had targeted.

Their dog, Abby, an Akita mix, had died almost a year earlier while they were getting married at the Hotel Figueroa. Her body had been found in the pet bed underneath the eaves of the back porch, but she'd probably picked up the poison in the front yard. A narrow breezeway connected the two yards, and the couple reported that Abby had the habit of running to the front whenever the intercom bell rang.

Jarsdel stepped out of the car, taking in the aroma from a nearby stand of honeysuckle, and approached the house. He stopped at the wall, then looked down the street to his right. He had a clear view downhill for a quarter mile until the street curved and was lost to view. Jarsdel looked to his left, where the road almost immediately vanished around a bend. He nodded to himself, then went back to the car, rapping on the passenger door.

Morales rolled down his window. "What?"

"I don't think the killer parked here."

"Why not?"

"Too exposed. Look at all these houses here. Middle of the day—anyone could've seen him. I'm betting he parked around the bend, then approached the house on foot."

"Okay. So what?"

"I'm recreating the narrative. He parks around the bend, out of sight—"

"The *narrative*?"

"Yeah."

Morales let out a pained laugh, looked pointedly up, presumably at God, and shook his head. "Go ahead if you want."

"You're not coming?"

By way of answering, Morales closed his eyes and hit the recline button on his seat. Jarsdel waited another moment, then walked back over to the house. He took a breath, then pressed the button on the intercom.

A woman's voice answered. "Yes? Hello?"

"Hello, Mrs. Andreotti? I'm Detective Jarsdel, LAPD. Would you mind if I had a word with you?"

"What's going on?" She sounded alarmed.

"I'm sorry. No, nothing's wrong. I've been assigned to your case. The death of your pet."

There was a pause. "I'll be right out."

Jarsdel glanced back toward the car, but Morales had reclined out of view. There was a click as the great studded door was unlocked, and Jarsdel turned back in time to see it swing open.

Aleena Andreotti was tall, standing nearly eye to eye with Jarsdel, and wore a sweat-stained, blue cotton T-shirt and spandex tights. Her shoulder-length brown hair was damp and tied back in a ponytail. She offered a slight smile. "I'd shake your hand, but you caught me in the middle of my workout."

"I shouldn't have come by unannounced," said Jarsdel. "And I didn't mean to startle you. But I've been reviewing the circumstances of your case and thought I'd catch myself up. You and your husband were the last known victims..." He trailed off, concerned he'd been rambling. He waited for Aleena to say something, but all she did was give a small, curt nod. Even beneath the flush of her cheeks, Jarsdel could see she'd grown paler as he spoke.

"I'm sorry," he said. "This must be a very difficult subject for you. I can come back some other time."

"No, that's okay," said Aleena. "Please, come in." She moved aside, and Jarsdel stepped past her into the courtyard. It was done in red tile, the same shade as the roof's heavy clay shingles, with a large fountain at its center—a statue of a half-nude maiden pouring water endlessly from a jug at her hip. It could have been tawdry, but the aged patina of the stone, along with the intricately mosaicked pool she stood in, put forward a quiet, subdued elegance.

Aleena closed the street door, then wove her way between Jarsdel and the fountain toward the front entrance. Jarsdel followed, and when he found his gaze lingering on the woman's toned and shapely backside, he felt a stab of shame.

"Can I get you something to drink? Some iced tea?"

"No, thank you." The inside of the house was cool and silent, and Jarsdel's first thought was of emptiness—of empty theaters or cathedrals. There was nothing on the walls but white paint, nothing on the floors but bare marble. It didn't feel like a home, a place to be shared, but like a museum that'd been looted and then forgotten. A built-in nook by the door held a small purse and a set of keys, but that was the only sign of life in the place.

"Let's go in the kitchen," Aleena said.

Jarsdel turned a corner and was struck nearly speechless. The slice of view he and Morales had glimpsed between the houses was expanded tenfold from Aleena's picture window. From Pasadena to Santa Monica and all the way out to the gentle rise of Catalina Island, the city was laid out before them. It was magnificent, yes, but also unsettling. As a child, when his parents used to take him up to the Griffith Observatory, Jarsdel had always felt more comfortable looking through the crummy pay telescopes that lined the observation deck than he did taking in the entire city. As a whole, it was overwhelming, perhaps even unbelievable, that there could be anything quite so big and complex as Los Angeles, that so many lives could be thrown together like that and still survive. It was too hard for Jarsdel not to imagine death when he looked at a view so tremendous, so mighty, so vast. Too hard not to believe that he'd see some terrific cataclysm, some great balance upset, the city destroyed before him as he watched.

Aleena must have sensed Jarsdel's awe; she glanced over her shoulder at him when she reached the refrigerator. "Oh yeah," she said. "I guess I kinda take it for granted now." She poured ice into a tall glass, then filled it with a bright-red tea. It looked good. *Hibiscus*, thought Jarsdel. *I should have said yes when she offered.*

As if sensing his thoughts, she asked, "Sure you don't want one?"

"Maybe I will. Thanks."

Aleena handed Jarsdel a glass and led him to the sitting room just off the kitchen. She directed him to the sofa facing the panoramic view. He wished she hadn't. It made him uneasy. He took a sip of his tea. It was tart and unsweetened but refreshing. He drank again and felt its cool fingers spread across his chest as it went down.

"So how can I help?" asked Aleena.

Jarsdel set his glass down on a painted tile coaster and took out his notepad. "You and your husband were the last known victims of the Dog Ca—I mean, the perpetrator of these crimes. I know you've answered these questions already, but it couldn't hurt to go over them again. You never know when something new might come out."

"It's not something I really like to talk about," said Aleena.

"Of course. I'll take up as little of your time as possible."

"What do you want to know?"

"If you could just take me back through that day. Did you have any deliveries to the house? Any flowers or anything?"

"David's family sent a couple arrangements by."

"Any idea what company they were with?"

"I think it was—oh, you know that florist on the corner of Franklin and Western?"

Jarsdel smiled. "It was called Floral & Hardy when I was a kid. Not sure what it is now."

"That's the one," said Aleena.

"And about what time did you leave for the ceremony?"

"It was in the late afternoon. Probably around three. We got dressed at the venue."

"What time did you get back?"

"Oh, had to have been close to midnight."

"You didn't go straight to your honeymoon?"

"No, we were going to leave the next day. Playa del Carmen."

"Near the ruins at Coba," said Jarsdel. "Nice."

"I wouldn't know. We never made it."

"You didn't go?"

"No. After David found Abby's body, we took her to an all-night vet to find out what happened. That's when we learned she'd been poisoned. Then we called you guys, and then..." She made a small gesture, then folded her hands in her lap.

"You missed your flight?"

"We weren't really in the mood to go celebrating. Spent the next few days just trying to deal with what happened. Kept going over it again and again. Who'd want to do this, why us—you know, all the usual questions."

"Did you come up with anything?"

She shook her head.

"What line of work are you in? Maybe something to do with that?"

"David comes from money. He works for his dad. And I'm a CPO, so not exactly a lot of conflict in what I do."

"CPO? Certified professional...?"

"Organizer."

"Oh. You work for companies? Or..."

"Sure, yeah. I specialize in human factors—time and motion study and industrial psychology—so I do a lot of corporate and government stuff. But if I have gaps in my schedule, I still like to take on private clients."

Jarsdel sat up straighter and gave a slow, considering nod. "Human factors. That's quite a field. Very involved."

For the first time in their conversation, Aleena broke into a wide and genuine smile. "You've never heard of it."

"I—I mean, it sounds really familiar. I'm sure I've read about it. Do you advertise?"

"Mostly word of mouth, and my website links to the national CPO credential registry, so I get found through there too."

Jarsdel nodded and made a note. "Before the wedding, did you notice anything strange? Anyone following you, weird phone calls, anything like that?"

"Uh-uh. No."

"What about your husband? He get in any arguments with anyone? It might not even have seemed like a big deal when it happened—a fight over a parking spot or maybe he cut someone in line at Starbucks? You never know."

"You can talk to him if you want, but I doubt it. We went over everything at the time."

"Do you know when he'll be home?"

Aleena looked away. "We're separated. I can give you his number."

"I'm sorry."

She shrugged. "Not the best way to start off a marriage, you know?"

"Yeah." Jarsdel didn't know what else to say. He looked down at his notepad. "Is there anything else you can think of that'd help us find out who did this?"

"I really wish there was," said Aleena. "It's the ugliest thing that's ever happened to me."

Jarsdel put away his notepad. "We'll do everything we can." But he knew as he said them that his words lacked conviction. She seemed to sense that as well and didn't respond.

Jarsdel's phone buzzed on his belt. He silenced it without looking at the screen. "Thank you for your time. And for the drink. Where can I put the glass?"

"Just leave it there," said Aleena.

They stood, and once again Jarsdel noticed how empty the place was. The only thing in the sitting room besides the two sofas and the coffee table between them was a flat-screen TV. The shelves on either side of it were empty, save for a few envelopes carelessly tossed there. Bills, probably.

The two of them made their way back to the front entrance. Aleena opened the door for him. On his way out, he turned to face her. He felt like he had to say something, to give her some assurance, but nothing came. Instead, he took his notepad back out again. "I'm sorry. I forgot to ask for a good contact number for you."

"Isn't it already in the file or whatever?"

"Just to be on the safe side."

Aleena gave him her number and that of her soon-to-be ex-husband. "I wouldn't call him, though," she added.

"Why not?"

"Abby was his dog. He said it was like losing a child. It makes him really upset to talk about it, so I wouldn't call him unless it's to tell him you found the guy."

Jarsdel's phone buzzed again. This time, he unclipped it from his belt and looked at the screen. One missed call, a voicemail, and now a text from Morales: We got the DNA. Hurry your ass up.

"Afraid I have to get going," he told Aleena. "Here's my card. If you think of anything, no matter how seemingly insignificant, please give me a call."

She took his card. "Detective Marcus T. Jarsdel."

"Yeah, but nobody calls me Marcus," said Jarsdel. "Friends call me Tully. Middle name's Tullius—Tully for short."

"Okay. Tully," she said, smiling now and holding out her hand. "I'm Aleena." Her hand was cool from the glass of iced tea, her grip strong and steady.

A blast from a car horn startled them both. "My partner," said Jarsdel. "Thanks for your time."

"I'm giving a talk this Friday, if you really want to know about what I do."

"A talk? Where?"

"You know the Philosophical Research Society? On Los Feliz? It's not really my scene—a bit crystal-rubby for me, but they're interested in the science of it. Anyway, seven o'clock, if you want to come."

The horn sounded again—three urgent bursts.

Jarsdel flushed. "Sorry. He's a... He's kind of a... Forget it. I'll definitely try to make it. Thanks."

———

"I don't get it," said Jarsdel as they came down out of the hills. "What does he mean it's inconclusive? I thought we had a hit."

"Familial DNA hit. Meaning we didn't get the guy exactly, but we know it's a brother."

Morales was driving. Jarsdel pulled out his iPad and found the email from Dr. Ipgreve. He clicked on the attached file, revealing a chart of DNA markers. It didn't mean anything to him until he got to the bottom, where it indicated a probability of 99.9998 percent that the subject in question was a full male sibling of a Lawrence Wolin. He punched the information into the dashboard computer.

"Here he is. Lawrence Wolin, DOB 8/20/77. Got a driver's license on here too. Priors for disorderly conduct and felony battery. Doing eleven months at County for assault."

"Tough guy, huh? Let's go see him."

The Twin Towers Correctional Facility was located at 450 Bauchet Street, right in the middle of downtown, and stood adjacent to the older Men's Central Jail. From the outside, it could have passed for a kind of sprawling, high-security office complex, albeit with very narrow tinted windows. It had its own Yelp page, and the reviews were unsurprisingly poor, many referencing the fact that the Towers had been ranked among the ten worst prisons in the United States. Jarsdel believed that part of the horror of being incarcerated there had to do with its proximity to ordinary life. State facilities like Corcoran or Mule Creek were mercifully located in the middle of nowhere. But like those poor souls in Alcatraz who could hear New Year's celebrations across the San Francisco Bay, inmates in the Towers had a perfect view of the Walt Disney Concert Hall, the Hollywood sign, and, most painfully, the Gordian network of freeways that carried Angelenos, however slowly, wherever they wanted to go.

Jarsdel and Morales checked their weapons when they arrived and informed the sheriff's deputy on duty that they were there to see Lawrence Wolin. The two detectives were escorted to an interview room, passing signs that read: *Attention: Do not discuss sensitive information when inmates are present* and *Do not proceed past this point with an inmate without first announcing "Coming through."*

The interview room was different from the ones at Hollywood Station. Those resembled tiny offices and maintained a pretense of neutrality. Just because you were being questioned in one of them didn't mean you were being accused of a crime, and you might be allowed to leave when the interview was over. This, however, was the other end of the justice system. Here, you were already guilty, and you could bet that anything the cops had to say to you in this room wasn't something you'd want to hear.

Jarsdel and Morales had come during lunch and had to wait twenty minutes before Wolin was brought out to them. He was a wiry, horse-faced man, his equine features enhanced by a mane of curly, shoulder-length hair. His cheeks were unnaturally hollow, suggesting missing back teeth. The deputy sat him across from the detectives and cuffed him to a steel bar affixed to the table. He instructed the detectives to call out when they were done, then left the room. Jarsdel pretended to smooth out his tie, activating his recording app.

"I'm not talking without a lawyer," said Wolin.

"We're not asking you to talk," said Morales. "Just listen."

Wolin shrugged. "Heard that one before."

"We have some difficult news for you," said Jarsdel. "We believe that someone close to you may have been involved in a serious incident."

"Fuck's that mean?"

"Hear about that body in Thailand Plaza a few weeks back?" asked Morales.

Wolin cocked his head and squinted, a parody of someone desperately trying to remember something. "Hmm. Let's think. Well, I was in here, so..."

"We know you weren't involved," said Jarsdel. "But we think the victim could be related to you."

"Why?"

"DNA," said Morales. That seemed to satisfy Wolin who, like most criminals, looked upon DNA analysis as a great but mysterious force.

"The indications are that it's your brother," said Jarsdel. "Have you been in contact with him?"

"Nope for both."

"Sorry, you have two?"

"Well, that is kind of usually what people mean when they say 'both.' Cops don't need a GED anymore?"

Jarsdel ignored the remark and pressed on. "Do you have any idea which of them the victim might be?"

"Eric's in the Corps. Okinawa. So it's probably Grant."

Morales was startled at the ease with which Wolin speculated on the violent death of a relative. "You don't seem very upset. You understand we're talking about a body, right?"

Wolin didn't answer.

Jarsdel had his notepad out. "You have a last-known address for him?"

"Some hole on Edgemont, south of the Boulevard. I don't remember exactly."

"You know of anyone who'd want to do your brother harm?"

Wolin laughed. "I wouldn't've thought anyone'd give enough of a shit about him to want him dead."

"I take it you weren't close," said Morales.

"He sucked at life. Big dreams. Always working some scam or another."

"*He* sucked at life? Who's the Joe Shitbag sitting up here in the Twin Towers?"

"What'd he do for a living?" asked Jarsdel.

"I don't fuckin' know, okay?" Wolin's voice took on an edge. Morales pointed a finger at him. That was all, just a finger, but it calmed Wolin down. "Check with the Wax Museum," he said with a shrug. "He was tight with a couple of ragheads who ran the place."

Jarsdel made a note. "The Hollywood Wax Museum?"

"That's the one."

"Any idea on a name of one of those—"

"Nope."

"Okay. Well, back to Grant, we'll also need any other vital details you can give us. Height, weight, birth—"

"Hey," said Wolin, brightening. "You think I could get out of here and ID the body for you? I could do that."

"Forget it," said Morales. "Burned beyond recognition."

"Burned, huh? Sucks to be him."

"Height, weight," Jarsdel repeated.

"Ah, fuck it. I'm done talking to you guys."

"Wait a second," said Morales. "You understand your brother was murdered, right? You tellin' me you so cold you ain't gonna help us catch who did it?"

"Hey, you know what I had for breakfast today?" said Wolin.

The detectives stared at him.

"No? Well, let me tell you. I got fake scrambled eggs—the powdered kind, okay? And some stale-ass bread, and a sticky little fruit cup with a spot of mold on it the size of a dime. What you guys have for breakfast?"

"Mr. Wolin," Jarsdel began.

"That's what I thought. Okay, so when you and I have the same thing for fucking breakfast, then we can talk. I'll talk to you all day long and sing you sweet music." He turned his head toward the door. "Guard!"

The deputy reentered. "Everything okay?"

"We're done," said Wolin.

The deputy stepped over, unshackled Wolin from the desk, then cuffed his wrists.

"You find the guy who barbecued my brother," Wolin said on his way out, "give him a big smooch for me."

———

Jarsdel had volunteered to drive back to Hollywood Station, and the two detectives pulled out of the parking lot reserved for law enforcement personnel. They headed south, then Jarsdel made a right on Cesar Chavez, away from the 101 on-ramp.

"Where the hell you goin'?" asked Morales.

"My treat," said Jarsdel, pulling onto Alameda. Next, they turned onto First, and Jarsdel found a vacant meter.

"What's this? Little Tokyo?"

"Yup." Jarsdel got out and, sighing, Morales followed.

"Trust me. My folks started bringing me here when I was a kid." He glanced over and saw that, in his enthusiasm, he'd walked far ahead of his partner. He slowed, letting him catch up. So far, Morales hadn't offered an explanation for his limp, and Jarsdel had thought better than to ask.

"How far's this place?" asked Morales.

"Just up ahead. See that crowd over there?" He pointed to a group clustered under a yellow awning printed with the words *Daikokuya Original Noodle & Rice Bowl.* "Don't worry. It's a quick turnover. And worth the wait." When they reached the restaurant, Jarsdel ducked inside and put their names down on a clipboard.

Morales was glowering at him when he came back outside. "We don't have all day to dick around out here."

"We gotta eat, right? Look, it's practically a sin to be so close to this place without stopping in. If you think I'm wrong, you can give me shit about it as long as you want."

Morales leaned against a parking meter, then migrated to a chair in the waiting area as people began to be seated. The wait was longer than Jarsdel had hoped. Twenty minutes, then half an hour. He glanced at Morales, but by then, the other man had seen the heaping bowls of ramen and smelled the rich pork broth, and his frustration had been overcome by hunger. By the time they were finally seated, his mood had completely changed.

"So what's the best thing here?" he asked, scanning the short menu.

"You want the original Daikokuya bowl."

After they put in their orders, the two detectives were quiet. Morales sipped a Coke and scanned the restaurant. It was designed like an authentic Tokyo ramen joint, with the kitchen located inside the dining area. Bar stools lined the counter, and customers seated there could watch their food being prepared. Jarsdel and Morales were at one of the red vinyl booths that abutted the opposite wall, on which hung vintage Japanese posters and exquisitely battered metal signs. The place was bustling and cramped but cozy.

Jarsdel was the one to break the silence. "Back when I was in uniform, my TO and I stopped by In-N-Out for lunch one day. So we get our food, and right away, his phone rings, and he goes outside to take the call. I don't want to be rude and start eating without him, so I decide to use that time to go use the men's room. I'm gone maybe a minute, that's it. When I get back, my TO's still outside, but now there's this string sticking out from my burger. It's an incongruous image, puzzling, and I didn't know what to make of it. Then I take the bun off, and then I'm even more confused. At first, I think it's a tea bag, but then I realize—"

Morales snorted. "That was you?"

"What was me?"

"The tampon in the burger. We heard about it all the way over in Wilshire. During roll call, Captain made a point of telling us never to leave our food unattended."

Jarsdel felt a peculiar sense of pride and nodded. "That was me."

"Probably not what you were hoping for when you joined up," said Morales.

"No, I guess not."

"What were you hoping for?"

"What do you mean?"

"You had a career before, right? History professor. Why would you trade that to be a cop?"

"I lectured at Pasadena CC, but it was always some entry-level survey class for freshmen. Not exactly the Sterling Professorship."

"Still," said Morales. "None of my business, but it just seems like you had a pretty good life figured out for yourself."

Jarsdel considered, unsure how much he wanted to tell Morales, who until now hadn't expressed the slightest interest in him. "I was twenty-nine," he said finally. "Six months away from my doctorate, and I realized my life would be exactly the same, year after year, until I retired. That I'd give the same lectures, grade the same papers, publish in the same journals, and that the most rewarding aspect of my job would be shepherding others through the same process. And all so they could do the same thing I was doing. Give lectures and grade papers and get published in journals."

"Yeah, that's some bleak shit, Tully," agreed Morales.

Jarsdel noticed he hadn't called him *Prof* and was glad. "I just didn't see the point," he went on. "I mean, I love history. I really love it, but—I don't know. It's something else to make it your life's work. And I couldn't imagine myself contributing anything new to it. It's hard to explain."

"I hated history," said Morales. "I always knew I wanted to be a cop, so what good was it gonna do me? No offense or anything."

Jarsdel nodded. "You have to come to it for the right reasons. The cause and effect of it, the story—that's it, really, above everything. The story of why."

"Why what?"

"Why we are the way we are. How far we've come, how much we've learned."

Morales smirked. "Come on, man. How far we've come? Tell that to Grant Wolin."

"Yeah, you see, that's exactly my point," said Jarsdel. "Look how shocked we are by that. There was a time when—and not that long ago—any regular person just woulda said, 'Oh well,' and not even given a shit. Instead, you're horrified."

Before he could continue, their food arrived. Aside from the noodles and the broth, Daikokuya ramen teemed with bean sprouts, seasoned bamboo shoots, scallions, thick slices of kurobuta pork, and a large, soft-boiled egg. The men ate ravenously and in silence. When they were finished, Morales leaned back and shook his head.

"Okay. You were right. Worth waiting for."

8

They made a deal: Morales would write up the warrant if Jarsdel conducted the initial search of the victim's property. They had the warrant signed that evening, and as Morales sat down to dinner with his family, Jarsdel was pulling up in front of Grant Wolin's apartment. Parking was scarce, and he finally gave up and grabbed a spot in the lot of a 99 Cents Only! store around the corner.

Wolin's jailed brother had been right about the apartment. It was located on Edgemont, between Santa Monica Boulevard and Lily Crest Avenue, a block west of LA City College. It was as drab and unremarkable as the building occupied by Dustin Sparks, if even more dilapidated. But unlike the other complex, this one had a directory at the front gate. The light that was supposed to illuminate the list of residents had gone out, and Jarsdel had to use his Maglite to read the names. He found the one labeled *Manager* and typed in the code. Through a mess of static, the line began to ring.

A man with a heavy Slavic accent soon answered, and Jarsdel did his best to explain who he was and what he was doing there. The manager continually asserted that no one had died on the premises and that if Jarsdel didn't go away, the police would be called.

"Sir, if you could just come out here and speak with me, you'll see that I have a warrant to search this man's residence. If you don't open the gate, I'll have to contact more officers to assist me." Even after years on the job, this was the hardest part—having to assert himself, and not with criminals but with ordinary civilians. It was in moments like this Jarsdel still felt like an impostor, someone playing cop, and they brought to mind all the things his parents had said to him when he enrolled in the academy.

He pushed the thoughts away as the man finally relented and emerged from the building. He was bald and hunched over, wearing a paisley shirt and khaki pants. Jarsdel badged him, then pushed the warrant through the gate for the manager to scrutinize.

"Who apartment?" he asked.

"It's on the warrant. Grant Wolin."

"Wolin," he murmured. "Wolin. He very much behind on rent. Six weeks."

"When's the last time you saw him?"

"I don't see him. Any tenant. They just push rent under door."

"Well," said Jarsdel, "unfortunately, he's going to continue to be behind. He's deceased."

"Is dead?"

"Yes, sir."

The manager handed back the warrant. "When can I clean place out?"

"We won't know until we take a look around. If part of the crime was committed in the apartment, it'll take longer. Otherwise, you can expect to have it back in about a week."

The man made a disgusted sound in the back of his throat and shook his head, but he finally opened the gate. The two then hiked up a dank, ill-lit staircase to the third floor. "By the way," Jarsdel asked, "do you by any chance have an on-site laundry facility?"

"No. Coin laundry block away."

They stopped in front of number fifteen. There were several notices taped to the door urging Wolin to contact the management, along with an intimidating legal document notifying the occupant that he was being given his final warning to pay his rent or face eviction. The manager knocked, waited, then knocked more loudly. No one answered. Jarsdel would have been surprised if anyone had. The manager fumbled through his keys until he found the one he wanted, then unlocked both the dead bolt and the knob.

Jarsdel gloved up. "I'll take it from here, please," he said, slowly pushing open the door. The first thing that hit them was the smell—high and rancid, like the noisome odor drifting from an open dumpster. It was dark inside, and Jarsdel felt along the wall to his right for the switch. He flipped it, but nothing happened. Once again, he used his Maglite for illumination. In its sharp beam, he saw a ratty-looking couch and a floor lamp arching crookedly to one side. He stepped into the room and hit the lamp's toggle switch. The cold light of a fluorescent bulb revealed a spare living room with poorly patched walls.

His first thought was that this was indeed a crime scene or at least that the place had been ransacked. A pile of clothing was bunched in a corner, and shreds of newspaper were strewn across the badly stained carpet. A painter's bucket had been knocked over, and its contents—which appeared to be dirt—were scattered everywhere. But then Jarsdel looked into the kitchen and saw that he'd been wrong. He also now knew that whoever had killed Wolin had inadvertently taken another life.

The cat lay on its side. It looked nearly flat, as if it'd been run over, but that was only because it had decomped pretty well in the stifling apartment and now rested in a dried pool of its own juices. Jarsdel felt no breeze and wondered if flies had managed to get in. Probably. They always found a way in. But now they were gone.

He sensed movement and saw that the manager had stepped across the doorway. "Fui!" the man said, wrinkling his nose.

"Sir, I'm gonna need you to stay outside."

"Something dead?"

"Now, sir. Outside."

The man turned and walked out, mumbling something in what sounded like Russian. Jarsdel didn't suppose it translated to "Have a nice day." He went back to his search, stepping over the cat and into the kitchen. The smell was much worse in there, and Jarsdel saw the litter box, full to overflowing with shit, in the corner by the refrigerator. Both the cat's water and food dishes were empty. On the kitchen counter was a small bag of kibble, and it too was empty, torn raggedly open along its side. The cat had tried desperately to live. There was nothing else of interest, and Jarsdel went back out to the living room.

Against the wall by the only window was a small breakfast table and a folding chair. Next to the dining setup, stacked waist-high, were several large cardboard boxes. One of the boxes on top had been opened, and Jarsdel pulled back the flaps to look inside. The box was divided into twelve compartments; most were empty, but a few held half-pint mason jars. Underneath these was a sheet of cardboard, and when he lifted it, he saw a dozen more jars. That made twenty-four per box.

Puzzled, Jarsdel continued to scan the room. On the coffee table in front of the couch, he came across a controller for a PlayStation 4 along with another, smaller box, this one about the size of a ream of paper. It was also open, and he pulled out a receipt from a company called Customize-It, detailing the order of one thousand canning labels. Jarsdel pushed aside the packing material to get a look at what Wolin had ordered. He pulled out a sheet of wax paper, on which were two medium-sized identical labels. Against a background of palm trees and searchlight beams were the words *Genuine Hollywood Dirt!* Then, in smaller letters, *Take a bit of the magic home with you!* The word *Hollywood* was rendered in the same font and eye-catching arrangement as the letters of the Hollywood sign. He replaced the labels and the receipt, curious if the bucket of dirt the cat had knocked over was destined to end up in the jars.

He opened a door to what he thought would be the bedroom but found it was only a closet. The apartment was a studio, and Wolin must have been using the couch as his bed. One corner had been designated as a hamper; threadbare briefs and stained gym socks made a small, dingy mountain.

On either side of the TV stood cheap pressboard bookshelves, bearing mostly action movies and games for the PS4. He scanned the titles, then did a double take when he reached a block of games that were each part of the *Call of Duty* series. Lined up against the spines of the cases were perhaps twenty shell casings of various calibers. Just eyeballing the find, Jarsdel was able to identify most of them as coming from 9mm rounds. The rest were a motley arrangement, from a .22 Long to a .38 Smith & Wesson all the way to a .45 Colt. They'd need to be collected individually to prevent them from marking each other up, and he'd have to get more evidence envelopes out of his car.

Jarsdel resumed his search of the apartment and was more impressed by what he didn't find than what he did. Nowhere in the room was there a cell phone, a wallet, or a set of keys. That kind of non-evidence was vital, indicating Wolin had most likely been grabbed elsewhere and his valuables disposed of after his death. But it also closed off yet another avenue of investigation, ensuring that no one in the complex would have been witness to Wolin's abduction.

The bathroom didn't look like it had been cleaned in years. A scum of greasy dust and cat hair covered the sink and the rim of the shower stall. The toilet seat was up, and Wolin hadn't flushed the last few times he'd urinated. The smell was terrible, and Jarsdel used a foot to lower the lid and depress the flush handle. He opened the medicine cabinet and found a large Ziploc of medical marijuana, complete with the sticker that identified the product as legal per the California Health and Safety Code.

Seeing nothing else of interest, he moved again to the living room. On the floor next to the sofa was a pink plastic milk crate Wolin had been using to hold his files. Jarsdel flipped through the folders, hoping for a photograph that would have better resolution than the grainy printout of the victim's driver's license. In a folder marked *MISC*, Jarsdel found what he was looking for: an eight-by-ten photo of Wolin posing with a wax dummy of Jackie Chan. The flimsy cardstock souvenir frame indicated that it had been taken at the Hollywood Wax Museum. "Come play with the stars!" it read in the margin. In the picture, the ersatz action hero had one foot raised as if about to deliver a kick, but his expression looked sleepy, even dazed. Wolin stood close by, grinning and pointing one finger at the dummy, as if he really were in the company of the celebrity. Jarsdel was captivated by the image. It was so endearing, so human, and it brought home the reality of Wolin's murder like nothing had before. Here was a real person, not the grotesque, unrecognizable corpse sitting in cold storage. For the first time, Jarsdel felt a surge of anger against whoever had murdered this man, who'd made him suffer so terribly. And for what? What could he have possibly done?

Jarsdel set the photograph aside. There was one more thing on his list he wanted to find. He opened drawers, fished through the jacket pockets in the closet, even checked beneath the couch cushions. But no matter where he looked, Jarsdel couldn't find a single red quarter. And the manager had said there was no on-site laundry, so that meant Wolin wouldn't have gotten hold of a red quarter meant for the washing machines.

Whatever its meaning, it had been known only to the killer.

9

The Wax Museum was located in Jarsdel's least favorite part of the city, just across the street from the outdoor mall at Hollywood and Highland. Day or night, the place swarmed with tourists, sidewalk vendors, star map tours, and street performers dressed to look like movie characters. Souvenir shops sold crude T-shirts, Academy Award replicas, and "Wish You Were Here" postcards featuring rows of bikinied, suntanned asses. The great irony, thought Jarsdel, was how these few blocks were advertised worldwide as epitomizing the Hollywood scene but were in reality the least authentic thing about the city. The movie industry that had once made the zip code its home had long since migrated to other parts of town or, when the tax incentives were great enough, out of California entirely. All that was left was a vague simulacrum of Hollywood, which in itself was a mere idea or even the dream of an idea. The whole scene, from the handprints at the Chinese Theatre to the giant stone elephants towering above the Hollywood & Highland Center, added up to yet another twisted mirror in the carnival fun house that was Los Angeles. Jarsdel found it all deeply depressing and more than a little creepy.

He arrived at the Wax Museum at ten, just as they were about to open for the day. A dozen tourists were already in line in the lobby, but their guide had made advance arrangements, and the crowd moved quickly inside.

Jarsdel was about to step up to the counter when something caught his eye. Nestled among the usual showbiz-themed souvenirs and knickknacks sold in the lobby stood a three-tiered wire display rack. He was familiar with the wares, though he'd never imagined any place would actually carry them. *Genuine Hollywood Dirt!* read the sign. *Only $14.99!* Even more surprisingly, it looked as if the rack needed to be restocked. Only five jars of Genuine Hollywood Dirt remained.

"How many, please?" The man behind the counter was in his midtwenties, wore a mustache, and spoke with an Indian accent. His name tag identified him as Ramesh.

Jarsdel showed his badge.

The young man looked fearful. "Is there a problem?"

"No, no problem. I want to know about the man who sold you those." He indicated the remaining jars.

Ramesh blinked. "Sold? He did not sell—I mean, *we* do not buy them. We sell them here for him, on consignment. As far as I know, it is well within the law."

"You're not in trouble," said Jarsdel. "I'm with Homicide. Is there a place we can talk?"

"Homicide? Who's dead?"

"Let's talk about it somewhere else."

"I cannot leave the counter. There's no one else to take over for me."

A voice spoke up from behind Jarsdel. "Excuse me?" He turned to see an angry-looking woman trailing a brood of four children. "If y'all gonna talk, you mind if we get our tickets?"

Jarsdel didn't see any other choice but to get out of the way and let her through. If this kept happening, it would be the strangest interview he'd ever conducted.

After the family had gone inside, Jarsdel approached Ramesh again, this time with a photograph of Wolin. It was the one of him with the Jackie Chan dummy, only Jarsdel had scanned and cropped the image so it would just be of Wolin's face and upper body.

He set the picture on the counter and slid it over to Ramesh. "Do you recognize this man?"

"Of course," said Ramesh. "His name is Grant. He's the one with the dirt."

"You're identifying this as the man you have a deal with? To sell his...souvenirs?"

"Yes. Is he okay?"

"When's the last time you saw him? Do you recall?"

"I'm not sure. It's been maybe two weeks. More, I think. He hasn't been answering his phone." Then Ramesh asked again, "Is he okay?"

"I'm sorry to tell you he's passed away," said Jarsdel.

Ramesh was silent a moment, then shook his head. "I don't understand. You say he's passed away. Why are the police involved? Was he killed?"

"It was a homicide, yes. Did you know him well?"

Before Ramesh could answer, Jarsdel had to step out of the way again to let another group of tourists through. It took about three minutes for Ramesh to pull up the reservation and complete the transaction. While Jarsdel waited, he observed the young man carefully. A change had definitely come over him. He didn't smile as he had before, and he went about his actions with the kind of robotic sluggishness typical of those in shock.

When the tourists had cleared out, Jarsdel once again approached the other man. "Were you and Grant close?"

"We were friends," said Ramesh. "It's hard news."

"I'm sorry to bring it to you," said Jarsdel. "But I'm going to need to speak with you further. Is there a time you could come by the station and give your statement?"

"I'll do anything I can to help."

Jarsdel pocketed the picture of Wolin and removed one of his business cards. He handed it to Ramesh. "When are you free?"

"I'll call my uncle. If he's okay taking my shift, I can come today."

Jarsdel nodded. "Good. And again, I'm very sorry."

Ramesh Ramjoo arrived at Hollywood Station that afternoon. Both Morales and Jarsdel were there to meet him, and the three of them went into one of the interview rooms adjacent to the squad room. After getting the preliminaries out of the way for the benefit of the recording devices, Jarsdel led the questioning.

"Can you tell us how long you've known the victim, Grant Wolin?"

Ramesh considered. "About two years."

"And how long were you in business together?"

"He got the idea for the Hollywood dirt a few months ago. He brought it to me and my uncle, and we agreed to sell them in the lobby."

"What was your end?" asked Morales.

"I beg your pardon?"

"Your cut. Of the profit."

"Oh. Twenty-five percent."

"What's your uncle's name?" asked Jarsdel.

"Suresh Malhotra."

"Spell that for us, please?"

Ramesh did so. Jarsdel referenced a legal pad where he'd jotted down his questions for the interview. "Did you spend time with Grant outside of your business arrangement?"

"We're both gamers. We'd hang out a couple times a week. Mostly at his apartment, since I live with my uncle."

"Did you know much about his personal life? Girlfriend or anything?"

"He didn't really care about girls."

"He was gay?"

"No." Ramesh looked uncomfortable. "No, he said—He told me the word once, because that was my worry, that maybe he was gay, and I don't feel that way, so..."

Jarsdel was flummoxed, but Morales spoke up. "Asexual."

Ramesh nodded. "Yes. Asexual. No interest."

Jarsdel gave his partner a curious look, and Morales shrugged. "They march in the LA Pride Parade now."

"Oh." Jarsdel gave his attention back to Ramesh. "Did Grant have any enemies? Anyone who'd want to harm him?"

"In real life? No, or if he did, he never said anything about it to me."

"What do you mean, in real life?"

"He'd talk trash online sometimes, during games. But in real life, he was always cheerful. Everybody liked him."

Jarsdel wrote down *Gaming console—forensics? Chat logs? Long shot.* He looked up at Ramesh. "What was his personality like? Other than being cheerful."

"He always had a lot of ideas. Things like inventions or business ideas. He also had a screenplay he was working on. Always wanted to make some money."

"Did he ever borrow money from anyone or have trouble with debt?"

"I don't think so. Once, his brother helped him out with his rent, but that was a long time ago."

"His brother? Do you know which one?"

"I don't know his name. Not the bad one. The other one—the one in the army."

"We were told he was in the Marine Corps."

Ramesh shrugged. "Okay."

"And you mentioned the other brother, the one you just called 'the bad one.' What was their relationship like?"

"He was afraid of him. When they were kids, he used to beat Grant up. When he was out of jail, sometimes he'd just come by and say he was spending the night. Grant never argued with him about it."

"What about you? You meet him?"

"A couple times, but any time he showed up, I'd leave. I didn't like him very much."

Jarsdel allowed a commiserating smile. "I don't blame you. What else can you tell us? What was Grant like socially? Did he like to get high?"

"He smoked a little."

"Marijuana?"

"Yes."

"Nothing stronger?"

"No, just that."

"Ever join him?"

Ramesh hesitated.

"We're just trying to get a sense of his lifestyle. You're not gonna get in any trouble. Legal now anyway, isn't it?"

"Okay," said Ramesh. "Sometimes."

Jarsdel nodded. "Back to the dirt. Did you have an exclusive arrangement with Mr. Wolin, or was he free to sell it wherever he wanted?"

"We didn't have a contract or anything. I think he tried to get Ripley's interested in it, but no luck. Oh, and Hollywood Museum and Cinema Legacy Museum. They weren't interested either."

"Is there any other place you know of that did decide to deal with him?"

"No. Sometimes he'd just set up a stand somewhere. He liked the spot in front of Cinema Legacy, but the owner would complain to the police, and he'd have to move. Didn't matter that he had a street vendor's license. They'd always come up with a reason for him to go. His stand was too big, or he was blocking foot traffic." He considered. "It wasn't an easy life. You know, dangerous. He didn't have any protection. One time, I was working the ticket counter, and he came running over to tell me he'd just been attacked. Some guy in front of the theater flipped over his cart and broke all his jars. And when Grant called the police, they didn't come."

Jarsdel made a note to talk to the owner of the Cinema Legacy Museum. "Was it the only way he made a living?"

"He also advertised for Fantasy Tours."

"What's that? One of those bus tours of celebrities' homes?"

"Yeah. This one is mostly for the Chinese market. He even learned a couple words in Mandarin so he could attract customers. But he didn't lead the tours, just advertised."

"Where'd he advertise?"

"He'd walk the Boulevard, hand out flyers."

Jarsdel nodded, copying down the information about Fantasy Tours and adding a note to contact Wolin's employer. "And how long had he been doing that?"

"Only about two weeks. Before that, he worked for another company. I think...maybe...the Hollywood Experience. Something like that."

"What's that, another tour company?"

"Yes."

Jarsdel wrote it down, and Morales picked up the questioning. "Did Mr. Wolin own a gun?"

Ramesh looked surprised. "I don't think so."

"Never went shooting or anything like that?"

"No. He liked shooting in games, but not in real life."

"If I were to tell you we found a red quarter in his apartment, would that mean anything to you?"

"I'm sorry, a what?"

"A quarter that was painted red."

Jarsdel could see by the expression on his face that Morales's question had truly puzzled Ramesh. The quarter was a vital piece of evidence, one they were holding back from the media so that only the investigators and the killer would know about it. But both he and Morales had agreed it was equally important that they learn its significance and that saying they'd found it in Wolin's apartment was a safe way to broach the subject.

"No, sir," said Ramesh. "I have no idea."

Morales pursed his lips in thought. He nodded to Jarsdel to resume his questions.

"I know it was a few weeks ago, but do you recall seeing Grant on October 2? That would've been a Thursday."

"I'm sorry, I don't. Was that the day he was killed?"

"Sometime between the second and the third, yes. We're trying to put together a timeline of his last few hours."

Ramesh looked up and wrinkled his forehead as he strained to remember. Finally, he shook his head. "I'm sorry."

"He didn't mention plans to meet anyone? Could have been a business meeting, something social... Anything come to mind?"

"It's hard to say," said Ramesh. "I mean, like I said, he was always wanting to make money, to expand his business. It's possible he was going around to the souvenir shops to see if they were interested, but I don't know for sure."

Jarsdel didn't have any more questions, and he glanced over at Morales. The other detective gave a single shake of his head, and Jarsdel turned back to Ramesh. "Is there anything else you can tell us? Something maybe we forgot to ask that you feel is important?"

Ramesh said there wasn't, and the detectives concluded the interview.

Grant Wolin's funeral was held the next day at Hollywood Forever Cemetery. His brother Eric—in formal military dress—had received special leave to be present, but not Lawrence, who remained in lockdown after fighting with another inmate. Both detectives attended the service just in case a new suspect might emerge from the crowd of mourners, but they could tell immediately that their hopes were in vain. Only three people besides Eric—Ramesh, his sister, and their uncle—had shown up. There was a brief, twenty-minute service, then Wolin's ashes were interred in a columbarium.

After the Ramjoo family had departed, the detectives introduced themselves to Eric Wolin. He looked like a stronger, healthier version of his late brother and stood with a soldier's iron bearing.

"Sorry for your loss," said Morales, shaking the man's hand.

Eric nodded. His eyes were dry, but his jaw trembled as he spoke. "What's happening with the investigation?"

"We're making progress," said Jarsdel. "Is there anything you can tell us that could help?"

"So what you're actually saying is you don't have any idea who did this."

"We don't have any suspects yet, no. Your brother seems to have been a well-liked man. He didn't move in large social circles, but the friends he did have spoke very highly of him." *Friend*, Jarsdel mentally corrected himself. *Just the one friend.*

Eric grunted. "You should check out the drug scene. Brother was a major pothead. Lotta lowlifes."

"We'll look into it," Jarsdel lied. Lowlifes put an elbow through your car window to get at the change in your ashtray or rummaged through trash bins, hunting for credit card offers. What they didn't do was kidnap you, cook you alive, and pose your naked corpse on Hollywood Boulevard.

"There's one thing we're wondering about," said Morales. "We found a red quarter among your brother's things. Any idea what that was for?"

"A red quarter?"

"Painted red, yeah."

"Don't some apartment managers use them? For the laundry?"

Morales nodded. "That's right. But can you think of any reason your brother would have one?"

"Why? Is it important?"

"Probably nothing. We're just following up on everything we can."

They spoke for a few more minutes, covering much the same ground as they had with Ramesh. No, Eric didn't know of anyone who'd have wanted to hurt Grant. He was a nice guy, and everybody liked him. Eric reiterated his belief that Wolin's death had something to do with LA's drug culture. The detectives thanked him, exchanged contact information, and headed to their car. On the way, they passed Mel Blanc's tombstone. Beneath a Star of David was the epitaph, "That's all folks."

"How're we doing with those shell casings? Anything yet?" Jarsdel asked.

"I told you. Three days at least, and that's a rush job. You really think they have anything to do with it?"

"It's the only thing in the apartment that doesn't fit."

They reached the car. As Morales lowered himself into the

driver's seat, he clipped his knee on the steering wheel and gasped in pain. "Jesus. Goddamn it."

"You okay?"

Morales waved him off. They pulled out of the lot and onto Santa Monica Boulevard, where they hit a traffic jam. Morales rubbed at his knee, and Jarsdel could see that despite the car's air conditioning, a light sheen of sweat had broken out on the other man's brow.

"Go ahead and ask," said Morales. "Looks like we're gonna be here awhile."

"It's none of my business," said Jarsdel.

"It's okay. We're partners."

"All right. So what happened to your legs?"

Morales thought for a moment, then asked, "You know what a ghost call is?"

Jarsdel didn't. "Sounds familiar."

"So this is when I was back in patrol, about ten years ago. I'm working out of Valley Bureau at the time, and my partner and me—You know Peter Van Hook? I think he transferred to Professional Standards down at the PAB."

Jarsdel shook his head.

"Anyway," Morales went on, "it's like three in the morning, and we get a call from dispatch. It's a bad one—caller says she's being chased down the 900 block of Saticoy by a guy with a kitchen knife. She's already been stabbed and thinks she might be bleeding to death. So we hit it, and since we're already on Roscoe, we make it there inside of two minutes. And we're lookin' around and lookin' around, and there's nothing. We can't find this girl. We double-check with dispatch to make sure we got the street right, and they say we did. We each get out and start jogging up and down the block with our Maglites. Nothing. No blood on the sidewalk, nothing out of place, just a quiet street. We check in with dispatch again, see if anyone else is reporting this, you know? I mean, girl getting chased down the street by a guy with a knife, and she's screaming; she's gonna attract some attention. But again, nothing. We're about to wrap it up and just circle the block a few times in case we missed something when Pete spots a house with the door open. The metal security door is still closed, but the front door—the wood door—is open, and we can see the TV flickering inside. Rest of the house is totally dark."

Morales paused to make a left on Western. He cleared his throat and continued. "Pete says we should ask the guy inside if he's heard anything, so we approach, not thinking anything of it. I'm in front, so I knock. It's loud, pounding on the metal like that at three in the morning, but no one answers. I identify myself and knock again. Then, all of a sudden, *boom!*—someone fires both barrels of a 12-gauge through the fuckin' door. I take it right across my legs. Lucky I didn't get my dick shot off. Anyway, I go down hard, and Pete's shouting, and there's another couple shots, and I black out. When I wake up, I'm in ICU."

Jarsdel didn't know what to say, and Morales continued.

"My wife and I used to dance. Bachata. You know bachata? Fridays at Club Bahia with a live band. I was good. I know I'm big now, but a lot of that's only 'cause it's hard to exercise. I was never a string bean, but I was fit, solid. And I could move."

"Who was the shooter?" Jarsdel asked.

"Some old guy. Dementia. Shouldn't've been living alone like that. And Pete had to take him out. Didn't know the shotgun was empty by then, and the guy wouldn't put it down. Whole thing shows you, you never know what's behind that door. Here we are, thinking we're gonna have a friendly chat with a citizen, and then I'm on disability leave three and a half months. Almost didn't make it back."

"But what about the call?" asked Jarsdel. "Was it some kind of setup?"

Morales shook his head. "Whoever made it had no way of knowing we'd pick that house. No, I still have no idea. We never did figure it out. Fuckin' ghost call. Changed our lives, though, both me and Pete. You never know what you're gonna sacrifice for this job till the moment it happens."

By the time he made it back to Park La Brea, Jarsdel was exhausted. Something about the funeral service, followed by Morales's story, made him feel emotionally drained. He wanted to do nothing more than curl around a bottle of wine for the rest of the night with a new slack-key album he'd bought. He had a Meiomi pinot noir in one hand and an opener in the other when his cell phone buzzed. He unclipped it and checked the display. It was a text from his father, asking if he could come at seven instead of six-thirty. Jarsdel stared in puzzlement for a moment, then groaned. His dads were having a dinner party for some of their academic friends, and Jarsdel had forgotten he'd promised to drop by.

"Shit." He was tempted to text back and cancel but knew they'd probably been looking forward to seeing him all week. At least Dad had been. He wasn't as sure about Baba.

Jarsdel put the bottle of Meiomi back in the closet under the stairs, where it would remain cool, and changed out of his work clothes. He put on a burgundy, fitted T-shirt Dad had bought him at Tankfarm & Co. in Seal Beach. It clung to his thin upper body, accentuating his slight, ungainly physique, but Dad would be so happy he'd thought to wear it. He left his gun and badge in his nightstand drawer and headed out, steeling himself for the cross-town drive.

There's no good way to get from the Fairfax District to Pasadena, even at the best of times, and this was five thirty on a weeknight. Jarsdel pressed southward until he hit the freeway, then crept along until he finally reached the 110 interchange. By the time he got off at Fair Oaks, he'd been on the road the better part of two hours. He'd had *Hawaiian Slack Key Guitar Masters* on repeat the whole way, but not even Ray Kane and Cyril Pahinui could stop him feeling tense and agitated when he pulled in front of his parents' house.

It was a two-story Craftsman bungalow, built in 1915 by the Greene & Greene firm, and was listed as a tour stop on the city of

Pasadena's website. It had also been in the Jarsdel family for three generations. The sight of the old house helped calm him down a little after the hellish drive. It was a part of him, that house, and growing up an only child in a neighborhood with no other kids, it had often been his sole friend. One day, it would probably be his, if his parents didn't disown him.

Jarsdel made his way up the curving brick walk to the front door and rang the bell.

———

Robert Jarsdel, professor emeritus of English literature at USC, had recently gotten into Moroccan cooking. That night's dinner had been prepared in a tagine, the conical clay cooking vessel, an apparatus so tall that it scraped the top of the house's old oven. What emerged was a kind of lamb and rice stew, and Robert had somehow managed to overcook the lamb and undercook the rice. The result was a dish that was both chewy and crunchy, but neither Jarsdel's parents nor their other guests seemed to notice. The wine, however, was good—a potent Rombauer zin that made up for the experimental cuisine. Jarsdel had put away two glasses before reminding himself he still had to make it all the way back across town.

"Like some more?" asked Robert, threatening Jarsdel's plate with a heaping spoonful of stew. He was handsome, in his late sixties, and a man whose coiffed silver hair and black horn-rimmed spectacles made him look like a B-movie scientist.

"Mm," said Jarsdel. "Maybe just a little."

Besides Robert and his husband—Professor Darius Jahangir—and Jarsdel himself, there were only two others at the table. He knew one of them. Richie Berman, a longtime friend of his parents who taught screenwriting at USC. Berman, in his fifties but as strong and fit as a college linebacker, had been in earnest conversation with an enormous, red-bearded man since Jarsdel entered. The beard was a showpiece, thick and luxuriant, an ordered companion to the mass of curls erupting from his head. A faded black sport coat struggled to contain the man's bulk, and a faux-vintage tee reading *Sawyer Family BBQ*—*"Our family has always been in meat!"* bulged across his belly. Taking in the scene, Jarsdel thought this was about what he'd expected when his parents had invited him to their "dinner party."

"When I sat down to watch it, I was totally resistant," the bearded man said. His voice was at odds with his size—high, even strident. "I'm thinking, 'Why are we remaking Tarkovsky? I mean, really? *Tarkovsky?* You know it's just gonna be painfully hip, right?' But I was actually pretty impressed. And this is what I've always been saying. You should do a remake only—*only*—if it's a significant departure from the original. It has to have something new to say. Otherwise, it's no different from fan art, you know? Just masturbation. Put some thought into it. I mean, the height of folly is Van Sant's *Psycho*. Yikes. I actually shouldn't even bring it up—such low-hanging fruit."

Berman shook his head. "I don't know. Can't think of a single remake I've been happy with. Not one."

"Serious? What about the '78 *Body Snatchers*?"

"It's okay."

"*What?* Man, I think it's completely solid. I mean, with the original, you've got this great but heavy-handed commentary about conformity, Red Scare shit, et cetera. But with the Donald Sutherland one, it's pure post-Watergate malaise and paranoia. And setting it in San Francisco's just genius. Dream of the Love Generation's clearly over, and now everyone's gotta join the zombie establishment. Brilliant."

Berman shrugged. "Okay."

"You know what? I don't know why I even bother with you." He turned to the others. "Yeah, this is the guy who called *Jaws* 'Wet Godzilla.' Frickin' *Jaws*, people. Right?"

Robert touched Jarsdel's arm. "I don't think you've ever met Jeff Dinan, have you?"

"Hmm? No, I don't think so," Jarsdel said, extending his hand across the table.

The giant half rose and gave it a bone-grinding squeeze.

"Meetcha," he said, then sat again. The solid oak chair groaned as Dinan's weight returned.

"Jeff curates the USC film vault," said Robert.

"Oh," said Jarsdel. "Cool."

"And," Berman put in, "despite his overall rock-bottom taste in movies, he's got a hell of a private collection too. Criterion actually borrowed his uncut print of *Phase IV* when they decided to do the remaster. Dary, didn't he screen some rare extended cut of *Satyricon* for one of your ancient studies classes?"

Darius gave a single nod. "Tried to talk me out of it for weeks beforehand. Assured me *Caligula* would've been a better choice."

Robert and Berman laughed, but not Dinan, who studied Jarsdel's face with naked fascination. "Whoa," he said, then glanced from Darius to Robert. "He looks like both of you. How the hell'd you guys pull that one off?"

"Ah," said Robert. "My...er...*seed*, I suppose one might say, and Dary's sister provided the egg."

"Sweet."

"A surrogate carried Tully to term," Robert continued. "In fact, our boy here—"

"Dad." Jarsdel lifted a hand. "Come on. No one needs to hear all this."

"But it's history! Living history!" He clumsily brushed a forelock from his brow and flashed a wine-stained smile. He'd already had too much, and soon, his bon-vivant routine would take on a forceful, mawkish flavor.

Robert turned back to Dinan. "So, our own boy was the very first gestational surrogacy in the state of California. The very first. Perfect arrangement too. I'd just come into some money from my father's passing, and the nice young lady referred to us had a tendency toward an eleemosynary lifestyle—a kind of Valley Girl incarnation of Blanche DuBois." He chuckled at his joke.

Jarsdel kept his head down and jabbed at his food. He'd never particularly liked this story, but it had grown even more irritating since his departure from academics. Now, Dad seemed to suggest, Tully's primary accomplishment in life was being the scientifically engineered progeny of two gay men in the mid '80s. Everything after that was simply a lead-in to the colossal betrayal of his parents' most sacred wishes.

Robert's facial expressions were always exaggerated when he drank, and now he did a perfect, vaudevillian pantomime of a man remembering something important. He looked over at his husband. "Dary, we need to send her a Christmas card this year. Don't forget."

Darius nodded, his mouth full of food. He was a very thin, severe-looking man, but one whose downturned mouth was capable, occasionally, of the most unexpectedly radiant smiles.

Not tonight. He swallowed with some effort. "I never do," he said.

"What about last year? Did we send her one last year?"

"Never forgetting is never forgetting."

Robert showed his purple teeth again and addressed the group. "Dary is Mnemosyne in the flesh."

Dinan perked up. "Hey, I know that one. Wasn't that the chick who boinked Zeus and gave birth to the Muses? You know, the goddesses of art and stuff?"

Robert beamed. "Absolutely correct. A well-read young man." He nudged Jarsdel. "Not the only one at this table who knows his Hesiod, I see."

"I actually have no idea who that is," said Dinan. "Only reason I know about the Muses is from *Xanadu*. Next to *Can't Stop the Music*—oh, and *The Apple*, can't forget about the ass-pounding *Apple*—*Xanadu*'s the most requested cheeseball musical I've had to screen at nostalgia fests."

"What..." Robert trailed off, baffled.

"The movie," said Darius. While Robert's speech came out in a sonorous baritone, everything Darius said was hard and clipped. The words themselves were doled out sparingly, as if he only had a limited supply. When he saw Robert still didn't understand, he exhaled softly. "It's not important."

"Okay." Robert brightened again. "It's a movie, I guess. Ooh, Tully, you'll find this interesting. Jeff moonlights as a projectionist at the Egyptian. Remember when we used to take you there?"

Jarsdel smiled. "Last time was *Ernest Scared Stupid*. So I guess it's been about thirty years."

"I remember. You used to *love* those Ernest movies."

Dinan looked at Jarsdel, horrified. "You mean you haven't been since the renovation? Oh, man. Stop by on Halloween. Me and a friend are doing *The Man Who Laughs*. One of my own prints. Pristine. Gonna be awesome. You guys should all come."

"Got an organist?" asked Berman.

Dinan looked annoyed. "You don't use an organist for that one. It's got a great original score." He turned his attention back to Jarsdel. "I'll put your name down."

Jarsdel started. "Wait, when is this? Halloween?"

"Frickin' *yes*. Halloween, man. 'Anything Can Happen on Halloween.' Remember that song?"

"It sounds great, but I'm not sure—"

"I'll put your name down. You make it, great. If not, no sweat. You got a plus one?"

"Sorry?"

Darius looked over at his son, the first time he'd done so all evening. "He's asking if you'd be bringing a date."

"Oh," said Jarsdel. "No. I don't think so."

"Speaking of which," said Darius, "I ran into Maureen at the faculty brunch today."

"Okay."

"Asked after you. Wanted to know how you were doing."

"Okay," Jarsdel said again, sensing a trap. He hadn't seen his ex-fiancée in two years, and that had been an accidental encounter at a Trader Joe's. Jarsdel wasn't in the mood to talk about her, but Darius went on.

"Wasn't sure what to say."

"I'm all right, Baba."

"Glad to hear it. I see her again, I'll tell her. She's married now. Theater arts professor."

"Well," said Jarsdel, "I guess you can't have everything."

Darius smiled wanly.

"Tell you what," Dinan cut in. "I'll put down two just in case. Maybe you'll bring a friend. No one should go solo on Halloween."

"I really doubt I'll be able to make it," said Jarsdel. "But—"

Darius interrupted. "How's work?"

"Ooh, I don't know if we want to talk about work," said Robert.

Dinan, grinning, glanced from Jarsdel to his parents. "I'm not in on the joke. What is he, like, an undertaker or something?"

Jarsdel looked straight at Darius. "I'm in law enforcement."

Robert sighed. Berman bowed his head, as though Jarsdel had mentioned someone who'd recently died.

Dinan's eyes widened with interest. "You're a cop?"

"Detective."

"No way. Really?"

"Sexy, huh?" said Darius. "No life as a dusty, luftmensch academic. Not for our boy. He's out there making a difference."

Jarsdel's mouth dropped open a little. Even he was surprised at the hostility behind the sarcasm.

Dinan went on as though Darius hadn't spoken. "Always wanted to be a detective growing up. What guy doesn't, right? What are you in—narcotics? Vice?"

"Homicide."

Dinan slapped the table with two hands, making Robert jump, then leaned back in his chair, shaking his head in awe. "Wow. Seriously wow. You working any cases right now? Probably can't talk about 'em, right?"

"Yeah, I don't think it's the best dinner conversation," Jarsdel said.

"No, please," said Darius. "Give us a taste. What'd you do today, for instance?"

"Baba, c'mon. Dad hates it when I talk about work."

"He can handle it. And our guest is interested."

Jarsdel sighed. "It was nothing. Lots of paperwork, and then I went to a funeral."

"A fellow officer of the peace?"

Jarsdel was taken aback. "No."

"Oh," said Robert. "I really—"

"To provide solace?" asked Darius. "Or to root out a suspect, like Columbo?"

Jarsdel took a measured breath. "Both, I guess. My partner and I thought there might be a chance that the kill—the...uh...perpetrator might show up."

"And was your supposition borne out? Did the dastardly villain show himself?"

"No."

Darius nodded. "So glad my son is making the most of himself. You know Marty called me from CSUN. They have a spot opening up in their history department this spring."

"Great," said Jarsdel. "I assume you told him I already have a job."

"I referred to you as a liminal figure—a seeker, poised between worlds."

"I'm not poised between anything. I assure you, I'm fully present in what I do."

"Tully speaks four languages," Darius said to the rest of the table. "English, of course. Farsi from very young—it's what I spoke to him as a baby. Fluent Latin by the time he was fifteen. Ancient Greek as an undergrad. He also knows how to read Akkadian, Aramaic, Hebrew." He glanced at his son. "Did I leave one out?"

Jarsdel didn't answer.

"I'm curious how often those skills aid you in your work. Perhaps a killer writes an incriminating note in cuneiform, and thank goodness, you're on scene to decipher it."

He'd gone too far. Jarsdel cleared his throat. "Actually, Baba, a guy was burned to death and dumped naked in the middle of Hollywood Boulevard. That's my current assignment, anyway."

Darius, smirking, shook his head. "*Épater le bourgeois*. But I think you'll find I'm a difficult man to shock. Even if you could, it wouldn't change my mind."

"About what?"

"What do you think? Your career."

"Wait, wait," said Dinan. "I heard about that. You're seriously working that case? Do you know who the guy is yet? The victim?"

"Dary," Robert broke in, "let's table this, huh?"

Darius gave an exaggerated shrug and stabbed a cube of lamb with his fork. A silence of several seconds followed. It was broken when Dinan swatted the table again, this time with just the meaty fingers of one hand. Even so, it was enough to rattle the dessert forks.

"You know what, though? Let's be real. You gotta love a good murder."

"Jesus, Jeff," said Berman. "C'mon."

"I'm serious. That's what Hollywood is, man. That's what we love about it. The toxic beauty. It ain't—you know—*Singin' in the Rain* Hollywood. It's *Swimming with Sharks*, it's *The Player*, it's *L.A. Confidential.* I mean, back in the '90s, there was this big push to clean it up, you know? Let's close down this, let's scrub up that, let's put in the metro, and all that other jazz. The whole Times Square thing. But it didn't work, because it wasn't the Pussycat Theater or—you know—unregulated food vendors that were the problem. How naive, right? You can't stop it from being Hollywood. It's like all the ferocity of the industry just feeds into everything else. The town's frickin' *alive* with resentment and suffering. I mean, New Yorkers think they're tough, right?" He clapped Berman on the shoulder. "Like this guy. I say live in LA for a while. New York kills you fast. Out here, it's slow. We eat people's dreams for breakfast. You work retail, do some cattle calls, get a half-assed degree in filmmaking or whatever, and before you know it, ten years have gone by, and you're out of options. Futureless. Every actor who couldn't get a break—and this isn't some small subset of the population. We're talking about hundreds of thousands of people, and then every PA who gets shit on every day by the line producer and every writer's assistant who just can't get that pitch meeting. And they go a little crazy. Because it makes you crazy to be that close to something and not have it happen. Whether you're in the biz or not, it touches you. It's this fury, this storm, always raging just below the surface, but every now and then, it breaks out, you know? *That's* Hollywood, man."

"Well." Darius plucked his glass from the table and held it out. In the low light, the wine looked more like ink. Or blood. "Hooray for Hollywood. And for amateur philosophers."

If Dinan noticed the dig, he showed no sign. He looked directly at Jarsdel. "We like it, you know. On some level. Our patron saints have always been dead celebrities. We like being reminded every now and then what the stakes really are. Keeps it real, knowing this shit can kill you."

Robert was about to speak, probably to suggest a change of subject, but Dinan steamrolled on. "And I guarantee: the place you guys found that body? The burn guy? It'll be just another tour stop in a couple years. Because if there's anything we're good at, it's not letting suffering go to waste."

———

After the guests left, Robert began clearing dishes. When Jarsdel offered to help, he was waved away. "Sit and relax. Talk to your baba."

"Okay, but I better hit the road in a little bit. Long way back."

"You could always spend the night here."

"Thanks, but I've got an early start tomorrow, and my place is closer to the station."

"Whatever you like." Robert left the room with a stack of dishes and some precariously gripped stemware.

Jarsdel looked over at Darius, who had leaned back in his chair, fingers interlaced behind his head. He appeared to be staring at the ceiling. Jarsdel wasn't going to get suckered into whatever game Baba was playing and resolved he wouldn't be the one to talk first.

He turned his attention instead to a small, freestanding bookshelf in the far corner. The top and middle rows were occupied with family photos, but the bottom held his parents' coffee-table book collection. The spines were a little blurry to him now, but Jarsdel had read them from where he sat so many times that he could probably name them all without looking. He was curious if one volume in particular was still there. Straining his eyes, he spotted it right where it had always been—sandwiched between a ten-pound Edward Hopper compendium and a copy of Carl Sagan's *Cosmos*. It was intended as a sober examination of how social mores affected art, but *Sex on the Screen: Eroticism in Film* had interested the twelve-year-old Jarsdel for a more basic reason. After a month of sneaking it up to his room, he'd been doing his homework at his desk one night when Baba appeared in the doorway and leaned against the jamb. It was meant to look casual, but the man was incapable of nonchalance. Jarsdel's defenses went up immediately.

"What you working on?" asked Darius.

"Reading comprehension," said Jarsdel. "For *O Pioneers!*"

Darius watched him in silence another moment, sighed, and was about to leave when a thought seemed to occur to him.

"Oh. By the way."

Jarsdel looked up, bracing himself.

"Around your age, a few things start to change for a boy." Darius shrugged. "All good things, but you might feel overwhelmed at times. There's an added responsibility too. A serious one. Young as you are, you have the capability now of being a father. You understand?"

Speechless, Jarsdel nodded.

"Good. And I want you to know you can ask us anything. Okay?"

Jarsdel nodded again and saw a hint of a smile on his father's lips.

"Okay," said Darius before turning to go. As he left, he spoke a line in Farsi, just loud enough for Jarsdel to hear. Its meaning escaped him at the time, but he understood it soon enough. It translated to something like *A dirty book is seldom a dusty one.*

It had been so long since Baba had looked at him with any real affection, and as Jarsdel regarded him now, he felt a sudden, desperate need to connect with him. To have nothing in the way and just be with him, like they used to be. Forgetting his resolution not to be the one to break the silence, Jarsdel spoke up.

"Please, Baba. I really wish you wouldn't get like this."

He didn't think his father was going to answer, but then Darius asked, "Like what?"

"You know. The whole 'my son is a disgrace' routine. It's tiresome."

"I would never think of you that way. As a disgrace."

"Ah, we're into semantics. A disappointment, then."

Darius turned to him. "You want me to lie to you? Of course I'm disappointed."

"Did you know," said Jarsdel, "that in my line of work, I'm actually considered a success? Five years in, and I'm already a homicide detective in one of the best departments in the world. That doesn't happen for everyone."

"Imagine a great pianist breaking his own fingers. How can you not be disappointed in that?"

"You see, I really, *really* don't like it when you do that."

"Do what?"

"You don't actually respond to me. You don't engage in conversation. You just keep on with the thread of what you're talking about regardless of what I say."

Robert had reappeared, standing in the doorway to the kitchen. "May I say something?" Neither Jarsdel nor Darius answered, so Robert continued. "It's hard on your baba and me when something like this CSUN job comes along, something we know you'd be good for, but you don't take it. It reminds us of what could have been."

"But see, that's always been *your* vision, not mine. You're both basically punishing me for doing my own thing."

"Your baba and I—"

"*Your baba and I, your baba and I.* Can't we have a single conversation where you don't say that?"

"What did we do to make you so angry with us?" Darius asked.

"I'm not angry at all."

"Then *why?*"

"Why what?"

"Why are you doing this, if it's not just a 'fuck you' to everything we've raised you to be?"

The words felt like a slap. "I'm really sorry you feel that way," Jarsdel said. "We've been doing this for years now, almost every time we get together. *Years*. It's nuts. Tell me what I need to do to convince you my job isn't some personal thing I did to you."

Darius gave a bitter laugh. "How can we not take it personally? You're our son. This thing you do, it could kill you, or you might kill someone else. It's no joke."

"Okay, now we're onto this part. Part two, the gravitas. Well, I'm not gonna kill anyone, Baba. You have any idea how rarely that actually happens?"

"And your partner? What about him? He ever kill anyone?"

"That's not something you ever ask. It's actually considered very rude."

"He ever get shot?"

Jarsdel struggled to form a reply.

"I take it by your silence that he has. Bravo. Makes me feel so much better."

"We love you, Tully," said Robert. "We love your heart, who you are, and we don't want to lose you. We don't want to lose you physically, and we also don't want to lose what makes you so special. You're not a parent, so you have no idea what it's like. Just try to put yourself in our position. One day, your son, who's one of the smartest people you know, comes to you and says he wants to be a policeman. You think he's joking, then you realize no, he's gone crazy. When will you say enough and come back to us?"

"I never left. I can't keep doing this. I'm sorry you guys feel like my job is an act of rebellion. I've told you a thousand times it has nothing to do with you, but you're not going to listen. I genuinely think what I do is important. I love you, but I'm not all of a sudden gonna go back to academia. Why does it have to be all or nothing with you guys?"

Robert wiped away a tear.

"Tully," said Darius. "You know what every parent's greatest wish is?"

Jarsdel sighed. "That their kids be happy, I know. And I am happy." He thought about the silence of his apartment at Park La Brea, about his solitary dinners at the Farmers Market, and added, "Happier than I'd be teaching."

Darius shook his head. "No. What all parents hope for is that the world will somehow come to love their children as much as they do. It's totally impossible, but there it is. And what you're doing, putting yourself out there as a cop, it hurts us on a level you can't imagine. People hate cops. And not just criminals. Everyday people too. We have reason to be not so fond, you know. Your dad was beaten with a nightstick. Gassed in protests. And I knew a boy who was killed in a terrible way by police in Tehran. You went from something in which you were universally appreciated to something that could snatch you away from us at any moment, and for what? For a society that loathes you. The thought of it breaks our hearts."

Tully rubbed his face with his hands. "I don't know what you want me to say."

"Say you'll at least think about finishing your PhD," said Robert. "It's all we ask. Get your doctorate. We'll support you while you work on it. If afterward you still feel that teaching isn't for you, we can explore other options. You could travel, join a research team, translate books."

"Just what the world needs. Another edition of *The Aeneid*."

"We'll figure something out. The three of us. Please."

Jarsdel stood. "The murder I told you about at dinner? Guy was tortured. Cooked alive. *Cooked alive*, Baba."

Robert closed his eyes. "Oh God, be careful. Please, my sweet son."

"We got another guy called the Dog Catcher. His idea of fun is poisoning dogs on the day their owners are getting married.

Charming, right? I mean, don't you remember what you always told me?" Jarsdel asked Darius. "That it was a privilege to be born here and in this time. You've said that ever since I was a kid. It's one of the things that got me interested in history in the first place. How much better everything is now compared to the way it used to be. That in spite of what's all over the news, people are measurably more loving, more compassionate."

"So?" said Darius.

"So if we're really going to move forward, you know, *as a species*... I mean, 'to be among those who renew the world...to make the world progress toward perfection.'"

"Ah. That. And you're a hero on a mission."

"Someone has to be. I can't go back knowing the stuff I know now. There's too much to be done. I don't want to sit on the sidelines."

"You're actually idealistic. You think that badge and gun have put a big *S* on your chest. It's a kind of idiocy. I never thought I'd say that, not to you."

Jarsdel remembered how when he was a boy, they would go to Seal Beach on weekends. During the winter months, the town would erect a berm—a tall, beach-wide dune—to protect the homes on the boardwalk from the higher tide. He and Baba would wrestle on the berm, and over and over again, Jarsdel would lose, getting tossed down the gentle slope, the sand packing itself deep in his hair, and he would laugh with a child's unique, wild joy. Baba was a force then, a titan to the young Tully, and Jarsdel loved the exhilarating helplessness he'd feel when he tried matching his own meager strength against him.

As Jarsdel grew, Baba remained a titan, but one of the mind instead of the body—one so certain of his authority that it was never a question of whether he was right or to what degree. There was no compromise. When Professor Darius Jahangir spoke, his words dropped with the finality of steel doors, and Jarsdel found he was as helpless battling him as he'd been on the berm.

"I'm gonna take off," said Jarsdel.

"Okay," said Darius. "Be well."

"We love you," said Robert. "Please don't be angry with us."

"He's fine," said Darius. "He knows what he's doing. Must be a terrific feeling."

Jarsdel turned and left. When he made it to his car, he looked back at the house he'd grown up in, marveling at how much comfort it had given him, how warm his life in there had been. And now, he felt that the structure itself—its broad porch, polished wooden beams, and intricate joinery—had divorced him somehow, had let him go.

As he pulled away, Jarsdel didn't think he'd ever felt quite so alone.

10

Jarsdel took Friday to immerse himself as much as possible in Grant Wolin's life. He located the victim's car in the Edgemont apartment complex parking lot but found nothing of interest—no more spent shell casings and no red quarters. He then drove to Hollywood, where he walked up and down the boulevard, in and out of shops, pop culture exhibitions, and cafes. Of the people he spoke to, only a scant few recognized Wolin's picture, and no one was able to tell him anything he didn't already know. He spoke to the managers at Ripley's and at the Hollywood Museum, both of whom recalled Wolin as the one who'd approached them as prospective distributors of Genuine Hollywood Dirt.

He had two more stops to make, but he thought he'd leave one of them—the office of Fantasy Tours—for next week. That left the Cinema Legacy Museum on Las Palmas, the place whose owner had repeatedly alerted the police when Wolin set up his wares.

From the street, Jarsdel could see it was a small showroom, nothing like the space at the Wax Museum, and the layout was more like that of an art gallery, subdued and elegant and devoid of any of the ubiquitous showbiz paraphernalia. It also looked to be empty.

A homeless man, dressed in a green, hooded parka, occupied an unused doorway to the left of the entrance. He was dug in and probably intended to stay awhile. A shopping cart was parked nearby, loaded with plastic bags stuffed with cans and bottles, and the doorway itself was heaped with blankets. As Jarsdel passed him, getting a strong whiff of urine, the man growled.

A security guard sat on a stool just inside the front door of the museum, reading a copy of *Helter Skelter*. He looked up when Jarsdel entered.

"How's it goin'?" He had an eager smile and close-cropped blond hair. His uniform strained around his midsection, and despite the coolness of the room, the armpits of his shirt were dark with sweat.

"Great," said Jarsdel. "I was hoping—"

"Good afternoon," said another man, this one emerging from behind a display wall. "Welcome to Cinema Legacy." He crossed the room and stood behind a small desk just to the left of the front door. On it were stacks of souvenir guides to the museum's collection, priced at fifteen dollars apiece. Next to these, arranged in a fan, were an assortment of brochures for area attractions and restaurants— the Egyptian, Mashti Malone's Ice Cream, Wacko, the Hollywood Experience, and the Tiki-Ti.

"Our requested donation is twenty dollars," the man said.

"Actually, I'm here to ask a couple questions," said Jarsdel, pulling out his badge.

Before he could introduce himself, the security guard spoke up. "Hey, can I see that?" Jarsdel showed him the badge, and the guard grinned widely. "Crucial, man. That's *crucial.* A detective shield. Never seen one in real life before."

Jarsdel turned back to the man behind the desk. He too regarded Jarsdel with a kind of naked fascination, as if until now, they'd both thought of policemen as semi-fictional. "Of course," the man said finally. "We're happy to answer any of your questions." He wore a dark-brown suit and a pendant of some sort featuring a smooth, startlingly white stone. He looked to be in his late forties, but his hair was raven black without a single streak of gray. A dye job, and one that made a startling contrast with his alabaster skin. When he spoke again, Jarsdel thought he detected a hint of an accent.

"Raymond Stevens, proprietor." He held out his hand, and Jarsdel shook it.

"Detective Jarsdel. I'm with Homicide. I'm wondering if you've—"

"Homicide—whoa!" said the security guard.

Jarsdel ignored him and produced Wolin's picture. He showed it to Stevens. "Do you recognize this man?"

Stevens took the picture. "Hmm. He looks like the man... What do you think, Brayden?"

The guard stepped over. "Yup, that's the guy."

"What guy?" asked Jarsdel, directing the question at Stevens.

"He tried to interest me in selling his product. Some sort of scam for tourists. Selling dirt, if you can imagine. I mean that literally. Dirt." Stevens shook his head. "When I refused, he tried peddling his goods out front. It's a prime spot. Lots of foot traffic and none of those costumed absurdities that parade out front of the once-great Chinese Theatre."

Now Jarsdel was certain the man had an accent, but he couldn't place it.

"I would say that at best," Stevens went on, absently rubbing his pendant, "we have an adversarial relationship. And since I'm well-liked by many of the patrolmen in your department, I'm frequently the victor in our little squabbles."

"Can you recall the last time you saw him?"

"Oh, I'd say it's been at least four weeks. Has he gotten himself into some sort of trouble? Because he did seem to have that air of desperation about him."

"Yeah," added Brayden. "A real dirtbag. A dirtbag who sells dirt."

Stevens held his hands out to Jarsdel, palms up, as if saying *What more do you need?*

"Actually," said Jarsdel, "this man is our victim. Grant Wolin. He was found a few miles from here, down in Thai Town. You may have seen it on the news a few weeks ago. It got a lot of coverage."

"*Oh*," said Stevens. His eyes widened, and he put a hand to his cheek. "*That.* Yes, I did. I'm very sorry. I didn't mean to be making light of the matter. My goodness."

"Our interest at this time is as to whether or not he had any enemies. Other than yourself, of course."

Stevens frowned. "He was no enemy. I regret having given that impression. He was just a sad Hollywood man, and there are so many of them. I bear them no ill will. It's natural that this town attracts that type."

"How do you mean?"

"You know, those without talent themselves, who use Hollywood to supply them with a vicarious allure. The business with the dirt, for instance. And now this disgusting thing happens, and it just drags the city down more. It's the last thing we needed for our image."

Jarsdel noticed that Brayden had drifted again to his place by the door and to *Helter Skelter*. He turned back to Stevens. "And you say you hadn't seen the victim in four weeks, is that correct?"

"Approximately, yes, though I can't be sure. Brayden? Would you say that's about right?"

Brayden grunted his assent but didn't look up from the book.

Stevens shrugged. "I think that's probably as much use as we'll be to you. I'm sorry we can't do more."

Jarsdel took out one of his business cards and was about to hand it over when he glimpsed a nearby exhibit. Affixed to the wall was a long, weathered spear.

"Is that a pilum?"

Stevens followed his gaze. "Ah yes! A pilum. Well, not an authentic one. This was a prop used in the film *Spartacus*. You're familiar?"

Jarsdel nodded, fascinated.

"Please, feel free to have a look."

Jarsdel stepped through the turnstile and approached the piece. The spear was taller than he was, consisting of a long wooden shaft and a cruel, two-foot iron shank with a leaf-shaped head. Hung nearby was a series of stills from the film, presumably depicting the scene in which the weapon had appeared. During the gladiatorial contest, the one that precipitated the great slave revolt, the spear was used to kill the Ethiopian gladiator Draba when he attacked the audience of Roman aristocrats.

"Not many know to call it a pilum," said Stevens. "You're interested in history?"

"Used to teach it," said Jarsdel.

"Really?" Stevens stepped closer. "Hard to believe something so simple practically conquered the world. Well, I suppose it's not so much the spear as the will behind it. Anyway, feel free to peruse the rest of our collection. We may have other pieces you'd find of interest."

Jarsdel gave the room a quick scan. It was large by Hollywood's standards, especially considering how old the building was. Prewar, probably. Space was at a premium, and Jarsdel thought the rent must be astronomical.

"Quite a place," he said.

"Hmm? Oh," said Stevens. "Yes. When I first came here, I rented out this floor to a souvenir shop, if you can imagine. It was a few years yet before I could afford to kick them out."

"You own the property?"

"I do, but I save a bit of money by not maintaining a separate home. I keep rooms right here, in the basement. It's quite comfortable, and that way, I can keep a close eye on my collection. To tell you the truth, it would be difficult to be away from it. These things are as much a part of me as my fingers and toes."

"I know what you mean," said Jarsdel.

"Do you? Perhaps so. Well, please, I'd certainly be curious to know what you think of my little gallery."

Jarsdel shook his head. "Maybe some other time." And now he did hand over his business card. "I know it's a long shot, but if you happen to think of anything that might help, please give us a call."

"Of course," said Stevens.

"Can I get one too?" asked Brayden. Jarsdel gave him a card, and he ran his thumb over the embossed LAPD logo. "Crucial."

Jarsdel was about to step around, but Brayden got off the stool and intercepted him.

"I gotta shake your hand. You guys're heroes, far as I'm concerned."

Jarsdel reddened but extended his hand.

Brayden pumped it enthusiastically. "I was gonna be a cop, but I had this misdemeanor cocaine thing. I do stunt work, though, when I'm not here at the museum."

Jarsdel nodded, as if those two thoughts made any sense together.

Brayden finally released him. "If there's anyone in your department," he said, "maybe like Media Relations? You know, if they're planning on making a movie about cops, I'd really appreciate a shot at doing some stunt work on it. Maybe I could call you?"

Stevens broke in. "Brayden, the detective isn't involved with things like that. Let the man go about his job." He turned to Jarsdel. "Forgive him. He gets excited."

"What's *not* to get excited about?" said Brayden. "Life is awesome." He clapped Jarsdel on the arm and went back to his stool.

Jarsdel waited an uncomfortable moment, then gave the two men a parting nod before exiting the museum. His cell phone buzzed—it was Morales.

"Got some news you're gonna want to hear. It's about your shell casings."

Jarsdel perked up. "What is it?"

"For most of 'em, nothing. But ballistics confirmed one of the cartridges featured breech markings identical to those found at the scene of a double homicide. Congratulations."

"But—what does that mean? Was Wolin there?"

"Don't know. We got a meeting first thing Monday with two detectives from Hollenbeck Division. Until then, they've asked us not to talk about it with anyone. So it should be interesting."

"But do we have a suspect? I don't want to lose any time on this."

"That's the thing. Suspect's a banger out of Ramona Gardens called Delgadillo, first name Bonifacio. But the case is closed. Hasn't gone to trial yet—guy's in lockup down at the Twin Towers, probably rubbing shoulders with our buddy Lawrence. So we don't have to worry. Not like he's going anywhere."

Jarsdel took in the new information, not sure what it all meant. "I don't wanna just sit on my thumbs. Three days is a long time not to have any movement. Can we bump the meeting to tomorrow?"

"Hey, you try coordinating between two different divisions, see if you can do better. Besides, I'm takin' my kids to the zoo tomorrow, and I'm not movin' that for the world, let alone for your fussy ass."

Jarsdel massaged the tense muscles of his brow. "Okay. I guess I'll just...I don't know. Okay."

"You're still single, right? It's Friday. Go have some fun. Get lucky even. Hey—library's still open, right? You could meet someone, talk about the Dewey Decimal System or some shit over a cup of tea. Never know."

Jarsdel considered the suggestion. "Actually," he said, "I think I'll go to a lecture on industrial psychology."

———

Los Angeles attracted seekers of all kinds. When the first movie producers descended upon the fledgling city, they were seduced by the year-round sunshine and variety of shooting locations. They also welcomed the chance to put three thousand miles between themselves and Thomas Edison, whose sue-happy grip on the East Coast film industry made entrepreneurship impossible.

But something about the land also beckoned to the spiritually ambitious, those who felt called to iron out the great universal truths. Once William Mulholland finished the aqueduct, delivering on his promise that Los Angeles wouldn't perish from dehydration, the city could expand as rapidly as it desired. Along with the soaring population, a kaleidoscope of churches, orders, temples, and fellow-ships sprang up across the basin. In 1934, a Canadian-born mystic named Manly Palmer Hall opened the Philosophical Research Society, which he envisioned as a home for spiritual students of all traditions. The Society's building on the corner of Los Feliz and

Griffith Park Boulevards soon became a neighborhood fixture and, true to the founder's vision, provided a haven to those hungry for ancient wisdom.

Jarsdel had taken a glance at the calendar of upcoming programs upon entering the modest lecture hall. Among them were "Saint Germain and Rosicrucianism," "The Kabbalistic Origins of the Tarot," and a three-hour seminar titled "Passages: Texts, Contexts, and the Ways to Wisdom—Sor Juana Inés de la Cruz." Jarsdel didn't understand how Aleena's talk fit with such esoteric company, but the room was filled to capacity, and many in the audience took notes as she spoke.

Most of what Aleena said was utterly foreign to Jarsdel—a crash course in time and motion study, with an emphasis on discrete units of action known as "therbligs."

"There are eighteen therbligs," she announced. "Eighteen components that may comprise a given task. So for instance, let's say I want a drink from this bottle of water, okay? First, I have to search for it, right? That's therblig one: 'search.' Then when I see it, that's another therblig, known as 'find.' It goes on like that, from 'reach' to 'grasp,' which then becomes what's called 'transport loaded,' and so on. I suppose at its core, my job is to locate and eliminate waste within that process, lessening the time required to achieve each therblig—or even reduce their overall number if possible— and thereby maximize productivity. Maximize productivity in both mechanized and human-driven systems."

She smiled self-effacingly. "Which all sounds, I know, like, creepy and authoritarian and heartless, right?"

There was general laughter, and a man sitting next to Jarsdel called out "Soylent Green is made of people!" Jarsdel glared at him, and the man reddened and dropped his eyes.

"And it definitely does come off that way with the language we use," Aleena went on. "Lenin said scientific management was merely a new way of wringing sweat from the working class. But I think after we're finished tonight, you'll come to understand that that's a major misunderstanding of what we do. And that's really the fault of my industry, our failure to connect with people. Because time and motion study isn't really about efficiency. That's its stated purpose, yes, but the real goal? The absolute real goal, I think, is beauty."

A screen behind her filled with three images, side by side. The first was of Mikhail Baryshnikov performing a grand jeté, the second showed the exterior of an industrial facility, with a focus on what appeared to be a large cooling unit, and the third featured a smiling family playing a board game.

"The one thing these three subjects share in common is efficiency. Baryshnikov demonstrates the apogee of physical efficiency—what's possible when the human body works in absolute harmony with itself. A wasted motion would have lowered the height of the leap, would have strained the posture with unneeded effort.

"This server farm," she said, pointing to the second picture, "requires a constant supply of cool air. As you may know, air-conditioning produces a tremendous amount of heat. That heat is normally wasted, just discharged into the environment. But what this business does is interesting: they reclaim the otherwise discarded heat with a simple recovery system and use it to provide hot water."

Aleena moved to the third picture, the pace of her speech picking up. "This family would not be considered privileged by most Americans. Both the father and mother lack a college education and work in unskilled professions. The two children attend public school and depend on a subsidized food program. Together, they live in a one-bedroom apartment in a not-so-nice part of town. But here they all are, on a weeknight, enjoying some leisure time. A hundred years ago, this moment they're sharing here just wouldn't have been possible. So what changed? Think of everything that had to line up for this to occur. Not just the washer and dryer in the closet or the dishwasher in the kitchen, but what about the advances in textile manufacturing that make it so these parents don't need to work so many hours to afford to dress their kids? Or what about the incredible upholstery foam packed into that couch behind them?

To get furniture even half that comfortable, the wealthy of Europe had to harvest mounds of goose down—a slow, labor-intensive, expensive process."

Aleena paused, considering her next words carefully. "I get it, believe me, that these ideas can be abused. Efficiency for its own sake can lead to some pretty horrific treatment of human beings and animals, and we've gotten so good at making stuff that we often don't anticipate the ecological consequences. But I maintain that those are perversions of a truly magical idea. I'm not the most spiritual person in the world—not by far—but I know enough to marvel at the...unique, divine beauty in material mastery. In other words..." She paused again, thought for a moment, then shook her head. "There's no way to say it that won't make me sound like a moonbeam. But I guess this is the kind of place that doesn't judge moonbeams too harshly."

There was more laughter, with Jarsdel joining in.

"Physical mastery, the mastery of the physical universe," Aleena ventured, "is a kind of prayer. Is a kind of meditation. Is a kind of love. It's loving God, if you believe in God, or whatever you understand God to be. Because physical mastery is honoring creation—matter, and the spaces between matter." She shrugged. "And, if you don't believe in any of that, I'll quote the great Frank Gilbreth, the father of time and motion study. When asked what the point was, what to do with all that extra time he was constantly trying to squeeze out of a process, he said, 'For work, if you love that best. For education, for beauty, for art, for pleasure. For mumblety-peg, if that's where your heart lies.'

"You see, if nothing else, it's still better to live in a world where energy and resources aren't squandered, where you spend less time on neutral or unpleasant tasks and more time on the things that bring you joy."

Jarsdel liked watching her, liked how she commanded the stage, how she'd use shifts in cadence and timbre to texturize her words. Even her pauses were artful—coiled springs of silence that propelled her onto the next point with renewed momentum.

When it was over, he waited until the crowd around Aleena thinned out before deciding to approach. A tall, elderly man in a bright-yellow suit took her hand in both of his and said, "Wonderful. Just wonderful."

"I'm glad it went well."

"Oh," he said. "Oh, it did."

He moved away, and Jarsdel stepped forward. "Ms. Andreotti. It's Detective Jarsdel. Tully—from the other day."

Her face brightened with recognition. "Tully. You came. I'm glad. So what'd you think?"

"I think I—"

"And please stop calling me Ms. Andreotti. It's Aleena."

"If you prefer, okay."

"I do. Go on. You were saying what you thought."

"I think," said Jarsdel, "that in theory, it's the most direct and practical application of Stoic principles I've come across."

Aleena looked uncertain. "Oh. I'm guessing that's a good thing?"

"I think so, yes. It's a way of mindfully engaging with the world, which can only lead to an increase in gratitude for one's material circumstances. Gratitude is one of the keys to happiness, to inner peace—according to Epictetus."

"Hadn't ever considered it quite like that," Aleena said, "but it's nice. I appreciate you coming."

The man in the suit returned and put a trembling hand on her shoulder. "Could we borrow you for some photographs?"

"Um, sure. Yes." To Jarsdel, she said, "I'll just be a few minutes. If you wanna hang around, we can talk some more." She was led off to join a group gathered near a bowl of lime-green punch. Someone set off a dazzlingly bright flash, and Jarsdel looked away, his eyes stinging. When he turned back, others were already crowding in to have their own photos taken. Whether any of them had actually gained a single insight from Aleena Andreotti's hour-long "Pursuit of Perfect: The Sacred Mission of Efficiency, from Taylorism to Tokimeku" wasn't the point, Jarsdel knew. Half the fun of attending an obscure lecture was in telling everyone you'd done so. It let your colleagues know that while their brains lay dormant, ossifying in front of the nightly news, yours was alive, electric, popping new axons and synapses into being.

Direct and practical application of Stoic principles, thought Jarsdel. *What pompous, turgid bullshit.*

Disgusted with himself, Jarsdel slipped out of the lecture hall and escaped into the forgiving night.

11

I t was the first time Tully Jarsdel had met Detective Gerald Cooney of Hollenbeck Division, but he understood immediately why the man's nickname was "Sleepy." Cooney was slumped in the chair across from Jarsdel and Morales and looked as if he might nod off at any moment. The tired pout started with his wildly bushy eyebrows, as if each weighed several pounds and were pushing his features ever downward. He reminded Jarsdel of Droopy Dog.

Seated next to Cooney was Detective Troy Rislakki, his partner, who smiled and nodded with the frequency of a brownnosing fifth-grader. He was called, also appropriately, "Happy." Together, the two men, though both were of normal height, had been christened "the Dwarves."

Rislakki spoke as Morales flipped through their murder book, the thick binder containing all information relevant to the Delgadillo investigation.

"No doubt about it, he's guilty. Stone-cold killer," he said brightly. "We got him in protective custody in the Twin Towers. Any of those 18th Streeters get ahold of him, and they'll tear him to pieces. Already got a bounty on him, far as we know."

"What can you tell us about the arrest?" asked Jarsdel.

"Typical barrio bullshit. No one wanted to give up a thing, but it didn't matter. We got it all on video."

"Right, but what actually happened?"

"Two bangers from 18 get off the freeway in the wrong part of town is what happened," said Rislakki. "But whether they don't know they're in Big Hazard territory or just don't care will forever remain a mystery. They pull up to a liquor store in their lowrider, music pounding away, like they're trying for attention, right? Anyway, our guy, Delgadillo, he's in the store and looks out and sees them through the front door. You can watch him just standing there, trying to think what to do next. Then he pulls the milli out of his waistband and goes to work. *Pop pop pop.* Goes to work some more. *Pop pop pop.* This isn't the old spray and pray game you usually see with these assholes. Delgadillo's deadly with that fuckin' thing, like he puts in time at the range. Who knows? Maybe he does. Anyway, other guys didn't even get a shot off. Dead where they sat, right through the windshield. So there's nothing up for dispute. Our guy did it, then got in his own ride and took off. Picked him up later off his license plate. Came pretty easy, considering he'd just blown away two vatos. Still had the gun on him even, which we match in record time. Open-and-shut case, right?"

"Until you two jokers show up," said Cooney.

"I'm sorry?" said Jarsdel.

"Bonifacio Delgadillo skated on at least two other killings we know about. Uncle's a cartel hitter down in Culiacán, and we think the nephew's up here making inroads for the organization. We want him bad, and this could put him away so as we don't ever have to see him again. LWOP. But then you guys come along and muddy the waters with your fucking shell casing."

"Wait a minute," said Morales, putting down the murder book. "This isn't exactly our fault. All we did was run some evidence from this vic's apartment. How were we supposed to know it would come back to you guys?"

Cooney didn't answer.

Rislakki sat forward. "I think my partner's point is that this cartridge isn't helping anybody. In fact, it could do our case some serious harm."

"How?" asked Jarsdel.

"Take your pick. Prosecution'll have to disclose it during discovery, and any attorney—even some shitty PD—will have a blast digging up enough reasonable doubt to get Delgadillo off. More likely, he'll have some slick cartel lawyer. Here's a scenario for you: The police weren't able to maintain chain of custody. The crime scene wasn't secure if one of the shell casings ended up on the other side of town. You know how evidence is. Any of it's tainted, and the rest gets thrown out. The OJ effect. Or how 'bout this? Even better, and this isn't as far-fetched as you might think. For whatever reason, our video gets excluded. Happens all the time. Then they can argue that your guy—what's his name?"

"Wolin," said Morales.

"Wolin. Okay, that this Wolin guy was at the scene and participated somehow. Maybe even pulled the trigger and then gave the gun to Delgadillo to get rid of. Without the video, they can make up any story they want. And I guarantee you the guy behind the counter won't testify differently even if we subpoena the shit out of him. You think he's more scared of us or Delgadillo?"

"You're right—it doesn't sound far-fetched. It sounds batshit crazy," said Morales. "Our vic was a two-bit Hollywood hustler, not a crazed banger hit man."

"But that's my point too," said Rislakki. "The wilder the story, the more the jurors will eat it up. It's good theater. You know as well as I do that whenever the defense wins, it's only because they managed to tell a better story."

"Come on, Happy," said Morales. "Our guy was probably killed by those cartel maniacs. He wasn't *working* for them."

"Can you prove that?" It was Cooney, and he looked sleepier than ever.

"We will. Our guy was obviously the only witness to this thing other than the store clerk. Why else would he have a shell casing? Probably intended on talking to you guys, which is why he ended up in the oven. If I were you, I'd get that clerk of yours some serious protection."

"We got a couple uniforms cruising his place regularly," said Rislakki. "Besides, I don't buy it. Put us together, and we got more than two dozen years in Central Bureau. Never heard of anyone getting baked before. Why go through all the trouble for one Hollywood loser, just to keep him from talking? Nah, they'd just pop him."

"This is a bunch of guys who stick peoples' heads on spikes, and what—you don't think they'd stoop to something like this?" said Morales.

"We're not getting anywhere," said Cooney. "We need to know what your next move's gonna be."

"Hey, all we do is follow the facts where they lead us. And right now, they're leading us to Delgadillo. It may not be as clear-cut a case as you got, but he's looking better than anybody else right now."

"Even though," said Cooney, "that by trying to link your case with ours, you'll more likely sink them both? Anyone ever tell you that a pound of shit mixed with nine pounds of ice cream is still just ten pounds of shit?"

"What do you suggest we do?" said Jarsdel.

"Easiest thing in the world. Nothing. Pretend you never found the goddamned thing."

"Ain't gonna happen," said Morales. "Guy gets cooked alive and left right in our backyard. Freaks everybody out. It's like a kind of terrorism. Nope. We're not gonna let that fly up here. This ain't Juarez."

"Look," said Rislakki. "This thing goes to trial in eight days. Eight. Unless you've got something you can file with, just sit on it. That's all we ask."

Morales and Jarsdel looked at each other.

"What?" asked Rislakki.

"Too many people know," said Morales.

"Who?"

"Councilman Peyser, Lieutenant Gavin, Captain Sturdivant. Not to mention ballistics, obviously. You'll have to disclose."

"Fuck," said Cooney. "You fuckin' clowns. I'll tell you something. If this goes tits up because of you, you'll have to live with it. Because the next time Delgadillo opens up on somebody, it might not be just a couple mopes from 18. Could be a citizen. Could be a kid. That's on you."

———

"Terrific," said Jarsdel as they got back in the car.

Morales grunted, undoing his belt and pants before he sat down. "Don't let old Sleepy get to you. Guy as tired as he is, sure carries lotta anger. Don't know where he gets all the extra energy."

"Is he right?"

"About what? About us fucking up their case? Nah, they're overreacting. If anything, we'll make it stronger, show what a maniac Delgadillo is."

"But in eight days?"

"What? You got doubts?" said Morales as he turned out of the station parking lot and onto First.

"A few things don't fit. I mean, think about it, what Detective Rislakki said. Why go through all that trouble to get rid of a potential snitch? Kidnapping, torture, then dumping him all the way over in Thai Town. What's the point?"

"Makes an impression," said Morales.

"Yeah, but on whom?"

"Everybody."

"Okay, then why not kill the clerk too? He's much more of an immediate threat. He was actually in the store when the shooting went down. If I were gonna get rid of any witnesses, I'd start with him."

Morales shifted in his seat, thinking. "They know he's too scared to talk now, so they're not gonna bother."

"I don't know," said Jarsdel. "Just seems a little thin."

"Thin? What d'you mean 'thin'?"

"I have a tough time believing that people brutal enough to cook a guy are going to all of a sudden feel a lot of restraint when it comes to the remaining witness."

"Okay. Then what about the usual explanation? They're criminals. Not everything they do makes sense."

"But what about our guy, then? What the hell was he doing in Boyle Heights at eleven o'clock at night?"

"Probably had a habit. Remember our special effects technician and his Oxy?"

"Medical marijuana. That's all we found."

"Okay, so we don't know yet. We'll figure it out."

"And the red quarter? What's that mean?"

"Some random cartel shit. Who knows what all their stuff symbolizes. I bet it has to do with making a phone call using a quarter, calling the cops, something like that." Morales pulled onto the 10 West, heading back toward Hollywood. Almost immediately, they hit a wall of traffic.

"That still leaves a major unanswered question," said Jarsdel.

"Yeah, I know. The other shell casings."

"Where'd they come from? What do they mean? They don't come back to any other homicides."

"That we know of."

"Yeah, but again, I just don't buy Wolin as being into anything heavy. Look at him. Other than a DUI, what's he ever done? And now we're saying he was somehow in on the Delgadillo thing?"

"*We're* not saying that. It's a defense attorney who's gonna make that leap. And in that sense, I see what the Dwarves are getting at. We gotta definitively tie Wolin to the scene or clear him completely."

"That's what worries me," said Jarsdel. "Because either way, we're going to need an explanation for how that cartridge made it from a crime scene in Boyle Heights to a guy's apartment ten miles away."

His phone rang. He didn't recognize the number, but it might've had to do with the Wolin case, so he answered.

"Jarsdel."

"Hello, is this the detective? Tully?" It was a woman's voice.

"That's right."

"This is Aleena. From the lecture last night? I didn't get a chance to talk to you again before you left."

"Oh." Jarsdel felt a tingle in his chest. "Sorry. You looked busy. What can I do for you?"

"I don't know exactly how to say this. Hmm. Okay. I guess I'll just come right out with it. Are you married?"

Jarsdel didn't think he'd heard her correctly. An MTA bus had come to a stop in the lane next to theirs, brakes hissing. "I'm sorry. Could you say that again?"

"Ugh. I have a feeling I'm about to be embarrassed. I'm calling to see if you'd like to have dinner with me."

There was no mistaking her words this time. The tingle in Jarsdel's chest blossomed into a sweet fire. "I, uh... I'd love to."

"You would?"

"Yes. Very much so."

Aleena sighed on the other end of the line. "Cool. Are you free tomorrow?"

"Tomorrow?"

"I know it's short notice, but—"

"No, tomorrow's perfect."

"Great. Come by my place around seven? You remember where it is?"

"I do, yes. Where would you like to go?"

"You like pasta?"

Jarsdel said that he did.

"Then I'm cooking. Just bring a nice red."

"Okay."

"You have my number now, right? In case anything comes up?"

"Nothing's going to come up. But yeah, I have your number." Then he added lamely, "Thank you for calling."

Aleena laughed. "See you tomorrow."

Jarsdel clipped the phone back onto his belt.

Morales shot him a sideways glance. "I don't get it. That shit never happened to me, man. Girl callin' you up. Take my advice—just try not to talk a whole lot."

When Jarsdel pulled up in front of Aleena's house, the sun had nearly set, spilling its last few rays across the sliver of the Pacific that could be seen in the distance. He chewed and swallowed a breath mint he'd been sucking on, then picked up a gift bag from the passenger seat. Inside was a bottle of Opolo Mountain zinfandel his parents had given him for Christmas. He'd debated bringing flowers but in the end decided against it. Jarsdel had always tried too hard and didn't want to scare Aleena off. Whatever impression she had of him, he had a feeling he could easily fuck it up just by being himself. The recent episode with Becca was just one example, and if he were in a masochistic mood, he was sure he could dig up others. He remembered Morales's advice and resolved to be a more aloof, subdued version of himself.

"No Rain Man stuff," he murmured.

The door opening onto the courtyard was ajar, and Jarsdel walked inside, passing the gurgling fountain on his way to the front door. He was about to knock when he realized his heart was pounding. He'd only been in one relationship since Maureen—a week-long fling of mediocre sex and alcohol-induced pledges of fidelity, even talk of marriage. Two souls in pain, both on the rebound, both trying to convince themselves they'd finally found their true mates. And one day, they'd woken up and had no idea what to say to each other. And that was it—a crash so fast and final they hadn't even exchanged a handshake. Now here he was, years since he'd last been with anyone, standing on the porch of a woman whose dog had been murdered by a serial killer.

The door swung open. Aleena stood there in a black cocktail dress, her tanned shoulders lightly spotted with freckles. She was barefoot, and something about that made Jarsdel feel a primal jolt of excitement. "Are you gonna come in or just stand out there all evening?"

"How'd you know I was here?"

"Kitchen window. C'mon inside."

Jarsdel stepped into the house, which was a welcome cool after the day's mugginess.

Aleena pointed at the gift bag he was holding. "That for me?"

He handed it to her, and she took out the bottle, cradling it against her forearm like a sommelier.

"Mm, zin."

"One of my favorites," said Jarsdel. "Hope it...uh...works with what you're cooking."

She studied him a moment, her rouged lips parting in a smile. "I'll pour us a couple glasses."

She turned toward the kitchen, Jarsdel following as he had the week before, and he was once again struck by the extraordinary view. And as it usually did, the sight of that sprawling expanse—tempered though it was by the dimming light of day—made him feel uneasy. *Somewhere in that city is someone who likes to cook people,* Jarsdel couldn't help thinking.

The fan above the stove was on full, sucking up the steam from the pan of pasta sauce simmering beneath it. Even so, the aroma of basil, garlic, and onions filled the kitchen. Aleena produced a wine key and sliced the foil from the top of the bottle. Jarsdel watched as her long fingers worked at the corkscrew. There was power in those hands, and they moved with a practiced assurance.

She caught him watching her. "Used to be a server. Three years at Cheesecake Factory."

Once the wine was poured and Jarsdel had his glass, Aleena went back to cooking, emptying a bag of spaghetti into a pot of boiling water. "So tell me about your name," she said. "How do you get 'Tully' again?"

"Oh," said Jarsdel. "My dads are both professors. They named me Marcus Tullius, after Cicero."

"The Roman guy?"

"Yeah. They had high hopes for me, I guess. Anyway, his nickname among those who study him has always been Tully. And that's what my dads have called me since I was a baby."

"Your dads? Plural dads? Are they... Or—"

"Gay, yeah."

"Cool. That's really cool."

Jarsdel smiled.

Aleena stirred the pasta. Billows of steam vanished into the vent. "So both dads are professors, and you ended up being a cop."

"I did."

Aleena poured a dribble of olive oil in with the pasta. "Were they freaked out?"

"Well, when I told my baba—that's 'father' in Farsi—that I joined the force, he wouldn't talk to me for months. And neither of them came to my graduation."

"Seems kind of harsh."

"It was, but you know, from their point of view, I'd joined the bad guys. Dad got teargassed more than once back in the sixties, and Baba won't even talk about the kind of things cops did to gay guys in Iran. Pretty dark stuff."

Aleena lifted a strand of spaghetti out of the water, pinched it to test for firmness, and dropped it back in. "I know what you mean. My mom's Lebanese, and she's the sweetest person in the world, but she's totally homophobic. Been here for, like, forty years and still can't shake it. It's just so ingrained in the culture over there. I mean, can't they still actually stone you to death for it in some places?"

"Yeah, they do."

"Shit. Crazy," said Aleena. "So with your parents, were you, like, *trying* to horrify them?"

"No." Jarsdel considered. "I don't think so. No, but...you sure you want to get into all this stuff? Not exactly pre-dinner, just-getting-to-know-you banter."

"Oh, see, I don't banter. It's what we in my field call 'avoidable delay.' So everything we say should mean something, else it's just noise. Besides, we can hardly go back to 'nice weather' and all that after you just told me about your amazing gay dads and their wayward, badge-carrying son."

"Fair enough," said Jarsdel, amused. "What's the best way to put this? Okay. You can be really good at something. Let's say you're the best horseshoe player in the world, but all you've really ever wanted was to play darts. And every time you toss that horseshoe, all you can think about is how much better, how much more fulfilling it would be to throw a dart."

Aleena thought about that. "Probably the worst analogy I've ever heard, but whatever—you wanted to be a dart player."

"I did. And it's not as if I didn't try to make my dads happy and do the academic thing. You know—Harris Tweed sport coat, copy of Plutarch's *Lives* under my pillow."

"So you're pretty much the perfect guy. Brains and brawn."

"Huh. I don't think 'brawn' and I have ever been in the same sentence before. Thanks."

Aleena dipped a long wooden spoon into the stockpot and collected a bit of sauce. She blew on it, took a tentative sip, and gave a nod of satisfaction. "Do you have a partner?"

"I do. He also thinks I should be in another line of work."

"You don't get along?"

"Not that well."

"Aw, bummer. In the movies, they always do. Or actually, I guess they don't, not at first. They have to clash and get on each other's nerves, but then by the end, they're total buddies. Mullets tend to be involved at some point. Maybe that'll happen with you."

"Working on it," said Jarsdel. "Took him for some good food the other day, and I think that softened him up a bit."

Aleena nodded at the pot simmering on the stove. "Never fails. Why do you think I'm doing this?"

Jarsdel felt himself blush. He took a large swallow of wine.

"Just so you know," she went on, "it's not my habit to call guys up and ask them to come over."

"No?"

"And I don't want you to get the wrong idea." She saw the disappointment on Jarsdel's face, then quickly corrected herself. "Oh no, I didn't mean it like that. That's not the idea I don't want you to get wrong. No, I'm totally attracted to you. What I don't want you to think is that I'm just lonely and rebounding from my husband. We've been separated a long time. I've made my peace with it, in other words."

"Okay," said Jarsdel. He'd never met anyone as direct as Aleena Andreotti, and he didn't quite know how to handle it. His resolve to be coolly aloof was crumbling.

───────

After they'd finished dinner, Jarsdel and Aleena sat side by side on the sofa, looking out at the city. It was fully dark now, and Los Angeles glittered silently before them. Jarsdel could even make out planes on their approach to LAX.

"You know what I'm thinking?" asked Aleena.

Jarsdel said he didn't.

"Our kiss good night won't be awkward. I'm taller than a lot of guys—taller than my soon-to-be ex, actually. He hated that, by the way. Being shorter. But you're just the right height for me." She considered. "Though I probably shouldn't have put so much garlic in the sauce."

Jarsdel's mouth was suddenly very dry. "It was delicious," he managed to say.

"Why thank you."

"Best vodka sauce I've ever had."

"Really? My father-in-law would always give me a hard time about it not being, you know, *authentic* Italian cuisine. But I don't care. It's good." She swirled the wine in her glass and took a sip.

Jarsdel detected the faint thrum of a helicopter. The sound grew louder as it approached, and looking out the picture window, Jarsdel glimpsed the beam of its spotlight skewering a line of deodar trees. He himself had done his share of chasing criminals up into the hills. It was a classic end run—a biological impulse to get to high ground. But it never ended well. He only hoped this helicopter wouldn't pick the Andreotti house to hover over. He was grateful when it banked to the left, out of sight.

"Can I ask you something?" he asked once it had passed.

"Sure."

"Why's your house so empty? No pictures or anything. Nothing that would say to me that anybody lives here."

Aleena was thoughtful. "Ever heard of William Morris?"

"I'm not sure. Which—"

"The arts and crafts designer. He was a poet too."

Jarsdel hadn't. "Okay, yeah, I think so."

"I have a quote from him on my business card. *Have nothing in your house that you do not know to be useful or believe to be beautiful.* There should be no such thing as stuff for stuff's sake, right? You've seen it. Some people will have, like, a vase with random dry sticks poking out of it, just because the idea of having some empty space in the house gives them this weird sense of anxiety. Neither useful nor beautiful, just displacing air. Empty space is like silence. Some people can't handle it."

Jarsdel nodded, looking down at his feet.

Aleena sighed. "But you know, that's only half of it. The house and pretty much everything in it were David's, and the things we shared—artwork and photos and whatever—it didn't make me feel good to have it all around, reminding me every day of him and the marriage and all that, so I made him take it. But even after that, I didn't feel like the house was really mine. I still don't. We haven't settled yet on what's going to happen to the place, so I guess I just want to be tied to it as little as I can. I'm already really picky about what comes into a house, and this way, if I have to move, it won't be so painful." Then she smiled. "Meantime, though, got a hella nice pad, don't you think?"

"Yeah."

"You ever married?"

"Engaged. A while ago. We don't even talk anymore."

"I'm sorry."

"I'm not. It felt like an arranged marriage. She was academic royalty, our families knew each other forever, and we played together growing up and—I don't know—I suppose on some level, it seemed like I was getting married to my cousin."

"What happened?"

Jarsdel hesitated.

"Sorry. Out of bounds?"

"No. It just doesn't make me look very good. What happened is I ended it. Then I quit my job as a teacher's assistant and enrolled in the academy. She said I broke her heart and that no one had ever broken her heart before and that it was worse than killing a person."

"Ouch."

"Yeah. But it's been five years. And hey, apparently now, she's doing great. Full tenure and married to a professor at USC."

The helicopter returned, skirting just shy of the house, firing its blinding spotlight somewhere out of view.

"Super romantic," Aleena sighed.

"If you want, I can call them up and tell 'em to beat it."

"Haven't had one of these in at least a month. Had to happen tonight, right?" Her fingers brushed his hand.

Jarsdel's heart sped up. "Those new copters are fitted with FLIR," he said. "Forward-looking infrared. They're so sensitive, they can detect thermal radiation on a dropped handgun. Bad guy ditches a gun onto a rooftop or whatever while he's running, and it'll actually glow on the monitor."

"Fascinating. Are you going to kiss me or what?"

Jarsdel had been wondering all night what it would be like—to kiss her, to hold her—and now he did, pressing his mouth against hers, tasting the red bitterness of her lipstick. She wove her fingers into his hair, heightening Jarsdel's passion. When they broke away, both of them were flushed, their breathing rapid.

"You know, there's something else I'm not in the habit of doing," said Aleena. "And that's inviting a man to bed on our first date."

"That's a good policy," said Jarsdel.

"Do you think so? I suppose. But I think there should be an exception to every rule."

Jarsdel swallowed. "Why?"

"I don't know." She touched his cheek. "I like you. A lot. What about you? Do you think I'm odd? Too forward?"

"No."

"Really?" She raised an eyebrow.

"Well, not in a bad way."

Aleena stood, taking Jarsdel's hand and pulling him to his feet. He let himself go then, surrendering to her as she led him through the strangely empty house. He felt wonderfully dizzy under Aleena's spell, drunk on the promise of what was to come. When they made it to her bedroom, she turned to him and, with two hands, gave him a playful shove onto the bed.

The bed frame caught Jarsdel behind the knees, and he went down harder than either of them expected. He tried not to grimace but couldn't help rubbing at his left leg, which had caught the worst of it. Aleena put a hand to her mouth.

"Oh my God, I'm so sorry."

"It's cool. It's cool."

"I'm such a doofus."

"No."

"I *am*. It's what I get for trying to be sexy." She climbed on top of him. "Forgive me?" Before he could answer, she began unbuckling his belt. "Here. I'll make it up to you."

Jarsdel gasped as she went to work on him, first with her hand, then with her mouth. And before he could protest that he didn't have protection, she lifted her skirt and drew him inside her.

"I'm on the pill," she panted, "and I'm clean." She moved her hips in tight circles, grinding herself against him, punctuating her movements with small cries of pleasure.

Aleena's enthusiasm for sex was something entirely new to Jarsdel, who came early and apologetically. As her breath slowed and she rolled off him, all Jarsdel could do was promise he'd be ready to go again soon. She didn't answer, just lay there, gaze fixed on the ceiling.

He waited until the silence became too uncomfortable, then tried again. "It's been a long time. I'm really sorry." When she still didn't answer, he asked if everything was okay.

"I don't know."

"Did I do something wrong? I know I wasn't good, but—"

"How badly did I just screw up?" she asked, turning to face him.

"What? Not at all. What do you mean?"

"Now that you've been with me, will you have any reason for coming back?"

"Why wouldn't I?"

"I was just thinking, maybe you feel like you got all you came for. I mean, we haven't exactly built up a relationship yet, so what's to make you...I don't know. I'm not articulating this well. I just really don't want this to turn into a one-night stand. I hate those."

"Aleena, no. It's not all I came for."

She put a finger on his chest, over his heart. "You promise? I'd rather you were totally straight with me."

"Absolutely. I want this to be—to be a thing. You know?"

She regarded him closely, looking for a hint of a lie, then nodded. "Me too." She fell back against the bed and gave a soft sigh.

"In fact," Jarsdel said, "what are you doing on Halloween?"

12

J arsdel and Morales reached the office of Fantasy Tours just after
eleven. The day was blazing hot, the Santa Anas blowing out
of the desert and giving the city the feel of a convection oven. As
Jarsdel stepped out of the car, something flew into his eye, and he
cursed, tearing up and blinking.

"Gotta love the Devil Winds," said Morales, stuffing his shirt
back in his pants and zipping up his fly. "Maybe we'll get some nice
wildfires too. Make those hose jockeys earn their paychecks."

Fantasy Tours was located on the second floor of a two-story
strip mall on Gower, between Lotus Massage and a branch of
Eastwood Insurance. Jarsdel caught the scent of seasoned meat
and fresh-baked bread from a kebab place on the ground floor.
The sign was in both Farsi and English, the latter part reading
Taste of Tabriz. Jarsdel saw it was a poor translation; the Arabic
letters actually spelled "Jewels of Tabriz," but the owners had
apparently decided an alliterative name would lure in more
Western customers.

Jarsdel and Morales exchanged a nod. They'd eat there once they
were done upstairs.

They climbed the steps, Morales white-knuckling the railing all
the way up. When they reached the top, a man emerged from the

massage parlor and gaped at the two detectives. He looked over his shoulder at the door closing behind him, as if considering a retreat, then appeared to slump in defeat. As they passed him on their way to Fantasy Tours, both Jarsdel and Morales greeted the man with a cheery "Good morning." He watched them go with the relief of someone who'd nearly been hit by a bus.

"We should check in with Vice," said Morales to Jarsdel. "Make sure this place is on their radar."

Jarsdel agreed. "Thought that guy was about to rabbit on us. Would've been a pain in the ass."

The blinds were drawn on the glass door of the tour company's office, but a sign indicated they were open. When Jarsdel pulled on the door, however, he found it locked. He rapped on the glass a few times and waited.

"Don't take no for an answer," said Morales, stepping forward. He gave a few robust backhand knocks, and Jarsdel thought he might crack the glass with his wedding band.

A moment later, the blinds parted, and the wide, alarmed eyes of a middle-aged Asian man peered out at them. "What the hell do you want?" His voice was oddly muted coming from the other side of the door.

The detectives pointed to the badges clipped to their belts. After considering for a few seconds, the man opened up but still didn't invite them inside. Instead, he stood with his arms crossed, scowling as he faced the detectives. He seemed well suited to it, with a bulldog's heavy jaw and jutting bottom lip.

"So what are you guys doing? Trying to break my door?"

"Sign says you're open," said Morales.

The man glanced at the *Open* sign and ripped it down. "There. Now you wanna tell me what's going on?"

"Can we come inside?"

"What's it about, huh? Why you guys bothering me?"

"What's your name please, sir?" asked Jarsdel.

"I don't have to talk to you."

"That's true, but I think you'll want to hear what we have to say. It could affect your business."

"Affect my business how?"

"It's about one of your employees. Can we talk inside?"

The man made a guttural sound of disgust but stepped out of the way. As soon as the detectives were in, he closed and locked the door behind them.

"Please don't do that, sir," said Morales. "We'd like the door to remain unlocked."

The man scowled but undid the dead bolt. "Now say what you need to say."

Jarsdel took in the space. The office was small, dark, and hot. Two desks lined a wall, but both phones were unplugged, their cords tangled on the pilling carpet. Boxes of promotional materials and multilingual brochures lay scattered around the room. Jarsdel couldn't tell if they were being unloaded or packed away. "Are you the owner of Fantasy Tours?" he asked finally.

"Yeah. So?"

"And can you tell us your name?"

The man sighed again. "Tony Punyawong."

"Is that a Thai name?" asked Jarsdel.

"Yeah. That a problem?"

"You have any ID?" asked Morales.

Tony jammed a hand into his back pocket and came out with his wallet. He flipped it open, showing his driver's license tucked behind an acrylic screen.

Morales smiled. "Can you take it out for me, please?" Wordlessly, Tony did as he was asked, handing the ID over to Morales, who barely glanced at it before handing it back. "Thank you."

"You don't have an accent," said Jarsdel.

Tony gave Jarsdel a withering look. "I'm from Diamond Bar. You ever gonna tell me what's going on?"

"You have an employee named Grant Wolin."

"I got lots of employees."

"This one walked the boulevard for you, handing out flyers." He took Wolin's picture out of his shirt pocket and held it out for Tony, who didn't take it.

"I don't know this guy. If he got into something bad, that's his problem."

"He's dead."

Tony hardly blinked. "Okay. That's got nothing to do with me. Anything else?"

"Sir, you need to chill out," said Morales. "We're just here trying to do our job—"

"Yeah, after breaking my door down—"

"*Trying to do our job.*" Morales raised his voice only a little above Tony's, but it was enough. The man took a step back.

"Okay. I been under a lot of stress, and when you knocked—"

"I get it. It was loud. Now can we focus on this here? Your employee ends up dead right over there in Thailand Plaza. See it on the news?"

Tony hesitated, then nodded.

"Okay, did it occur to you it might be your guy?"

"No. Why would it?"

"Didn't you notice your employee was missing? Did you call him? Did you call us?"

"There's something you need to understand about this business."

"Enlighten me," said Morales.

"People come and go. I'm lucky if I have someone working for me more than two weeks sometimes. I don't know everyone who hands out the flyers. There's no regular payroll or anything."

"What do you mean you don't know them? How do they get work from you?"

"I find 'em on Craigslist. They come down to the office and get a color-coded stack of ten-percent-off coupons. The guy you're talking about was yellow. Every voucher he handed out had a little yellow sticker on it, so when the tourists turned them in, that's how he got paid."

"How much?"

"Two dollars for every coupon turned in to make a sale. It's a good deal. Ask anyone."

"And I guess he just had to trust you, right? I mean, he had no way of checking you were being up front about how many coupons you were getting back."

"I don't rip off my guys."

Jarsdel spoke up. "How's business?"

"What?"

"Looks like you might be moving."

Tony seemed uncertain how to answer him. He crossed the room and folded down the flaps on a box of flyers. "I'm looking at other ventures at this time."

"No more tours?"

"Market saturation."

"What's that mean?" asked Morales.

"It means there's too many people in this business for me to make a profit." Tony bent down and began winding up a length of telephone cord that stretched across the room and disappeared into a pile of electronics. Soon, a black desk phone emerged like a hooked fish and whispered across the carpet toward him.

"Funny timing," said Jarsdel. "I mean, closing up so soon after one of your guys gets killed."

"I didn't even know him."

"We heard he was a pretty good worker. Even learned some Mandarin so he could get you more customers."

"I don't know. Maybe." The phone finally arrived at Tony's side. He secured the cord with a rubber band, picked up the phone, and set it in an old Amazon Prime box. He looked around for something else to do and set his sights on a LaserJet.

"When's the last tour you gave?" asked Morales.

Tony shrugged, removing the paper from the printer and laying it in a neat stack nearby. "Few weeks."

"And you're just closing up now?"

"Takes time. Fantasy Tours isn't the only thing I run out of here. Got a real estate broker's license and also operate as a travel agent. Help lots of people in the Thai community." He flicked open a hatch and checked his toner levels.

"I'm confused," said Jarsdel. "If the tour business isn't going well, fine, but why shut down everything?"

"What do you guys care?"

"I thought you were gonna chill out," said Morales. "And do you mind giving us your full attention?"

"It just seems like a big coincidence," said Jarsdel. "You say you hardly knew our victim, but you're packing up now he's dead."

Tony returned to where the detectives stood, glowering. "Again, nothing to do with it. I'm moving out of state."

"Where to?"

Tony shook his head. "I feel like you guys are hassling me. I didn't do anything wrong."

"Where to?" Jarsdel repeated.

"Bangkok."

"Thailand?"

"No, man. Bangkok, Minnesota. What do you think?"

"Got another question for you," said Morales, "long as you're in such a helpful mood. What does a red quarter mean to you?"

"A red quarter?"

"Yeah. If we were to tell you we recovered a red quarter in the course of our investigation, would that mean anything to you?"

Something in Tony's attitude changed. "Where'd you find it?"

"Doesn't matter," said Morales. "Mean something?"

Tony straightened up. "No. No, it doesn't."

"Really?" asked Jarsdel.

"No. I mean, it's just a weird question. Red quarter."

Morales stepped closer to him. "Mr.—what was it?"

"Punyawong," said Tony.

"Mr. Punyawong. My best advice for you right now is to tell us everything you know. Because if we find out later you were holding something back on us, that's what's called obstruction of justice."

"But I don't know anything!" said Tony, his voice rising. "You're asking me about a quarter and making threats. I'm sorry if I'm not handling it perfectly, but I've never been in a situation like this before. I'm not used to police guys asking me lots of questions. I was just going along with my day, and now you want to make trouble for me. It's crazy. It's—" He seemed to realize he was rambling and stopped himself.

Morales nodded slowly. "Okay. Remember what I said, though, about obstruction of justice."

The detectives each gave Tony their cards. "Do us a favor," said Jarsdel. "Let us know when you plan on leaving the country. We might want to talk to you again."

As soon as the detectives made it outside, Punyawong locked the door after them.

"Skittish," said Morales.

"What do you make of it?" asked Jarsdel.

"He's scared."

"Of us?"

"I don't think so."

"Me neither. Delgadillo, maybe?"

"Makes sense to me," said Morales.

"What should we do? Another trip down to Twin Towers, take our own crack at him?"

Morales shook his head. "He's lawyered up. Forget it."

"Can at least try."

"You want to spin your wheels down there, go ahead."

"I still don't get it," said Jarsdel. "What's the connection between Delgadillo and Wolin? And now this guy? It doesn't hang together."

"Look for the simplest explanation," said Morales. "How about this? Wolin saw Delgadillo blow those guys away in Boyle Heights and picked up one of the shell casings. The cartel tracks him down, kidnaps him, kills him. Maybe his boss Punyawong in there witnesses the abduction somehow, which is why he's so scared."

Jarsdel was baffled. "That's the simplest explanation?"

"I didn't say it was perfect," said Morales. "We're still missing one or two pieces."

"Yeah. One or two."

They began down the stairs, the smell from the kebab place beckoning.

13

Jarsdel pulled up in front of Aleena's just after six and texted her that he'd arrived. She was out a moment later, wearing a short, flower-print dress, belted across the middle, and knee-high, brown leather boots.

"You look amazing," said Jarsdel as she got in the car.

She leaned over and kissed him. "Thanks. So what exactly are we doing tonight?"

"I'm serious," he said. "Amazing."

She put a hand on his knee and slowly brushed her fingers up his leg, causing him to hit the gas too hard as they drove away from the curb.

"Okay," he said. "That's probably good. Thanks."

Aleena laughed, giving his thigh a final squeeze.

"Ever been to the Egyptian?" asked Jarsdel.

"Not since I was a kid. Didn't even know it was still open."

"Yeah, kind of fell apart for a while. But then in the mid-'90s the city sold it to a group of film historians for only a dollar. Gave it a major renovation. Heard it's really something."

"But what are we seeing? I don't like scary movies."

"Don't worry," said Jarsdel. "It's old. From the '20s. Besides, we don't have to stay long. Just thought it would be a fun night out."

The Hollywood Hills made poor roving grounds for trick-or-treaters. Many of the homes were tucked away beyond security gates and steep driveways. The few that were accessible and advertised their participation in the holiday were far enough apart to encourage most kids to migrate to the flatlands below Los Feliz Boulevard. Still, Jarsdel and Aleena passed a minuscule Iron Man being led down Bonvue by his father, and a little farther on, a Harry Potter and Hermione.

Aleena waved as they passed. "So cute."

They made it onto Los Feliz and headed west, passing the entrance to Griffith Park and the statue of its curiously named benefactor, industrialist Griffith J. Griffith. When they turned onto Hollywood Boulevard, Jarsdel saw they'd be in for a long drive. Halloween always brought the street its worst annual traffic jam. There was no way around it, he knew. Franklin and Sunset would be just as bad.

"Sorry about this," he said.

Aleena watched a small parade of sparely clothed teenage girls in goth makeup waiting outside an eighteen-and-over club. A man in a devil costume lunged at them, threatening them with his plastic pitchfork. "No prob. It's kinda what we signed up for, living in this city. What part of town you in?"

"The other end, pretty much. You know Park La Brea?"

"By the Farmers Market? Wow, how long'd it take you to get over here?"

Jarsdel smiled. "Wasn't that bad. Had this to keep me company." He turned up the music, one of his favorite Sonny Chillingworth albums. It made for a queer juxtaposition with the scene unfolding around them on the boulevard. A club security guard approached the man in the devil costume, shaking his head gravely.

"What is this?" asked Aleena. "Hawaiian music?"

"*Authentic* Hawaiian music. None of that 'Mele Kalikimaka' crap. Do you like it?"

"I don't know. It's different."

"I can put on something else."

"No, it's okay. Kinda relaxing." She thought for a moment, then added, "I woulda pegged you for a classic rock guy."

"Yeah, why's that? My rugged good looks? John Mellencamp olive jacket?"

"Ah, he was still just John *Cougar* on that album cover. No, I don't know. You just seem like the kind of guy who'd really appreciate a mean guitar solo. You know, really get into the technicalities of what makes a song *great*. I can see you giving a lecture on Frank Zappa or something."

Jarsdel laughed. "I promise I'll never give you any lectures."

"Oh, don't say that. I bet I'd love to hear some of the stuff you used to teach."

They sat in silence for a while, inching forward in the long stretch of traffic. The cars moved so slowly that pedestrians crossed the street at will, weaving through the cars and grinning made-up faces at the drivers. Some wore masks. A man dressed as Leatherface glanced in at Jarsdel and Aleena and shook a small sledgehammer at them before moving on.

"Ugh," said Aleena. "I hate Halloween. What about you?"

Jarsdel shrugged. "I kinda love it. Get to be someone else for an entire day."

"Is that why you became a cop? To be someone else?"

"Hey, therapy territory here."

"Just curious. Can't say I've met many cops. And I've definitely never been out on a date with one before."

"What do you call the other night?"

"Well, we didn't go out, did we?"

"No," he said, smiling. "I guess we didn't."

It took them another half hour to reach the Egyptian. Jarsdel offered to drop Aleena in front while he hunted for a parking spot, but she said she'd rather stay with him. They spotted a pay lot on Selma that was charging an astounding thirty dollars to get in, but Jarsdel didn't think he'd be able to find anyplace else. He grudgingly paid the attendant and they headed toward the theater.

"Wanna go into business together and open a parking lot?" asked Aleena. She slipped her arm through his, and again, Jarsdel felt a galvanic charge in being with this woman. She was lovely and strong and beautiful, and he felt he could fall in love with her if given the time.

The theater's exterior was done in the Egyptian Revival style, a product of the surging fascination with all things Egyptian when it was built in 1922. Hieroglyphs—linguistically nonsensical, Jarsdel quickly determined—along with paintings of the gods Horus and Seth adorned the courtyard walls. A crowd of people milled between the four large columns at the entrance, most of them costumed, waiting to get inside.

By the time they made it to the door, Jarsdel was afraid he'd made a mistake. So far, this date had consisted of sitting in traffic, looking for parking, then more waiting to get into a silent film Aleena didn't even want to see.

"Tickets?" asked the doorman. He was about twenty and wore plastic press-on fangs and a black turtleneck. Twin streaks of fake blood had been applied on either side of his mouth, but they made him look more like a ventriloquist dummy than a vampire.

"I think we're on the list," said Jarsdel.

The doorman consulted a clipboard on a nearby lectern. "Name?"

"Jarsdel."

The man nodded and made a note. "Reserved section, right in the middle. Hands, please?"

Jarsdel and Aleena held out their right hands, and the doorman stamped the backs of them with a blood-red crescent moon. *Red like the quarter*, it occurred to Jarsdel. He pushed the thought away.

The doorman waved them in. "Enjoy the show."

"VIP, huh?" said Aleena, squeezing Jarsdel's arm. "I thought police officers weren't supposed to use their position for preferential treatment."

"It's got nothing to do with me. The guy who runs this thing's a friend of a friend of my folks."

They followed the crowd into the largest of the two theaters, where they showed their hand stamps to an usher. She directed them to a section of seats cordoned off with painter's tape. Jarsdel was about to head toward the middle of the row when Aleena stopped him.

"Can we sit on the aisle? In case we decide to leave?"

"Sure." He lifted the tape, and they took their seats. "Shit, I'm sorry," Jarsdel said. "Did you want any popcorn or anything?"

"You're sweet. No, I'm good."

"Yeah? It's no trouble at all."

"I'm fine, really."

The room hummed with conversation. Someone shouted something and was answered with a raucous laugh. Jarsdel glanced at Aleena, but her head was turned away. He tried to think of something funny to say, but everything that came into his head fell flat.

Then the lights dimmed, and there was a smattering of applause. The screen's footlights came on, and a man stepped out of the shadows and moved center stage. He wore a tail suit, complete with white tie, cummerbund, top hat, and white gloves. It took Jarsdel a moment to recognize him as Raymond Stevens, proprietor of the Cinema Legacy Museum.

"I actually know that guy," Jarsdel said to Aleena.

"Who?" she asked. "Count Dracula up there?"

Stevens raised a cordless mic and smiled broadly. "Good evening." A few people in the crowd returned the greeting, but not many. Stevens didn't seem to mind. "I'm immensely gratified that so many have decided to join me on this most special of nights. I won't talk long, but as a confirmed pedant, I can't resist providing you with a brief introduction to tonight's presentation. I hope you'll forgive me this bit of indulgence. The film you're about to see is very dear to me, and in sharing it with you, I feel as if I'm making a roomful of friends."

Aleena leaned close to Jarsdel. "Ze children of za night," she said in a Lugosi accent, "vhat beautiful music zey make. Vine? I never drink...*vine*."

Stevens closed his eyes and held up his free hand in the manner of a revivalist preacher. "The Comprachicos traded in children. And what did they make of these children? Monsters. Why monsters? To laugh at. The populace must needs laugh, and kings too. What are we sketching in these few preliminary pages? A chapter in the most terrible of books; a book which might be titled *The farming of the unhappy by the happy*."

Stevens opened his eyes. The room was quiet now, waiting for him to continue. "So writes Victor Hugo in his 1869 novel, *L'Homme qui rit, The Man Who Laughs*." He began to pace the stage slowly as he spoke, directing his attention to any part of the room that wasn't yet with him. "The master writes with great insight, mocking our drive to impose ourselves, to *thrust* our will upon the world. The loathed Comprachico mutilators are merely a symptom, a product of our amusement seeking. Consider the man who docks his Doberman's tail. He does not do it himself but hires it out to one who is experienced in those matters. Is such a thing horrible? If not, when does horror enter into it? By what degree does the shaping of the world according to power and privilege become repellent, become abominable?

"And so, what makes this a horror film is not the chain-rattling ghost, nor the hand creeping from behind a curtain to squeeze the life from a nubile throat." Stevens extended his hand and mimed the gesture, then went on. "The horror lies in the poisonous wake of an ego given to whim and caprice and possessed of the power to indulge itself. And it echoes in the eyes of the king's political enemy, Lord Clancharlie—Gwynplaine's father—as the door of the iron maiden closes upon him. For it is not his own fate that torments him but that of his young son, whom he's just learned has been handed over to the Comprachicos. What that band of mercenary surgeons has done to his dear Gwynplaine is left to Clancharlie's imagination, producing an agony far in excess of the embrace of the maiden. That"—Stevens held up a finger—"is horror. The horror of a father's love turned against him, made into a weapon of exquisite torment. Pay attention to his eyes! My God, those haunted eyes.

"But the king's vengeance is still not complete, for Gwynplaine, our unlikely hero, must live out his life marked with the ghastly work of the Comprachicos: a rictus of a grin carved across his face." Here, Stevens swept a finger from one cheek to the other. "All because a king thought it might be amusing. To force the boy, as a title card from the film reads, 'to laugh forever at his fool of a father.'" He stared out at the crowd, letting a long few seconds go by.

"Before we begin, put your hands together please for our marvelous projectionist, Jeff Dinan, who was so kind to lend his own print for tonight's screening." Stevens gestured to the projection booth.

The crowd turned as one, applauding lustily. Jarsdel looked too and, from his angle, caught a flash of Dinan's bright-red hair and a wave of his hand.

"And now," said Stevens, once again drawing the crowd to him, "I urge you to think of Gwynplaine—now, and later on, as you make your way home safely to your beds. On this night of masks, consider the fate of one who wears a mask not of his own choosing and that can never be removed. That, too, is horror. My most gracious ladies and gentlemen, happy Halloween."

———

Jarsdel and Aleena stayed for the whole movie, holding hands through most of it. It was more a tragic love story than anything else, despite Stevens's macabre speech, which suited Jarsdel just fine. Aleena even applauded as the lights came up.

"Amazing," she said, turning to him. "Conrad Veidt is my new hero."

"Wish I could take more credit," said Jarsdel, "but it was the only semicool thing I could think to do tonight. And the guy who—" A thought occurred to him. "Hey, I want you to meet someone. He'll love it that we showed up." He led her past the throng streaming out the exits and to a stairway marked by a sign reading *Projection Room—Employees Only Please*. He glanced around but didn't see the vampire doorman.

"Up there?" asked Aleena.

Jarsdel took her hand. "It'll round out the evening nicely. You'll see. That way, you can say you met a real live berserker."

"What? Like a crazy man?"

"No, Viking warrior. S'what he looks like anyway. C'mon. You'll love this guy. He's a real LA character."

They climbed the staircase, which ended in a pocket of darkness. To their left was an open doorway. Faint light spilled out, and they could also hear voices, low and resonant. There was a hitching, snorting chuckle, and someone said, "That was the *worst*."

They approached, and Jarsdel was amazed by what he saw. The theater they'd just left had been immaculate, slick, the benefit of a multimillion-dollar renovation—ergonomic seats, a flawless, bone-white screen, and a state-of-the-art speaker system. But the similarities in here stopped at the shiny twin projectors. The rest could've been mistaken for someone's basement rec room.

Finish your beer—there's sober kids in India, advised one poster, but the rest were all for horror films. In one, a bikinied teenager was shown reflected, screaming, in the blade of a butcher's knife. Another—this one more stylized—featured a giant, cruel-looking hand cradling a girl in a nightgown. The caption above read, *To avoid fainting, keep repeating: it's only a movie, only a movie, only a movie...*

A collection of empty liquor bottles lined one shelf. Another held action figures—mostly big-breasted fantasy heroines wielding broadswords. One—Jarsdel squinted to make sure—was of a wide-eyed manga schoolgirl, ass arched high, being taken from behind by a tentacled, winged demon.

Jeff Dinan sat splayed on a battered, threadbare sofa, his massive figure making it appear abnormally small, like something to be found in a child's room. In his lap, he cradled a twenty-four-ounce can of Murphy's Irish Stout. A few feet away, Raymond Stevens was studying several dozen reels of film arranged on a low shelf, his pendant swaying below his chin as he went.

"You actually have the trailer for *The Stuff*," he said in a tone somewhere between awe and disgust.

"You have no idea how popular that one is," said Dinan. "Gets laughs every time I play it. Probably worth five-hundred dollars, maybe more."

Stevens made a sour face. "Something is only worth what people are willing to pay. I have trouble believing you'd find a buyer with just the right blend of base desires and fiscal profligacy."

"Dude, first of all, it's not for sale. Second, it's ironic. Postmodern. That's the whole *point*."

Jarsdel rapped softly on the doorjamb. "Hey, sorry to interrupt. We just wanted to come by and say hi."

Dinan looked up, his expression confused. Stevens threw a glance over his shoulder, then went back to flipping through the reels.

"My name's Tully. We met a couple weeks ago. My folks—"

"You came! Awesome!" Dinan's face was alight with joy. His smile broadened even further when he saw Aleena. "And this must be the 'plus one' you told me not to bother putting on the list."

Aleena gave Jarsdel a quizzical look.

"Before we started dating," he assured her. "I didn't have anyone to bring, so—"

"Detective Jarsdel?" Stevens had by now recognized him. He stood uncertainly, holding a reel in one hand and a bottle of Strongbow cider in the other.

"You guys know each other?" Dinan turned to Stevens. "How does a guy like *you* know a badass LA homicide cop?"

"Long story," said Jarsdel, changing the subject. "Anyway, we just wanted to say thanks for the movie. It was—"

"Perfect," finished Aleena.

Both Dinan and Stevens looked at her in astonishment.

"Ray," said Dinan, "you seein' this?"

"I am," said Stevens.

Dinan grandly lifted a hand, indicating a mini fridge in the corner. "We are well met, Lady of Jarsdel. I offer you full use of my stores. A flagon of mead, perhaps?"

"He really does have mead," said Stevens.

Aleena nodded in the direction of Dinan's beer. "Any more of those?"

"Tully," said the giant, beaming. "She doesn't by any chance have a sister, does she?"

"I do, actually," said Aleena, crossing the room to the fridge. She took out a can of Murphy's, flicked its side a couple of times, then cracked the top. "She's got the Serenity Prayer tattooed on her hip, looks like our dad, and hates me. Oh, and her favorite movie is *Crash*. Want her number?" She took a long pull of the stout.

"I retract the question," said Dinan, bowing his head. "All the same, please join us."

Aleena sat in a squeaky black swivel chair facing the sofa, and Jarsdel leaned against a worktable piled high with strips of film and splicing tape. "We don't want to take up a ton of your time," he said. "Just wanted to thank you for the movie and everything."

"Stay long as you want. Every minute you're here is one less I gotta spend alone with Comrade Eurotrash. Guy's actually more of a snob than I am."

"Yeah yeah yeah," said Stevens. He'd again gone back to perusing the shelf of trailers. "Just because I said Scorsese was sometimes a bit pushed."

"That's not what you said. You said he was unchallenging—the go-to director for people who want to pretend they're film buffs. Then you went on to slam Tim Burton."

"I also said *Stripes* isn't all that funny. Don't forget that."

"I *don't* forget. I don't."

"Good."

Dinan leaned close to Aleena. "You know what it is? These ex-Stasi guys just have no sense of humor. Get it beat out of them in basic training."

Stevens didn't bother turning around. "I'm from Montenegro, you ignorant, beer-swilling oaf."

Dinan threw back his head, and there again came that porcine laugh. He gradually recovered, sighing loudly, and clapped his hands. The sound was startling in the tiny room, like the crack of a whip.

A silence followed. Aleena took another long swallow of beer. Stevens continued his perusal, pausing occasionally to hiss and shake his head. Only once did he find something that interested him enough to take out for inspection, but this too he returned to the rack with a sad little grunt.

Jarsdel's gaze drifted to the wall opposite, on which hung an inflatable moose head. Beneath it, in identical cheap black frames, were tacked perhaps thirty autographed headshots. Jarsdel recognized a couple of names, but the rest were a total mystery. One image was a close-up of a man grinning evilly and drawing a straight razor across his tongue. *To Jeff*, read the caption. *You're next!* The signature was illegible. Dinan followed Jarsdel's gaze.

"Those're all originals," he said. "No eBay bullshit. I met each and every one of those guys in person. Some I screened their movies right here in the Tomb. I once did a double bill of *Frenzy* and Polanski's *Macbeth*, and John Finch was actually fucking there in the audience. Wouldn't sign anything for me, though."

"Wasted career," said Stevens.

"Huh?"

"He turned down *Live and Let Die*. Could've been James Bond. So because of him, we're stuck with Roger Moore."

Dinan was about to argue, but Jarsdel interrupted. "Sorry, tomb?"

The big man looked at him, confused.

"You said something about showing their movies in a tomb."

"Oh." Dinan smiled. "My little nickname for the projection booth. Egyptian Theatre...Egypt...King Tut's tomb. I know it's a reach, but I always wanted to have a place with an actual *name*, you know?"

"Like the Shire," said Stevens.

Dinan ignored him. "Houses used to have names, the way ships do. Everything had names. Swords, violins, guns, famous pieces of jewelry and mirrors and even goblets, right? Because everything was unique, you know, so with the scarcity of the thing, it made sense to come up with a name for it. Now there are a billion copies of everything, so who cares? Me, I like things unique. Custom. Like, I got a sling at home—a real sling—made by this guy in the South who does these Bible reenactments. And he makes slings. I got the best one. Parachute cord, and with a pouch made of supersoft deer skin. My initials are branded on the leather. Guarantee you—only one on earth like it.

"But that's about it, though, for me—stuff like that. Little things. 'Cause I live in an apartment, right? You can't name an apartment. It's not yours, and when you go, they'll slap on another coat of Swiss Coffee, and it's off to the next drone. And that's apartment life, right? And everything you own *in* that apartment is mass-produced, just mass-produced, but this"—he gestured broadly at the room around him—"only place in the world like it. The Tomb."

Aleena nodded. "You gotta hold on to the things that define you."

"*Yes.*"

"I'd rather have nothing than a bunch of stuff that doesn't speak to me."

"Absolutely. But that's very advanced thinking. Most people it's just gimme gimme gimme. It's the acquisition that fires them up, but it doesn't last, and then they're left asking themselves why they're no happier."

Jarsdel wondered where the fornicating demon/schoolgirl statuette fit into Dinan's philosophizing, but didn't ask. He saw that Stevens had stopped examining the movie trailers and was watching the exchange with interest, all the while rubbing at the milky stone pendant hanging from his neck.

"A rare moment," he said when nobody filled the silence. Everyone turned to look at him. "I mean, my dear Jeff, how often do we ever agree on anything? But in this case, I'd have to bow to your wisdom. Such as it is."

"Hey, even a stopped clock's right twice a day, right?" asked Dinan. He turned his attention back to Aleena. "I'm not gonna pretend anything I just said is profound. But you're nice to humor me."

"No," she protested. "I totally agree—"

"I'm sorry, but I have to say it: you are just so fucking cute."

Aleena cocked her head and surveyed him, her face suddenly unreadable. Jarsdel felt a surge of protectiveness but didn't know what he should do or say. He looked over at Stevens and found no help there. The pale man was focused on Dinan and Aleena, expression vague and distant, fingers still working at the stone.

It was Dinan himself who broke the strange impasse. He lifted his hands, palms raised, then dropped them heavily at his sides. "Does it make you uncomfortable I said that? That you're cute?"

Aleena put down her beer and continued to regard the big man. Jarsdel thought perhaps she narrowed her eyes a little, but that was all.

Dinan shrugged. "I played a lot of D&D in high school. Probably not a huge shock, right? Played D&D, was on tech crew. People thought I was a *type*, you know? I *looked* like a type. No denying that. So this new kid comes to school. 'Troubled' was the official term. 'Asshole' was what I would've called him. And he spots me and just zeroes in like a fucking missile. First, it's just little things. Swats my books outta my hands, steps on my shoe when I'm walking, bumps me with his shoulder—'Watch it, fag.' The classics. Then he starts slamming my locker when I'm getting stuff—nearly cuts my fingers off a couple times. The shoulder bumps start to get a little harder. I just sense it. I just sense it, and it's like, whoa, wait a minute, this guy's really not gonna be happy until he causes me some serious damage. And on the heels of that, I said no. No, wait a minute. I'm just floored by the arrogance of it. So I look at my body in the mirror and I'm like, 'Well, God gave me this soft personality, this D&D personality, but he gave me this body to defend it. So I'm gonna use it.'

"Well. I can't act on my newfound resolve right away, 'cause there's always too many people around, so I gotta just suffer in silence the next time the cunt biscuit goes for my fingers with the locker door. But eventually, he tries for me when it's only the two of us."

Dinan smiled, allowing the memory to come back to him fully. "I knew they'd look at the backs of my hands if I got caught. Look for bruises and scrapes, you know, to show I'd been in a fight. So when King Dickface comes after me that day, I don't punch him. Instead, I give him a slap, right on the chin. Whap! Guy goes down like he's made of nothing. Even I'm surprised. I could've left it at that. But I want him to remember me. I want him to remember all those shoulder bumps, all the locker slams, everything. And even more than that, I want to—as they say—eliminate his capacity for making war. What good is it if he just comes back tomorrow even more pissed off, right? I stand over one of his ankles and bring my heel down hard as I can, right on the bone. Crack! Then really quick, because he's already screaming, I do the same to his wrist."

Dinan looked from Aleena to Jarsdel, then back again. "The end."

Aleena finally spoke. "Is there a reason you're telling me all this?"

"By way of explanation," said Dinan. "Not that I owe you one. But ever since that day, I haven't had any trouble saying what's on my mind or doing what I needed to do."

"Mm. How's that going?"

"Look, with me, what you see is what you get. No surprises. Some people find it refreshing."

"Others find it rude."

"Fair enough, but consider how fuckin' goofy it is, how worked up we get over little bits of social protocol. What could actually be an invigorating conversation turns instead into an absolute minefield. So I basically say 'you're beautiful,' and that bothers you. That puzzles me, because you knew I was thinking it anyway, so why does it matter if I come out and say it?" He held a hand out to Jarsdel. "And I'm not even trying to move in on your territory—"

"*Territory*," Aleena spat.

"—but I do get to say you have a hot girlfriend." He turned back to Aleena. "That's my right. And you can take it or leave it, but no one gets to tell me what I can and can't say. Think about it. All I did was make an observation."

"So if I were ugly," said Aleena, "you'd tell me that too?"

"No, probably not. It doesn't interest me to point out what's common in the world. *Most* people are ugly, or at least forgettable." He yawned. "Look, I don't want to expend any more intellectual fuel on this conversation. I'm sorry you were offended, and I'm sorry if that means we can't be friends. Woulda been wicked having you in my entourage."

"Okay," said Jarsdel, reaching for Aleena's hand.

She brushed it away and stood on her own.

Stevens approached the couple, looking grave. "I'm very sorry about this. He can get very back-and-forth emotionally sometimes. The alcohol doesn't help."

"You know I can hear you, Gomez," said Dinan. "That's me—mister big drinker, mister volatile, unpredictable *man*." He spoke the last word with barely checked fury. "You know what? Why don't you go ahead and fuck off? All of you."

"We should go. Let's go," said Stevens, ushering them toward the door.

"We should *go*. Let's *go*," Dinan imitated in a squeaking falsetto. "Let's get away from the terrible *man*."

"You're gonna feel pretty silly about this tomorrow, Jeff," said Stevens on his way out.

"Good. Then I'll have a glimpse of what it's like in your head *all the fucking time*."

Jarsdel, Stevens, and Aleena made their way wordlessly down the dimly lit stairs. Stevens took the lead and showed them out through a set of double doors. Jarsdel wanted the night air to be cool after the mugginess of the projection booth, but instead, it was tepid and heavy on his skin. He didn't feel like he was outside at all, even though he could see the moon.

"What a clod," said Stevens, producing a cigarette and lighting it in a single fluid motion.

"Is he manic-depressive or something?" asked Jarsdel.

"Who cares?" said Aleena. "You can be bipolar and still be a decent person. What an *asshole*."

Stevens nodded and took a drag on his cigarette. He blew a beautiful smoke ring that rose in the warm air and quickly twisted out of shape. "I agree."

"But you guys are friends?"

Stevens flicked a curl of ash onto the sidewalk. "He's probably the only person in Los Angeles I can talk film with. Like me, he's seen everything—has a holistic approach to the medium. Good and bad, high art and trash, it all comes together to create a fuller picture of what film can do. And he's not like that all the time. Only when—"

"Only around women?"

Stevens frowned. "I can't apologize for him, nor would I. He's not my responsibility. But I am sorry he ruined your evening. Most of all, the movie."

Jarsdel was puzzled. "The movie?"

"*The Man Who Laughs.* It's a truly great film, and sadly, you'll now associate it with this stupid episode. He had no right to do that to you. *No right.* He thieved the experience. Is that right to say? In English? 'Thieved' it?"

"'Stole' is more common, but 'thieved' is fine."

"Fine, then. He *stole* what could have otherwise been a really special thing. That upsets me."

Jarsdel took Aleena's hand. "Yeah, well. I think we're gonna take off. Have a good night, Mr. Stevens."

"Raymond, please." He shook his head bitterly. "God. How humiliating. And you an historian. You knew what my pilum was."

Jarsdel had started back toward the parking lot but now halted uncomfortably a few yards from Stevens. Aleena was farther ahead of him and gave his hand an insistent squeeze. "Not a big deal," he said. "Like you said, he's not your responsibility."

Stevens gave him a sad, doubtful look. "I don't think that matters. You'll still on some level associate this incident with me."

Aleena squeezed his hand again. "Let's go."

"We really gotta run," he said to Stevens, who gave a resigned nod and sagged against the double doors. Jarsdel was reminded of a grade schooler who'd just been picked last for a game of kickball. "The movie was really great. We loved it."

Stevens looked up, his expression hopeful. "You did? Really?"

"Yeah. Couldn't believe I hadn't even heard of it before."

The man's eyes glittered with happiness. "Yes. A true gem. I'm actually trying to get ahold of one of the dental prosthetics used to create Gwynplaine's unearthly grin. Same makeup artist, you know, who did *Frankenstein*. Jack Pierce. A genius. Ah—I have an idea! Why don't the two of you stop by sometime? As my guests, of course. I'll give you a private tour of the museum, even show you some pieces unseen by the public. Guaranteed the most filmically sincere experience in the city."

"Sounds great."

"Tremendous. What a turnaround from the way I felt a couple minutes ago. Thank you. And I still have your card! Is the same number—"

"Yeah, there are two numbers on there. One's my desk at the station, but my cell's under that. Call me on that."

"Good, good. I'll certainly be in touch."

This time, Aleena pulled on Jarsdel's hand, and he nearly lost his footing. He gave Stevens a final, reassuring smile and went with her.

———

Jarsdel expected a chilly drive back. He didn't think he'd known Aleena long enough to have a right to share in her anger and indignation. Worse, the whole evening had been his idea. Going up to meet Dinan had been his idea. There was no way to duck the blame, and crippling embarrassment seemed the only reasonable response. He only hoped his humiliation might offset some of Aleena's resentment, though he didn't suppose that was likely.

But he was wrong. Aleena was electric with fury, true, but none of it directed at him. "Fucking misogynistic *troll*."

"I don't know what to say. I'm really sorry that happened."

"What? No—don't you dare apologize for him. I hate that, when people apologize for someone else's bullshit."

"Okay, I'm just—"

"*Ugh*. And that disgusting story he told, posing as a badass, like he was trying to intimidate me—I mean, I don't know what else to call it—intimidate me into, I don't know, thinking he was *justified* in being a complete dick. And did you see that statue thing? Of the schoolgirl getting raped? Real nice. I mean, Megan's Law, anyone?"

"Yeah."

"You should look into him, seriously. I know that's not how things are done, investigating people without, like, any real cause. But I don't know. Or can you?"

Jarsdel opened his mouth to speak, but she plowed on.

"Am I totally overreacting?"

"No. But like my TO said—"

"What's a TO?"

"Training officer. Said there's no law against being an asshole."

"I guess." She exhaled forcefully. "Okay. I'm done. No. Wait." She rolled down her window, stuck out her head, and shouted, "Fucking *troll*!"

"Fuck you!" someone called back from somewhere.

She rolled the window back up.

"Better?" Jarsdel asked.

"Better," she agreed.

They drove the rest of the way in silence. The traffic heading east wasn't nearly as bad, and it wasn't long before they were back at Aleena's. She was out of the car and about to shut the door when she noticed Jarsdel still had the engine running.

"Aren't you coming in?"

"I don't know. I feel really awkward."

"Why?"

"This wasn't exactly the evening I had planned. Especially when you said how much you hated Halloween, you know, I thought, 'Hey, I'm gonna show her a great time.'"

Aleena sighed. "Are you honestly gonna do a pity party over this?"

"What do you mean?"

"I mean if you really want the whole night to be a wash, you can be all mopey and go home. Then I agree, that *would* be super awkward. But if you can let it go and come inside, we can still have a good time."

"We can?"

"If you lighten up."

Jarsdel thought for a moment, then nodded. "Okay, you got it."

"Good. Because I was thinkin' reverse cowgirl. I'm seriously horny, and that usually does it for me."

—————

Their lovemaking was much better than before, less hurried, the two enjoying each other's bodies fully. And afterward, as they lay together, Aleena was far from the darkly pensive person she'd been the last time. They'd gotten past something together, and there was a sense in both of them of letting go, of releasing old demons. Aleena spoke with her usual intoxicating frankness, but there was a fresh ebullience to it. Jarsdel matched her, slipping with ease into the rhythm of the conversation.

"You bring your gun with you?" said Aleena.

"No."

"Why not?"

"Didn't think I'd need it. Was I wrong?"

"Thought you guys were always supposed to have your guns on you. Just in case."

"It's not a rule. They want us to, but I try to spend as little time with it as possible."

"Huh. A cop who's antigun."

"It's not a political thing. I'm just not much good with it, so it's like having a little reminder of a personal inadequacy glued to my hip all the time." He grunted. "You know something funny? When we're in the academy, we have to practice shooting these targets—more like posters, I guess—of bad guys. They're actually these big blown-up photographs of real people. And the thing is, they're all pictures of cops. I mean, not in uniform or anything. They're in civvies, looking mean and pointing guns at you, but it's real cops from departments all over the country who pose for them."

"Why?" asked Aleena.

"Ah, interesting. Because here's the thing. If it was pictures of civilians dressed up like bad guys, and you ran into the actual person somehow in real life, they don't want to take the chance that you'd be conditioned to just start shooting at them."

Aleena laughed. "For real?"

"Well, maybe not shoot them exactly but, you know, automatically think they're criminals or something. Hassle them and not even realize why. Because you spend so much time emptying clips at these posters that you get to know the faces very well. I'd easily recognize them if I saw them on the street."

"That's funny," said Aleena. Her hand brushed against the top of the nightstand, where Jarsdel had dumped his things before they'd gotten into bed. "Why'd you bring your badge?"

"Oh. Yeah. Force of habit, I guess."

"Can I see it?"

"Sure. Of course."

Aleena held the badge up so that it caught the low light spilling in from the bathroom. "Detective," she said, running her fingers across the lettering.

"Yup."

"Hmm. They made city hall look like a giant penis. I wonder if that was intentional."

"It does not," said Jarsdel. He took the badge away and squinted at it. "It's symbolic."

"Of a penis."

"No, it has real meaning. The tower symbolizes the enduring spirit of the city's founders, standing tall—"

"*Erect.*"

"—while the wings of the building signify the expansion from the first El Pueblo, and the base—"

"What *penetrating* insight you have."

"Better show some respect," said Jarsdel, "or you're looking at a lewd conduct beef."

"Sounds like something at a fusion restaurant. 'Lewd conduct beef.'" Aleena took the badge back from him, studying it more closely. "Does everything on here mean something?"

"Of course."

"Well, don't say it like that, like I'm supposed to know."

"Sorry. No secret why I'm slow to make friends. Ever heard of the Shield of Achilles?"

"No, but I know who he is. Invincible Greek guy, except for his heel."

"Right. Well anyway, the god Hephaestus makes him his armor—long story as to why—including this incredible shield, to fight with in the Trojan War. What makes the shield so impressive—you know, other than being made by a god—is that it depicts a microcosm of the known universe in all these little scenes. You've got basic human activities, like people picking grapes or farming sheep, but you've also got a siege going on over here and a wedding going on over there. You've got the best and the worst and the mundane side by side, and it's all juxtaposed with the eternal constants, all those things greater than us—the sun, the moon, the constellations. You get what I mean. Anyway, scholars like to debate the significance of the shield, but to me, there was always only one good answer."

"And that is?" asked Aleena.

"*To be among those who renew the world...to make the world progress toward perfection.*"

"What's that?"

"Zoroaster. My baba, my Iranian dad, he was from an old Parsee family, and Parsees are Zoroastrians, not Muslims. Zoroaster said that was the main purpose in life: 'To be among those who renew the world,' and 'to make the world progress toward perfection.' That's what the shield is reminding us of. It represents what Achilles is fighting for. Not just humanity as the Greeks saw it, but the whole cosmic balance. If he loses, then all those things depicted on the shield, good or bad, fall into chaos."

Aleena placed the badge over her bare left breast, over her heart. "And you're saying this is like that shield? Representing what you're fighting for?"

"Check out the border," said Jarsdel. "That design comes from the fasces—Ancient Roman symbol of authority. There in the middle's the city seal, and you've got little images symbolizing the last two hundred fifty years of LA's history. And behind city hall, those are the rays of the sun, because hey—West Coast."

"Cool," said Aleena, "but incomplete. They got no one from the Walk of Fame on there. Like that Wonder Woman I always see in front of the Dolby. Or maybe a tranny hooker or two." She was quiet awhile, then asked, "How do I look?"

Jarsdel raised himself on an elbow and took her in. She lay atop the covers, her curly brown hair fanned out behind her on the pillow, naked except for the badge.

"Like something worth fighting for," said Jarsdel. He kissed her fully, dipping his free hand to the moist cleft between her legs. She arched her back to meet him.

"Ready for round two?" Aleena gasped.

"Sure." He picked up the badge and moved to set it back on the nightstand, then paused, frowning.

"What's wrong?"

"Thanks a lot, Aleena. Now every time I look at this, I'm gonna see a giant dick."

She smiled. "My gift to you."

14

The call was passed along to Hollywood Station late the following afternoon. An emergency animal hospital in Toluca Lake had sent a vet out to an address in the hills above Ventura Boulevard, where a dog had been reported seizing in the backyard. By the time the doctor had arrived, the animal was dead. Its owners, she noted, had just returned from their wedding ceremony.

Above the tree line and across the plodding concrete snake of the 101, an orange flare arced into the sky, chased by a cloud of pale smoke. The burst of pyrotechnics signaled the climax of the Universal Studios stunt show, and Jarsdel watched with some longing as the flare cooled and winked out, dropping harmlessly somewhere backstage.

It couldn't have been more than two miles as the crow flew—a giddy audience sitting enthralled as muscle-bound actors threw looping stage punches, dodged explosions, and plummeted from high scaffolds. Jarsdel knew he could get back in the car and be at the gates of the theme park in under five minutes—plenty of time to spare before the next show, maybe even get a ride in beforehand. When it was over, he could take the backlot tour. He hadn't done that since he was in grade school and wondered if they still had the shark, the town square from *Gremlins*, and—his favorite—that big tunnel of churning ice that made it look like you were caught in the barrel of an avalanche.

Jarsdel had only been out of the academy a week before he was called to his first death scene. It was a classic shotgun suicide—barrel under the chin and toe on the trigger. The blast had taken off the front half of the man's head and distributed it on and around his white faux-leather couch. A piece of skull was even discovered in a nearby fish tank, leaned right up against a mini treasure chest. What remained after the buckshot had done its work wasn't remotely recognizable as a face—just a splayed mass of pulverized gristle, bone, and bright-yellow fat. On its own, it wouldn't have been any more upsetting than a pile of roadkill. But the body it erupted from was whole, untouched by the rampage of lead pellets, so the final effect was one of absolute horror, one that lay between what the eye expected to see atop a human form and what it actually beheld.

That had almost been Jarsdel's last day. It was obvious he wasn't ready, not for what the job really called for. He was faking it, playing dress-up, and was certain everyone could tell, that they could see it in his ill-fitting uniform and shiny new badge and the way his gun hung awkwardly on his hip. All he wanted to do was run, run back into the arms of what was warm and familiar. He'd tell his parents they were right, that he'd made a terribly foolish mistake, and promise he'd somehow manage to piece his old life back together. Maureen too. They'd only been apart half a year, and he thought he might have a chance at winning her back. Not a good chance, perhaps, but it was worth a try. Anything was worth it to get away, to be anywhere else other than standing over the shattered remains of a man he'd never known and didn't want to know.

He struggled to remember how he had conquered that moment and moved past it, but that was almost five years ago now, and the answer didn't come. He hadn't scampered home, and he hadn't called Maureen—that much he recalled—but his actual method for mining some hidden reserve of resiliency remained beyond his reach. That was too bad, because at the moment, he could use whatever wisdom he could tap into.

Morales moved into his periphery.

"Let's go."

But Jarsdel didn't want to go. He could hear the sobbing even from where he stood, the kind of long, braying squalls that only sounded from the absolute depths of misery, like the cries of the damned.

It was an old and surely tired axiom—one trotted out at every police academy in the world—that when everyone else flees from danger, it's the cop's job to run toward it. That arrangement was fine with Jarsdel, was something he'd made peace with, even if it should one day cost him his life. That might very well be the price of being among those who remake the world. But attending to the grieving held no appeal for him. Grief and despair were such fluid and adaptable monsters, and he had neither the skills nor the weapons nor the desire to meet them on the field. He wanted foes he could touch, ones that could be contained by a pair of handcuffs and a reinforced steel door.

Jarsdel followed Morales up the short path to the front door. Along the way, he noticed a painted iron lawn sculpture of a sleeping Saint Bernard, front paws curled around an oversized bone. Stuck in the grass next to it was a warning sign, red lettering on white: *Beware of...oh, never mind.*

The door began to open before Morales could ring the bell. It did so slowly, as if nudged by a gentle wind, but soon the detectives could make out a figure in the murky light of the front hall. He was young, perhaps in his midtwenties, with close-cropped dark hair and pale skin. Tattoos twisted their way out of the sleeves and collar of his T-shirt; Jarsdel saw claws, teeth, and tentacles, the faces of Gothic horror authors, and scattered words done in Courier font. There was *Apep, Leviathan, Jörmungandr, Vritra,* and *Cthulhu.*

"Cameron Dysart?" asked Morales.

"Hey," the man said. "I guess you'd better come in."

The detectives stepped inside just as another wail rose from somewhere in the house. It reached its peak, hanging high for a moment like the urgent blast of an air-raid siren, then broke apart into a hitching, gasping staccato that, on its own, might have passed for laughter.

The door shut behind them, and Dysart spoke. "It's this way."

Jarsdel and Morales followed him through the Craftsman bungalow and into the living room, where dozens of wrapped wedding gifts were stacked in front of the hearth. To their left, French doors opened onto a patio and a small, fenced-in yard. The wail started up again, and Jarsdel was grateful when they were led outside. He shut the door softly behind him, which at least robbed the cries of their sharp clarity, and descended the three steps to the lawn.

Beyond a pair of handcrafted Adirondack chairs—the kind made from repurposed wine barrels—Morales and Dysart stood over something draped with a mint-green bedsheet. Jarsdel slipped in beside them and looked down at the oblong shape. He glanced at Morales, who gave a single nod, and squatted, slipping a glove over his hand. He pinched the sheet on the hem nearest a dark stain— brick red on its way to crimson—and peeled it carefully back.

The dog's head was enormous, more like that of a bear cub than a canine, and it stank of bile and blood. The muzzle was thick with both. The huge jaws had clenched violently in the animal's death throes, nearly severing the blackening tongue that poked from its mouth. The eyelids were drawn up halfway, exposing filmy corneas caked with the residue of thick, cloudy tears. A leather collar was fastened around the neck, ID and blue plastic registration tag hanging from its metal loop. The ID was in the shape of a paw, the name *SAHJHAN* printed in all caps, a smear of dried blood obscuring the owner's phone number beneath.

Only a few flies had managed to work their way under the sheet, but now many more descended to light on the encrusted fur of the dog's face. Jarsdel wondered how they'd arrived so quickly and spotted several piles of pinkish vomit scattered about the yard.

These squirmed with flies, and Jarsdel guessed they owed their hue to the dog's ravaged insides.

The suffering would have been total, the terror felt as the poison ran its maniac course unimaginable. Jarsdel believed that the extremes of emotion were felt more acutely in an animal. A dog lived purely in the moment, could not conceive of the timeline it had ridden to the present and would from there split off into one of countless abstract futures. A dog could rocket between the poles of joy and fear without effort and without the tempering influence of deliberation.

"He was gonna be the ring bearer," said Dysart. "But at the last minute, Amber was like, 'We should see if T.K. wants to do it.' That's her nephew. He's nine and does ballet."

Jarsdel laid the sheet back in place and stood up. "Who found him?"

"She did."

"She being your wife?"

"Amber, yeah. Someone gave us as a wedding present this whole box of bully sticks, and she was gonna run one outside for him here before we went to the dinner thing tonight. The reception." He made a strange sound, a plaintive sigh of some sort that ended with a rasp of unvoiced air. "My question," he went on, "is, like, what are you guys gonna do about this? The vet said this has been going on for years? And you guys did nothing?"

"Sir," said Jarsdel. "I understand this is an extremely upsetting time."

"Upsetting?" Again came the sigh, and Jarsdel used the time to try to think of something to say.

But Morales spoke up and in a tone Jarsdel hadn't heard from him before. It was gentle, with the same soothing cadence he used when addressing grieving family members, but there was something more. Good law-enforcement officers were born with the potential for mental toughness, the ability to proceed with the job at hand without getting derailed by revulsion, shock, and anger. But veteran murder cops like Morales, whose lives had been defined by death for so long, were other creatures entirely. They required more than naturally hard shells. No feeling human could withstand an onslaught that constant and remain aloof. It became a daily labor, a wrestling match between a finite mortal body and an ever-vigorous, eldritch horror, whose bouts—at best—ended in a draw. In Morales's words, Jarsdel could hear that he'd lost this one.

"I'm sorry this happened to you."

Dysart looked at him. "Yeah. Yeah, me too."

There was silence for a while, and Jarsdel realized the crying from the house had stopped. He turned to look in that direction and found himself face-to-face with a slight woman standing barefoot in the grass and wearing an oversized bathrobe—her new husband's, Jarsdel supposed. Her nose and cheeks were bright red, a color made more startling by the dark hollows running beneath her eyes. Her sandy-blond hair hung damply around her face.

"Hi," she said.

Dysart took a step toward her. "Amber. Babe. You should go back inside."

His bride put her palm out to stop him. Dysart hesitated but made no further move.

"Excuse me," said Amber and made her way through the group to her dog's side. She knelt there, putting a hand on the rigid form beneath the sheet.

"I'm so very sorry," said Jarsdel. "But the more we can find out from you this early on, the better chance we have of catching the person who did this."

Amber gave no reply. Just swept her hand in small, slow circles.

"If you'd prefer, we can just talk to your husband."

Still nothing. Jarsdel and Morales exchanged a look and were about to suggest to Dysart that they come back another time when Amber stood. She regarded the detectives, brushing the hair from her face.

"Go ahead."

Morales already had his notebook out. "Thank you. What time did you get home?"

"Hour and a half ago, I think."

"And your dog was still living when you arrived?"

"Barely. He was on his way out, and I don't think he could see me. Could smell me, though. I hope he could, anyway."

Morales made a few notes. "And that's when you called the vet?"

"Yes."

"What's her name, please?"

"Dr. Lindy. That's her first name. What everyone calls her. I actually don't think I...Cam? Do you know her last name?"

Her husband looked down at his feet. "No. Sorry."

"We can get it for you," Amber told Morales.

"No prob. We can figure it out. Can you think of anyone who'd want to do something like this? Any enemies or, you know, unbalanced individuals?"

"My ex doesn't like Cam. But he lives way up in Alameda. And he also loves dogs, so..."

Morales turned to Dysart. "Sir? Can you think of anyone? It could've been something relatively minor. Maybe you got into an altercation recently? Rear-ended someone or fought over a parking space?"

Dysart thought about that but soon shook his head. "Nothing like that. Not that I can remember."

"What about anything out of the ordinary? Get the feeling someone was following you? Hang-up phone calls? Prowlers?"

"No."

Jarsdel jumped in. "Deliverymen? Someone who rang your bell with a package, then when you answered, maybe said they had the wrong address?"

Dysart and Amber silently checked in with each other, then both answered no. Morales and Jarsdel continued the questioning, getting the locations of the ceremony and the reception—which would now be canceled—along with the names of their wedding planner, officiant, and DJ. Jarsdel had read the case file so many times that he already knew none of them had come up at any other point in the investigation.

This had been the freshest Dog Catcher crime scene so far, but by the time Jarsdel and Morales left, they were even more mystified as to the killer's identity than they'd been before. How did he pick his victims? How did he know so much about them, down to the start time of their wedding ceremonies?

The detectives made their way back to the station in morose, frustrated silence.

15

Morales was back in court on his Hollywood nightclub stabbing case, this time under a defense subpoena. It was a desperate move on behalf of their client, a clumsy Hail Mary, their case hinging on making Morales appear he had bungled key aspects of the investigation. He'd been livid when he received the summons. "They are going to repent at motherfucking leisure for this."

That left Jarsdel by himself to interview Bonifacio Delgadillo.

Jarsdel hadn't been sure what to expect. A monster, certainly, but what sort? Would he be ferocious, teetering on the brink of explosive violence, as his actions at the convenience store suggested? Or would he be cold and glib like Lawrence Wolin?

It turned out he was neither. When he took his seat across from Jarsdel, the first thing he did was apologize for not being allowed to shake hands. And though he was young, no more than nineteen or twenty, his voice was low and hushed, in the manner of a funeral director.

"No offense, but you understand I gotta have my lawyer here," he said, nodding to the man at his side.

Delgadillo's attorney had already introduced himself to Jarsdel while the two of them were waiting for him to be brought out. He was a weary, rumpled-looking man, clothes worn and tired, suit jacket shiny at the back and the elbows. But Jarsdel thought it was an act—the beleaguered public defender burning the midnight oil for an endless roster of indigent clients. In fact, he knew Barry Chavanne had an office on Wilshire and billed $350 an hour, and Jarsdel guessed it was cartel money that had put him on retainer.

Now the three of them would play a delicate game. Jarsdel, without revealing how little he actually knew, would ask as many questions as he could about Delgadillo's connection to Wolin. Chavanne and Delgadillo, in turn, would answer as few of them as possible while still trying to work out what kind of case the police had.

"Okay, Detective," said Chavanne, "just to set a couple ground rules, we're not going to talk at all about the incident in Boyle Heights, nor will we discuss allegations that my client has ties to any criminal organizations. This is strictly a friendly meeting. It's my hope that we can clear up any misunderstandings that my client is involved in whatever brought you here today. Put it to bed before wasting your time and ours. If all that's agreeable to you, then we can proceed."

"Certainly," said Jarsdel.

"But if I sense you're abusing this meeting in any way, I'll immediately call it to a close, and you'll never speak to my client again. So I urge you to be on your best behavior."

Jarsdel nodded.

"Okay," said Chavanne. "How can we help you?"

Jarsdel turned to Delgadillo. "Thank you for agreeing to see me."

Delgadillo shrugged. "Got lots of spare time."

"I'm here because we've uncovered some evidence from a deceased person that indicates you may have known him."

"What evidence?" Chavanne broke in.

"We can get to that. For now, we're just trying to figure out how exactly you knew him."

"Who is he?" asked Delgadillo.

Jarsdel reached for a manila folder he'd brought with him and produced the picture of Wolin in the Wax Museum. He slid it across the table.

Delgadillo reached for it, but Chavanne put his hand on his shoulder. "Don't touch it. Just look."

Delgadillo leaned forward and squinted down at the photograph. He took a long time before shaking his head.

"No?" asked Jarsdel.

"Never seen him before. Looks like a nice guy." He made a dismissive gesture toward the picture, but Jarsdel left it where it was.

"His name was Grant Wolin. That sound familiar to you?"

"No." Delgadillo's soft voice seemed weighted with regret, as if he really had wanted to help.

"Hmm, that's a puzzle."

Chavanne held up a hand. "Please, Detective. Let's dispense with the usual bullshit. Or are we finished already?"

"Apologies," said Jarsdel, then, to Delgadillo, "Do you recall where you were on October 2 of this year?"

"No. What's that, like a month ago? That when your guy got killed?"

"Let the detective ask the questions," said Chavanne.

"What about the early morning hours of October 3?" asked Jarsdel.

"Still no," said Delgadillo. "Probably in bed, man."

"You ever been to Thai Town?"

"What's that? Like Chinatown?"

"Yeah, but a lot smaller. And Thai. Thai Town. In Hollywood."

"I been to Hollywood, but I don't know no Thai Town."

"I'm gonna show you something." Jarsdel opened the folder again and brought out a photograph of the Wolin crime scene. It was a full body shot, taken at a forty-five-degree downward angle. Wolin's head was wrenched upward and a little to the right, and his black eye sockets seemed to be staring straight into the camera. His mouth yawned open, pulled taut into a perverse imitation of high good humor. Jarsdel waited a moment, holding the picture so only he could see it, then slowly turned it around. He pushed it across the desk until it was level with the photo of Wolin alive and happy in the Wax Museum.

An expression of disgust flashed across Delgadillo's face. It was brief, but it was there. "What's this, man?"

"Detective, I warned you," said Chavanne.

"This is why we're here," said Jarsdel.

Delgadillo shook his head vigorously. "No way. I didn't have nothing to do—"

"Let me handle this," said Chavanne. He turned to Jarsdel. "I told you to be on your best behavior. Now you're trying to intimidate my client with this ghastly photograph."

"I'm not trying to intimidate anybody," said Jarsdel. "But I do need to know what happened to this man."

"And what makes you think my client has any information on the matter?"

"I don't think I should say."

"And why not?"

"Because you just warned me to be on my best behavior. And you're not gonna like the answer."

Chavanne sat quietly for a moment, chewing his cheeks in thought. Jarsdel knew he was weighing the pros and cons of allowing the questioning to continue. In the end, the lawyer decided he wanted to know what the police had.

"All right. For my client's best interest, I'll let you continue. But our proceeding with you in no way concedes any involvement in this—this horror show."

"Understood. Mr. Delgadillo, when you were arrested, a firearm was found in your possession. A Browning HP, 9mm." He saw Chavanne about to protest and quickly added, "But I'm not alleging anything having to do with the Boyle Heights shooting. My interest is specific to the gun itself. Can you tell me where you got it?"

Chavanne answered instead. "That gun did not belong to my client. It happened to be in the car, which he'd borrowed from a friend."

"Who?"

"That's not important. Suffice it to say it's not his gun."

"Okay. Then my advice is that Mr. Delgadillo contact his friend, whoever it is, and explain that we'll be wanting to speak with him about the death of this man here." Jarsdel indicated the pictures.

"Guy doesn't look shot," said Delgadillo. "Burned or something."

"A shell casing was found among his possessions," said Jarsdel. "This casing has since been matched to the gun recovered from the vehicle you were driving."

"That don't mean nothing."

"Really? Because if a cartridge from my own weapon were found on a dead man, I'd want to know how it got there."

"Detective," cautioned Chavanne, "I've already explained to you that it wasn't *his* weapon. Are we going to be able to get past that or not?"

"Mr. Chavanne," said Jarsdel, "put yourself in my position. Whether the gun belonged to your client or not, we still need to figure out how that casing ended up with our victim. So unless you have someone else for us to speak to, I'm afraid he'll be the focus of our investigation."

"And that concludes the interview," said Chavanne, pushing the photographs back across the desk to Jarsdel. "I thought we could cooperate on this, but it looks like the same old, same old from you guys. My client had nothing to do with this, and you'll only embarrass yourselves by pursuing this angle of investigation. That casing could have come from anywhere. Your victim could've worked at a shooting range and collected them. Maybe I should even thank you. You've certainly proven that gun got around. And I'll be interested to find out why this hasn't been disclosed to us by the district attorney's—"

But Jarsdel had stopped listening. Something Chavanne said was bothering him, and he was trying to figure out what it was.

Shooting range, he thought. *Something about a shooting range.*

Jarsdel stood suddenly, stuffing the photographs of Wolin back in the folder. "I'm sorry," he said, cutting off Chavanne midsentence. "Thank you both for your time today. We'll be in touch if anything else comes up."

"That's not going to hap—," Chavanne began, but his words were drowned out by Jarsdel calling for the guard.

———

Once he was outside, Jarsdel put a call in to Hollenbeck Station's homicide unit.

"Rislakki."

He was glad it wasn't Cooney, the one known as "Sleepy."

"Hello, yes. This is Detective Jarsdel from Hollywood. We met last week about the Delgadillo case?"

There was a long pause on the line, and Jarsdel thought the other detective had hung up. Then the man said, "What can I do for you?"

"You said something before about the Boyle Heights shooting—how Delgadillo hit the guys in the car like he knew what he was doing. No spray and pray. You said he might have put in time at a range. Did you by any chance ever look into that?"

"Sure," said Rislakki. "Thought it might help tie him to the gun in case he tried the whole 'it wasn't mine' routine. Weren't able to confirm anything, though. Canvassed a couple ranges in his area, but they didn't recognize him by his picture, and he didn't have any membership cards on him or anything."

Jarsdel felt himself deflate. "Nothing?"

"Not that we found. And the ranges we didn't visit personally, we emailed his picture. Nothing in SoCal. Why?"

"Then how was he so accurate? Military trained?"

"Ha. No. He's just a punk."

"But he had to have practiced somewhere."

"Or got lucky. Or plinked cans out in the desert. Or a combination of the two. Tell you what—you figure it out, you let us know. That it?"

Jarsdel couldn't think of anything else, so he thanked Rislakki and was about to hang up when the other detective spoke. "You know we go on trial day after tomorrow, right?"

"Yeah."

"Good. Just a little reminder in case you forgot."

"Uh-huh. And you didn't tell the DA's office about that shell casing, did you?"

"What do you care?"

"I just got out of a meeting with Delgadillo and his attorney, and—"

"You did what? You fucking did what?"

"We have our own investigation to follow. I'm sorry if that bothers you, but we still have to go where it takes us."

"You may have just fucked this whole thing, you know that?"

"Hey, look, it's not my problem you didn't disclose—"

Rislakki hung up. Jarsdel let out a shaky breath and made his way back to the car. He'd considered going back to Daikokuya for lunch, but the conversation had cost him his appetite. After leaving the lot, he turned onto the 101, intending to drive back to Hollywood Station. Still, the shell casing nagged at him. He'd been so certain the gun range was the answer—that somehow it would connect back to Wolin. It would explain everything, including why he had so many different cartridges in his apartment and only one of them had been tied to a crime. But if Rislakki and Cooney couldn't place Delgadillo at a single range in southern California, Jarsdel didn't think he'd be able to do any better.

His mind wandered back to what Rislakki had said, that Delgadillo might have been doing his target practice out in the desert. Fine, but how would Wolin have come across any of his casings? An idea lurked somewhere in the tangle of his thoughts, but he couldn't quite grasp it. A car swerved into his lane, and he had to slam on the brakes. "Goddamn it," he muttered, swatting the wheel and stinging his palm. "No, come on," he said. "What is it? The desert. Out in the desert. Why is that important? Sand, lots of sand. No way to..."

And then he had it.

Instead of getting off at Sunset, his exit for the station, he turned off the freeway on Cahuenga, then headed south until he hit Hollywood

Boulevard. In five minutes, he was in front of the Wax Museum. He parked in a red zone and turned on his police lights, then hurried to the ticket counter. Ramesh Ramjoo wasn't there. Instead, there sat an older man in a tall black turban, wearing a heavy beard. The tips of his mustache were molded into precise curls.

"Is Ramesh here?" asked Jarsdel as he approached.

"How you know Ramesh?"

Jarsdel pointed to the badge on his belt. "Please, it's urgent. I need to talk with him."

"Everything okay?"

"Everything's fine. It's about the case he's helping us with. You were at the funeral, right? You're his uncle?"

The man nodded, then gestured to the entrance. "Inside somewhere. Walking the floor."

"Thanks." Jarsdel stepped through the turnstile and into the museum. He hadn't been inside since he was ten or eleven years old. The wax Yul Brynner and Deborah Kerr waltzing in *The King and I* had been replaced by Ace Ventura, his expression more psychotic than gleeful. Farther in, where he remembered a beefy Rambo dummy, there stood in its place a figure of Jackie Chan about to kick. Jarsdel realized it was the same spot at which Wolin had been photographed and felt a chill.

He walked quickly through the exhibits, looking for Ramesh. Each room had its own music playing to match the scenes being depicted, and as he made his way through, the sounds and images blurred together into a discordant, dreamlike soup. He passed Dorothy and her friends, and it was "We're Off to See the Wizard," then *Terminator*, then *Back to the Future* and *Titanic* and *Forrest Gump*.

By the time he reached the exit, he felt a little dizzy, and he still hadn't found Ramesh. He went back outside, approaching the man at the ticket counter.

"I didn't see him. You sure he's inside?"

"Check everywhere?"

"Pretty sure."

"Horror Chamber? Crypt Keeper not working today. Maybe he's fixing."

Jarsdel wilted a little. He never had liked the horror section. When he was a kid, he'd test himself to see how far inside he could go before retreating. He'd made it all the way through only once, and it was at a light jog, eyes squinted nearly shut, hands clamped to his ears. And now at the mention of the place, a voice that had been dormant within him nearly thirty years began to protest.

Jarsdel thanked Ramesh's uncle and went back inside, walking more slowly this time. He wasn't sure if he'd ignored the horror section deliberately or not, but now he was careful not to pass it. And there it was, just off the superstars of music exhibit—Michael Jackson and Madonna and the Beatles in their Sgt. Pepper outfits—a passage snaking off into darkness, marked by a glowing, red-lettered sign reading *Chamber of Horrors*.

He stepped inside, making his way down the narrow hallway, which turned sharply left before opening into a large, dimly lit room. Upon entering, he was greeted by a sharp blast of air and a tinny cackle of canned laughter. A recording of scraping chains and low moans played behind Bach's Toccata and Fugue in D Minor. The figures of Dracula and Frankenstein's monster stared down at him from a raised platform, and off to his right was Regan from *The Exorcist*, her head turning slowly around and around.

It took Jarsdel a moment to realize that he felt nothing—no fear, not even the slightest tingle of apprehension. The Chamber of Horrors was quaint now, its ersatz demons with their fangs and pale, clutching fingers holding no thrall alongside a knowledge of the world's real monsters and the carnage strewn in their wake.

Jarsdel started forward, cautious of any more hidden sensors. At the far end of the room, a man was bent down, a penlight clamped between his teeth, fiddling with something attached to the wall.

Jarsdel approached. "Hey, Ramesh."

Ramesh looked up at the sound of his name, startled, and the beam from the penlight shined into Jarsdel's eyes.

"Oh, it's you. Sorry," said Ramesh, flicking the light off. He stood, brushing his pants. "Some damn kid kicked the sensor that works the Crypt Keeper. It's all bent. What's going on? Did you find the murderer?"

It was the kind of question, Jarsdel reflected, that he never would have been asked had he stayed a history teacher. "No, but I need your help with something."

Ramesh shrugged. "Okay."

"I need to know where Grant got his dirt. You know, for his Genuine Hollywood Dirt business."

"Oh, the dirt, yes." Ramesh thought for a moment. "He tried different soils, different colors. Some sold better than other ones. At first, I think he just dug around the rental property, but the dirt was too dark. Didn't look good with the label."

"Okay, so what'd he do?"

"Well, it's hard to find just *dirt* in a city, you know—all the cement—so he'd bring a bucket up to the park and get it from there. Same place we'd go to smoke. Sort of sandy dirt, very nice shade. Tan."

"The park? You mean Griffith Park?"

"Yeah."

"Where?"

"It's hard to describe. Up by the fire road. I guess I can show you."

"When? Now?"

Ramesh made a face. "No, I have to fix this. We have a big tour coming in an hour, and—"

"Ramesh, this is important."

The other man considered. "It will help? With finding the murderer?"

"Yes."

"Then okay, but you have to drive. I don't have a car."

After a brief argument between Ramesh and his uncle at the desk, the two were in Jarsdel's car and heading up Highland toward Franklin. They drove mostly in silence, Ramesh staring in fascination at the dashboard computer and throwing glances over his shoulder at the shotgun racked behind the front seat. When they turned onto Los Feliz, Jarsdel asked for additional directions.

"Left soon. Not here. There, coming up," said Ramesh, pointing at Nottingham. They made the left and began to climb up into the hills, winding their way past old Hollywood mansions and robust stands of bougainvillea. They weren't too far from Aleena's place, Jarsdel realized. The road turned and dipped often, and progress was slow. When they'd come to a fork, Ramesh would point the way, and Jarsdel would follow. Finally, he directed them up Glendower Road, which quickly dead-ended. "Now what?" asked Jarsdel.

"Now we park."

They got out, and Ramesh led them to a restricted-access gate and a sign reading *Emergency Vehicles Only*. Beyond, a single, narrow road snaked farther up the mountain and disappeared from view. The Griffith Observatory, the restored deco masterpiece, looked down on them from a vast plateau. Past that, the land swept upward again, rising to the peak of Mount Hollywood.

The gate, Jarsdel saw, allowed a small gap for pedestrians to pass while still blocking the road to cars. Ramesh slipped through, and Jarsdel followed. Off to their left, the city lurked behind a shroud of haze.

The two men made their way along the road for several minutes, avoiding the occasional pile of coyote dung. Jarsdel noticed an old air-raid siren standing sentry, its dark mouth poised to cast a blanket of sonic terror over the houses below.

Eventually, they reached a sharp rise, at the top of which stood a lone metal pole, the remnant of a gate that'd long ago been removed.

"Here," said Ramesh.

"Here? This is the place?"

"Where we'd smoke. Best view of the city."

Jarsdel noticed the area was overgrown with dry shrubs and other desert plant life. A stray blunt dropped here at the wrong time would've sent the whole mountain up in flames. He resisted pointing this out and asked instead, "But this is where he'd go digging?"

"Off down that way." Ramesh pointed to where the road bled into a dirt footpath.

"Show me."

They followed the path, which wound around a large water tank and stopped abruptly at the base of a granite cliff face. Something crunched under Jarsdel's foot, and he looked down to find he'd stepped on the remains of a broken bottle. Shards large and small peppered the area, glinting dully in the muted sunlight.

"Here? With all this broken glass?"

"All around," said Ramesh. "Wherever he found good dirt."

Jarsdel frowned and walked the area. Gaudy red and blue graffiti marred much of the cliff face and had even been used to mark nearby boulders. Jarsdel peered down at the tops of the boulders and saw more glass particles, but much finer, like dust, as if someone had smashed the bottles against the rocks with great force.

Excited, Jarsdel bent lower and began scouring the ground. Almost immediately, under the shadow of one of the boulders, he found what he was looking for. Grabbing a nearby twig, he teased it out into the light where both he and Ramesh could see it.

A shell casing. He'd found Delgadillo's shooting range.

16

Morales prepared the package for the Dwarves at Hollenbeck Station. Thirty-one casings recovered from the makeshift target range in Griffith Park, including photographs and a report from Jarsdel detailing how he came to locate the site. Ramesh provided a statement, and both detectives were confident that taken together, the evidence proved overwhelmingly that Wolin had acquired the 9mm cartridge on one of his digging expeditions. Whether or not Delgadillo or someone else had fired the weapon in the park was unimportant; what mattered was that it closed a major loophole for the defense. They'd found the connection between Delgadillo and Wolin, and it amounted to nothing the prosecution couldn't handle.

"Never seen Sleepy look so alert," said Morales upon returning to Hollywood Station. "And Happy looked happy again. He'd been on his way to becoming Grouchy."

"You mean Grumpy," said Jarsdel.

"Whatever. So what do we got now?"

"No idea. Tough to know where to go from here now that Delgadillo's out of the picture."

"I kinda like the boss for it," said Morales.

"Tony Punyawong?"

"That his name? Yeah."

"Why? Why possibly?"

"You remember the way he was about the red quarter? Definitely knew something. I think we should take another run at him."

Jarsdel thought about that. "Okay, but let's come at him with a fresh angle. That quarter was glued to Wolin's hand. Wasn't there by accident. So if Punyawong had anything to do with it, even if it's only that he knows what it means and that's why he was spooked, we'll get further with him if we give him a little more. Let's see what he does when we tell him the quarter was actually found on the body. Not where specifically—I know we don't want to tip him to that—just on the body."

Morales agreed, and soon they were back at the office of Fantasy Tours on Gower. Morales pounded on the door as he had on their previous visit, and when there was no answer, he cupped his hands against the glass and peered inside.

"Take a look."

Jarsdel did and saw the place had been completely cleaned out. "Gone. Well, he did tell us he was folding his tent."

"Yup. But I want to know why. And I don't want to hear any more from him about 'market saturation' or whatever."

They went back to the car and pulled up Punyawong's DMV record. He lived in Santa Monica, just off the Third Street Promenade, a large outdoor shopping center.

Morales groaned. "Other ass-end of town. Take an hour to get there."

"Think of it as a field trip," said Jarsdel. "Besides, we can either sit at a desk at the station or sit in the car. Personally, I'd rather be near the ocean."

Morales shook his head. "Closest we're gonna get to the ocean is a traffic jam on PCH."

———

They took Sunset most of the way, despite Jarsdel's protests that it would have been twice as fast to go down Wilshire to San Vicente.

Morales now seemed to actually be enjoying the drive, pointing out places he used to hang out when he was younger.

"Used to be a Tower Records right there," he said wistfully. "Don't get to come over this side of town much anymore. It's nice. Those fuckin' WeHo cops got a pretty slick beat."

They continued west, passing the Beverly Hills Hotel and, farther on, UCLA. They crossed the 405 freeway, and Jarsdel gazed down at the cars gridlocked in both directions. It was only one thirty, but there didn't seem to be an official rush hour anymore. Or maybe it was always rush hour now.

Jarsdel wished they'd gotten something to eat before they left. By the time they made it to Tony Punyawong's duplex, he was starving. Morales apparently felt the same way. "Shoulda hit Fred's or House of Pies first," he said as they got out. "I don't know this area at all. Anything good around here?" He stood and buttoned his pants as he spoke, tucking in his shirt and cinching his belt.

Jarsdel glanced around to make sure they weren't being observed. "Hey, you know I've been meaning to ask, can't you do that before you get out of the car? Anyone watching's gonna think I've been servicing you or something."

"Are you actually bitching at me?" said Morales. "What? Get laid or something? Feelin' your oats?"

Jarsdel hesitated too long, and Morales grinned. "That's it, huh? Well, good for you, partner. Finally loosened up a little."

The two detectives approached the door, noting a *For Sale* sign in the yard, and Morales gave his usual teeth-rattling knock.

No one answered. Morales was about to knock again when a voice spoke from somewhere above. "Left a few days ago."

Jarsdel and Morales took a few steps back and looked up, shielding their eyes. Leaning over the balcony of the adjacent unit was a fleshy, shirtless man of about sixty, face and body red from the sun. His hair and beard were long, stiff, and matted, like something soaked in brine and left to dry. He took a sip from a collins glass in which a handful of mint leaves danced in bubbly liquid.

"You know the man who lives here?" asked Morales.

"What're you guys, tax collectors?"

"LAPD," said Jarsdel, showing his badge.

The man took another sip and nodded. "Used to be in the Coast Guard Reserve myself."

"Sir, do you have any information on the whereabouts—"

"Cleared out. Told ya so."

"And when was that?"

The man tilted his head in thought. A light breeze blew past, lifting his beard like a flap. "I wanna say five, maybe six days ago."

"Any idea where?" asked Morales.

"Nope. Haven't seen him since. You could talk to his son, though. Works just down the pier."

"The pier? Where on the pier?"

"Video game arcade, I think. He's a surf bum, 'bout twenty or so. Gets up at five in the goddamn morning."

"And he lives here with his father?" asked Jarsdel.

The man nodded, downing the rest of his drink.

"Do you happen to know the son's name?"

He thought for a moment, then shook his head. "Ran into him a thousand times, but it's just not one of those names you hold onto. Plain sort, like Bob or Tim or Tom or something. Doesn't fit him. You ever meet someone whose name doesn't fit their face? This kid's like that."

"Tell you what, sir, if you could give us a call if anyone comes back here, we'd very much appreciate it." Jarsdel brought out one of his business cards. "Do you mind taking this, Mr...?"

"Hank Lind. Nah, I don't wanna come all the way down there. Just drop it in my mail slot."

Jarsdel did so, then turned to Morales. "Might as well walk it. We're close enough, and the parking at the pier's murder. You up for it?"

"How far?"

"Two, three blocks. But they're long blocks."

"I don't wanna go hunting for another parking spot. Yeah, let's do it."

The two detectives set off on foot, crossing the promenade. A street performer juggled flaming torches while onlookers watched him through their phone cameras. Jarsdel and Morales wove their way through the crowds, making a left on Second and a right onto Colorado. It took them only a couple more minutes before they were heading down the ramp at Ocean Avenue toward the water.

The Santa Monica Pier was originally built as part of the city's sewage disposal infrastructure, running pipes a quarter mile out to sea to jettison their contents beyond the breakwater. Despite its unglamorous function, it had the distinction of being the first concrete pier on the West Coast, and its unveiling had been accompanied by the self-congratulatory pomp typical of Gilded Age achievements. The festivities culminated in a sort of play in which a boastful and appropriately hunky Rex Neptune declared his intention of battering the pier to scrap. Queen Santa Monica, unperturbed, pointed out that the whole of Neptune's fury was no match for modern civic engineering. The chagrined Olympian conceded his defeat, mounted a sixty-five-foot tower, and dove back into the sea.

A few years later, the Pleasure Pier was added onto the existing structure, bringing games and roller coasters and the magnificent Looff Hippodrome, which housed a grand wooden carousel. In 1996, the amusement center reopened as Pacific Park, with children's rides, a new roller coaster, even a solar-powered Ferris wheel. And of course, there was also the Playland Arcade.

They passed the Santa Monica Pier Aquarium, then a series of restaurants and food stands—Jarsdel eyeing them hungrily—before finally arriving at their destination. It was dark and noisy inside, the din, Jarsdel thought, much like a casino. Quarters clattered into the collection trays of change machines while sound effects and electronic music, tones rising and falling, blasted from the game cabinets.

Against one wall in the large gallery stood a glass prize counter, its surface scratched and scarred from years of abuse. Behind it, a ponytailed teen was counting out a batch of tickets for a little girl wearing a cardboard crown. When he finished, the attendant said something to the girl, who pointed to a box of Chinese finger traps. The young man reached underneath the counter, picked one out—the wrong one; she wanted green—put it back, and gave her the one she'd asked for. The girl moved off, delighted, her fingers already firmly stuck.

Jarsdel and Morales approached the attendant, whose name tag read "Chris." He wasn't Thai—his skin was a cheesy white, except his cheeks and forehead, which were ravaged by blooms of acne. Around his waist, he wore a belt of steel barrels, each one loaded with quarters, from which he could dispense change by flicking a small switch. It must have weighed at least ten pounds.

Chris saw the detectives coming and stared at their badges. Before they could speak, he took an involuntary step back and asked, "What's up?"

Morales held out his palms to reassure him, but it only made him flinch. "We're looking for someone. Maybe you could help us out."

"Okay," said Chris. "I mean, I want to, but I don't know anything."

"Relax," said Morales. "Nobody's in trouble. We're looking for a kid, a Thai kid. Got a Thai name."

"Punyawong," said Jarsdel. "We don't know his first name, but he works here. Surfer?"

Chris was already nodding. "Yeah, cool. Um, yeah."

"What's his name?"

"Oh. Dan. His name's Dan."

Jarsdel smiled in what he hoped was a reassuring way. "Like we said, he's not in trouble or anything. We just want to talk to him. Is Dan here?"

"No. I mean, not that I know of. Haven't seen him in, like, a week."

"Is that unusual?"

"Well, he missed his shift. That's why I'm here. Last couple shifts, they called me in. I'm just covering. Normally, I work nights."

"Is he okay?" asked Morales. "Last time you saw him, how was he?"

Chris shrugged. "I don't know. Seemed fine, I guess."

"He give any indication where he might be going or why he wouldn't be coming in?"

"No, man. I mean, like, I hardly know him. We just cross paths and stuff. I come, he goes, that kinda thing."

"What sort of a guy is he? Moves around a lot?"

"I dunno."

"Well, listen," said Jarsdel. "If he comes back, will you tell him to give us a call? Maybe give him this?" He was about to hand over a card, then paused and added another. "You know what? Take two, just in case. And call us, okay? If he comes in."

Chris nodded, taking the cards and putting them in a pocket on his change belt. The detectives thanked him and left.

They were almost outside when Jarsdel froze. Morales walked ahead a few feet before realizing he wasn't beside him, then turned, frowning.

"What? Thought you were hungry. Got some old Skee-Ball tickets you wanna cash in?"

"Something."

"What?" Morales came back into the arcade and stepped closer. "Say again?"

"I thought..." Jarsdel crossed back to the prize counter.

Chris was rearranging a tray of cheap sunglasses, making sure all the lenses faced outward.

Jarsdel peered at his coin belt. "Excuse me," he said when Chris looked up. He pointed at the coin belt. "What're those?"

"Huh?" He looked to where Jarsdel was indicating. "These? Just change. For the customers."

"I know that," said Jarsdel. "I mean *those*." He leaned over the counter, almost touching one of the steel cylinders at the teen's waist.

"Oh. These are for testing the machines. Like when someone tells me one of the games is down and I have to check it out. Or when a game eats someone's quarter and I have to give him a credit. You know, so we don't count 'em along with the rest of the money."

"Makes sense." Jarsdel dug in his own pocket and brought out a quarter. "You mind if I trade you for one of those?"

"What for?"

"It's a long story."

Chris hesitated. "Okay," he said. "I guess." He flicked a tab at the base of the cylinder, dispensed one of the coins, and handed it to Jarsdel, who gave him his own in exchange.

"What was that about?" asked Morales when the two met up again.

"Here," said Jarsdel, holding out a closed fist. Reflexively, Morales put out his palm to receive it, and Jarsdel dropped the red quarter into his hand.

17

One of the fluorescent bulbs in Gavin's office was dying. It hummed behind its frosted plastic screen, flickering in erratic little fits. As Morales and Jarsdel spoke, the lieutenant continually shot angry glances at the fixture, once glaring at it with such ferocity that Morales paused.

The flickering eventually stopped, and Gavin turned to the detectives. "Yeah? Okay?"

"I was saying, sir, that it's looking like a longer road ahead. We don't have nearly enough to begin extradition proceedings on Punyawong and the kid, so for now, they're out of our reach, even for questioning."

Gavin cleared his throat and straightened in his seat. "And you're pretty sure they're in, uh…"

"Thailand, yeah. We got the flight info."

"Do we even have an extradition treaty with Thailand?"

"Yes, sir."

"Fine. But what I'm not getting is what your theory is at this point. What exactly do you think happened? Who's the responsible party?"

Jarsdel and Morales exchanged a look, then faced their superior. "We don't know," said Jarsdel.

Gavin nodded as though he'd expected nothing more. "What *do* you know?"

"We know that Punyawong was Grant Wolin's employer and that shortly after the murder, he began liquidating all his U.S. assets. Now both he and his son have left the country. And also, of course, there's the red quarter that was glued to Wolin's palm, which we can now link to *Dan* Punyawong—"

"That's the son?"

"Yes, sir. We can now link the quarter to where he works—the arcade on the pier."

"Well, you're right, Detective," said Gavin. "You don't know a whole lot. There isn't a case here, guys, just more questions."

"There's something else," said Jarsdel. "A search on Dan Punyawong turned this up." He produced a computer printout of an article from the *Seal Beach Sun* and handed it across to Gavin. "They had a week of particularly high surf there. Attracted people from all over. That picture is him, riding the wave."

"So?"

"The name, sir."

Gavin scanned the article, then read the caption accompanying the photograph: *Dan "Brahma" Punyawong, of Santa Monica.*

"So?" Gavin asked again.

"His nickname—'Brahma'—that was the statue the body was left in front of in Thai Town. Put that together with the red quarter—which also happened to be minted in 1996, same year Dan Punyawong was born—and we definitely think we're on the right track."

"On the right track to what? To this kid as a suspect?" When Jarsdel didn't answer right away, Gavin grunted in exasperation. "You know what? I happen to know Captain Sturdivant gave you a way out of this and you didn't take it. Could've let Morales here determine the course of the investigation. Now we're more than a month into this thing, and all you've got is the weakest kind of circumstantial evidence, no motive, not even a working theory. The only thing you've actually accomplished is nearly derailing someone else's investigation and almost setting a killer free. Good work."

"If I may, sir," said Morales. "Detective Jarsdel did everything I would've done. I don't feel he left out anything or made any procedural errors. That business with the shell casing was just bad luck, and he cleared it up. It was a solid piece of police work."

Gavin was shaking his head vigorously. "Oscar, you know better, okay? You know what the captain cares about. You know what Chief Comsky cares about. Math. Closure rates up, crime stats down. Avoiding catastrophic fumbles should be par for the course, not something you expect praise for. I tell you x, y, and z, and you tell me, 'Hey, Lieutenant, it could've been worse.' That's basically all you're saying. Well, that doesn't impress me. And where are we with that goddamned Dog Catcher thing? Do you realize how badly I want that fucker buttoned up? I'm just so tired of hearing about it. One meeting after another, I have to listen to jokes and all kinds of bullshit. So how 'bout it? How 'bout a single actual piece of news?"

The meeting continued in that vein for several more minutes, concluding when Gavin resolved to make a report to Chief Comsky recommending the disbanding of HH2, despite its overall success. "Nothing Olympic Division or RHD can't handle. We're just burning city funds." Then, on an oddly conciliatory note, he said to Jarsdel, "Look, I'm not singling you out. It's not your fault you don't have the years. Put some time in at Auto Theft or Vice and work your way back to Homicide when you're ready. For now, keep going and just try not to fuck up too much."

Back at their desks in the squad room, Morales was philosophical. "Don't listen to that brasshole. Ultimately, it's Chief Comsky's decision, so we'll make it as tough on her as we can. Let's close it up. I think we're almost there."

Jarsdel nodded in the direction of the other two detectives who made up HH2, who were working nearby, filling out paperwork. "Maybe we should give it to Barnhardt and Rutenberg. Seems like they clear everything they get handed."

At the mention of her name, Detective Kay Barnhardt raised her head. She looked around, spotted Jarsdel, and gave him a smile. She was only a year older, but premature wrinkles and the severe, regulation women's hairstyle made her look to be more in her midforties. She was pretty, if a bit plain, her petite physique offset by a heavy bosom she did her best to conceal under conservative business attire. Barnhardt pointed a finger at herself and raised her eyebrows, asking if she was needed. Jarsdel returned her smile and shook his head, and she went back to her work.

"Here," said Morales, getting out the murder book for the Wolin case. "You were a history teacher. Let's look at some history. You take half, I'll take half. Nine times out of ten, the answer's already in there somewhere."

"History," murmured Jarsdel, but he took the offered pages. They sat and read for an hour. One look exchanged between them was all it took to communicate that neither had had any revelations. Jarsdel poured them some old coffee, and they listened to a drunk rave for a while in the prisoner intake area, then switched their stacks of paper and went back to work.

Jarsdel started by reviewing Wolin's cell phone records. His last call had been to Ramesh Ramjoo on October 1 and had lasted three and a half minutes. Before that, Wolin had received two incoming calls—one from a tire store on Franklin, probably to tell him his car was ready for pickup, and the other from an 800 number they'd determined was a solicitation call. Going back further in the records revealed pretty much the same pattern, with the exception of several calls made to Tony Punyawong's cell phone. These, Morales had highlighted.

Abe Rutenberg, Barnhardt's partner, sixty, with a shiny bald dome framed by wiry brown hair, stopped behind Morales's desk and read aloud over his shoulder. "According to Dr. Ipgreve, victim was baked alive in a large container but not exposed to a direct flame. Trauma was uniform, and the body—"

Morales turned the page facedown with a sigh. "Help you, Abe?"

"Just fascinated," said the detective. "And a little hungry. Could go for some brisket."

"Ha, that's funny."

Rutenberg shrugged. "What do you want? It was either that or something about your Dog Catcher case. You guys really excel at catching the weird shit. Just got regular old homicides over here. Any time you wanna switch, let us know. Love to take a walk on the wild side."

Rutenberg spotted Jarsdel, gave him a slight nod, then went back to join his partner.

"Prick," said Morales with affection.

After another hour passed, the men conferred again. "White van," said Jarsdel. "Any way we can get back to that white van?"

"Don't see how," said Morales.

"I feel like we're missing something obvious. Let's go over the timeline again. Who was the last person to actually see Grant Wolin alive?"

"Hard to say for sure. Because we weren't able to ID him for about two weeks after he died, no one seems to know exactly when he disappeared."

"But we do know," said Jarsdel, "that it couldn't have been any later than the night of October 2. Ipgreve said it would take time for the body to end up like that. No charring. Slow-cooked, then more time for it to cool to the temperature we found it at. I mean, I guess it's possible he was snatched sometime after midnight on the third, but for our purposes, let's say it was the second."

"I'm with you," said Morales.

"Body gets spotted early next morning by Sparks when he's out hustling Oxy. He waits to call it in because he doesn't want to get involved but breaks down and makes the call at"—Jarsdel checked his paperwork—"7:03. You and I roll on it around eight, maybe a little before. Talk to Sparks just after nine. Tells us about the van and the guy driving it. Just one guy, right? Says he gets out, dumps the body at the Brahma statue, gets back in, pulls a U-turn."

Morales nodded. "Then we're at sea until Ipgreve comes back with the DNA. We talk to the piece-of-shit brother at the Towers, who puts us onto the Indian guy, then there's the whole mess with the shell casings..."

"Slow down," said Jarsdel. "Go back to Ramesh for a second."

Jarsdel leafed through his stack of papers, didn't find what he was looking for, then sifted through the one in front of Morales. "Here," he said, pulling out a few sheets. "Transcript of our interview. He's vague about when he last saw Wolin."

"Vague or not sure?"

"Not sure, I guess. I don't think he was being cagey, but it'd been almost three weeks since they'd seen each other, and their last meeting obviously wasn't that memorable. Probably just hung out and smoked."

"Potheads," growled Morales. "Life's a blur to them at the best of times. Add a couple weeks on top, and you can forget about it."

Jarsdel scanned the transcript. "Fantasy Tours. Okay, so we get Fantasy Tours, and that leads us to where we are now. What else do we know about them?"

Morales checked a printout on his desk. "Permit approved by the city, July 9 of this year. Owned in totality by Anthony Punyawong of Santa Monica."

"July 9," said Jarsdel. "That puts them in business for only about three months before he decides to shut it all down. Why?"

"Because his son kills a guy."

"Okay. Then why does an arcade attendant, a *surfing* arcade attendant—if you can conceive of a mellower-sounding person, please let me know—kidnap one of his father's employees, cook him alive, then leave clues to his own identity at the crime scene? The red quarter? The Brahma statue?"

"Kid's cuckoo for Cocoa Puffs." But Morales said it without conviction.

Jarsdel stared at the transcript, as if willing the answer to come to him. "Couldn't have really been any more theatrical, right? What do you think? Ever seen anything this carefully staged before?"

Morales shrugged. "Worked a stabbing once. Dead hooker, posed like Jesus on the cross. Lying down on a bed, but other than that, it was perfect. Arms out to the sides, wounds on the hands and feet, gash in the side. In place of a crown of thorns, the killer'd wrapped a cell phone charging cord around her head. Everyone thought we had a religious nut on our hands, you know, out there convinced he's doing the Lord's work, and we're all bracing ourselves for the next body. But it was all a big show. Ended up being her pimp boyfriend. Wanted to scare her with the knife, ended up killing her instead, then tried covering it with the phony Passion play."

"That's what you think all this is? A big misdirection?"

"Could be."

Jarsdel thought about that, then shook his head. "I don't buy it. It's too organized. Too ritualistic. This was about satisfying the killer's fantasy, his ego. I think sending a message or making a statement or whatever was second to that."

"You sound like one of those wannabe FBI profiler guys."

"No, it's just..." Jarsdel trailed off, embarrassed. He actually had been trying to recall some of the behavioral analysis techniques he'd learned through his informal study of FBI textbooks. He began stuffing pages back into the murder book and was about to suggest a lunch break when he noticed something in the Ramesh transcript. He studied the section more closely, reread it, then dragged a highlighter across the lines of text. He handed the paper across the table.

Morales took it and read aloud. "'It wasn't an easy life. You know, dangerous. He didn't have any protection. One time, I was working the ticket counter, and he came running over to tell me he'd just been attacked. Some guy in front of the theater flipped over his cart and broke all his jars. And when Grant called the police, they didn't come.'" Morales set it down and looked at Jarsdel expectantly. "So?"

"I wonder what theater he's talking about."

"Theater?" Morales skimmed the paragraph. "Probably the Chinese or the Dolby. Who cares?"

But Jarsdel already had his phone out. It rang twice before Darius answered.

"Hi, Son."

"Hey, Baba."

"Everything all right?"

"Yeah. I was actually wondering if you could get me your friend Richie Berman's number."

There was a long pause, then, "What for?"

"I'd like to ask him something. About that guy he brought over to dinner that night. The big guy. Jeff."

"I suppose I was hoping you were calling about something else."

"About what?"

There was a heavy sigh on his father's end. "Oh, I don't know. Reconciliation."

Jarsdel marveled at how a single word could carry so much baggage. The man was a master.

"I think it might take more than a three-minute phone call while I'm at work to solve all our problems."

There was an even longer pause this time. "Do you have a pen?"

"Yeah. Go ahead, please." Jarsdel took down the number and was about to say goodbye when Darius changed tactics.

"We were hoping you'd come by to dinner again soon."

Now it was Jarsdel's turn to let a long moment go by. "Why?"

"Because we miss you."

"I miss you guys too, but not when you get the way you did last time."

"We're concerned about you. About what you do."

What you do. It was said with the kind of contempt reserved for people who robbed corpses for a living. "And that's always your refrain," said Jarsdel. "You're concerned."

"It's true. You think it comes from a place other than love?"

"Baba, I can't get into this right now. I got work. Can we talk later?"

"Now you're angry."

"I'm not angry. I'm busy. I love you guys. Can we just talk later? I'll call tonight before bed."

"Don't call too late. Your dad's getting over a cold."

"Okay."

"Love you, Tully."

Jarsdel glanced at Morales, who watched him expectantly. He

turned away and cupped the phone with his other hand. "Love you too." After he hung up, he sat down at his computer, typing rapidly.

"So what's goin' on?" his partner asked. "Got me in suspense."

Jarsdel skimmed the website he'd brought up. "Wanna go to the movies?"

———

It was a two-tone poster, magenta and white: *Mods and Rockers!— 19th Annual Film Festival.* There was a line of maybe a hundred people, even though show time wasn't for an hour. The first of them who caught Jarsdel's eye wore a dashiki and drainpipe jeans, while others wore bell-bottoms, chain belts, go-go boots, Jesus sandals. A girl, perhaps sixteen, wearing a tie-dyed headband and purple teashades, sported a peace sign medallion the size of a salad plate. Toward the back of the line, a barefoot woman in a flower-print caftan moved her arms in slow, swimming gestures.

"This was a whole scene I never got into," said Morales, watching the woman with rare curiosity.

"I'm shocked." Jarsdel looked back at the poster. A double bill tonight. At six thirty would be *The Jokers*, with Oliver Reed and Michael Crawford, followed by *Privilege*, starring Paul Jones and Jean Shrimpton. Jarsdel hadn't heard of either movie.

They started toward the box office, making their way around a few ticket holders who'd broken from the line and set up a portable speaker. They held hands, circling it as if it were a bonfire, and swayed clumsily to "Crystal Blue Persuasion."

They reached the ticket window, and Jarsdel badged the attendant, whom he recognized as the vampire doorman from Halloween. They explained what they were doing there, and the man looked first amazed, then troubled.

"You know he's got a show tonight, right? In an hour? He's probably getting set up. I don't know if he'll be in the mood to talk."

"Let us worry about that," said Morales. "Can you open up?"

"It's unlocked. Just..."

They moved away from the window and pushed through the lobby door. A teen behind the concession stand looked up from wiping down the counter. "Hey, we're not open yet."

Before Jarsdel could answer, the ticket attendant emerged from the box office, arms stiffly at his sides. "It's okay, Scott. They're... um...uh. He's..." He couldn't seem to bring himself to say "cops" or "police officers," as if doing so would only summon more.

Not interested in prolonging the moment, Jarsdel led the way across the lobby and up the staircase toward the projection booth. It was dark, as dark as it had been on Halloween, but he was able to make out the faint outline of the projection booth door.

Morales grunted his way up behind him. "If I fall down these *pinche* stairs, I'm takin' you with me."

Thinking of his partner's epic knocks, Jarsdel bunched his fist and rained three punishing hammer blows upon the wood.

"Uh, what the *fuck*?" came a voice from inside.

Jarsdel touched the button to activate his recorder.

The door swung open to reveal Dinan, immense and furious. His normally volcanic hairstyle had been sculpted with hairbands into half a dozen shaggy protrusions. It made him look maniacal.

"Easy, Jeff. That temper's gonna catch up with you some day."

Dinan's twisted features softened as recognition set in, first into surprise, then unease. "Oh. What are you doing here?" He saw Morales and added, "Who's *that*?"

"We came to have a talk."

Dinan exhaled and leaned on the doorjamb. "Hey, look, okay, I was a dick on Halloween."

"Yes."

"That why you came? To give me shit about the whole thing?"

"What if I did?"

"I'd tell you with all due respect that I was a little bit inebriated, and all in all, it wasn't even that big a deal."

Jarsdel turned to Morales. "I think I'll do this one alone," he said. "Wait for me downstairs?"

Morales looked at Dinan, then back to his partner. "You sure?" he said, keeping his voice low. "Guy decides to play, he'll make you into a little stain."

"I'm sure."

Morales shrugged "You got it. Gonna go get some Red Vines."

After he was gone, Jarsdel faced Dinan again. "Just us now."

"Who was that? Your bodyguard?"

"That," said Jarsdel, "is one of the finest detectives working in law enforcement today. Helped catch the Bell Gardens Butcher. It was his idea to use low-angle sun photography to find the clandestine graves of the victims. Smart, right?"

Dinan's confidence began to return. He stood straighter, using his bulk to fill the doorway. "Look, I got a show soon. And I would say that you coming here, you know, with a gun and badge and everything isn't really all that cool. You're taking a personal incident and making more out of it, under color of authority. I bet that's way against police regulations."

Jarsdel stepped closer. "Let's talk inside."

"Dude—"

"Believe me, I'm doing you a favor. This could just as easily happen downstairs in front of all your friends, or it could happen over at Hollywood Station. I'm giving you an opportunity to salvage a little dignity."

Dinan stared at him, and Jarsdel could see fear, uncertainty, and ego playing tag across the big man's face. Finally, Dinan moved aside and let him pass into the booth, then shut the door. It was just the two of them now. Jarsdel took a seat on the threadbare couch, stretching out, taking up as much room as he could.

"So this is some kind of intimidation ploy? Some kind of 'Hey, I'm a cop, and you can't talk to my woman like that' kind of thing? What do you want? A formal apology? Fine. I'm sorry. So very, very sorry. Okay?"

"What can you tell me about Grant Wolin?"

"Who?"

"Guy you threatened out front."

"I didn't. What guy?"

So it would be that way. Jarsdel didn't mind. "I'll make it easy, so you won't feel the need to bullshit me. I have a source who can positively identify you as the man who assaulted Grant Wolin, right in front of this theater."

That wasn't strictly true. When he'd gone to see Ramesh after rereading the transcript of their interview, all he'd gotten was confirmation that the Egyptian was the scene of the incident involving Wolin and the jars of Hollywood dirt. Jarsdel was taking a gamble, but he could already see it was paying off. Dinan was rattled, off-balance.

He pressed on. "You flipped over his cart, chased him off the property. Said you'd mess up his face if he ever came back." That was also a fabrication, but it too seemed to have hit home.

Dinan sagged onto a stool, obscuring it with his colossal mass. It made for a peculiar illusion, as if the man were somehow hovering in a sitting position. "Look, whatever he said, he wasn't on the sidewalk—he was on Egyptian property. That's private property. I asked him nice if he would go, but he didn't go. I never touched him. Why do you care? What does this have to do with you?"

"Because—"

"I mean, he's complaining? He's complaining to the cops? You know what? I think that fucking sucks. Guy was on private property. And that was, like, six months ago. I don't get it."

"He's not complaining. He's dead."

"I mean, isn't there a statute of limitations on that kinda shit? Wait—huh?"

"The body in Thai Town. The one you asked me about at my parents' place."

At first, Dinan just looked at him blankly. Then, slowly, understanding set in. His expression became one of pained disbelief, the skin around his eyes and mouth creasing deeper and deeper until Jarsdel feared his face might collapse in upon itself. The great beard shuddered, then gave a few quick jerks as the lips beneath struggled to form words. Jarsdel was impressed. If it was an act, it was a good one.

"Are you *serious*?" Dinan finally asked, voice barely above a whisper. The beard jerked again—once, twice.

"I'm serious he's dead, and I'm serious you're the only person I've met who's gotten physical with him."

"I didn't—I didn't *touch* him. Okay? I knocked over his crap. You know?"

"I do know. I also know you warned him never to come back. But I guess he didn't listen, right?"

"That was just *schoolyard* shit, man."

"Uh-huh. You told me what you once did at school, remember? First the guy's ankle, then his wrist, right? I'm sure you get up to even more sophisticated stuff now you're all grown up."

"Wait, just stop. Stop. I'm not...do you honestly think I killed this guy?"

"I think you might have had something to do with it, yes."

Dinan hung his head, shaking it in slow, ponderous arcs.

Good, thought Jarsdel. *Here it comes. Easier than I hoped.*

But when Dinan looked up, he was smiling. "You're fucking with me."

"Nope."

"You are. This is revenge for Halloween. Who told you about the thing with the dirt guy? One of your cop buddies? Figures that motherfucker would've called the cops. So they told you, and you knew *I* already knew about that body in Thai Town, so you thought, 'Hey, this is perfect.' Well." He slapped his thighs, then stood. "I've got a show tonight, and I still have to check the perfs on one of the trailers. I'll thank you to leave now."

Jarsdel gave him a hard, steady look. "You sure this is how you want to play it?"

Dinan raised a hand, pointing a tree branch of a finger at the open doorway.

Jarsdel took his time getting to his feet, surveying the room with affected disinterest. The wall of autographs, the inflatable moose head, the posters. *I Spit on Your Grave, Hell of the Living Dead, Cannibal Ferox*. The last boasted of being banned in thirty-one countries. Below the tagline—"Make them die SLOWLY"—the tableau was dominated by a predictably busty blond, blouse torn and ravaged, lying supine, screaming and streaked with blood. A muscular, dark-skinned man in a grass skirt stood over her, gripping a machete. His face was hidden, the top half of his body vanishing beyond the poster's border.

"Charming," said Jarsdel. "Anyone in that movie get cooked alive?"

Dinan flinched. He opened his mouth, about to say something, then reconsidered. He jabbed his finger in the direction of the exit.

Jarsdel nodded and crossed the room. He stopped in the doorway and turned back. "You sure got a thing for death as art. I'm betting there're some pretty whacked-out fantasies crawling around in that head of yours. I don't know, maybe you're tired of them. Tell you what..." Jarsdel approached the demon/schoolgirl rape statue, taking out one of his business cards. He balanced it carefully against where the demon's engorged cock plunged between the girl's pale cheeks. "You want some relief, you want to stop this, gimme a call. Can't be a whole lot of fun seeing the world through a mind like yours."

18

When Tully Jarsdel was a PhD candidate, he'd shared an office with thirteen other teacher's assistants, their name cards stacked on the door like a movie's closing credits. The plastic slab of a desk assigned to him was his only on Tuesdays and Thursdays from eleven to one, and even then, the other ones in the room were usually occupied with conferences, which so often included the tearful pleas of a freshman who'd just been handed her first C.

Jarsdel hated that room. It felt like a betrayal. After years of visiting his dads in their offices, he'd pictured dark, rich woods, books with nobly battered spines, a rolltop bureau with a bottle of Buffalo Trace tucked away in the bottom drawer. No—something European. Sherry, or maybe calvados. And frowning down on it all, a gaudily framed oil of some long-forgotten academic.

Instead, he'd been dumped in a kind of customer-service boiler room. No partitions, no windows, just buzzing fluorescents and plenty of oscillating fans. Certainly no art, except for, incredibly, a motivational poster depicting a bald eagle in flight. Jarsdel hadn't known whether it was supposed to be amusing in a postmodern way, but he tore it down the day he left.

He hadn't thought of any of that in years, but the wound reopened easily enough when he stepped through Richie Berman's door. The USC Millard Rausch Screenwriting Professorship came with a six-figure grant and a private office that would've suited Louis B. Mayer. Antique chairs of burgundy leather were arranged around an exquisite custom poker table, complete with carved chip wells and inset cup holders. The walls were white plaster, save for one, which a muralist had transformed into a trompe l'oeil of a nocturnal beachscape. The painting was sumptuous, almost photo-real in detail. Coconut palms swayed over moonlit sands, while in the distance, couples in formal evening dress danced on a raised stage flanked by tiki torches. Nearby, a jazz quartet played under a fronded canopy. Behind Berman's desk—not a rolltop, but an art nouveau wonder—a built-in shelf showcased an assortment of Emmy, Golden Globe, and Writers Guild awards. Framed posters of the corresponding film and TV projects, autographed by the actors in silver Sharpie, hung on either side. Finally, the capstone, the real gut punch of Jarsdel's envy, came in the form of a crescent-shaped wet bar occupying the far corner. Beneath the mahogany top, illuminated, frosted-glass windows allowed for discrete glimpses of the bar's wares.

He'd been waiting in the anteroom, watching Berman's assistant send off a flurry of double-thumbed texts, when the man himself swept in. He glistened with sweat and wore a starched karate uniform with a dragon patch on the right shoulder. A tattered black belt, so faded it appeared gray, was cinched around his waist, and the hand gripping the straps of his gym bag bore hard, flat knuckles. He flashed a gleaming smile.

"Hello, monsieur." He stuck out a hand.

Jarsdel shook it, wincing inwardly at the man's startling strength, and followed him into the office. He'd been overwhelmed at first, unable to take in the scene in its entirety, until Berman sat him down while he changed his shirt. Then Jarsdel had enough time to survey the room, between glimpses of Berman's coiled bundles of sinew, to feel sufficiently inadequate.

"Thanks for fitting me in on such short notice," said Jarsdel.

"Sure." The screenwriting professor slipped on a fitted white tee, then fastened a Patek Philippe onto his wrist. Instead of sitting behind his desk, he grabbed one of the poker chairs and dragged it over. "Sorry about the outfit. I teach a Chinese Kenpo class at the gym on Wednesdays. You probably did lots of hand-to-hand in the academy, right?"

"Basic stuff, mostly holds and locks. All nonlethal. Very little striking."

"Figures. Post Rodney King, you guys've had to do your jobs pretty much with your hands tied behind your backs."

Jarsdel didn't answer, just made a vague, noncommittal sound in his throat. He hadn't forgotten the look on Berman's face when his career had come up at his parents' dinner. Sadness, with just the right hint of disdain. And as was the case with most people who didn't like cops, Berman turned sycophantic when confronted with one.

"What do you carry?"

"Glock 40."

"Nice. Got one of those myself." Berman's smile returned. "So what's up? How you been? How're your folks?"

"They're great."

"Okay." He chuckled. "That's it for small talk, huh? Gotta admit, I'm pretty curious about what's goin' on. Something about 'one of my colleagues.' I'm gonna have to save that voicemail. Sincerely hope you're talking about Bud over in animation. Even if you're not, I'm still gonna play it for him."

"No," said Jarsdel. "What can you—"

"Oh, hey, sorry. You want a drink?" Berman pointed at the wet bar.

"No, thanks. Jeff Dinan. What can you tell me about him?"

"Jeff? Film guy Jeff?"

"His name came up in an investigation, and I'm following up."

"*His name came up in an investigation.* If this were a screenplay," said Berman, "I'd say that's a lousy line. I'd say let's rewrite it."

"How'd you meet?"

"God, I don't know. New Beverly, maybe. Yeah, Richard Fleischer double feature. *Compulsion* and *10 Rillington Place*. You serious about this? You actually sitting here asking me about Jeff Dinan? Officially?"

"He's a person of interest."

"Jesus. You are serious. What the hell could he've possibly done?"

"I can't say at this time. But it would be helpful if you could give me a feel for him. What can you tell me?"

"Not a whole lot. I mean, we're not extremely close. He's just a fun guy. His bona fides come from that projectionist gig at the Egyptian. He's not a professor or anything, but he's sharp. Knows a lot about movies. A real fan, like me." Berman paused a moment before adding, "Maybe even more. Movies are his whole life."

"How do you mean?"

"You *know*. Always quoting this or that. Doesn't want to talk about anything else. Corner you for hours with Kurosawa or Satyajit Ray. Smart, though, like I said. Knows his stuff."

"In your interactions with him, you ever notice any unusual behavior?"

"Like what? Jerking off into his pudding?"

"Like a temper. Anything like that."

"Jesus," Berman said again. "He hurt somebody?"

"I'm sorry, but I can't—"

"Yeah, yeah. Right. Okay. Wow. Uh, I've seen him get pretty worked up during a discussion, stuff like that. He's a passionate guy. Loves his little corner of the world. Defends it if he feels he's dealing with someone who's ignorant or doesn't appreciate it."

Jarsdel nodded for him to go on.

Berman exhaled, thinking. "Worst I saw was an argument he had with one of my grad students. It was about the Oscars. Jeff hates the Oscars, and this guy was bragging about how he could name all the Best Picture winners in order. Jeff said something way outta line, and—"

"What? What'd he say?"

"I didn't really catch it, but you could tell by the reaction. The other guy was all 'Excuse me? Excuse me? The fuck you say?' And Jeff doesn't say anything back, but he gets up and just kinda *looms* at him, and you know he's a pretty big guy. You've seen him. And with that beard and everything, he's like something outta *Game of Thrones*."

"What happened?"

"Nothing. Once the kid saw how outsized he was, he made some snarky remark and bounced. But it was a little hairy there for a second."

"You think—"

"To be honest, *I* wouldn't want to fight him. And I'm a fifth-degree black belt. Because with a guy that big, you'd have to kill him to stop him. Take the knee out, break a wrist, he can still put you in the morgue. That's the thing with big guys. They think they own the world, but what they don't realize is that no one's gonna show them any mercy once push comes to shove. Lights out is the only way. He keeps up like that, and one day, someone's just gonna shoot him." Berman gave a strained laugh.

"So you think Jeff's dangerous?"

"Do I think he's dangerous? You mean, more than just a bigmouth but actually *dangerous*? I don't know...it's one thing to maybe not have the greatest social skills in the world, but...man. I have no idea."

Jarsdel changed his approach. "You remember that Halloween screening of his?"

"Boy, do I. I couldn't make it, and he gave me endless shit."

"I took my girlfriend." Jarsdel hadn't yet had occasion to refer to Aleena by that title, and he liked it. "We were having a good time. Then when we went up to the booth to say hi, he got very strange."

"Strange how?"

"A lot like what you described. Aggressive. Told a story about a time he kicked the shit out of a schoolmate. That, plus all the posters and stuff..." Jarsdel shrugged. "Seems like he gets a little turned on by violence."

Berman fell quiet. Jarsdel let the silence play out. He sensed there was something coming and didn't want to push any harder. He glanced at a bookshelf stocked solely with copies of Berman's *The No Bullshit Guide to Screenwriting*. For propriety's sake, the *i* in *bullshit* had been replaced with a dripping fountain pen. Jarsdel's dads had told him the book cost nearly twenty dollars and was required reading for anyone enrolled in Berman's undergrad introductory class. "Easiest A on campus," Baba had said. "Only gets you two units, but it's basically impossible to fail, so everyone takes it. Lecture hall filled to capacity. Three hundred kids, and he teaches two sections every quarter. Summer too. An army of TAs, so he never has to grade a single paper, just gets up there and talks about movies. If he's feeling especially lazy, he'll actually just read sections of his book aloud and then analyze them for the students, as if it's goddamn Joyce or Tolstoy." Baba had shaken his head in amazement and, with a reluctant admiration, added, "He's on a sixth edition with that fucking thing. That *madar kharbeh* prints his own money."

Berman cleared his throat and leaned forward, his face suddenly anxious. "Look, I'm taking this conversation very seriously. And because I'm taking it seriously, I don't want to get a guy in trouble based on something stupid. Because for all his nonsense, I've never seen Jeff hurt anybody or directly threaten anybody. I like him. I do. And I really don't think there's any more to his quirkiness than just a guy who's maybe compensating for not being that popular in high school."

Jarsdel waited to a count of five, then asked, "But there is something else, isn't there?"

Berman leaned back and drew in a long breath. When he spoke, he didn't meet Jarsdel's eyes, instead fixating on a point on the carpet somewhere between them. Jarsdel had seen it before, the guilt of giving someone up, the shoulders hunched, head bowed.

"Few years back, he came to me with a script," said Berman. "Wanted me to give it to my agent. Which I told him I would, but I never actually did. I just couldn't. Lou woulda read three pages and never spoken to me again."

"Why's that?"

"I've actually done my best to forget it. It was some period piece about a crazy emperor. Unreadable. Funny thing was he had the format down perfectly, had the right screenwriting software—it *looked* professional is what I mean. Most amateurs don't get the basics right, you know, filling the pages with CUT TO's and FADE OUT's and all the stuff they think goes in a screenplay. Well, this was clean, not even a typo, but an absolute mess storytelling-wise. No through line, no hook, no real story, even. Just, like, a week in the life of this despot. So you've got this terrifically overwritten dialogue, kinda wannabe period dialogue, you know? 'Ho ho, pass the wineskin, thou salty knave.' Shit like that. And the rest of it was all beheadings, gougings, boilings, burnings. On and on. I'm not squeamish, but this was basically, like, let's focus on all this stuff in the most lovingly realized way, let's really get into this and show it all in real time. Serious Grand Guignol shit. It's one of those screen-plays that comes along and just makes you think, wow, what are you trying to say here? What's the message? Because it was clearly a labor of love, but to what end? Just to be gruesome? He said it was a true story, but who cares? Lot of true stories out there don't need to be made into movies."

Jarsdel felt excitement building within him. He was near to the golden thread again, could almost touch it. "Do you still have a copy?"

Berman shook his head. "Into the shredder. Bad juju." He forced a laugh, but Jarsdel could see the effort he put into it, as if perhaps he really did think the screenplay had been in some way malefic.

"You mentioned an emperor," said Jarsdel. "Remember which one?"

"No, like I said, this was a while ago."

"Domitian? Nero?"

"I don't know. Which of them ate babies?"

"What?"

"That was one of the scenes. Has this big banquet, and the main course is a human baby. Actually shows it. Cuts into its—you know—its butt. Eats it. Eats the whole thing."

Jarsdel felt his stomach turn. "I...don't know of any Roman emperors who did that."

"Greek, I think. Always going on about the power of Greece, the majesty of Greece."

"The Greeks didn't have emperors. They had kings or archons."

"What do I know? Maybe it was one of those."

Jarsdel strained to think of whom Berman could be talking about, but his grasp of Greek history was mostly limited to Athens and Sparta. He knew little about Paeonia, Lydia, Kommagene, and the myriad other city-states of the Greek world. Dinan's character could be one of hundreds of men. "If I wanted to read this thing," he said, "how would I go about doing that? You think it's online somewhere?"

"Nah, doubt it. Odds are the worse the script, the more the writer is afraid someone'll rip it off. He actually wanted my agent to sign an NDA before reading it, but I talked him out of that. Told him it was bad form. Why don't you just ask him? I'm sure he'd be delighted."

"I'd rather he didn't know I was looking at it."

"Okay." Berman sighed. "Well, he's definitely got it registered. First thing an amateur does is get a WGA reg number to protect against copyright infringement. Never fails. Soon as they're finished with a draft. No rewrites, no notes. No, first the reg number. Gotta get that."

"How's that work?"

"You pay a fee—ten if you're in the Guild, twenty if you're not. You send in your manuscript, and they hold on to it for you. Establishes legal proof of authorship should anyone steal from you—which, incidentally, I haven't seen happen a single time my thirty-five years in this business."

"Do people upload their files, or—"

"Mostly, but the guild still takes hard copies. Lot of writers prefer that. Feels more real to them."

"And I'm assuming you can't just go in there and ask to read someone's script."

"Ha, no. Think of it like a bank, but instead of money in the vaults, there's a million unproduced screenplays. Hell of a lot less valuable."

Jarsdel wondered what the procedure would be for getting the Writers Guild to release one of them. "Is there anyone over there you could refer me to? About seeing the script?"

"No, you'd probably need to talk to the registration staff or the depository custodian. Never heard of a situation like yours, so I don't know what the protocol would be."

Jarsdel stood. "Thanks, Richie. I'm sorry for having to come to you with all this."

"Yeah. It's...unexpected." He got to his feet and shook Jarsdel's hand. His grip was much softer than it had been earlier.

"And I probably don't need to say this, but I'd appreciate it if—"

"If I didn't tell Jeff you came to see me. Yeah. Okay."

Jarsdel turned to go, pausing for a last look at the beachscape mural—the warm tropical night, the mellow surf lapping the white sands, the dancers embracing in the glow of the torches.

Berman followed his gaze. "I know," he said, though Jarsdel hadn't spoken. "Beautiful, right?"

Jarsdel nodded.

"Rough day and I just stare into it and let time pass. Every now and then, almost like I could walk right in and never look back."

———

Aleena called Jarsdel after work and asked if he wanted to join her for an early dinner at Little Dom's on Hillhurst. Afterward, the plan was to go back to her place, where she was going to make them kettle corn and put on a movie. She'd been astonished to learn he'd never seen *Real Genius* and insisted they watch it.

The restaurant was cozy, the air heavy with the smells of garlic and basil. Jarsdel had over-ordered and doubted he'd be able to finish his meatball and provolone sandwich. He offered Aleena the rest of his appetizer—grilled corn with parmesan—and she took it gladly.

"You know," she said, "I was thinking. For someone who grew up in LA, your knowledge of movies is pretty sad."

"I'm from Pasadena. We read books over there."

"B...b...how do you pronounce it? *Books*?" Aleena put on an expression of absolute bafflement. She shook her head. "No, don't know 'em. Are they French?"

Jarsdel smiled. He watched as she spooled a tight forkful of angel-hair pasta in the bowl of her spoon. She offered it to him.

"Mm," he said, chewing, "delicious."

"Yup. So simple, yet..." She squinted at him. "I feel like you're not here."

"What do you mean?"

"You know what I mean. Your mind, it's elsewhere."

"Sorry. I'm a little preoccupied with work stuff."

"Can I help?"

"I don't think so. Just ruminating."

The busboy came over and refilled their waters. Aleena thanked him and asked for more bread. "How's this gonna work, then?" she said when he'd gone.

"How's what gonna work?"

"You and me. You have to be able to talk about your job. The good days, the shitty days. I want to know you. It's kinda what couples do."

"I don't have a problem talking about it. A few things I'm not supposed to discuss because they might be on their way to trial or they're sensitive for other reasons."

"Then what about the rest, the things you *can* tell me?"

Jarsdel took a drink of water and thought it over. "I don't wanna ruin the mood. It's ugly, a lot of what I see. Not everyone likes hearing the details."

"Try me."

"You sure?"

She gave him an exasperated look.

"Okay. Right now, I'm mostly working that thing in Thai Town. Little over a month ago."

"Ew, the burned guy?"

"Yeah, that's why I didn't want to bring it up."

"I can handle it. Do you know who did it yet?"

"I have a suspect. No real proof, though, he's not in custody."

Aleena smiled. "*Custody.* I just think it's so cool. My boyfriend's a detective. Like Magnum."

Jarsdel had to stifle a laugh around a mouthful of wine. He swallowed painfully, then said, "He was a private detective, not a LEO."

"LEO?"

"Law enforcement officer."

"Ah, *LEO.* Very cool."

The busboy came back with some bread. Aleena peeled the crust from one of the slices until all she had left was the soft center. This she buttered, sprinkled with salt, and popped into her mouth. The song that had been playing—"You're Nobody Till Somebody Loves You"—gave way to Sinatra singing "The Way You Look Tonight."

"Ugh," said Aleena when she'd finished chewing.

"What's the matter?"

"Nothing."

"You look upset."

"I'm not. It's just this song. I hate this song."

"Why?"

"It was our wedding dance song. David and me. Social foxtrot."

Jarsdel understood. "Oh. I'm sorry."

"Yeah." Aleena tried a smile. "Can't help thinking of Abby whenever I hear it. Obsessing over whether she was already dead by then, when we were dancing to it, or if it was happening at that moment. You know, just torturing myself."

"Are you okay? Want to go?"

"No, it's fine. It's just music."

"Music can be pretty powerful." He thought it sounded lame, but Aleena nodded.

"Yeah, definitely."

They let the rest of it pass in silence. Over the last few weeks, Jarsdel had almost forgotten—perhaps deliberately—the circumstances of how he'd come to meet Aleena. Now he felt a sudden, hot wave of anger at the Dog Catcher and the anguish he left behind him. The killer had even managed to reach out through a harmless old song and inflict a little more misery.

When it was over, Aleena swirled her wine and took a thoughtful sip. "I've been thinking about something. Ever since Halloween. Not that asshole in the movie theater. Afterward, when we were at my place. You remember?"

"I'm not sure. What specifically?"

"When we were in bed, and you were telling me about your badge. And what it represented and how you never had any doubt that it was like cosmic balance and the proper order of things and stuff like that. That you were fighting for reason against chaos. I know I'm not saying it exactly right, but—"

"No, that's pretty much it," said Jarsdel.

"Okay, so the thing that bothers me is what if you're wrong? I don't mean your motivations, but your whole—I don't know—*thesis*, I guess. That there's any such thing as balance, or even any such thing really as right and wrong."

"That's a...uh...that's a pretty intense argument. Do all certified professional organizers dabble in philosophy?"

Aleena's face hardened. "Don't do that."

"Do what?"

"Don't be a dick. You don't have to undercut me."

"I'm sorry. Wasn't trying to. I guess I'm just trying to keep things light."

"Like I need a certification in a subject to express an opinion."

"Really, Aleena—"

"No. You're being condescending. Like you've got all the answers and you're just sort of smugly observing everyone else. That *lecture* you gave me about Achilles. I'm not your student, okay?"

"You're right. It's a bad habit. Please say what you were going to say."

Aleena looked at him coolly.

"It's my security blanket," Jarsdel went on. "It's what I do when I feel vulnerable or, I don't know, uninteresting. I have this need to be interesting. It sucks. You're right, and I'm working on it. Please, accept my apology."

Aleena gave a reluctant nod. "So," she said, exhaling, "that's all I was thinking. About what you said. And if you were kind of—I can't think of a nice way to say this—kidding yourself, I guess?"

"How do you mean?"

"Do you know what moral luck is?"

"Maybe...I—"

"It's okay if you don't know. Just say 'I don't know, Aleena. Please tell me.'"

Jarsdel blushed but nodded. "Okay. I don't know. What is it?"

"It's a theory—yes, from philosophy, which was my minor by the way—that what we think of as right and wrong are really matters of circumstance and not a true measure of a person's worth. So like, if you take a person who, let's say, ends up participating in a riot. He gets caught up in the crowd and the energy and the excitement and ends up looting a store or joining a crowd that beats someone up. You have this person, right? We'd say he's, I don't know, not exactly evil, but not a great guy. A criminal. Lower down on the spectrum of relative worth to humanity next to a person who didn't do those things."

Jarsdel thought it over a moment. "Yeah, okay. I'm with you."

"But then let's say instead that on the day of the riot, he happens to be sick with the flu, so he doesn't go out and get caught up in the madness and therefore doesn't do anything wrong. He's still the same guy, but this time, the opportunity didn't present itself, so he didn't do the thing that in the other scenario we'd look at and say, hey, this is a bad dude. So in the new scenario, he gets a pass, right?"

Jarsdel frowned, then shook his head. "No, I don't think I buy it. I mean, that may be the case some of the time, but crimes of opportunity make up only a small spectrum of the stuff people end up in jail for. What about premeditation? And what about people who *put* themselves in situations where those opportunities keep arising? You could say a mugger is an opportunistic predator, because he wouldn't be able to commit the crime without the appearance of the victim. But he's good at what he does. He makes sure to put himself in places where victims come along and *create* those opportunities for the crimes to take place."

"But that's my point—"

"No, wait, hang on. Gimme a chance to respond. Because this is something I'm knowledgeable about, or at least really passionate about. I think what you're saying is a cop-out, because you're ignoring the fact that it takes a certain kind of person *in the first place* to take advantage of an opportunity to do wrong. You have to have it in you. Whether you act on it or not, it's still in your bones."

"You're going to arrest people for what's in their bones?"

"Of course not, and I think you know that's not what I mean. But a criminal is—and forgive the cliché—like a ticking time bomb. If he hasn't committed a crime yet, it's only because the right set of circumstances haven't aligned in the right way to entice him. Think about this. Think about repeat offenders, right? In and out of jail. Whatever the crime—assault, robbery, fraud—it doesn't matter. According to your model, they're just morally unlucky? Wrong place at the wrong time? There but for the grace of God go we?"

Aleena's gaze didn't falter. "Yeah. Pretty much."

Jarsdel exhaled between his teeth. "Okay. I don't think I've ever disagreed with someone so strongly on any point, ever."

"That's kind of an honor."

"I just don't know what to say. It runs contrary to everything I know about criminal psychology, history, everything. The wickedest people in the world were already wicked. Circumstances arose through which they could wield their terror, yes, but the ingredients were already there."

"Exactly."

"I don't get it—what do you mean?"

Aleena paused to peel the crust from another piece of bread. She buttered and salted the spongy center and took her time eating it. Jarsdel waited. Aleena took a slow sip of wine, then finally spoke. "That was just a basic example I was giving you. But the thing with moral luck is that you can go deeper with it. Constitutive moral luck, it's called. It's those ingredients you were talking about. How much control do you have over them? You're surrounded by abuse, cruelty, self—"

"This is nature-versus-nurture stuff, I know—"

"No, you don't know. Listen. I was going to say that those things are typical of the nature-versus-nurture argument. As in, whatever nurture we receive is out of our control, whether we're beaten or caressed. We can't choose our environments; everyone agrees on that. But isn't the *nature* we receive, the nature we're born with, also outside our control? Let's say I'm born a narcissist. I only care about others to the extent that they figure into my life, with me at the center. But I didn't choose to be a narcissist, right? I was built that way. It's genes. I didn't make a choice to be a selfish asshole, but it's how I came out."

"Ah, so it's just the hand you're dealt. Bad luck. Free will is out the window, and it isn't your fault for being horrible."

"What does it matter to assign fault? What does that do for us? That wasn't even what we were talking about. We were talking about there being some kind of higher realm of right and wrong and that the side of righteousness is directly connected to cosmic balance, whereas the side of what we'd call wickedness is in opposition. Perverse."

Jarsdel's assurance wavered, and Aleena smiled. It was a sad smile. "You see what I'm saying, don't you?" She went on before he could answer. "Whether it's nature or nurture doesn't matter, because neither are within our control. We're either shaped by our environment or by our DNA. Either way, we're shaped. And if that's true, then what part of a person's moral character can we isolate and say that it's truly them? You know—pure, truly untouched by any other factor. I don't think we can."

"So no one's responsible for anything?"

"We're in the body that does what the mind attached to it tells it to do. And that body is held responsible, rewarded or punished according to the standards of our culture and our time. But this idea that there's some objective goodness that's counting on you, that's counting on the righteous people of the world to fight on its behalf... I don't know. Because what we think of as wickedness is just another expression of natural processes, a product of the same system that made goodness. Isn't it all the same to the universe? Does it actually care if someone's nice or not?"

Jarsdel could tell by her urgency that the question wasn't rhetorical. She was waiting for an answer. "I just think," Jarsdel began, then swallowed, buying himself more time. "No, I'm certain that living for the benefit of others is...that it's a more rewarding path. Both for yourself and for the people around you."

"But I'm talking about a person's value," Aleena pressed. "Their core, below all the influences. How do you really know what a person's value is, their worth? If they're good or bad or if it even matters at all?"

Even in the dim light of Little Dom's dining room, Jarsdel could see her eyes were wet, the lashes flecked with tears. He wasn't sure if it was for the dog, Abby, or for something bigger—her dead marriage and the entire life it had represented, a life that was now and forever out of reach, one that had been cheated of its possibilities, aborted. Jarsdel wondered if it haunted her and directed another surge of fury at the man who'd robbed her of it. Even though, he knew, that same killer was largely responsible for the relationship he now shared with this woman.

Aleena reached across the table and squeezed his hand. "Hey. Forget it. You still in the mood for kettle corn and Val Kilmer?"

19

An elk's head was mounted on the wall behind Judge Lori Monson's desk. It gazed at Jarsdel through blank, black eyes that were somehow compelling, hypnotic even, and he found himself staring into them whenever the judge's attention wasn't on him.

Monson was in her seventies, with gray hair done in a marcel wave and cheery, pleasant features. She resembled what an artist's conception of what Mrs. Claus might look like, down to the gold, wire-framed glasses. But Monson was one of the most hotly disliked jurists in the Stanley Mosk Courthouse, maybe the entire city, by the defense attorneys unlucky enough to draw her on a case. Morales had told Jarsdel that she had once been a member of the defense bar herself, specializing in civil rights, and in the '70s and '80s was as loathed by the LAPD as she was now loved by it. The reason for her dramatic change was a single client—Stuart Boyett—whom she'd helped acquit on a murder charge after proving a patrolman had planted evidence in his car. Boyett celebrated his release by abducting and murdering a four-year-old boy. Monson shuttered her law practice shortly thereafter and started working for the district attorney's office. Once a staunch opponent of the death penalty, she went on to successfully prosecute no fewer than a dozen capital cases. Later, as judge, Monson sentenced an equal number of men to San

Quentin's Green Room before the state put a moratorium on executions. If anyone was going to sign their warrant, it would be her.

But Judge Monson looked up from the paperwork and frowned. "I'm not seeing a lot of hard evidence here."

Morales shifted in his chair. "That's right, Your Honor, but we have reason to believe the item we're after will provide us with what we need to move forward."

"Wouldn't it be grand if it worked that way, Detective. Unfortunately, you need evidence to uncover more evidence. I don't approve of fishing expeditions."

"Your Honor," said Jarsdel, "we think the circumstantial case is strong enough to support this warrant. Mr. Dinan is the only individual we know of who's had a physical altercation with our victim. In broad daylight, right in front of the Egyptian. That's a movie thea—"

"I *know* what the Egyptian is, thank you, Detective. I didn't fall off the turnip truck yesterday."

"Forgive me, Your Honor."

Monson turned a few pages of the warrant application. "I see you have an affidavit here from a Ramesh Ramjoo. Is that a male or a female?"

"Male."

"Mr. Ramesh Ramjoo, then. States that his friend, the late Grant Wolin, was the one who came to him with the tale of this alleged assault."

"That's right."

"He didn't see it take place himself."

Jarsdel hesitated. "No, but—"

"No police report?"

"None was filed at the time."

"And I imagine you don't have any actual witnesses, or they'd be on this application."

"No, Your Honor, but I—"

"Detective Jarsdel, how is it that you can present me with such a textbook case of hearsay? Come now. 'A man, who's now dead, alleges you once struck him.' That would be setting quite a precedent. Just imagine the swarm of new civil and criminal cases that could be brought before the bench, depending solely on anecdotal evidence gathered from the deceased."

"Pardon me, Your Honor," said Morales, "but Mr. Dinan freely admitted to the assault during an interview with Detective Jarsdel."

Monson shuffled through the pages again. "I see he admits to knocking over a cart. Property damage. Not assault." Monson steepled her fingers and leaned back. "It's not good enough. Not nearly."

Jarsdel bit his lip. He had another card to play, a gift from Detective Barnhardt and her background in psychotherapy. "Your Honor, if I may."

"You may."

"We have a credible source who affirms that the document in question contains scenes of mayhem and graphic death. Our victim was tortured, perhaps for hours, until he expired. We think the screenplay could paint a valuable picture of how this man's mind works, perhaps establish a pattern of violent thoughts or obsessions."

Morales cut in. "And let's emphasize that we're not asking to violate anyone's privacy. We don't want to search his house or his vehicle or his person. All we want to do is read a script—a script that's been kicking around Hollywood for years. Something he's freely shown countless people."

Monson's frown of concern lifted slightly at its corners. "And you know for a fact this script is where you say it is? At the Writers Guild?"

"Yes, Your Honor," said Jarsdel. "I talked to them on the phone. There's only one script registered by a Jeffrey Dinan. But they won't give us access to it without a court order."

"It says here," said Monson, referring to the warrant application, "that you're requesting a copy."

"That's right."

"Hmm. Tell you what I'll do..." She handed the application back across the desk, unsigned.

Jarsdel took it, unhappily. His eyes met the elk's again, and he wondered if Monson had been the one to bring the noble beast down.

She went on, "Bring that back to me, rephrasing that you'd just like to read it at the Guild. No copies. If you end up finding what you're looking for, we'll proceed from there. Do that, and I'll sign."

Jarsdel brightened. "Certainly, Your Honor."

"Good. Will that do it, gentlemen?"

The detectives thanked her and left to rewrite the warrant.

—————

Something was bothering Jarsdel. He tried to sleep but couldn't. At first, he thought he might be too hot and stuck one leg out from under his blanket, but then he was too cold. He liked the pressure, the weight of the sheets on his body, and having a limb naked and exposed felt strange.

He'd had a full day, and it should have been good, deep sleep. But now he thought he'd need a glass of something to help him nod off. Frustrated, he got out of bed and went into the kitchen. He opened his liquor cabinet and eyed a bottle of Bulleit Rye. Maybe that and some TV would do the trick. The clock on the microwave said it was quarter to eleven, and he had to be up by five.

He thought of the way the alcohol would feel, hot on his tongue and in his throat, and decided he wasn't in the mood. He closed the liquor cabinet and stood there, thinking.

What was it? It had started the night before, after his dinner with Aleena. Some quiet but nagging little voice insisting he'd missed something, like catching a few scattered notes of music and then trying to place them.

He replayed the conversation they'd had at dinner. Most of it had been casual, nothing too significant, until that Frank Sinatra song had come on. Then she'd been upset, and instead of comforting her, Jarsdel had managed first to insult her, then engage her in a debate about moral responsibility. The irony was that of all people, he should have been the most helpful and compassionate. He understood what it was like to leave a life behind, to make a vicious, sudden turn and abandon what was old and familiar, only then to have it run beside you, dogging you, a sputtering film strip that every now and then came into bright and terrible focus. The life you could have had.

The difference was, of course, that Jarsdel had made a choice. Leaving Maureen, his career, it had all been up to him. For Aleena, that decision had been made by a killer, a phantom who'd dropped out of a clear, blue day to wreak devastation and heartache. A fairy-tale ogre, a plague sent by a spiteful god.

Jarsdel asked himself, selfishly he supposed, whether he'd always have to contend with Aleena's unrealized life with her ex-husband. Or how many times a perfect moment would be ruined by a trigger of some kind, like the song, and pull her away from him.

The song.

Something about the song. She'd begun to cry because it had been the first dance at her wedding. A dance they'd probably rehearsed for weeks on end. And she'd had to listen to the song dozens of times. No wonder she'd been so well-conditioned to associate it with the day their dog had been murdered.

Her wedding day. How had the killer known it was her wedding day? In each case, he'd known. The couples had been picked completely at random, according to the computer, yet they were all drawn together by that single commonality. Their wedding day.

The song.

What about it?

And then he thought he might know. Depending on what the other couples told him, he really might. He checked the clock on the microwave again. Almost eleven. Aleena could already be asleep, but it didn't matter. He grabbed his phone.

———

Early the following morning, a fight broke out between two arrestees in Hollywood Station's main holding area. After repeated attempts to break up the scuffle, a nearby officer chose to deploy her pepper spray—a by-the-book decision that had the desired effect of sending the combatants into a state of groaning, mucousy compliance. Only then was it discovered that the station's supply of baby shampoo—the most effective over-the-counter neutralizing agent for capsaicin—was missing. While a patrol officer sped to Rite Aid to pick up some more, the desk sergeant raided the break room fridge and seized two quarts of half-and-half, which he used to alleviate some of the prisoners' suffering.

The mess was mostly cleaned up by the time the detectives arrived to start their day, but a tiny bit of pepper spray residue had made it onto the handle of the men's room door. Abe Rutenberg discovered this the hard way and so also required a dose of baby shampoo. When Jarsdel found him in the break room, the webbing of his thumb was a bright, angry red, and he still hadn't stopped scratching.

"You're probably not in the mood to hear this," said Jarsdel, "but I'd like to run an idea by you."

Rutenberg had the fridge open and used his good hand to hunt through the contents. "Most of this shit oughta get dumped. Someone's gonna die of food poisoning. Where's the goddamned, mother-jumping half-and-half?"

Jarsdel told his story while Rutenberg grimaced his way through a cup of coffee lightened with nondairy creamer. After he'd finished, Rutenberg called his partner in to join them and had Jarsdel repeat it for her.

When it was over, Rutenberg and Barnhardt exchanged an amused look.

"What do you think?" Jarsdel asked.

"I don't know," said Barnhardt. "All the couples so far were in their twenties. I don't think Abe and I fit the profile."

"I know," said Jarsdel, "but I don't think he's picking them based on age. It just happens most couples who get married are going to be in their twenties. You guys'll do fine. Just make sure you're clear you have a dog. Bring it up however you can. Naturally, of course. I don't know, maybe one of you asks the other if wherever you're going on your honeymoon takes pets. Or talk about how you're going to board the dog while you're away. Whatever, just make sure you do it in front of him."

"I actually do have a dog," said Barnhardt. "My husband got me one two Christmases ago."

"Big?"

"No, a Maltese."

"Great, maybe even bring it with you a time or two. Do you have a crate or a carrier or something?"

"I'd die if anything happened to her."

"It won't. He only goes after them on the day. And we won't even need the dog to be there when he makes his move."

She turned to her partner. "What about you?"

Abe shrugged. "Gotta admit, it's the best theory come along since Rick Jackson and his dog park idea. You HH2 whiz kids, raising the bar around here. If you're good with it, Kay, I'm with you. Besides, might actually be fun."

Barnhardt considered, then began working her wedding ring loose from her finger. "Guess I'll have to keep this in my nightstand for the next few weeks."

———

The Writers Guild of America building was located at 7000 West Third Street, less than a block from Jarsdel's apartment at Park La Brea, making the trip the one and likely only time in his career he wouldn't have to drive on an official errand. Armed with his warrant, he entered the lobby and approached a young receptionist who would have been pretty if she weren't so alarmingly thin.

She gave him a reserved smile. "Good afternoon. Can I help you?"

"Hi, yes, I'm Detective Jarsdel with the LAPD." He showed his badge and went on, "I'm not sure exactly who I need to talk to, but I need a script recovered for me. From the depository."

Her eyes widened, meerkat-like, at the sight of the badge. "Oh. I... uh...I don't know either. Let me call our depository custodian."

Jarsdel waited on a sofa bench and thumbed through an issue of *Los Angeles* magazine. After a few minutes, a man stepped out of an elevator and crossed to the front desk. He was middle-aged, with a belly that stood out in relief under an otherwise loose-fitting polo shirt. He had a brief, whispered conversation with the receptionist, who pointed a tremulous finger at Jarsdel. The man turned, spotted Jarsdel, and approached. The detective stood, and the two shook hands.

"Leon Buxbaum. Understand you're looking for a script?"

"That's right. I have a warrant here." Jarsdel handed it over.

Buxbaum raised his eyebrows. "Never actually seen one of these. My predecessor had to deal with a court order once for a copyright case, but that was a civil matter. You're not asking to go into the actual depository, are you? Because I don't see that on here."

"No, I can't think why it would be necessary," said Jarsdel. "I assumed you'd just bring it to me and I could read it somewhere."

"Sure. We have a room you could do that in. Or I could just make you a copy, and you'd take it with you."

"Actually, I'm not allowed to have a copy. The warrant's explicit on that, I'm afraid."

Buxbaum shrugged. "Okay. Follow me, please." The two took the elevator to the second floor, and Buxbaum installed Jarsdel in a small conference room while he went to find the document.

Jarsdel didn't have to wait long. Buxbaum came back with a large, sealed envelope. He pulled a tab near the flap, breaking the seal, and removed a second, slightly smaller envelope. This too he opened and was about to reach inside when he stopped and looked at Jarsdel.

"I can touch it, right? No worry about fingerprints or anything?"

"Oh, sure. You can touch it. It's fine."

Buxbaum tilted the envelope and gave it a gentle shake, and the script dropped into his waiting hand. He laid it on the table as carefully as if it were a rare first edition. "You're lucky. This had one more month on it, then it was off to the shredder."

"What do you mean?"

"We only keep screenplays five years unless the artist extends the registration. This was about to lapse."

"Does that happen often?"

"Sure. People forget they've got their work here. Then all of a sudden, for whatever reason, they need a copy, and we have to tell them sorry, it's gone."

"You don't let writers know when their work's about to expire?"

"You have any idea how many scripts we've got in the vault?"

Jarsdel didn't, but he saw Buxbaum's point.

"Anyway, take your time. When you're finished, just bring it down to Lisa at the desk. Like a glass of water or anything?"

"I'm good, thanks."

"Okay. Well, it was nice meeting you."

Buxbaum left the room, and Jarsdel turned to the last page of the screenplay to see how much he'd have to read. It was nearly two hundred pages long. He didn't know much about screenwriting, but that seemed like a lot. He went back to the title page.

KINGDOM OF SORROW

BY JEFFREY M. DINAN

This was followed by a WGA registration number, the words *writer's draft*, a completion date, and a copyright warning. Jarsdel opened to page one and began to read.

───────

By page twenty, Jarsdel was grateful he'd only had a light lunch. As far as he could tell, the story was about the rise of Phalaris, a Greek general who'd been granted absolute rule in the town of Akragas, Sicily. He seemed to spend most of his time either pontificating or putting suspected traitors to death, and these in the most gruesome ways possible. One man was hung upside down while two executioners sawed him in half. Another was condemned to be boiled in urine. Jarsdel had managed to shrug off most of it, but a moment toward the end of the third scene sent a queasy twist through his stomach. A guard had been accused of abandoning his post so he could be at his wife's bedside as she gave birth.

                    PHALARIS
          Be not gentle with him, for his
          weakness offends me.

                    EXECUTIONER
          What would you have me do, o Lord?

                    PHALARIS
          Remove the flesh that houses such
          a feeble soul, but take care! Peel
          first each finger to the bone,
          then each toe, and from there treat
          similarly the hands and the feet.
          Slowly, mind, but continue on until
          naught but the face remains. If he
          cries for food, give it, and if he
          cries for water, give it also. It
          will displease me much should he
          gain rest premature. Let him live as
          long as he may, a tortoise without
          its shell.

Jarsdel read on, skimming the following pages where the torment was actually depicted, then happening upon the scene Richie had warned him about—Phalaris eating the newborn baby of the doomed guard. Jarsdel wanted to take a break but reminded himself he still had nearly 150 pages to go. He took a breath and dove back in.

—————

PHALARIS

You've journeyed far. From Athens, I
am told.

PERILLOS

Yes, My Lord.

PHALARIS

And you wish the patronage of this
court?

PERILLOS

I do humbly ask it, My Lord.

PHALARIS

Why should such privilege be granted?

PERILLOS

I am well-schooled in the arts and
have cast many great figures in both
bronze and stone. I would do likewise
for Your Lordship and any person-
age he so deems worthy. It would be
my crowning honor to be known as the
sculptor of the great Phalaris.

PHALARIS

Very well then, here is your task. I
take delight in small amusements but
have grown weary of late and find no
joy in old games. Craft for me a tool
to wring fresh sport from the bodies
of mine enemies, and you will be
rewarded with the position you seek.

Jarsdel turned the page and continued reading. Something about the scene struck a chord with him—some long-ago lecture, back when he was an undergrad, about the sculptor Perillos. He paused, trying to dig up a dormant bit of trivia, but it didn't come. He went on. The next few pages weren't any more illuminating, and Jarsdel found himself skimming again until Perillos reappeared on page 110.

PHALARIS

You come before me once more, and
at a time when I am in the most ill
humor. Did you bring me what you
promised? Your life may well depend
upon my satisfaction.

PERILLOS

Yes, My Lord. If I may flatter
myself, I have brought you a
unique gift, one whose construction demanded the utmost in
skill and ingenuity and which you
shall find unsurpassed in all the
Mediterranean. You will be the envy
of kings, and your enemies shall
quake with fear.

PHALARIS

(aside) He dares to presume both are
not already so? Perhaps he wishes
to try his invention firsthand! (to
Perillos) Bring it before me.

Jarsdel felt a kick of excitement and read faster. And at the top of the next page, without any more ceremony, there it was. Yes, he now saw why the name Perillos had seemed familiar. He'd heard the story once but tucked it away at the very back of the storehouse of knowledge he'd accumulated since. Why would he have any use for it, other than as a ghastly curiosity? Even now, it was almost impossible to believe Dinan had actually gone through with it. But everything fit. Tully Jarsdel took out his phone, centered the page in his viewfinder, and snapped a picture. He now knew, in painstaking detail, exactly how Grant Wolin had died.

20

Based on Jarsdel's discovery, Judge Monson happily authorized as many copies of Dinan's script as were requested. By the next day, *Kingdom of Sorrow* could be found on all four desks in HH2. Abe Rutenberg highlighted some of his favorite passages and lured over curious detectives from Vice, Gangs, and Auto Theft. The results usually involved his prey retreating after a minute or two, faces bunched in disgust, as Rutenberg called after them, "Whatsa matter? I just set up a Kickstarter page for it. Five bucks. C'mon, let's get it *made*." Eventually, Morales yelled at him to get some new material.

Command personnel were also each provided a copy, though neither Jarsdel nor Morales expected Captain Sturdivant to bother reading it. They thought the same of Bruce Gavin—when Jarsdel first brought him the script, he'd taken it without a word and tossed it on a pile of forlorn papers near the edge of his desk. Soon, however, glimpsed through the glass walls of his office, he began carving his way through Dinan's house of horrors. For the next two hours, HH2's division commander was riveted. Bent over the script in his pressed black uniform, lieutenant's silver bar glinting on his arm, he resembled what a movie producer in a totalitarian regime might look like.

Jarsdel was preparing the file they'd present to Dinan when they brought him in. There were crime scene and autopsy photos, the postmortem report, a copy of the incriminating scene from *Kingdom of Sorrow*, and a letter from Dr. Ipgreve affirming that the state of the victim's body could be explained by the manner of death described in the script. The finishing touch was a stack of miscellaneous dog-eared reports and circulars Jarsdel had intercepted on their way to the shredder. They wouldn't be shown to Dinan, of course, but they'd add weight to the folder and imply the police had been building its case against him for some time.

Morales sat heavily across from him. "Kinda funny, all this."

Jarsdel looked up. "How do you mean?"

"I was just thinkin', here you have this writer who can't get a break, movie doesn't get made, but now he's got some of the most important people in the city reading it. Finally got some attention."

"Probably not the kind he'd hoped for."

Morales picked up his copy of the script and opened to a page he'd marked with a sticky note. He read for a moment, then exhaled, shaking his head. "I don't get it, man. Life's hard enough, you know? And then guys like this come along and they're like, 'Hey, you really wanna see how fucked up shit can get? Let me show you.' You get the same feeling working serials. You just want them to go away. Enough already. Life's hard enough without you assholes. You work a serial case yet? Besides Dog Catcher, I mean?"

"No."

"Then you're lucky."

Jarsdel selected the last of the dummy documents, an intradepartmental memo outlining the penalties for failing to follow grooming guidelines, and shoved it into the folder. He stood, leaving the inflated case file on his desk, ready for the interrogation soon to come.

Morales got to his feet. "You sure you wanna play it like this? We got no physical evidence. No way we can charge him just with what we got. Best we can hope is to scare him into a confession. He doesn't crack, it's your standard forty-eight-hour hold, then he walks."

"True," said Jarsdel, "but while he's on that hold, we've got Judge

Monson's warrants for his car and apartment. You can't do what he did without leaving some major evidence behind."

Morales picked up the script and pointed to the page he'd been reading. "And you actually think he did *this*? For real? What are we looking for, then? A storage unit somewhere? Maybe his grandmother's basement?"

"We'll find it, wherever it is. Pretty tough to hide."

"I don't know. I got doubts, man. Maybe we should sit tight just a couple more days, see what else we can turn up. Can't hurt, 'specially if he decides to give us the silent treatment in there. Or gets a fuckin' lawyer."

Jarsdel knew Morales was right. A few more days on top of the months that had already elapsed wouldn't make a difference. A deeper investigation could only strengthen their case and increase the chances of pushing Dinan into a confession. But then he thought of the twisted, tormented body, its eyes two hollow pits, cooked muscles wrenching the mouth into a jack-o'-lantern's grin.

"No," he said to Morales. "I want him in custody. Once he's in an interview room, he'll want to know what we're finding on those warrants, and we can tie him in knots with any story we like. Make him sweat. Meanwhile, we'll have two days' carte blanche to dig through his life. If we can't find anything to charge him with after that, we never will."

Morales shook his head. "Nah, I see what you're sayin', but I'd still wait. Do some more field work. See what he was up to as a juvenile. Sealed court records and shit. A guy who does something like this has to have a history, but we got nothin' on him as an adult. We're missing some major pieces."

"I don't care. I want him in here. What if he does it again? Could you live with that?"

"We could put a tail on him. That'd—"

"Gavin won't okay that, not on what little we got, and you know it. We have to bring him in. Besides, it's my call. You made me lead on the case, remember?"

It was early, not quite six, and still mostly dark. Heavy clouds had rolled in during the night to blanket the sky. Hopefully, Dinan would still be asleep and wearing nothing more than his briefs. If all went well, he'd wake to the pounding on his door feeling groggy and confused. Confronted with the surprise show of force—two detectives, plus the pair of uniformed officers backing them up—he'd be shocked into acquiescence.

"Maybe in my prime I coulda taken him," said Morales as they rode over to Dinan's apartment. "Did Golden Gloves in my teens. Now, though..." He gestured at his legs in disgust.

Jeff Dinan was a very big man—a towering hulk somewhere in the neighborhood of three hundred pounds. Jarsdel and Morales figured it would take two sets of cuffs to span the width of his back. They also figured that if he became combative, they'd be in serious trouble. Richie Berman had been right about that. To stop someone that big, you had to go beyond the application of mere pain. You had to either cause a major dysfunction in the body, which the Taser usually accomplished, or resort to lethal force. The prospect of the arrest ending in Dinan's death gave Jarsdel a feeling of tightness in his chest.

Morales glanced at him from the passenger seat and seemed to pick up on his thoughts. "Never had to draw on a guy, huh?"

"Once. Had a note robber at a bank on Western—you know, no gun, just a piece of paper with 'Gimme the money or die.' The teller hit the 211 button and stalled him long enough for our patrol car to show up. Also threw in a dye pack, which exploded in his bag just as he was coming out the door. So he was on edge, and we didn't know if he had a weapon or not, and he just stood there staring at us. It was pretty tense."

"Was he armed?"

"He was high. Turned out he'd just fled from a complaint a block down the street where the manager of a Burger King caught him stealing all the ketchup packets. It was actually because of that call that we were already on our way to the area."

"But no weapon?"

"No."

"So in the end, nothing happened."

"We just kept yelling at him to get down on the ground, get down on the ground, then a backup officer flanked and tackled him. He'd soiled himself by then, so I'm glad it wasn't me who had to do that."

Morales nodded. "Don't think they'll be telling that story at any of our recruitment drives."

At those words, Jarsdel felt a profound wave of sadness and doubt pass over him. He thought of the pledge he'd made to Brahma—to the universe as a whole—to be among those who renew the world. It had been a reaffirming of the reasons Jarsdel had decided to become a police officer in the first place. A pledge to fight the tide of entropy, to act as an agent of order and sanity and justice. To not merely theorize and pontificate from a professor's lectern but to actually do something, however small, to help speed humankind toward a new age of enlightenment—one he believed could be predicted with near-mathematical certainty.

Just look where we once were, what we used to do to each other, and look at us now. If we could chart human cruelty on a graph, the line would step ever downward, barring the occasional plateau. If the trend were to continue, violence and its terrible fallout would someday retreat toward the realm of statistical insignificance, of anomaly. Eventually perhaps, they would pass into history as a strange relic of our species' evolution.

But Morales had just pointed out, correctly, that one of the most fraught episodes of Jarsdel's career in law enforcement—and of his entire conscious existence—was hardly worth recounting. What, then, had he accomplished? His last five years had seen him take on an endless stream of shoplifters, identity thieves, petty fugitives, noise complaints, DUI stops, he-said/she-said domestic abuse cases, and unsolved car break-ins. Even the murder cases he'd worked as a detective, even the ones he'd solved, had felt somehow primitive, offering no sense of achievement or progress.

At a nightclub, a man feels slighted when another steps on his foot. After an argument, he shoves the offender, who strikes his head on a table leg and suffers a fatal subdural hematoma. A dozen witnesses identify the pusher, whom Jarsdel arrests early the next morning. He is charged with involuntary manslaughter, pleads guilty, and is sentenced to three years' probation.

A pair of muggers attack a woman as she leaves an ATM. They yank on her purse. She yanks back. One of the attackers produces a steak knife and plants it in her neck. The ATM's security camera records the whole thing. The footage is processed using facial recognition software, and the thugs—who both have extensive criminal records—are apprehended within a week. It's a charge of first-degree murder with two special-circumstances enhancements—lying-in-wait and commission of felony robbery. The trial is short, and the sentence is death. The state hasn't executed anyone since 2006, however, so the men expect to spend the rest of their lives in CCI, outside Los Angeles, where they'll find some protection as associates of the Mexican Mafia. The judge sends them instead to San Quentin, deep in rival Nuestra Familia territory, while they await execution. The men are very quiet as they're led from the courtroom.

A twenty-eight-year-old addict drops out of rehab for the third time. Ashamed, she can't face her parents and finds a spot near the LA River where a band of homeless people live under the shade of a rumbling overpass. A charity van stops there each morning to drop off day-old sandwiches. That's plenty of food for her; she's gone much longer with much less and hardly even noticed. She has heard, however, that these encampments can be dangerous, so enlists an alcoholic Iraq War veteran to protect her in exchange for sex. He's out one day, scrounging money to buy liquor, when his charge is raped and strangled by one of the other men living in the camp. He throws her body in the river, but it snags on a tangle of marsh plants and is quickly discovered. The vet returns to camp and learns of the murder. He quickly deduces the identity of the killer—the only one who's suddenly abandoned his tent. The vet tracks him all the way to MacArthur Park, where he proceeds to shove a beer bottle, neck first, into the man's mouth. It doesn't fit, but the vet is strong, and eventually, most of the bottle is in there. The screams of bystanders attract police, who confront him with guns drawn. He gives a crisp salute and allows himself to be taken into custody. The charge is first-degree murder. It's later reduced, with the help of a plea bargain, to voluntary manslaughter. The sentence is only six years, but the vet dies of cirrhosis in the Kern Valley infirmary after just a month.

Jarsdel reflected upon these and other cases he'd worked. Very quickly, his promise to Brahma—to "make it right"—seemed not merely naive but arrogant. What had he meant by "it"? The grand human condition? Did he really believe he could improve its overall character by locking up a handful of the lost and desperate? That by some mysterious mechanism, fewer of the lost and desperate would therefore be produced? Baba had referred to his zeal as a kind of idiocy. It appeared the man, right as always, was right yet again.

But surely Dinan was different. His brand of mayhem wasn't an understandable—if not excusable—product of moral weakness or addiction or social pressure. There weren't a million others like him born every year, ready to take his place, until the conditions that helped create them were changed. Dinan's darkness was organic, innate, and decadent. If there was indeed such a thing as evil, then Dinan, like his hero Phalaris, was evil. Removing him from society would be akin to purging a toxin from an organism. It would, in the purest sense of the phrase, make a difference.

The unmarked detective car and the black-and-white slipped into a red zone in front of the Chiswick Arms on Hyperion. Officer Will Haarmann, he of the "Sexiest Cops in America" feature in *Los Angeles* magazine, climbed the short flight of stairs and woke the manager. The rest followed, and soon a bleary-eyed woman in a bathrobe was leading them to Dinan's room on the second floor. Morales got into position, standing to the side of the door in case

Dinan decided to put a bullet through it, and raised his fist. Jarsdel gestured for the manager to stay back, and Morales struck the door—one, two, three heavy blows.

"LAPD! Open up!"

Silence.

Three more knocks. "Open up, Mr. Dinan. This is the police."

A door opened across from them, and a young man's lean, irritated face poked out. "Okay, do you have to, like, wake up the entire fucking *building*?"

"Get back inside," snapped Haarmann.

"Don't order me around. You *can't* even, legally." He turned away, speaking to someone behind him. "It's the cops. They're gonna arrest the cave troll. Oh yeah, totally. That's an awesome idea." He stepped out, clad only in boxer briefs and a ragged white tee, pocked here and there with cigarette burns. He was soon joined by a short, androgynous woman with close-cropped hair dyed an electric blue. She was pointing the lens of a smartphone at them.

The landlady frowned. "Hey. Hey, guys. That's not helping."

Morales tapped her on the shoulder. "I need the key."

She didn't seem to hear him. "What you're doing is—"

"*Ma'am.* The key."

She handed Morales the key but didn't take her eyes off the couple. "Just have some respect, you know?"

"I'll respect a cop when they learn to respect *us*," said the man. He pointed at Haarmann, who was watching Dinan's door as Morales undid the dead bolt. "Look at him. He's just *achin'* to—"

Then the door was open, and they charged in.

───────

Dinan's bed was unmade. Haarmann ran his hand over the sheets. "Cold. If he was here, he left a while ago."

Jarsdel had Monson's warrant with him, and he and Morales began conducting their search. The woman with the blue hair appeared in the doorway, scanning the room with her smartphone.

"Wow, look," she said in a flat, bored voice. "It's the LAPD in their natural habitat. Someone's private shit."

Morales glanced over at her. "You step one foot in here, I promise you an obstruction of justice charge."

"Love the Orwell lingo. Are you from the Ministry of Truth?"

Jarsdel shut the door in her face.

Rain began to fall as they resumed their search. Streaks of water appeared on the window overlooking Hyperion. The streaks soon fattened and, before long, sheets of water moved down the glass. The weak light passing into the room washed the walls in ghostly shimmers.

Morales called Jarsdel over. "What about all this?" He'd opened a desk drawer and discovered a cache of receipts.

The drumming of the rain became a hammering. Jarsdel glanced up, hoping the flimsy roof could withstand the onslaught. "Good. Might be something in there tells us where to look next." He used a gloved finger to poke some of the papers aside and found a checkbook. "That too."

Morales brought over a large evidence bag. After removing the receipts and checkbook from the drawer, the detectives poked through the remaining contents—piles of keepsakes, trinkets, and plain junk. There was a small Tupperware bowl overflowing with bottle caps, a snow globe depicting Santa tanning himself under a palm tree, and a memo pad bearing the letterhead "Edward R. Rooney, Dean of Students." Marbles, Ping-Pong balls, and the contents from an open bag of wasabi peas fled from the detectives' fingers as they sorted through the mess.

"Could take all day," said Morales. "Think it's worth it?"

Jarsdel sighed.

"Lotta possibilities. Key to a storage unit, a red quarter, maybe a note sayin' *I did it and here's why*. Whatsa matter? Don't feel like doin' real police work?"

"Just empty the whole drawer," said Jarsdel.

Morales did, slowly and carefully. The last to go into the evidence bag were hundreds of loose staples, sounding like the rain as they went in.

———

Dinan's wallet and keys were missing from the apartment, and his parking spot in the garage was vacant. A BOLO went out for a black 1980 AMC Eagle with vanity plate FLMNUTT. It was the only vehicle Dinan owned—no van, Dodge Ram or otherwise. Jarsdel had to concede that their only witness to the body dump, Dustin Sparks, was probably unreliable. That would be an enormous hurdle if the case went to trial.

They returned to Hollywood Station in torrents of driving rain, passing two serious accidents along the way. Waiting for Jarsdel on his desk were copies of Jeff Dinan's Verizon records going back six months. An attached note from a Sergeant Pokorny reported that efforts by the Technical Investigation Division had been made to ping the phone, but either the battery or the SIM card had been removed. The last call Dinan made had bounced off a cell tower on McCadden and Hawthorn, about a block south of the Egyptian.

Jarsdel referenced the last page of Dinan's records and found the call. It had been made three days ago at 5:40 p.m. and lasted just under a minute. He looked across at Morales, who was filling out a report for Lieutenant Gavin.

"I gotta go out again."

"Hell you are," said Morales, continuing to type. "You ain't leaving me to dig through all that evidence. I got a FSD guy comin' in twenty minutes to photograph it."

"It's not that much. Just paperwork from the file cabinets and those tchotchkes we found."

"The whats?"

Jarsdel slid the call log onto Morales's desk.

The detective stopped typing, glanced sourly at his partner, and adjusted his reading glasses. "No calls for three days."

"Uh-huh."

"Makes sense if he's runnin'. Watch one episode of *Law & Order* and you know to ditch your phone."

"Look at the time, though. That's maybe five minutes after I asked him about the altercation with Wolin."

Morales scanned the page. "Who's Raymond Stevens? Why do I know that name?"

"He's the guy owns the Cinema Legacy Museum. I interviewed him about Wolin's Hollywood Dirt thing, remember?"

"Right, right. Okay, so why don't I go talk to him, and *you* stay here with FSD?"

"You could, but I already have some rapport with the guy. We're on a first-name basis. If he knows anything that'll help, he'll probably be more likely to open up if it's me."

Morales sighed. "Fine, go talk to him. Goddamn it." He thrust the paper at Jarsdel, who got to his feet. "You're bringing me back some lunch, though. I want a triple XL Fatburger with the works. And some onion rings."

"No, that's in Barnsdall Park. I'm going the other direction."

"Don't worry. I'll be patient."

"C'mon. It's pouring rain. That'll tack on another hour."

"You know what they say, partner—freedom ain't free."

———

The lot on Cherokee was full, so Jarsdel was forced to park in the bowels of the Hollywood & Highland complex. By the time he got off the elevator at street level, the rain had slackened to a faint drizzle, and the costumed street characters had emerged from under eaves and awnings to mingle with the tourists. Jarsdel wove his way around a boy and girl having their picture taken with Shrek and had to stop suddenly when a Minion in full body costume crossed his path without looking.

Jarsdel's phone buzzed. It was a text from Morales: HomeSec says no one with Jeff Dinan passport left US last three days. Checking domestic flights now.

There was a hard tap on his shoulder. Jarsdel turned, irritated, to find himself face-to-face with Catwoman. Even though a cowl masked half her face, he could see she was too old for the role. Her lips—thin and bloodless—were pinched into a frown that bunched the flesh of her chin into a gray prune.

"Yes?"

"You're a cop," she said, revealing an upper row of crooked, stained teeth.

"Do you need help?"

"I've been trying to get one of you guys to listen to me for, like, a *year*."

"Okay, I'm sorry. Is everything all right?"

"No!"

Jarsdel held out a calming hand. "I hear you. Please tell me what the problem is."

She exhaled hard, delivering a blast of fetid air into Jarsdel's face. "It's *Bruce*. That's what I been telling you guys. Bruce is *gone*."

Jarsdel brought out a memo pad and pretended to write. "Bruce, okay. Bruce who?"

"Bruce *Wayne*."

He looked up, his expression weary. "Batman?"

"But his real name is *Bruce*."

"Yes, I've heard." He put his memo pad away. "I'll run it up the ladder to Commissioner Gordon."

"No. No, no. Not this again. That's his fucking *name*."

"All right, just ease up on the language—"

"Dora!" Catwoman beckoned to someone over Jarsdel's shoulder. He turned to see Dora the Explorer waddling their way, her great round head bobbing as she wordlessly greeted passing tourists. The frozen foam smile spread across her face told everyone she was amazed and delighted to see them.

"Dora!" called Catwoman again. "C'mere."

Dora saw her and gave a dainty wave. When she got close enough, Catwoman pulled her by the arm so they were standing together, facing Jarsdel.

"This is a *cop*," Catwoman said, slowly and deliberately.

Dora looked up at Jarsdel and put both of her hands to her mouth in a pantomime of surprise.

"I want you to tell him that Bruce is his *name*."

Dora glanced at Catwoman, then back. She gave two exaggerated nods.

Catwoman fixed Jarsdel with a look of righteous satisfaction.

"Got it," he said. "Batman's real name is Bruce Wayne."

"You don't *get* it," Catwoman said, the anger creeping back into her voice. "He's a real *person*."

Dora nodded again, vigorously, then had to stop and adjust her head.

"I'm sorry," said Jarsdel. "I don't understand. Are you talking about one of the superheroes here? Who work this block?"

"That's what I've been trying to tell you guys. For a *thousand years*. No one *listens*."

"You're saying that a gentleman who dresses up as Batman has disappeared?"

Dora held two thumbs up, then skipped an imaginary hopscotch grid.

"And his name is actually Bruce Wayne?"

"*Yes*," said Catwoman. "He had it legally changed."

Out came the memo pad again. "What's your name?"

"Why do you need to know that?"

"For my report. And if I need to contact you again."

"Can't I make it anonymously?"

"You can, if that makes you more comfortable. But it could slow things down if we end up investigating."

She gave another frustrated, fragrant exhale. "Marcy Kremer."

"Address and phone number?"

As they spoke, Dora began getting restless. She blocked a family as they tried to pass, putting her hands on her hips in a gesture of spunky assertiveness.

"Excuse us," said the father.

Dora motioned pulling out a camera and taking a picture.

"Not today." The man led his wife and two children around her and moved on. Dora watched them go, then shook her fist at their departing backs.

"I'll see what I can do," said Jarsdel, putting his pad away once more.

Catwoman rolled her eyes. "Yeah, I'm really counting on that." She turned and stalked off westward toward the Chinese Theatre. Dora watched her go, then regarded Jarsdel a moment, unmoving.

"Hi," said Jarsdel.

Dora lifted a hand, wagged a finger at him in sharp disapproval, then headed down the block after Catwoman.

———

The homeless man who'd been camped out in the doorway adjacent to the Cinema Legacy Museum was now gone. His shopping cart and blanket were still there, but there was no sign of their owner. *Probably getting lunch somewhere*, Jarsdel thought. Strange, though, that he didn't take his recycling with him. That stuff was like gold to the vagrants who roamed the area.

When he entered the museum this time, the security guard wasn't at his usual spot by the door—just his book, which was open facedown on his stool. He'd apparently finished *Helter Skelter* and was now reading Ann Rule's *The Stranger Beside Me*.

As before, the place seemed pretty much empty, though Jarsdel could overhear some murmured conversation behind one of the displays. "Hello?" he called.

Raymond Stevens leaned his head from behind a partition. "Yes?" Then he recognized Jarsdel, and his expression lit up. "Tully! Just a moment, please." He disappeared for a few seconds, then reemerged, striding toward Jarsdel with his hand out. The polished white stone of his pendant bounced jovially as he approached.

"I was just giving a personal tour. Always enjoy doing that if I'm able." The two men shook hands. Stevens went on, "We've recently come into a very exciting acquisition. One of the portraits of Jonathan Frid from the *Dark Shadows* series. I know, I know, it's technically not a movie. But how could I pass it up? Anyway, what can I do for you?"

"I—"

"Did you by any chance bring your lady with you? I've been eager to take you on that tour we talked about."

"No. Actually, I'm here about something a bit more serious."

Stevens affected a somber mien. "More serious than *Dark Shadows*?"

His security guard emerged from somewhere in the back of the museum, spinning a key ring on his finger.

Stevens touched Jarsdel's arm. "Sorry, one moment." He turned to the guard. "How did it go?"

"Fine," the man said, then recognized Jarsdel and broke into a grin. "Hey, whatever it is, I didn't do it."

Jarsdel had heard that joke before, usually from high schoolers back when he'd been in uniform. It hadn't grown funnier with time, but Jarsdel gave a dutiful grunt. "Remind me, what was your name?"

"Brayden. Brayden Wouters. What's up? We wasn't supposed to meet or anything, was we?"

"Brayden was just returning a piece we had on loan," explained Stevens. "Shame to have to give it up. I might end up making an offer on it, but I think the tentacled old bitch wants to gouge me."

Jarsdel flinched, though he had no idea who was being discussed. "Oh? What was it?"

"The actual blade from *The Pit and the Pendulum*, if you can imagine. I'm speaking of the 1961 version by the way, with Vincent Price, not the French one. It doesn't have any of the cranking apparatus or any of that stuff with it, just the blade at the end of a long pole. It's dull, of course, but my goodness, quite heavy."

"Hmm," said Jarsdel. "That's wild. Anyway, I was hoping—"

"Of course, the serious issue. Please."

"Thanks. Jeff Dinan's been missing for a couple days, and—"

"Jeff? Really?"

"Yes."

"Why would you be looking for him to begin with?"

"I need to talk to him."

"Has he done something, or…" Stevens's face fell. "Oh. This has something to do with the call, doesn't it? The other day."

"What? What's up?" asked Brayden.

Jarsdel stayed focused on Stevens. "What can you tell me about it?"

Stevens seemed to grow paler, if such a thing were possible. "Did I do something wrong?"

Jarsdel glanced between the two men. "I don't know. I can't advise you on anything. I just need to know what you talked about."

"I don't *think* I did anything wrong," said Stevens. "He was just so desperate sounding."

Jarsdel looked again at Brayden, who appeared to have gone back to his book. Jarsdel wasn't convinced. "Can we talk alone for a sec?" He took Stevens by the shoulder and led him through the turnstile and past the small reception desk. They stopped under a canoe paddle, mounted horizontally, with an accompanying still from the film *Deliverance*. There was no rhyme or reason to the museum, Jarsdel thought, just one man's jumble of semi-collectables, lovingly displayed.

"The reason I'm here," he said once he and Stevens were alone, "is because you're the last known person he spoke with."

Stevens looked horrified. "The last? And for three days?"

Jarsdel let silence answer for him.

Stevens clutched at his pendant, rubbing at the stone with the pad of his thumb. "He was very upset. Wouldn't say what was going on, just that he was in some kind of trouble, and would I lend him some money."

"Did you?"

"Not at first. I thought it was a very strange call to get. Like a prank. And we hadn't really reconnected after that silliness on Halloween. But after we talked a few minutes, I realized he wasn't faking it."

"What happened?"

"I told him to come over. He sounded so desperate, you understand, and he wasn't asking for that much money."

"How much?"

"Five hundred."

"You keep that kind of cash in the museum?"

"No, I have a small safe down in my quarters."

Jarsdel nodded. "All right. So he came over, and you gave him the money."

"*Lent* him the money. He promised to return it."

"Has he borrowed money from you in the past?"

"No. But I've suspected for some time that he's been developing a gambling addiction."

That was news to Jarsdel. "Why do you think that?"

Stevens considered. "He fancies himself a brilliant poker player. Perhaps this time, he bet more than was on the table. Just a guess."

That seemed awfully pat. There wasn't a big underground poker scene in LA, much less the mob-run, potentially lethal variety. "Did he also borrow a vehicle?"

"Strange you should ask. He wanted to, but I told him it wouldn't be possible."

"Raymond, I'm going to tell you why he approached you, and maybe that'll give you some ideas about where he might have gone."

Stevens's customers, an elderly couple, had stepped into view and were examining the spear from *Spartacus*. "Basically just a big pointy stick," the man said.

Stevens looked pained. To Jarsdel, he said, "Let me just tell them I'll be a few more minutes."

"Sure."

He approached his customers, unleashed a fusillade of hushed apologies, and returned.

"Thank you. I'm sorry, you were saying?"

"I went to see Jeff about a case we're working on. Unfortunately, he's a person of interest."

"What, you mean, like a suspect?"

"That's right."

"But you're a homicide detective. So..." Stevens was incredulous. "You're joking."

Jarsdel shook his head.

"My God."

"It was just after I talked to him that he called you. You say you lent him some money—"

"But I didn't know!"

"No, no. You're fine. Relax. Based on what you told me, you're not in any kind of trouble. So you lent him some money—"

Stevens sighed. "My God."

"Did he give any indication where he was going?"

"No."

"Maybe just what his next stop was going to be? A friend's house? A relative?"

"Nothing. He said nothing like that."

"Is there any place you know that he likes to go? Towns or cities? Maybe where he grew up?"

"He's from Chicago, I think, originally."

That was some help. He could find Dinan's family with a DMV search, then have Chicago PD cruise by and have a talk with them. In the meantime, a quick call to the Illinois state police would put a BOLO on the Eagle. "Think of anything else? Any other place?"

"He likes Tijuana."

That was one word Jarsdel was hoping he wouldn't hear. Being in Mexico would effectively put Dinan out of reach. Unless some damning new evidence emerged from the morning's search, they couldn't file charges against him, which meant he wouldn't qualify as a fugitive. As long as he didn't break any laws, the Mexican police had no cause to detain or extradite him. And with a three-day head start, he could have easily made it all the way through to Guatemala, maybe even Belize. He pulled out his phone.

Check bank withdrawals.

Morales's reply was immediate and in all caps: THANKS. NEVER DONE THIS BEFORE.

Jarsdel put the phone away. "Anyway, I appreciate you talking to me. It's been a big help."

Stevens made a vague gesture with his hands. "It's the least I can do. You must believe that if I'd known any of this, I wouldn't have given him the money."

"I know. And like I said, you don't have anything to worry about." He took a card from his wallet. "Please call if there's anything else you think of."

"Oh, I already have the one you gave me before."

"Take another."

Stevens shrugged and took the card. "Brayden's unloading some new pieces. Real finds. Oliver Reed's shirt from *Curse of the Werewolf*. A devil mask from *Black Sunday*—the Mario Bava film, not the John Frankenheimer thriller. Lots of horror, I know, but they do make me happy. As a policeman, you may be interested to see the hat worn by Gene Hackman in *The French Connection*. Fox was very kind to lend it to me. Van's just out back if you'd like to go see."

"Sounds cool, but I better follow up on what we talked about. Thanks."

"Of course. Well, I hope to see you again under more pleasant circumstances. Perhaps with your lady?"

"We'd like that." They shook hands once more, and Jarsdel started outside. But then he halted, one foot on the sidewalk. An idea had suddenly wormed out of his subconscious and now lay in his mental spotlight, demanding action.

Absurd.

He made it a few more paces before stopping again. It might be absurd, but it wasn't going away. Besides, it would only take a minute to see for sure. He could surely spare that, couldn't he? Besides, with all the time he was taking arguing about it with himself, he could have already—

"Fine," he said aloud and went back into the museum.

Stevens was back with his customers. They'd moved on to the *Deliverance* paddle. "Gave me nightmares," the woman said. "And that *scene*—oh, you know the one I mean. Where Warren Beatty—"

"*Ned*, Sheila," her husband said. "That was Ned Beatty."

"Hey," said Jarsdel, stepping through the turnstile.

They all turned to face him.

"Sorry to interrupt, but that actually does sound pretty fascinating. The hat from the movie."

Stevens puffed up with pride. "Of course. Brayden's getting it now. Just straight toward the back, and there's a door opening onto an alley. He's parked there."

"Great." Jarsdel passed several exhibits, most of which were small in size and from films he'd never heard of, on his way to the door. Each item was accompanied by a still from the movie depicting a scene in which it had appeared. A pair of earrings, a ring, a cane, a derringer pistol, a playing card. There were some original posters in sleek black frames, their colors too lurid, too dreamlike for contemporary billboards. There was *Taste the Blood of Dracula*, *Vampire Circus*, and *A Hatchet for the Honeymoon*.

To his right, a stairway led down into darkness. The top was cordoned off with a heavy velvet rope, like the kind used in old movie theaters. A sign stood behind the rope reading *No Entry Please*. Jarsdel guessed the stairs led down to Stevens's rooms.

Up ahead, he saw a door propped open with a brick, late afternoon sunlight spilling across its threshold. As he reached it, Brayden nudged it open with his elbow and stepped inside. He carried a medium-sized cardboard box.

"Hey," he said upon seeing Jarsdel. "Boss is up front, I think."

"Yeah, I know. Changed my mind. He said I could come back here and check out some of the new pieces."

"Sure. This is the hat. Had to leave a three-thousand-dollar deposit for it—you believe that?"

"Wow."

"Yeah. And I had to sign a form saying only the museum's curator would handle it, so no touchy. Goes for both of us."

"Understood. Let's crack it open."

Brayden set the box down on the floor between them and bent to undo the flaps. "They didn't tape it up, probably to stop some knucklehead from slicing the box open and cutting the merchandise. I guess I'm that knucklehead, 'cause that's exactly what I would've done."

While Brayden carefully brushed packing peanuts aside, Jarsdel slipped around him toward the exit. The door was still propped open, but he couldn't see much through the meager opening, so he leaned against it—casually, he hoped. It began to swing outward. He went with it for just a little bit, then looked over his shoulder into the alleyway.

And there it is.

"Crucial," said Brayden.

Jarsdel glanced back at him, but Brayden was staring awestruck into the box. Jarsdel chanced another look outside.

It was strange, he reflected, even a bit unreal. Like seeing a celebrity in a supermarket. Unexpected and jarringly noncontextual but undeniably there.

"Hey. Here's the hat. The real deal. Popeye Doyle, man. Hello?"

Jarsdel turned to see Brayden regarding him with naked concern. "Hmm? Oh, yeah. Wow. That's really something."

Brayden picked up the box and walked it the few feet over to where Jarsdel stood. "It's the hat," he said. "Seriously. This is it."

"Yes. I can see it. It's great."

"You don't believe me?"

"Of course I believe you. It's definitely the hat."

"It is." Brayden held the box between them and peered down into it. "You wanna put it on?"

"That's kind of you," said Jarsdel. "But I've really gotta run."

"Is it because I said we weren't allowed to touch it? Don't let that be the reason. I don't think they got, like, a hidden camera in there or anything." He laughed, shaking his head. "Man, I really wanna put it on."

"Thanks for showing it to me." Jarsdel began to move away when Brayden reached out and touched his arm.

"Hey, I didn't say something that pissed you off or anything, did I?"

"Sorry, what? No, not at all."

"Because I know that's a thing with me sometimes. I'll say something, and people act funky, and I won't know why. And you being a cop and everything, a homicide detective, I'd be really embarrassed if that happened. You guys, you're my heroes. I think I told you that."

Jarsdel summoned what he hoped was a reassuring smile. "No need for the slightest concern. I really appreciate you taking the time to show me this. It's quite a piece."

"It is, right?" He once again dropped his gaze to the hat. "Wonder if it smells like the '70s."

"Take good care of it," said Jarsdel, making his way back toward the museum's exit. He tried to resist the temptation to look back, failed, and caught a final glimpse of Brayden. He'd put the box down and was at the back door, looking into the alley and probably trying to figure out what Jarsdel had found so fascinating out there.

"Nothing," Jarsdel murmured as he stepped from the museum's antiseptic cool and into the sunlight. "Just some old, beat-up Dodge Ram."

21

M orales was at his desk, his expression sullen. It grew darker when he saw Jarsdel's hands were empty.

"I'm not seein' any Fatburger."

"I found the van."

Morales stared at him.

"I mean," said Jarsdel, "I think I found it. I don't know for sure, and we'd have to get FSD in there to prove it, but it would be a pretty big coincidence if it wasn't it." He went on to explain where and how he'd seen the vehicle and that it probably belonged to Raymond Stevens.

"Goddamn it, I'm hungry," said Morales. "Gonna have to get one of those shitty-ass granola bars from the break room to tide me over."

"Sorry."

"And the guy from FSD decided he'd rather come tomorrow. Our case isn't ringing a lot of bells at the Cal State crime lab, apparently, and he was needed elsewhere. Oh, we found Dinan's car by the way."

"We did? Where?"

"Right here in LA. It'd been sitting in a parking garage by the Egyptian for more than two days, so they had it towed. Now it's at that big impound lot downtown. I'm having it moved to Cal State for processing. But again, though, that's not gonna happen today."

"So Dinan's just gone," said Jarsdel. "Car abandoned, didn't fly anywhere, no phone or credit card activity—"

"No ATM stuff either. Banks with Wells Fargo but hasn't touched his balance since last week. That means if he really did boogie on us, he must've had a go bag ready. But you know, he doesn't exactly strike me as the type."

"Supposedly got five hundred from Stevens."

"That's nothing. Wouldn't last him more than a couple days, even south of the border. Nope, I'm thinkin' our friend's no longer among the living."

They thought about that for a moment. An arrestee in the intake area began singing "Sweet Home Alabama." Someone shouted at him to shut the fuck up.

"So what's up with this Stevens guy?" asked Morales. "You say you know him?"

"Met him a couple times. He seemed, I don't know, harmless, just some effete film historian."

"*Feet*?"

"Effete."

Morales blew out a mouthful of air. "Whatever. Anyway, so what's this harmless guy doing with our van? And how come he's the last person Dinan talks to before pulling a Copperfield?"

Jarsdel drummed his fingers on his desk, then said, "Can I ask you a favor?"

"No."

"There's an incentive."

"Hey, I'm not even supposed to work today. I came in special for that warrant."

"I know."

"I was gonna leave when you got back. I got errands. And I'm cooking tonight. Got some nice asada to grill up, and then we were gonna watch the new Pixar movie. Steaks been marinating all day."

Jarsdel nodded. "I won't screw up your family time, I promise. I don't even need you that long, but you've got more experience with this stuff than I do. The systems and everything. Just run this guy for me, deep as you can, see what comes up."

"And you'll do...?"

"Fatburger. Triple XL and a side of onion rings, right?"

———

When Jarsdel returned an hour later, Morales was standing over the printer, catching the pages as they spat into his hands. It was a larger stack than Jarsdel had anticipated—perhaps thirty sheets. When the printing had finished, Morales traded them for the offered bag of food.

"Enjoy," he said. "I'm outta here."

"What is all this?"

"As much as you'll get without dealing with the feds. You'll have to get in touch with USCIS if you want to see his original immigration stuff. Assuming they still have it."

Jarsdel thumbed through the stack. He saw what he expected to see on a normal check—driver's license, social security, vehicle information, DMV records—but Morales had also gotten him pages and pages of permits that had been issued by the city for Stevens's various business ventures. Attached to these permits was supporting documentation listing current and former addresses, financial information, and personal history.

"Hey," he said to Morales's departing back, "appreciate it."

Morales lifted a hand in acknowledgment, and Jarsdel sat down to read.

———

Raymond Stevens was originally Radovan Stefanović, formerly of the Republic of Montenegro, who'd immigrated to the United States in 1996 and become a naturalized citizen in 2001. He was forty-nine years old, had no family, and was the sole owner of his businesses, which included the Cinema Legacy Museum, the Hollywood Experience, and something called Exclusive Imports. On his earliest permit application, he'd listed foodservice as his occupation, but in all later paperwork, he identified himself as a businessman. He operated two vehicles, a 2012 Cadillac CTS, silver, and a 2002 Dodge Ram van, white. There was one point on his license from an illegal U-turn in January of 2014, but otherwise, his record was clear—no outstanding warrants or criminal history in the United States. His most significant contact with law enforcement was a complaint he'd once made of vandalism to his museum's display window.

As biographies went, it certainly wasn't a showstopper. Despite all Morales had given Jarsdel, it still painted the barest outline of a life. Before he could move forward, he needed to know more about Stevens's connection with Wolin and the Punyawongs.

He did a search for Exclusive Imports, but it was such a generic name that he came up with dozens of companies from all over the world. Nothing in California, though, that he could see. He again checked the paperwork from LA's business licensing office and saw he'd been wasting his time. Exclusive Imports had canceled its permits in 2010, the proprietor citing liquidation of company assets as the reason.

Jarsdel moved on to the Hollywood Experience. The website's banner was done in Broadway typeface, and the company promised to provide a taste of the *real* Hollywood, touring the residences and hangouts of the major stars of yesteryear. A VIP ticket included a professionally taken photograph of the customer while on the tour, a keepsake frame, and a poolside martini at the Sunset Tower Hotel. Conspicuously absent was any talk of celebrity crime scenes, overdoses, or suicides. It seemed the Hollywood Experience wanted to distance itself as much as possible from the more sensational tours operating in the city.

Its patina of class seemed to be paying off. The company only gave a "select" number of tours each day—whatever that meant— and offered both Mandarin- and English-speaking guides. Jarsdel wrinkled his nose at the redundancy of the phrase, "Advance reservations recommended."

He yawned, scrolling through the site. The "About Us" page

boasted that the business had won a Heroes of Hollywood Award from the chamber of commerce. There was a picture from the awards luncheon, and a caption below it read *Hollywood Chamber Community Foundation honors The Hollywood Experience, 2014.* There was Stevens, receiving the plaque and smiling at the camera with unabashed pride.

Jarsdel picked up a jumbo paperclip and carefully worked it until it was straight. Then, slowly, he began bending the metal into segments, back and forth, feeling them grow hot beneath his fingers before snapping off. He flicked the pieces into his wastebasket.

The desk phone rang, and he snatched it up, grateful for the distraction. "Detective Jarsdel." He waited, but no one spoke. "Hello?" A soft click, and the line went dead. Jarsdel jammed the phone in its cradle and went back to staring at his computer screen.

The Hollywood Experience. It sounded familiar. He brought out the murder book and began turning pages, not sure what he was looking for.

His cell buzzed. "Fuck's sake," he mumbled, unclipping it and checking the screen. Aleena. "Hey, what's goin' on?"

He heard her take a shaky breath.

"Hey," he said, growing alarmed, "what is it?"

"I'm sorry," she said, her voice strained. "I know you're probably at work. I could just use a friend today."

"Why? What's up? Are you safe?"

"I'm safe. It's not that." She sniffed. "Today's my anniversary. Of the wedding. I thought I could get through it okay, but—"

"Oh, Aleena. Why didn't you tell me? Yeah, um…" He checked the time—quarter of five. "You want me to come over?"

She blew her nose. "No."

"Why not?"

"I don't want to be that high-maintenance girl who needs her man to come running and—"

"Whoa, whoa, whoa. I think you're…" He hunted for the right thing to say. "I think that's a bit of extreme thinking, right? And you know, it's kind of expected for couples to help each other out from time to time."

"But *I'm* always the one who needs help."

"What? No you're not."

"I fucked up dinner the other night with my drama. And the first time we had sex, I was all clingy, and now—"

"Aleena, gimme an hour, okay? I gotta wrap something up, and it'll be slow going in the rain."

"You don't have to."

"I want to. I officially insist."

She gave a weak laugh, but there was relief in it. "Okay."

"Okay. See you soon."

Jarsdel put the phone back on his belt and stared down at the murder book. It was hard to focus. He kept thinking of Aleena in that silent, empty house. He should go to her, just take off and leave this all for tomorrow. There wasn't anything exciting in the package Morales had given him. They needed probable cause to get a warrant to sic Forensic Sciences on that van, and Stevens hadn't given them any.

Jarsdel again went back to the murder book, this time skimming the interview with Ramesh. He was the only one they'd spoken with who'd been at all close to Wolin, and maybe there was another detail in there that could help.

And there was.

```
Ramesh:    He also advertised for Fantasy Tours.

Jarsdel:   What's that? One of those bus tours of
           celebrities' homes?

Ramesh:    Yeah. This one is mostly for the Chinese
           market. He even learned a couple words in
           Mandarin so he could attract customers. But
           he didn't lead the tours, just advertised.
```

```
Jarsdel:   Where did he advertise?

Ramesh:    He'd walk the Boulevard, hand out flyers.

Jarsdel:   And how long had he been doing that?

Ramesh:    Only about two weeks. Before that, he
           worked for another company. I think…
           maybe…the Hollywood Experience. Something
           like that.
```

Jarsdel called up Morales, unsure about whether he would even answer when he saw Jarsdel's number come up.

Three rings. "I'm off duty," Morales said.

"The guy I went to see today. Raymond Stevens, owns Cinema Legacy?"

"Yeah?"

"Turns out he also owns the Hollywood Experience."

"What's the Hollywood Experience? Get your dreams shattered and Greyhound it back to Iowa?"

"Another tour company. Like Fantasy Tours, but classier."

"Okay. I'm trying to care."

"Grant Wolin worked for the Hollywood Experience. It's in the interview with Ramesh."

Morales chewed on that a moment. "What else?"

"A month ago, when I showed Wolin's picture to Stevens, he said he only knew him as a guy he'd have to hassle out of his doorway every now and then. Never said Wolin worked for him."

"I'm not sure that means a whole lot. Maybe they never actually met. My wife works at Williams-Sonoma, but you know, she never actually got to hang out with Chuck Williams."

"Yeah, maybe," said Jarsdel, a little deflated. "But that plus the van. I think it's suspicious."

"Follow up with it tomorrow. If my onions burn 'cause I'm on the phone with you, you're gonna come over here and apologize to Leticia yourself."

"I get it. I'm gone. Have a good night."

"Hey, hang on."

"What?" Silence stretched over the line for a full ten seconds. "Morales?" Tully checked his phone to see if the call had been disconnected.

"Look, why don't you?"

"Why don't I what?"

"Come over. Got a full spread and a twelve-pack of Modelo Negra. Wife wants to meet you." A voice murmured something in the background. "And apparently my oldest wants to show you his ball python."

"Shit, I can't. I really want to, but I promised my girlfriend I'd go over to her place."

"So bring her."

"I'll talk to her about it. She's having kind of a rough day."

"Okay, whatever. I'll text you the address in case you change your mind. We're eating at seven."

"Thanks. If not tonight, then soon, okay?"

But Morales had hung up.

22

Aleena's face was puffy, her eyes red-rimmed. An empty bottle of wine stood on the counter, and she was halfway through another.

Jarsdel had declined his own glass, thinking it would be better if one of them remained sober, but she'd insisted, overpouring it nearly to the top. He sipped at it occasionally, but mostly, he listened.

They were at her kitchen table. She had a tissue knotted around her fingers, and she worried at it while she spoke. She told Jarsdel the story of how she and her husband met and how even though his family was wealthy, he worked for everything they had. Her narrative meandered as it got closer to their wedding day, and then her voice began to break.

"I have to tell somebody. I can't live with this...fucking...I can't live with this..." She brought the sodden tissue to her face and began to cry.

Jarsdel got up, hunting for the tissue box, and settled for a roll of toilet paper from the hall closet. He returned, putting his arm around her shoulders. When he offered her the toilet paper, she gave an exhausted laugh.

"How appropriate. Good for cleaning up bullshit."

"What're you talking about? Why're you being so hard on yourself?"

"Because I deserve it."

"Why do you say that? Because the marriage didn't work out?" When she reached for her wine glass again, Jarsdel took her hand. "Hey," he said. "Leave it just a minute, okay? Let me tell you something. What happened with you and your husband was this terrible, crazy thing you had absolutely no control over. You do not—listen to me—you do not have a single thing to feel bad about."

Aleena tore off a few squares of toilet paper and blew her nose. She then closed her eyes and took a deep breath. When she looked at him again, her expression had cleared somewhat, and she seemed more composed.

"I'm sloshed."

"You are."

She smiled. "Want me to go down on you? I give good head when I'm drunk. Most girls don't, but it relaxes my throat and I can—"

"Aleena."

"What?"

"Come on. Let's talk this through."

"You're no fun." The smile went away, and she lowered her eyes. "It's my fault David's dog died."

"No."

"It is. You don't know. I hated that fucking dog. He had Abby before we met, right? So from the beginning, I was always a little bit like the other woman. I know that sounds stupid, but..." Aleena blew a strand of hair out of her face. "We'd be cuddling on the couch, and *yap-yap-yap*. Or we'd laugh about something, and more yapping. These awful, piercing yaps, and every time, he'd have to pick her up to calm her down, and it was always 'Ooh, Abby, ooh, sweetie.' When we had sex, David actually had to lock her in a room at the other end of the house, because she'd yap the entire... fucking...time."

Aleena took her wine glass before Jarsdel could stop her and put away a long gulp before setting it down. "But the best part was the way she'd piss on the floor to make a point. She especially loved doing it whenever David and I went out together, her way of punishing us—mostly me—for having a good time without her. Her way of saying 'Okay, bitch, you want a night out with my man? This is what it costs.'"

She shot Jarsdel an annoyed look. "And she had pee-pee pads in her box in the laundry room, so don't think it's like she couldn't hold it in and that I'm just being paranoid."

"I wasn't thinking that."

"Sorry. I'm just...so yeah, I hated her. I've actually—wow, I've never said this out loud—I've actually never hated a human person as much as I hated that dog."

"That doesn't mean you're to blame," Jarsdel said, his voice low and soothing. "It's not as if your hatred acted as some kind of prayer, you know, summoning the sick asshole who poisoned her."

"You're defending me. It's sweet. Check it out, though." She gestured to the house around them. "See any doggie doors?"

He gave a quick scan of the room. "I don't."

Aleena nodded. "Never got around to putting them in. David would just let her out when she wanted, and while we were gone, we'd keep her inside. That's why we had the litter box with the pee-pee pads. Ah! But, you see, on my wedding day, I did not feel like coming home to a nice puddle of piss drying on the living room floor. I was firm about it. I was...forceful. I gave him my little speech about avoidable delay. So David, even though he didn't want to, and even though he knew how much she hated being locked outside, agreed. We put out her water and her food and closed the doors, and I was...I was just happy. Triumphant. On the most important day of my life, I'd won, and she'd lost. Yeah. Well, I won all right." Aleena took another swig of wine. "Moral luck, huh?"

———

Jarsdel said everything he could think to say, but Aleena wouldn't be consoled. The wine and the misery had put her firmly beyond his reach.

After complaining of a headache, she stood up and immediately began swaying. Jarsdel got to her before she could fall and led her down the hall to the bedroom. He helped her lie down, tucking a pillow beneath her head, and left to get her a glass of water. She'd soon be miserable if she didn't start hydrating.

When he returned, she was already passed out. Jarsdel set the water on the nightstand and gave Aleena a light kiss above her brow. Her flesh was clammy.

In the drawer of the nightstand was a pen and a pad of paper. "Please call me when you get up, no matter what time. I love you." He considered, then tore the page off and stuffed it in his pocket. "Please call me when you get up. Let me know if you want me to bring you anything." He drew a heart and set the note next to the water glass.

The rain had abated a little, and it took Jarsdel only a half hour to get home. He opened the door to his apartment and was as usual greeted by overwhelming silence. He hesitated in the doorway.

Aleena might be down for the night, but that didn't mean he had to suffer. He could go across the street. If Becca was in the food court, he'd go to one of the restaurants—Monsieur Marcel, or maybe even Du-par's for some of their famous pancakes.

Then he remembered Morales's invitation and checked his watch. Ten to seven. He'd be late but not terribly so. The thought of going to the Morales house, warm with food and laughter and the vitality of children, seemed at once not merely appealing to Jarsdel but essential. Urgent.

He brought out his phone and fired off a text. I'll be there ASAP. Forty-five tops. Cool?

Morales's response was immediate—Fine.

His spirits renewed, Jarsdel jogged across the street and ducked into Monsieur Marcel's adjacent gourmet market just as the rain picked up again. He selected some milk chocolate bars for the kids and a bottle of Burgundy for Morales and his wife. The cashier wrapped the purchases in tissue paper, set them into gift bags, and tied the handles together with shimmering purple ribbon.

Jarsdel was soon back at Park La Brea and about to strip off his rain-spattered clothes and rinse off when he saw he had just over twenty minutes before his promised arrival time. He'd spent too much time agonizing over which bottle of wine to get his partner. He stood there, uncertain what to do, then decided it would be more embarrassing to be late than to arrive looking a little haggard. He grabbed his keys and locked up, making it all the way to his car before realizing he'd left the gifts behind.

"Shit." He ran back down the block, nearly wiping out on the wet sidewalk, and hurried inside his apartment. He flicked on the lights, but the presents weren't on the kitchen counter where he thought he'd left them. Then he remembered how he'd almost taken a shower and raced into the bedroom to find the Monsieur Marcel bags on his dresser.

He was just about to turn off the lights in the front hall when his phone buzzed.

It's Morales, Jarsdel thought. *It's Morales, and he's canceling. They're tired, and the kids want to hit the sack.*

He pulled the phone from his belt, already resigned to another night alone.

But it wasn't Morales.

Hey.

Aleena. Jarsdel blinked. He was sure she was going to be out cold until late morning at the earliest. Maybe she'd woken to throw up and that had sobered her a little.

How are you feeling? he wrote back.

Not so great.

Yeah, but at least you're okay. I'll come by after work tomorrow.

Actually I need your help. Can you come outside?

Jarsdel frowned. You're here?

He opened the front door and looked upon an empty street. He texted, I don't see anything. A moment passed, and there was no response.

He checked the time. Fewer than ten minutes to make it to Morales's on time. Annoyed, Jarsdel slipped the phone back onto his belt and picked up the gift bags.

He had his key in the lock when his phone buzzed. "Come on, Aleena," he said. He checked the screen.

I don't feel good. Please help.

Alarmed, Jarsdel set down the bags and looked around. It was dark, but the streetlights showed the block was deserted. Everyone was inside where it was warm and dry.

What the hell was she up to? He hoped to God she hadn't somehow driven over here in that condition. She could hardly stand up.

He was about to text that he still didn't see her when a new message appeared.

To your right.

He snapped his head in that direction. A few dozen yards away was the pedestrian gate opening onto South Fairfax. He caught a flash of movement, something in the shadows, but then it disappeared from view. Jarsdel hurried to the gate and looked around. Hesitant, though not certain why, Jarsdel turned the knob and stepped through. He lingered there, listening.

"Aleena?"

Nothing. It occurred to him she might be on medication of some kind and that it was reacting with the alcohol. That would explain the unusual behavior. He sent her another text.

Aleena, come on. What are we doing here?

He waited, but there was no answer. The security gate was flanked by high, green bushes, so Jarsdel's line of sight was limited. He took off his jacket, bunched it up, and shoved it between the jamb and the gate itself. It would swing shut otherwise, and he'd left his keys in his front door. Then he stepped past the bushes, first looking north up Fairfax, then south.

The white van rolled up beside him. The passenger window was down, and Brayden leaned across the seat, giving Jarsdel a broad grin. He wore a brown porkpie hat. The Popeye Doyle hat.

"What up, Detective?"

Jarsdel stared at him, then down at his phone. Aleena hadn't answered his last text.

"Oh, hey," said Brayden. "Check this out." He picked a cell phone out of his drink holder, tapped at the screen a few times, then looked at Jarsdel expectantly.

The phone buzzed in Jarsdel's hand—Eat shit, followed by a smiley face.

The van had stopped in a red zone, and cars were already stacking up behind it. There was a long and indignant honk from the lead car before it swerved angrily around. Brayden didn't appear to notice.

"Hop in. Mr. Stevens wants to talk to you."

"Where's Aleena?"

"Now that," said Brayden, "is kinda the whole point." He seemed charged with barely contained excitement, his head bobbing in quick little nods as he spoke. "And if that's not enough, we got this…"

He reached over and opened the glove compartment. Glinting dully back at Jarsdel was a snub nose .38. He felt an icy stab in his chest, reflexively dropping his hand to his own weapon, but he caught only air. He'd taken it off to go to dinner.

"Hope you have a permit for that."

Brayden shook his head. "But that's what's cool. I don't even need to use it. You'll come with me anyway. If you're still interested in where your girlfriend is, and I believe you are. So here's what I'm gonna need you to do. Take your gun and hand it to me, butt first. Once you've done that—"

"Wait, wait."

"No wait-wait." Brayden snapped his fingers and held out his hand. "Pronto." There was another long honk from behind the van. Someone yelled "Come on!" Brayden stuck his head out the driver's side window. "It's cool. Just gimme a minute. Just a rinky-dink little minute."

Jarsdel looked up and down the street, hoping for a traffic cop to come along.

Brayden turned back to him. "Don't try and stall me out. Anyone shows up, and I'm gone. Gone and you don't know what happens to her." Brayden leaned closer. "Or maybe you do know, right? Only you can stop it. But we gotta get going."

Jarsdel thought of Aleena, her smooth, tender flesh browning and crisping like parchment, her agonized screams, her fists beating helplessly at the thing that imprisoned her.

"How do I know you have her?"

"Well," said Brayden, "I'd say call her, but as you can see, I've got her phone. What do you think, she just decided to lend it to me?"

Jarsdel needed time to develop a strategy. If he could just talk to Brayden for a little while, he could convince him this was absurd. No one kidnapped police officers on Fairfax at eight o'clock on a Sunday. It just wasn't possible.

"So long then," said Brayden. "You get to live with this. Enjoy."

"Okay, wait."

"Your gun, then," said Brayden. "Nice and easy. Butt first, just how I like my girls."

"I don't have it. It's in my apartment."

"Back up. Let me see."

Jarsdel obeyed, lifting his arms and turning around.

"Put your fuckin' arms down, man," Brayden snarled. "Get back over here. You got anything on you 'sides that phone? Anything weird? Panic buttons or anything that'll let the boys back in the precinct know you're in trouble? I read a lot, so don't fuck with me."

"No…" His phone vibrated. He had it at his side, and Brayden wouldn't be able to see the screen. But he might be able to hear it. Jarsdel muffled it against his leg in case it buzzed again, then glanced down. It was from Morales.

When you get here just park behind me in the driveway.
Shit's all permit around here and they'll tow your ass.

"Better not be lying to me," said Brayden. "That's a sincere threat. You better not be lying."

"I'm not."

"Then get in, but toss that phone away first. I know all about that tracking shit."

Jarsdel shivered. He was getting soaked. "How do I know she's still alive?"

Brayden pulled the .38 from the glove box. "I'll give you the count of three," said Brayden. "Then I think I'll put one in your guts just for fun before I take off."

Jarsdel touched the button behind his tie, activating the microphone. "Can you at least tell me where we're going?"

"One."

"The museum?"

"Two."

Jarsdel touched the button again, stopping the recording. His phone chimed, letting him know he had a new audio file. Without looking, he tapped the reply bar on Morales's text. He knew that made an options menu appear, but he had to look at the screen to do the next part; he couldn't do it blind.

Brayden steadied the gun with his free hand and closed one eye, like someone aiming in a cartoon. "Center mass, right?"

"All right. I'm doing it." As Jarsdel raised the phone to throw it, he thumbed the attachment icon. A list of file names filled the screen. Only one of them was untitled. He clicked on it and turned to Brayden one last time as the file began uploading to the message. "Where do you want me to throw it?"

"I will blow your fuckin' skull apart if you don't throw that phone."

Jarsdel wasn't sure if the MP3 had uploaded or not, but it didn't matter. Brayden would kill him before he could send it. Jarsdel tossed the phone away, and it vanished into the night.

———

There were no seats inside, just straps, furniture blankets, and eye-bolts set at intervals along the floor. As he'd climbed inside, Jarsdel had clipped his knee on one of them but barely registered the pain.

The bite of adrenaline in his blood made him feel sick, and his heart pounded in anticipation of what would happen when they got to where they were going. His inability to act, to help himself or Aleena, to do anything but wait, made the trip feel endless.

The van took a corner too sharply, and Jarsdel slid across the floor and into a pile of blankets. He scrambled to his hands and knees and crawled back toward the front of the van so he could see out. They'd just turned onto Hollywood and were heading east, toward the museum. He glanced at the back of Brayden's head, where a roll of flesh bulged at the base of his skull.

"Is she hurt?" asked Jarsdel.

"Huh? Speak up."

"I said did you hurt her?"

"Who, your girlfriend? Just enough to get her in the van. Feisty little bitch, isn't she? Look." Brayden held out his right arm, where Jarsdel could make out some teeth marks. "Hope she's had her shots. She was drunk as shit, by the way."

Jarsdel thought he might vomit up the dregs of his late lunch and had to close his eyes until the feeling passed. It eventually did, but reluctantly.

Brayden snorted. "But if you're asking if I was, shall we say, less than a gentleman, I'm here to tell you I don't roll like that. Not that I'm not into girls—I am—but I got two rules. Never pay for it, and always respect it if she says no. That's why God gave us our hand, right?" He made a fist and jerked it up and down a few times.

Jarsdel didn't think he could stand to listen to any more and changed the subject. "Why'd you pick us up?"

"I told ya. Mr. Stevens told me to."

"I know, but why?"

"Oh, you gotta give me a little credit. The way your eyes bugged out when you saw the van, back at the museum. You didn't even look at the hat, the one you *said* you went back there to see. Shithead. I was out back for a while there, trying to figure what got you so hinky. I told the boss about that, and boom, you should have seen his face. None too pleased. I got in a little hot water myself over that, considering I told him no one saw me dump the body. Guess there must've been a witness, though, huh? ID'd the van?"

"And Aleena? Why her? She's got nothing to do with this."

"Boss figured you'd come easier that way. And he was right, wasn't he? You'd've put up a big fight if we didn't already have her."

"How'd you know where we live? Where we'd be?"

"Wish I could take credit, but again, that was Mr. Stevens. You by any chance remember a hang-up phone call today?"

At first, he didn't, but then it came to him. At his desk in the station. "Yeah."

"That told us where you were without having to ask anybody. Then I just sat on the station until you left, followed you, and... boom. Your girlfriend had your address. Gave it up fast, you should know. Kind of a cunty move, you ask me."

"What happens now?"

"Whatever the boss wants. He is kind of a scorched-earth guy, though, gotta say. Went through all kinds of shit back home. I always forget the name. One of those weird European places that went to hell in the '90s."

As Brayden spoke, Jarsdel looked around the van for something that could work as a weapon. A screwdriver, pencil, anything he could hide in his pocket until he had the chance to use it. He crawled over to the blankets and began rifling through them, hoping to find something small and sharp.

Brayden glanced in the rearview. "Don't know what you're hopin' to find back there, but good luck. Checked it over pretty good before I picked up your fuck buddy."

They came to a sudden stop. Jarsdel slid forward and slammed against the back of the passenger's seat. Brayden cursed the traffic, and a moment later, they were moving again. "Almost there," he said.

"Listen," said Jarsdel. "You realize what you're doing, right? I'm LAPD. Anything happens to me, and they won't stop until they nail you guys. And they will. They know what I was doing today. They'll put it together. But if you end it now, help us out of this, it'll make a big difference. It'll change everything for you. Don't let Stevens destroy your life."

"Dude. Dude." Brayden shook his head. "I'm touched, but it ain't *my* life you need to worry about." He made another turn, quickly followed by another, then put the van in park and cut the engine. Brayden turned around in his seat and regarded Jarsdel gravely. "Okay. This is it. I'm gonna come 'round and open the door, and you're gonna get out of the van." He opened the glove compartment again and took out the snub nose. "You fuck with me, I'll give you one in the knee. But you won't fuck with me, will you? Because then the girl goes, and she goes hard. Questions?" He waited, eyebrows raised, until Jarsdel shook his head. "Cool," said Brayden. He got out of the van and appeared a moment later as the sliding door swept open. He trained the gun lazily on Jarsdel. "Now."

Jarsdel stepped out into the rain. He glanced around and saw they were in the alley behind the museum. The back door was propped open with the brick again. Brayden closed the van door, then jabbed him in the back with the muzzle of the gun.

"Can you be careful with that, please?" said Jarsdel.

Brayden prodded him again, harder this time. Jarsdel went inside the museum. The lights were off, and it was cold, the air-conditioning blasting, even though it already had to be in the mid-60s.

"Couple more yards," said Brayden. "And to your left."

Jarsdel continued on until he came to the staircase leading to Stevens's quarters. The rope and the sign asking visitors to keep out had been moved to the side.

"Down," said Brayden.

Jarsdel started down the stairs into total darkness. He stumbled when he came to a turn and descended farther. He could soon make out faint light, and when he made it to level ground, he saw that its source was a small lamp perched upon a table. He was in an anteroom of some kind, cramped and dim. Ahead stood a stout wooden door.

Brayden slapped him on the back of the head with the gun, a swift, glancing blow that made Jarsdel's eyes water. "Go 'head. Knock."

Jarsdel knocked. Before long, there was the click of a heavy dead bolt unlocking, and the door swung inward. It was dark in the hallway beyond, and Stevens's face floated ghostlike before them. He looked deeply sad.

"Hello, Detective. Come in, please."

When Jarsdel didn't move right away, another blow landed, this time on his crown. His surroundings blurred with tears; faint colored dots popped and danced at the corners of his vision. He staggered to the side, bracing himself on the doorjamb.

"Brayden," said Stevens, his voice chiding.

And now Jarsdel did vomit, his body's last, desperate protest against the terror and the pain. The two men on either side of him stepped away, disgusted.

"Guess who'll be cleaning *that* up," said Stevens.

"Got any sawdust?" Brayden asked.

"Why would I have sawdust? This is not a saloon."

"I dunno." He sounded stung. "Some people have sawdust."

"Is that—no, you wouldn't. Is that Gene Hackman's hat?"

"So? I was just borrowing it for this mission."

"Give it here."

Jarsdel heaved again and again, though by now, there was nothing left in him, while Brayden and Stevens continued to argue. He strained through the shudders that racked him, through the dizziness that threatened to spill him to the ground, and tried to think of something to do. If he could somehow overpower Brayden and get hold of the gun, he'd be free. Stevens appeared to be unarmed, and Jarsdel could force him to let Aleena go while he called for backup. He exhaled shakily, sending a thick strand of saliva to the floor, and looked over his shoulder at his captors. They were both staring back at him.

Brayden pointed the gun at Jarsdel's leg. "Go."

Stevens held out a hand, directing him down the hallway. "The very last door." To Brayden, he said, "As soon as this is done, you're taking that hat upstairs and putting it away. I have to say I'm feeling very frustrated with you."

Jarsdel pushed off from the doorjamb and stumbled forward. The strength had gone out of his knees. They felt jellylike, insubstantial. Behind him, Stevens ordered Brayden to leave the door to the anteroom open so it wouldn't swing shut on the puddle of vomit.

It was a short hallway, with only a single door on either side and one straight ahead. There was nothing differentiating it from the others, but if it led to what Jarsdel feared it did, it was the doorway to hell itself. He nearly turned and ran the other way then, Aleena's fate and Brayden's threat to kneecap him notwithstanding.

He reached the door and stopped, breathing as rapidly as if he'd just sprinted there.

"It's open. Go ahead," said Stevens.

Jarsdel turned the knob and entered.

———

The floor was bare cement, the walls naked drywall, huge patches of it missing to reveal faded pink tufts of insulation. A single caged

construction light lay on the ground, plugged into an orange exten-
sion cord. The bulb cast a murky glow over the room and lit from
below the obscenity crouched at its center. Something in Jarsdel
broke at seeing it—an ordered and reasoned mind faced with an
anachronism, a nightmare made real.

It was a gleaming, red-gold structure of polished brass—a life-sized
replica of a bull, face twisted in a snarl, head topped with imperious,
curved horns. Its eyes stared emptily into space. On the side facing
Jarsdel was a hatch, now locked by a heavy-duty surface bolt, big
enough to admit a person into its hollow body. The legs of the beast
were thick and solid to support its immense weight and ended in wide
hooves. Beneath the belly of the bull was an enormous burner system.
A ribbed yellow connector hose snaked away from the apparatus, fed
by a nozzle that jutted from the wall. Suspended from the low ceiling
above the bull was what looked like an industrial exhaust hood.

Stevens strode past him into the room. "You've surely read the
script, so I'm assuming this isn't much of a surprise. But still, as an
historian, you must agree it's impressive. The Brazen Bull. As close a
replica as possible to the original, with just a few modern upgrades.
Wood fires are romantic but impractical." He tapped the yellow
hose with his foot. "These burners run on natural gas, not propane,
so it can get up to well near 50,000 BTUs per hour. The brass, of
course, conducts the heat marvelously."

Jarsdel turned and saw Brayden pointing the gun at him. The
security guard seemed to know that if he were going to make a
move, it would be now. Brayden jutted his chin in Stevens's direction, as if encouraging him to put his attention back on the man
speaking. Jarsdel obeyed.

"I can control the temperature very effectively with the gas,"
Stevens went on. "Phalaris would've been impressed. The one thing
that bothers me is that you can see the welding joints. I wanted it
cast all in one piece, like the original, but it couldn't be done. I can
say, however, that it is completely lightproof inside. Utter darkness,
so that's good."

"Where's Aleena?" asked Jarsdel. His voice didn't tremble, as he'd expected it to.

"In a moment," said Stevens. He patted the bull, then fixed Jarsdel with the same woeful look he'd given him in the hallway. "I'm very sorry about this, Detective. And you enjoyed the movie I screened. I do believe you were being genuine when you said that. Tell me now, honestly, what did you think of the script?"

Jarsdel wasn't sure he'd heard the question correctly. "What?"

"Jeff's screenplay. I presume you read it all the way through?"

Jarsdel's eyes flicked to the torture device in front of him, then back to Stevens. *Stall him. That's all you can do.* "I...uh...thought it was a hell of a read."

"You mean it was entertaining? Or..."

"Yeah, very entertaining. And I really appreciated the attention to detail. To historical detail. The research really showed."

Stevens made a face. "But it's a little overwritten, right? The dialogue in particular. It was my idea, you know, for a movie. I don't want to self-aggrandize, but I'm very much an historian as well. The story of Phalaris is one I'd always been fascinated by, but I have the humility to recognize I'm not a writer. Jeff liked the concept, so I told him to run with it. If he sold it, I'd be attached to direct. But of course, as we all know, that didn't happen."

"Is that why you killed him?"

"Because his dialogue is lousy? Don't be ridiculous. No, his mistake was getting in trouble with you. He told me all about it when he called. He got in some stupid fight with the dirt sales-man, and you were investigating. That's when I knew it was only a matter of time before you read the script, and then, of course, he would tell you the whole thing came from me, and..." He made a flicking gesture with his fingers. "Had to go. Anyway," he went on, "the way the studio system is today, I think it would've been a tough sell even if the names Goldman or Kasdan were up there where it says 'Written By.' There's just pathetic little interest in projects of real substance. I mean, say what you will about those old Jews who ran Hollywood, they knew story. There was a care, a real care, and love of the art of storytelling. You know, it taps into something in us, something so special when we're challenged and moved by a story. It's essential to our souls. You know what I'm saying?"

"Yes."

"As important to us as food. I really do mean that. And what they're doing today is giving us empty calories. Just a light show and some sound effects. It's not merely that it's bad art, but I think it's really harming us, depriving us of what we need as human beings."

"It's awful."

"It's beyond awful, and who knows what the consequences will be, on a broader level, for the generations to come?"

"I agree."

"So you see what happens. You read the script. Historically accurate, entertaining, if perhaps a bit sensational, but with a real message. Something to say. And yet no one wants it because, you know, it's not 3-D and it doesn't have a built-in brand. No tent-pole movie, right? What do you think?"

Jarsdel nodded, perhaps a bit too eagerly, but he wanted to keep the conversation going. The more they spoke, the more Stevens would think of him as a human being, and the more he'd hesitate in torturing him to death. At least in theory. "You're probably right. They're always playing it safe. Sequels and remakes, right?"

"Exactly. But even so, it's hard to let it go. My little baby, you know? What do you think? Is it worth revisiting? Give it another pass?"

"You could try. I guess it might be a little long. Maybe—"

"I know. I know. That occurred to me too. I could make some trims..." Stevens waved a hand and allowed himself a rueful little smile. "Fuck it. They'll never buy it anyway. And I've gotten way off the point. What I want you to know is I'm not happy with the way things turned out. Between us, I mean. And mostly, I just don't understand you. Why invest so much effort into someone like Grant Wolin? He was a nothing, less than a nobody."

"You tell me," said Jarsdel. "You're the one who took the time to torture him to death. He obviously wasn't a nobody to you."

"Show some respect," said Brayden from behind him.

Stevens raised a palm. "It's all right. The detective is entitled to his opinion. But I should tell you, Tully, that I had very good reason to do what I did. That Wolin character did work for me, that much is true, and was very effective in roping in Chinese tourists for my Hollywood Experience. And I was fair with him. His commissions were substantial. But his disloyalty was shocking. Shocking. Am I right, Brayden?"

"Yup," said the security guard. "Big-time asshole."

"He goes to this other company, this Punyawong company that does these trash tours. Action stars' homes mostly, if you can imagine. I'm providing something that's equal parts entertainment and edification. Punyawong is all snap and flash. But he wants to expand, add some class. What does Wolin do? For a bit of money, he gives up my route, even the exact, *exact* script my tour guides use. All of a sudden, these places that were exclusively mine are crammed with these other buses. What was it called, Brayden? Some Fantasy something?"

"Fantasy Tours."

"God. Right." Stevens shook his head. "Fantasy Tours. Even the name offends, don't you agree? And Wolin starts working for him, telling customers this new company is better—actually better— than mine. Advertises right in front of my storefront, handing out flyers. So now he's costing me money. And I don't need to tell you, do I, how competitive this town is. Men far more patient than me would've broken under the weight of such treatment. But even all that isn't enough for him. He then gets this incredible idea, and I'm using the word 'incredible' not in a good way, to start selling dirt to tourists. Genuine Hollywood Dirt, he calls it. It's insulting, disgusting, emblematic of everything that's wrong with this city. A malignancy. The Wolins, the Punyawongs, the street characters, and the raving derelicts, all just sucking at Hollywood's teats. So unworthy of this place."

So that's what happened to them all, Jarsdel thought. *The Riddler and Ghost Rider and Batman. And the vagrant in the doorway probably, and who knows how many others.*

"I'm trying to restore this town to what it once was," said Stevens. "Inject it with a new passion for the arts, for history, and along comes this nothing man peddling dirt. It was more than I could bear. So then Brayden tells me, how did you put it?"

"Two birds with one stone," said Brayden.

"I love that expression. Yes. Two birds with one stone. Get rid of my Wolin problem and fold up Fantasy Tours all in one go. And this Punyawong has a son, Brayden tells me. Wonderful. So I decide to send a strong message, just like we used to do during the war. Put on a real show. I thought the red quarter was a particularly nice touch." Stevens smiled broadly. "I made a call to Punyawong, letting him know his son was next. And it worked! No more Fantasy Tours! No more Punyawong!" His smile faded back into his expression of sadness. "But then you." He turned back to the bull. "The hardest thing to get right was the head. Said Perillos, the sculptor, 'His screams will come to you through the pipes as the tenderest, most pathetic, most melodious of bellowings.' The tubing in the bull's head had to be specially calibrated to produce that effect but resilient enough to stand up to the tremendous heat. Here, I'll show you."

Stevens bent down and picked up a stainless-steel box affixed with a large black dial. A cord ran from the box into the side of the burner apparatus. He gave the dial the smallest of turns, and there was the clicking sound of an ignitor, followed by a soft *whump!* as the gas jets caught. Low blue flames sprouted upward, and Jarsdel could already feel their heat.

"I'll keep it on low for now," said Stephens. "But I can have those flames up and licking the bull's body if I like. When that happens, make sure you stand far back. It can get quite hot in here. Really, it was made for outdoor use. The fan helps a little, but it's mostly there for the smoke. You see," he continued, "Wolin was an unusual case. I needed a body to scare off Punyawong, but most times, I get it really cranked up so there's nothing left at all, just bits of bone that I throw into the greens bin. Contemporaries of Phalaris said they 'shone like jewels.'" He fingered his milky white pendant. "See? Remarkable. All that's left of a Bosnian sniper who killed an officer in my unit. His death was a big favorite in Foča. We all drank rakia and sang while he burned."

Thinly at first, but growing in volume, the bull began to moan.

"Sounds just like the lowing of cattle," said Stevens, marveling. "Man or woman inside, it always comes out the same on this end."

There was the faint sound of something scrabbling inside the bull, the slap of feet and hands against the increasingly hot metal. And over it all, the screams of pain and fear transformed into that terrible moaning. Despite the room's increasing temperature, Jarsdel experienced a violent chill. It began somewhere in his chest and spread outward, sapping the strength from his muscles and making his limbs tremble.

"You know what I find interesting?" said Stevens. "Human nature. Specifically, the mechanism of choice. It's a powerful thing, watching people make choices under pressure. You can't guess or imagine what people will do when faced with those grand life choices."

Jarsdel started toward Stevens, then felt an arm clamp around his throat. "Easy," whispered Brayden, jamming the gun's muzzle into his lower back.

The bull's moans increased in volume and urgency.

"You can make one of those choices now if you like," said Stevens. "My bull is going to sing for me today, but it doesn't have to be her in there. You could take her place."

The banging inside the bull sped up as Aleena struggled to get away from the heat. Stevens touched a finger to the side of the bull, held it there for a moment, then snatched it away, grimacing. "Could almost cook an egg on it."

"Turn it off."

"So you'll go in, eh?"

Jarsdel didn't know what he was going to do. He just had to have it stop. "Turn it off," he said again.

The bull wailed. Stevens regarded Jarsdel for a moment, smiling faintly, then turned the dial on the box to the off position. The blue flames sputtered and vanished. Stevens slid back the heavy bolt and pulled the hatch open. Aleena's screams filled the room as she tried to fling herself from the bull. Her hips caught on the lip of the hatch, and she hung there, clothes soaked through with sweat, her skin a high scarlet. Sobbing, she clambered out the rest of the way, swatting Stevens's hand when he held it out to her, and spilled in a heap to the cement floor. Jarsdel tried to go to her, but Brayden held him fast.

"She holds quite a distinction," said Stevens to no one in particular. "The first person to emerge from my Brazen Bull alive." He turned to Jarsdel, then gestured to the open hatch, which yawned into blackness. "Your half of the bargain, yes?"

"And Aleena?"

Stevens gave a sorrowful shrug. "No happy endings, I'm afraid. Not tonight. But at least it won't be this." He knocked the bull's flank, which gonged sonorously.

Jarsdel felt Brayden's arm around him loosen, and the gun's muzzle prodded him forward. His legs gave out, and he stumbled and fell flat. The concrete was cool against his palms, and he thought about what it would be like inside. What would kill him first? Would the heated air burn him from the inside out, cooking his lungs with each breath? Or would it be even slower, his nerve endings shrieking under his skin as he tried in vain to get away from the metal?

Brayden pulled him roughly to his feet. "Hey." Brayden's whisper was hot in his ear. "You wanna piss him off? Don't scream when you're in there. No matter what. No one's been able to do that before. I wanna see his face."

There was a squeak of suppressed laughter, and Jarsdel was pushed forward again. Now he did go to Aleena, kneeling beside her. She was still facing the ground, weeping at the sight of her hands, which were swollen and misshapen with blisters.

"Aleena, it's me. It's me." He reached out to touch her but stopped himself, afraid of frightening her further. "You're gonna get out of here." It was all he could think to say, and he knew it wasn't true.

She looked up at him then, through the damp, stringy hair that had spilled across her face. Jarsdel saw vivid purple bruises below her left eye and along her jaw. Her lip was split, and a smear of dried blood ran from her mouth to her chin.

It seemed to take her a moment to recognize him. When she did, a strangled sound escaped her, and she seized him in an embrace, wailing as she clung to him.

Jarsdel looked up at Stevens, who made another gesture toward the bull. "You know," said Jarsdel, rubbing Aleena's back gently. "Your hero Phalaris didn't make it."

Stevens cocked his head. "Hmm? How do you mean?"

"Overthrown. Cooked in his own bull, as I remember. Very poetic."

Stevens nodded. "At least so says the prevailing theory. What's your point? You think I too am destined to spend my final moments in there?"

"It'll catch you one way or another. One day. This isn't gonna end with me. My partner knows you lied about Wolin working for you, and he knows you're the last person Dinan called before he disappeared. And when I don't show up to work tomorrow morning, he's gonna get a warrant to tear this place down to the studs."

Stevens stiffened. "Thank you for the warning. An acetylene torch can take the bull apart, and I can always put it back together some other time. That's how I got it into this country, you know. It's a bit of a hassle, but it doesn't seem I have a choice. Oh well. Better get inside, then. I'll turn the heat on full for you. Much quicker that way. Up."

"No."

"We made a deal. Honor it, or I'll have Brayden persuade you."

"Let Aleena go."

"Up."

"Not until you let her go."

A new voice broke in, full of authority and, it sounded to Jarsdel, barely checked fury. "Freeze. Nobody moves. I will put bullets in the first of you motherfuckers so much as twitches."

Jarsdel wasn't sure if that warning included him and decided to play it safe. He stayed still, his hands resting on Aleena's back. Even she'd become quiet. Jarsdel snuck a look up at Stevens and saw the man staring in surprise in the direction of the doorway.

"Partner," said the voice. "You hurt?"

Jarsdel got to his feet, pulling Aleena up with him. Morales was standing behind Brayden, who'd been disarmed and now had his hands in the air. Jarsdel led Aleena to the corner so she could rest, her back supported. He then turned his attention to Stevens and moved toward him, reaching for his handcuffs before remembering he didn't have them. He didn't care. He'd pin him to the ground until backup arrived if he had to.

It was just as Jarsdel was crossing in front of the bull that it happened. The burners came to sudden, roaring life, shooting blue-and-yellow flames as high as his elbows. He instinctively dove away as the terrific heat hit him, but not before losing the hair on the left side of his body. Jarsdel landed hard, rolling in case his clothes had caught.

Stevens dropped the burner control and darted toward the open door as Brayden spun on Morales, clouting him with the back of his hand. The detective, who held both his own gun and the one he'd taken from Brayden, stumbled back against the doorjamb, striking his head. Brayden pressed his advantage, grabbing one of Morales's wrists in each hand and wrenching them toward the ceiling. Morales was strong and fought back, and Brayden hurled a clumsy but powerful kick that caught him on the knee. Morales's eyes bulged as the fight went out of him. He sagged to a sitting position as Brayden grabbed one of the guns and stumbled away, twisting it free. He quickly regained his balance and began leveling the weapon at Morales. But the detective, though wheezing in pain, brought his own weapon up faster. Morales fired six rapid shots. The first two were wild, one of them clipping the bull with the sound of a bell being struck. The remaining four rounds lifted Brayden off his feet, carrying him backward, his blood arcing in bright crimson streams. His body slammed against the bull and slumped sideways into the flames, and the Popeye Doyle hat caught as if it had been dipped in gasoline. The room began to fill with the smell of burning hair and clothing.

Jarsdel scrambled to his feet and looked at Aleena, who sat frozen in shock. He picked up the burner control and snapped the dial to *Off*. The flames guttered out, but Brayden's body continued to smolder.

Jarsdel went quickly to Aleena. "You okay?"

She blinked but didn't answer.

"Aleena!"

She turned toward him, eyes wide and haunted. Jarsdel glanced at Morales, who remained on the ground. He still held the gun and, with his other hand, gripped his knee. The pain had drained the color from his face. "Can you walk?" Jarsdel asked.

Morales shook his head, then held out his weapon. "Go. Get him. I'll take care of her. Backup's coming."

Jarsdel took the gun, threw one last look at Aleena, then raced from the room.

———

As he bolted up the stairs, Jarsdel realized he'd been burned worse than he thought. The left side of his face throbbed painfully, and the back of his hand felt as if it were on fire. His pant leg on that side hung in charred ribbons, the skin underneath taut and shiny. A feverish shiver ran through him, and he was almost sick again. He stumbled when he reached the top of the stairs, and that probably saved his life.

The spear point that had been aimed at Jarsdel's throat instead took him just above the ear, glancing off bone and opening up the flesh in a long, jagged line. His glasses snapped off and scattered across the floor. He clamped his free hand to the wound and turned toward his attacker, raising the Kimber, but Stevens charged forward again. The spear flashed, its dull tip punching through Jarsdel's right bicep, and the gun dropped from his hand. He gasped. There wasn't much pain, not yet, and he watched with remote fascination as Stevens wrenched the spear free.

I'm going to be killed with a movie prop, Jarsdel thought. *Only in Hollywood.*

It was hard to see with only the light from the streetlamps outside coming through the museum's display windows, and the spear was practically invisible. Stevens lunged, aiming at his chest. Jarsdel ducked to the side, and Stevens followed up with a vicious swipe toward his face. Jarsdel flailed out his hands and seized the shaft of the spear, keeping the point away from his body, and threw a kick at Stevens's groin. The other man dodged it easily, alternately shoving and yanking the spear to try to get it free. He didn't look angry; instead, his expression was one of deep concentration, as if he were trying to solve a troublesome problem.

"It's over. Let it go," said Jarsdel. The order lacked confidence. He was overmatched, fighting for his life. Even his most frenzied struggles with suspects had never progressed beyond the simple arrangement between criminal and cop, one trying to get away and the other trying to stop that from happening. But this man wanted to kill him. He'd first wanted to kill him slowly, torturously, and now that had failed, he was trying to skewer him like a fish. It was unbelievable that he could die today, and die like this, right now, the blade taking him in the windpipe or the lung or the heart. It could happen easily. He didn't think he'd be able to fight Stevens much longer. His neck and shirt were sticky with blood from the head wound, and more had run down from the puncture in his arm, making his grip begin to slip. He was weakening, while his opponent remained strong and unharmed.

Stevens gave an especially hard push, then let go of his end of the spear. Jarsdel, suddenly finding himself without any resistance, nearly fell backward. As he regained his balance, Stevens bent down to pick up the gun.

Jarsdel swung the spear two-handed in a sharp downward arc. It whistled through the air, and the base of it caught Stevens on the shoulder. There was a crack, and Stevens let out a loud, mournful sigh as he sank to his knees. Jarsdel turned the spear around so the shank was pointed at Stevens, who reached for the gun again, this time with his left hand.

"Don't." Jarsdel prodded the blood-slick blade at Stevens. "Back away from the weapon."

Stevens shook his head. It was a slow, weary gesture. Then he smiled, wiggling his fingers in the direction of the gun. *Dare I?* the move seemed to say.

Jarsdel took a step forward, intending to kick it away, but Stevens was faster. Stevens rolled forward and grabbed the gun, then spun around as he rose to one knee, already firing.

Jarsdel ran at him, squinting at the loud reports, and something thrummed past his ear. He shut his eyes then and felt the spear meet a brief resistance before bursting forward again. Then he hit something hard and unyielding and came to a sudden halt.

The gunfire had ceased. Jarsdel opened his eyes and was startled to see Stevens looking back at him. He was frowning, his forehead creased in concern. His unnaturally black hair had come loose from its meticulous part and now lay crazily across his brow.

Jarsdel had run Stevens into the wall, just to the left of a poster for a movie called *The Stranglers of Bombay*. The head of the spear was sunk into his body just above Stevens's pelvis, and Jarsdel could feel the point scraping against the wall where it exited out the other side. Jarsdel let go of the shaft, and Stevens sank slowly to the floor, the long wooden pole bobbing a little as he went.

The smell of blood was heavy in the air, along with something else, foul and sharp, the smell of shit, and Jarsdel wondered if it was coming from him, if he'd soiled himself. Then he saw something brown and syrupy seep from around the blade buried in Stevens's belly and realized he'd punctured the man's intestine. He stepped forward and took the gun from Stevens, who didn't seem to notice or care. He debated whether or not to try to remove the spear but decided it would be better to wait for the EMTs. He could hear sirens now. His backup. In a moment, the officers would be inside, and then later the Force Investigation Division, and he'd have to explain how he'd ended up impaling another man with a prop from *Spartacus*. A wild laugh bubbled inside him. He tried stopping it, and what came out was choked and strange, like a suppressed sneeze. Stevens raised his head.

"It *is* funny. Yes."

Jarsdel felt suddenly very faint. His legs buckled, and he sat down hard, groaning at the pain that now seemed to be everywhere at once. The gun felt heavy in his hand, so he rested it on a bent knee.

Stevens closed his eyes, and Jarsdel thought he might have passed out. Or died. But then, though it seemed to take great effort, he began to talk. "First movie I ever saw was *Singin' in the Rain*. Father bought a print from a Frenchman...screened it on a bedsheet on our back patio..."

Stevens bunched his features, then gripped the spear with one hand. He pulled, but the shank didn't budge. More fluid, red and brown, burbled around the wound. Stevens gasped, then let go. His skin was almost as white as his pendant now, his face covered in a sheen of sweat.

"Only had one projector," he continued, "so every twenty minutes, the movie would stop, and Father would have to change the reels. Like being awakened from a beautiful dream..."

The sirens grew louder.

"Watched it every week for six months, until the projector broke. Still have the print somewhere..."

Jarsdel didn't know where Stevens was going with all this, and anyway, the only thing he wanted now was to shut his eyes and not think about anything for a while. He felt something trickle down his wrist and was startled to see that a pool of blood the size of a dinner plate had formed beneath his hand.

"You can't imagine," said Stevens, "the love I had for that magical place in the movie. Promised one day I would go there...and when... finally arrived, saw the grand lady Hollywood was now just an old whore. But I felt her spirit. It's still here, calling to those with the right ears. It calls from the Roosevelt Hotel...from the curves of Mulholland Drive and Sunset Boulevard...the Polo Lounge. Even those handprints in the cement. She's still here."

Jarsdel's breathing slowed as the urge to sleep grew greater. Stevens seemed determined to explain something to him, something he felt was important, but Jarsdel didn't have the strength or the desire to follow his meandering story any longer.

There was a bang and the tinkle of breaking glass and shouts, but the sounds were so very far away. The last thing he heard was Stevens's strangely melodious voice. "Try holding onto a dream with both hands, Tully, and see if you don't have to kill a few people along the way."

23

There were five new arrivals that night at Hollywood Presbyterian, all from the Cinema Legacy Museum. One went to the burn unit, two to ICU, another to orthopedic services, and one to the morgue. Detectives from LAPD's Force Investigation Division were dispatched to speak to the survivors, but even the least injured among them, Oscar Morales, wouldn't be available for several hours. The kick Brayden had delivered to his knee had damaged his meniscus replacement plate, and surgery was required to repair it.

Jarsdel experienced the first night in the hospital through a fog of pain and the drugs used to keep it at bay. It was impossible to know at any given time if he was dreaming or not, so he decided it was best to treat every encounter as if it were real. He answered questions when they were asked of him but otherwise didn't speak for fear of saying something nonsensical or self-incriminating. Mostly, he just lay there, fading in and out of consciousness, stirring occasionally at the sound of hurrying feet and raised voices or the stick of a needle or the squeeze of a blood pressure cuff. But soon even these ceased to wake him, and he slept.

In the morning of the next day—or at least Jarsdel assumed it was morning—he woke to find his parents at his bedside. Both had been crying. Robert clutched a tissue, and the tip of Darius's nose was red—something that only happened when he was upset. At first, Jarsdel pretended he didn't see them and closed his eyes again. He didn't know what to say, how to justify his near death to these people. But Robert must have seen a flicker of movement.

"Tully? Tully, are you awake?"

Jarsdel took a deep breath and opened his eyes.

"Hey."

"Oh God, Tully." He grabbed his hand, mashing the damp tissue against his fingers. Darius, not wanting to push his husband out of the way but still needing contact with his son, grasped Jarsdel's foot.

"I'm fine, guys."

Darius made a sound somewhere between a laugh and a sob. "Yeah, you're fine. Nearly got killed by a maniac."

"Oh, Tully, Tully," Robert said. "Your dear sweet arm. And your *hair*."

"It would've destroyed us, Son. Just destroyed us," said Darius.

"I'm really tired, guys. I feel funny."

"You need the nurse?" Robert asked, immediately alarmed.

Jarsdel shook his head and immediately regretted it. A wave of dizziness rolled over him, and he grimaced.

"Nurse! Or a doctor? Doctor!"

"I'm fine, Dad, please."

"Are you sure?"

A man in an immaculate white coat appeared at the foot of his bed. The cursive stitching on his breast identified him as Jonathan Gray, MD.

"How're we doing?"

"I keep telling them I'm fine."

The doctor nodded but checked Jarsdel's vitals and fluids before departing.

"Please don't call the doctor again."

Robert squeezed his hand. "We love you. Oh, we love you so much."

"I love you too."

"We want you to stay with us after you get out of here. Just until you get better."

"Okay."

Robert squeezed his hand again. "The docs say your arm doesn't have any tendon damage. You should have eighty-percent recovery in two weeks. Jesus God, you got so lucky."

"Could've been bad, Tully. Very bad," said Darius.

"Well, his *head*, Dary. The head is not good. It's *not* good."

"No. No, it isn't."

Jarsdel reached up a tentative hand and began touching his face. "Why? What's wrong with my head?"

"Oh, Son," said Robert. "When that *man*, that"—he lowered his voice—"that son of a bitch attacked you, he cut a nerve in your head."

"Occipital nerve," offered Darius.

"Your occipital nerve, yes. The doctors say you could get a neuroma and then terrible headaches. For the rest of your life." He sniffled and wiped his eyes. "That bastard. I hope he's suffering. I know it's not right to say that, but it's how I feel."

Jarsdel blinked. "He's alive? Stevens?"

"Is that his name? Yes, he's alive. The police are guarding him."

"He's here?"

Darius nodded. "I'd like to go over there and put a pillow over his face. They're saying they don't even know how many people he killed. He's a monster."

"I saw people who looked like government agents too," said Robert. "You could tell by their suits and by the way they interacted with everyone. They just felt different from regular police."

If that were true, it probably had to do with some of the things Stevens had told him he'd done during the Bosnian War. That would spell federal involvement, maybe deportation to Montenegro or The Hague for trial. He speculated on what that would mean for the Grant Wolin case, then decided that at least for the moment, he didn't really care. Stevens was caught; that was what mattered.

I'm here, to be among those who renew the world.

And he supposed that was true, though the cost had been nearly unbearable. "Is Aleena okay?"

"Who's that?" asked Darius.

"Must be the young woman he came in with," said Robert. "They told me he saved someone's life."

"I want to see her," said Jarsdel.

"Do you know her? Other than from this terrible thing?"

"Where are my glasses?" He started to get up, but Robert put a hand on his chest.

"Shh, it's okay. I'm sure she's fine."

"Please tell them to let me see her."

"We will."

"Please."

"We will, Tully."

Reluctantly, he lay back down.

"Your baba and I asked about the best way for you to leave the police. They said you could get something like a disability thing—I suppose it's like an honorable discharge from the army—and you'll get paid good money."

"Why?"

"What do you mean, sweetie?"

"Why would you ask them that?"

"You should be compensated for what you went through. You can retire for disability reasons, and you still have your whole life ahead of you to pursue something else."

Jarsdel didn't speak for a while.

His parents exchanged a look, then Darius spoke. "You're not thinking of staying, are you?"

"Oh, Tully," said Robert, "you have such an extraordinary, loving, and lovely mind. You're built for better things than this."

"It's all taken care of," said Darius. "Too late for the job at CSUN, but there's a TA position open under Professor Bodman. You'd have to grade undergrad papers again, but it'd get you right back on track with your doctorate. He'd love to have you. Told me so."

"And with the money you'd be getting from the police, you'd be in really good shape."

"I'm very tired," said Jarsdel. "I'd like to go back to sleep for a little while."

"Did we upset you?" asked Robert.

"No, just please. Please let me get some sleep."

Darius put a hand on Robert's shoulder. "He's okay. Let's let him rest." Then he turned to his son. "Let us take care of you. Let us make everything right."

———

On the day Tully Jarsdel graduated from the police academy, one of his instructors had advised the class not to smile in their police ID photos.

"Same picture they use on the news if you shoot someone. Imagine—you just killed a guy. You got an FID team looking into your case, see if it was a good shooting or not, and citizens too are questioning whether what you did was right. You also, probably. Doin' some soul-searching. And now every time you're on TV, you're this grinning asshole. Last thing you want."

Tully had followed the advice and was glad for it. When his story made the front page of the *Los Angeles Times*, the photograph that accompanied it showed a bespectacled man with full, boyish cheeks, a prominent Adam's apple, and a haircut that wouldn't have been out of place on an aide in the Johnson administration. No smile, though. A smile would have been absurd, even profane, next to the headline "A Killer's Dungeon of Horror."

Morales had brought the paper, and Jarsdel now set it on the tray beside that morning's inedible omelet. "Thanks," he said to his partner. "I'll read it later."

"Most of it's bullshit and speculation," said Morales, who was still wheelchair-bound after his surgery. "But it makes you look good."

"Yeah? You're right. That would be bullshit, considering I nearly got myself and two other people killed."

"You got the bad guy. Stuck a fuckin' spear in his guts. Don't think the state's gonna be able to top that, especially now the Green Room's outta order."

"How'd you find me that night, Oscar? Nobody can tell me."

Jarsdel had been moved from ICU to a private room in the transitional care unit, and they had the place to themselves. Still, Morales wheeled closer, as if he were about to share a deep secret.

"I get visions sometime. Like flashes of divine inspiration."

"Huh. That's really something."

"Yeah. Gonna open my own place on the boulevard. Do readings and shit. Make more than I do as a cop."

"Okay. Seriously, though, how?"

Morales shrugged. "You didn't show up. Didn't answer my text about the parking or anything. I called, and you didn't pick up. Just wasn't like you, not like the professor we all know and love. Thought maybe you were in an accident or something. So I had the station check the GPS tracker on your phone, which didn't move. Right outside your complex, and it just blinked and blinked. Went to go see what's up—which was dangerous as shit, by the way, four beers in and with the goddamned rain. Meanwhile, I actually get WeHo sheriffs to do a welfare check on your apartment. Keys in the door. Car still there. Then I find your phone in some lantana bushes and listen to that little message you were gonna send me. Got to the museum, saw the van, and the back door to the place was open, so I went in. Called for backup when I heard the girl screaming. Everything else you know."

"Thank you, Oscar. For everything."

"How's the arm?"

"It's okay. Could've been a lot worse."

"That's our motto, man."

The two men were quiet, and Morales pretended to find the art on the wall interesting while Jarsdel stared at the blank television set.

"You gonna come back, right?" his partner finally asked.

"I don't know." He expected Morales to protest, to tell him he was a coward for thinking about quitting, but instead, the older detective gave a small nod.

"You do what you need to do," he said and wheeled out of the room.

———

Aleena had been placed in a specialty unit a floor down from Jarsdel's own, but before going there, he'd stopped in the lobby gift shop and picked up a dozen roses. Because of his arm, he had to depend on a nurse to guide his wheelchair. On the way back up the elevator, she'd asked about the flowers.

"For my girlfriend."

"That's sweet. I'm sure she'll love them."

The door to Aleena's room was open, and Jarsdel could see her lying in bed. She wasn't asleep and seemed to just be staring down at her hands, which were wrapped in bandages. Jarsdel was glad to see the bed next to hers was unoccupied.

"Hello," said the nurse, knocking on the doorjamb.

Aleena looked over at them, then quickly again at her hands.

"Someone's here to see you." The nurse pushed Jarsdel into the room. "I'll let you two talk. Just have her ring the call button when you're through." She left the two of them alone.

Jarsdel was too far away from the bed to hand Aleena the flowers, which she couldn't take anyway. He should've thought of that. It looked as if she were wearing giant white oven mitts. By using just his left arm, he was able to successfully wheel toward her side table and set the roses there.

"Hey," he said. "Hope it's okay I'm here."

When she didn't answer, he went on. "I missed you. You're all I think about in here. And I wanted you to know I'm gonna leave the department. Take my disability and go back to academics."

Aleena's gaze remained fixed on her hands, which lay one atop the other in her lap. When she spoke, her voice was almost unrecognizable. There was no life in it, none of the vivacity that colored her normal speech. "Please go."

"What?"

Aleena began to weep, and she mashed furiously at the tears with her bandages.

He wasn't sure what to do. He wanted to go to her, to hold her, and began to get out of his chair when she spoke again.

"No. Just go."

"Aleena. I'm trying to tell you I'm gonna give it up. It's not worth it. I just want to be with you."

She took a shaky breath and did her best to speak, though her voice hitched and trembled. "I hear you... I...just...can't look at you."

It was as if he'd been struck. "But we can get past this. We can get past it."

"No..."

"Don't let this ruin it for us. I'll help you. We'll do it together."

"I can't—"

"Aleena."

She screwed her eyes shut, lifted her hands, and brought them down hard on her thighs. She spoke rapidly now, in a single unbroken stream. "No, please just go. I can't look at you. I can't be around anything that reminds me of that day. I'm sorry. I'm sorry." Once the words were out, she lost what little control she had left. She covered her face and gave in to harsh, wracking sobs.

Jarsdel opened his mouth to speak, but nothing came to him. Only her name, so that's what he said. "Aleena."

She didn't move, didn't respond. Just continued to cry, her giant, oven-mitt hands shaking up and down in front of her face.

Jarsdel turned and saw the nurse had returned. She was standing in the doorway now, watching the scene, and gave him a reproving look. "I think it's time to go," she said, stepping forward and taking his chair.

Jarsdel gave no reply.

He thought about what it must have been like inside the bull. The darkness, the unbearable pain, the hopelessness of escape. And his the first face she'd seen when she was let out.

Before he was rolled out of the room, Jarsdel gave the woman he loved a final glance and silently wished her well.

Two Months Later

Derek Bonda, known to some on the LAPD as the Dog Catcher, pulled off the I-5 freeway in the direction of Silver Lake. His silver '99 Daewoo Nubira, which was due for a smog check he feared it wouldn't pass, took the turn onto Glendale Boulevard followed by a cloud of blue exhaust smoke. Bonda considered postponing his day's activities in case his car attracted the attention of a cop, then decided he'd rather take the risk. "Fortune favors the bold," someone had once said. He liked that. He also liked, "Pain is temporary, glory is forever." Translated to his current situation, it meant that the agony of the dog might only be a passing thing, but the suffering caused by its death would haunt its owners forever. That was good. That, in fact, was just what he wanted.

Bonda lived in Toluca Lake, and his ballroom dance studio was in Burbank, so he didn't spend much time in this part of town. Still, he knew the area well enough, had even reconned his destination weeks earlier to make sure the property suited his needs. He'd use Google Maps to direct him the last little bit of his drive; it was confusing up in those winding residential streets between Sunset and Riverside. He headed down Hyperion, passing a few upscale restaurants, a cheese shop, a Gelson's, and a pizzeria he remembered being pretty decent. He'd stop there afterward, he decided. These errands always seemed to leave him hungry.

He made a left up Micheltorena, slowing to read the numbers on curbs and mailboxes. The address the couple gave on their sign-up sheet was 6120, and he still had a ways to go. He checked his rearview and saw he was alone, no cars following him, and that made him happy. Bonda knew crimes committed during the day were considered higher risk for the offender, but experience taught him there were advantages too. Most people in a given neighborhood were gone during the day—that was a plus. Second, neighbors who *were* home were apt to be less suspicious than they were at night. A strange car on the street could go unnoticed for hours, and Bonda had got his routine down to just about a minute from the moment he shifted into park. In and out, slick as you please.

He was in the four thousands now and remembered the even numbers would be on his right. He began to get more excited as he got closer. This would be a treat and a real departure for him. The couple who'd come to him to learn their wedding dance was much older than he was used to. The woman looked like she was in her forties, with crow's feet around the eyes and enormous, matronly jugs, but she was still pretty in a kind of bookish way. Her fiancé was at least ten, maybe fifteen years older, mostly bald, and as forgettable and dull a client as Bonda had ever had. He was only their dance teacher, so they didn't confide in him too much, but they'd both hinted at previous marriages. At one point the woman—Katherine—said she'd all but given up on remarrying until she'd met Bill. And oh, how fabulous he was, and oh, what a gentleman, and oh, how he even looked forward to doing a wedding dance when so many men dreaded them. Bonda had smiled and congratulated the couple, had even given Bill a manly clap on the arm and told him he was thrilled to work with such an enthusiastic groom. And all the while, in his heart, he wanted nothing more than to destroy this couple, to rip apart their second chance at marriage like a rototiller through a flowerbed. He wanted to grievously wound that boring, unremarkable man, a man who despite his crippling ordinariness and ridiculous, shining head seemed strangely confident and even—somehow—tough. And the woman, with her bubbly optimism and shelflike tits, how Bonda wanted to hurt her the most, to kill her spirit and leave her broken.

He'd wished and hoped for two things, and they'd both come true. His first wish was that they lived together. It seemed about half his couples did, but just as many did not, waiting for that special day to move in with each other. And bingo, they did live together, at 6120 Micheltorena. His second wish, and this was the biggie, was that they were the proud and happy owners of a dog. And oh yes, they certainly were, of a scurrying little Maltese that'd demanded all of Bonda's acting ability to pretend he thought was cute. They'd brought the yapping puffball into the studio on more than one occasion, cooing over it between run-throughs of their dance routine while he, Bonda, imagined the little fucker writhing on its back, blowing fluid from its mouth and its ass until respiratory failure finally killed it.

He harvested the poison from the banks of the LA River, where *Cicuta douglasii Calflora*—California water hemlock—grew in wild profusion. It was such a pretty plant: a tall, branching perennial that blossomed with small, white, umbrella-shaped flowers. All parts of it were highly toxic, but the most concentrated poison was in the roots. All you had to do was shave off a chunk, and you'd start to see a yellow-ish oil begin to flow. That was the good stuff, the real deal. Toss that with some ground round and you'd have quite the "spicy meat-a-ball."

Bonda chortled. He was almost there now. 6080, 6090, 6100... and then he saw the house. It was drab, slate-colored, and boxy, surrounded by a high wooden fence—what homeowners called a good-neighbor fence, because you couldn't see between the slats. The last time he'd staked the place out, it had been nighttime, and he hadn't been able to tell just how ugly it was. What was important, though, was the way the house was built. It had a large front yard, which you could easily see down into if you drove a little farther up the hill. There was no backyard, just a deck that hung over a steep drop. That meant the dog had to play in the front, something that was also confirmed by the chew toys strewn about the grass and the doggie door cut into a side wall. It was ideal. Not that Bonda hadn't had to deal with backyard dogs before, but he preferred it this way. It was more certain the meatball would land intact and in a place accessible to the animal.

He glanced in his rearview again. A Jetta was making its way up the hill behind him. Bonda pulled over, and soon the car passed him, the driver not sparing him a glance as he continued upward. Bonda liked this street. There were no pedestrians about, and the sight lines were terrific; he'd know far in advance if anyone was approaching from either end. Only a few cars were parked along this stretch, and there was plenty of empty space in front of 6120.

Bonda pulled in front, slipped on a pair of vinyl food-prep gloves, and was about to go to work when he noticed something. About a block ahead of him, on the other side of the street, was parked a service van. *Neptune Pool & Jacuzzi*, it read on the side, followed by the slogan, "Keepin' you in blue since '72!" Bonda frowned. He didn't like workmen being around when he did his thing. They kept records of their jobs, when they arrived and when they left, and if—worst case scenario—they spotted Bonda, they could easily help an investigator put together both a timeline and a suspect description.

He drummed his fingers on the steering wheel, his frown deepening. Should he go get some food and come back in an hour? He checked the time, nearly three in the afternoon. The wedding ceremony would be starting soon, and after that, there'd be champagne and canapes while the happy couple took pictures, then dinner, then drinking and, of course, the wedding dance. A bland nightclub two-step he'd choreographed years ago and recycled for every couple that came to him with a ballad. (Bill and Katherine had picked "Crazy Love" by Van Morrison. Not exactly original folks, hate to tell ya.) And after all that, there'd be cake and the usual silliness with the garter belt and the bouquet and the requisite drunk uncle swatting a bridesmaid's ass. Bonda knew he had plenty of time before the newlyweds, ready to boink their little hearts out, came back in the limo and found their dog cold and stiff. But four o'clock would be right around the time the assholes in this neighborhood began coming home from work, first just a few, then a flood. There might even be kids playing in the street. Probably not, as steep as it was, but you never knew.

Shit.

No, he'd do it now. And not just because he'd been looking

forward to it ever since he'd met this couple. The risk was greater if he waited. For the reasons he'd already considered, but also because a car leaving and coming back had a higher likelihood of being noticed. It was better to do it now. He could be pulling away from the curb and back on his way in a minute—a measly little minute—and Mr. Neptune Pool & Jacuzzi could just go fuck himself.

It was decided. Breathing a little faster now, he opened his center console and took out the Ziploc bag of meat. He'd already mixed in the poison back at his apartment, and this was all ready to go—eight ounces of raw ground chuck finished with an eyedropper-full of hemlock oil, more than enough to send a Maltese to doggie heaven. He opened the bag and dumped the meat into his waiting right hand. It was pure death he hefted there—death and a misery that would last for years, hopefully a lifetime.

Using his still-clean left hand, Bonda pulled the door handle and stepped into the street. He glanced both ways, keeping his handful of meat out of sight inside the car. Nobody either on foot or on wheels. He gave the Neptune van a lingering look. No technician heading toward it for a part or an invoice, not yet anyway.

Bonda stepped around the back of his car and approached the house, moving quickly. *This is for you*, he thought. *This is for you, you fucking bitch.*

His divorce had cost him exactly five hundred and twenty thousand dollars, a staggering sum. Now, instead of owning his dance studio free and clear, he'd be paying off the mortgage until the day he died. His retirement? That was a laugh. Gone. Gone along with everything else. It'd all been his money to begin with, his savings, not hers, and now he had to teach six days a week to stay afloat. Six days a week of stumbling beginners who could barely clap out a rhythm, let alone move to one. Six days of fat-assed women who always wanted to be lifted like ballerinas, of horny single men hoping to get lucky in his group classes. It was endless. The faces changed, sometimes anyway, but the people were always the same. And it would go on and on and on.

But it was the wedding couples most of all. The wedding couples didn't merely depress him; they infuriated him. Of course, he hated the bitchy ones and the occasional screamers, those who fought in front of him like he was their shrink, but the lovey-dovey ones were the worst. It was the promise in their eyes—the promise of a bright, happy future, one that in Bonda's mind always included a little house with a tire swing and a new kid getting farted out every couple of years. Oh yes. And, of course, the family dog. Well, he couldn't do much about everything else, but he could certainly fix that last part.

He wound back his arm, looking first left, then right. *If only I could stuff this right into your lying, whoring mouth.* He threw. The tennis-ball-sized hunk of meat sailed in a graceful arc over the fence and disappeared. Bonda was on his way back to the car before it even landed, feeling full of giddy life, ready to hop in and grab a pizza and think about the look on Bill and Katherine's faces when the vet told them yes, Plushy or Muffy or whatever the fuck it was called had in fact been poisoned. Killed while they celebrated the happiest day of their lives.

Bonda gave a squawk of laughter and was reaching for the car door when there was the whoop of a siren and the purr of a fast-approaching engine. He looked up and watched openmouthed as a police car came roaring down the street.

It's not for me. It can't be.

There was another whoop, this time from behind him. Bonda turned and saw another police car ascending the hill, also moving fast. Then the back doors of the Neptune van opened, and several people got out. First, there was a beanpole of a man with a dopey haircut and glasses. Bonda could see he had a gun and badge on his hip, and so did the next two who followed him out. They were the couple he'd known as Bill and Katherine. They looked right at him, and they smiled.

The police cars came to a stop on either side of him, and four officers leapt out, guns drawn and shouting commands. Bonda did as he was told, getting down first on his knees, then full on his stomach. His hands were cuffed behind his back, tightly, one of them biting into the skin of his wrist and making him shout. Then he was hauled to his feet and pressed against the side of his Daewoo. Hands moved briskly up and down his body then, finding nothing but his wallet and cell phone, and kept him pinned in place.

"Don't move," a voice commanded.

"I'd like a lawyer."

"Shut the fuck up."

"I want those bagged right now," said a different voice.

"On or off?" another asked.

"On. Leave the gloves on him. I want pictures back at the station."

An officer drew paper bags over his hands and secured them with rubber bands. The cops turned him around then, and the beanpole one was there, flanked by Bill and Katherine or whoever they were.

"The Dog Catcher," Beanpole said.

A uniformed cop reached inside the Daewoo and switched off the idling engine. He hit the unlock button, and a second cop opened the passenger door and began photographing the interior of the car.

"Get a good close-up of my Del Taco receipts," Bonda said but without as much vitriol as he'd wanted to muster.

Another car joined them—obviously a cop car, but the kind detectives drove. A fat Mexican in an ill-fitting suit got out and limped over, joining the trio who were sizing him up. After staring at Bonda for half a minute, he spoke up.

"I got a dog."

Bonda gave no response.

"Belgian Malinois. Took him in after his handler was killed in the line of duty. Had him six years." He stepped closer.

Bonda's natural instinct was to retreat, but his back was already pressed against his car. All he could do was watch as the fat cop took one step, then another, until Bonda could smell the man's Speed Stick.

"Fuckin' coward," the cop said and stayed in his face for a few more seconds, as if daring him to do something. He finally moved away, and Bonda realized he'd been holding his breath.

"He ridin' with us?" the fat cop asked Beanpole.

"Yeah. Think so."

Another uniformed cop strolled into view, smiling and carrying a transparent plastic bag. Inside, Bonda recognized his meatball. It was a little worse for the wear from its trip over the fence, and a few blades of grass clung to its misshapen body, but there it was.

"I want a lawyer," Bonda said again.

Beanpole gave a nod, and two more cops—there were about ten of them milling around now—closed in on either side and shepherded him to the back of the car driven by the Mexican. Just like on the TV shows, they pushed his head down so he wouldn't bang it on the doorframe.

It wasn't like the normal cop cars—no grate between the front and back seats. There was even a shotgun near him, but it was locked into a mechanism that looked like it needed a special key to release it. He glanced up as the passenger door opened and Beanpole got in. The fat Mexican cop was still outside, talking to the uniformed ones.

"You're breaking the law," Bonda said.

"How's that?"

"Didn't read me my rights."

Beanpole let out a thin, mirthless laugh. "I haven't asked you anything yet. Don't have to read your rights till then."

"I want a lawyer," Bonda said for the third time.

"Okay."

"I'm not saying anything."

"Okay."

They sat in silence, watching the activity outside. A few neighbors had stepped out of their homes by now and were gathered in clusters, chattering, pointing.

"Get me out of here."

"In Zoroastrianism," the cop said, "dogs are considered sacred. Did you know that? They guard the bridge to heaven. In fact, if a dog is pregnant on your property, whether she's yours or not, you're required to make sure she and her puppies are safe."

Bonda sighed, a little shakily.

"I got you," Beanpole murmured.

"What?"

"I said I got you."

Bonda still didn't think he'd heard the man correctly and leaned forward.

Beanpole met his eyes in the rearview. "I made a promise that I would. You see"—he turned around now, so that he was looking right at Bonda—"you're only this big." He held out two fingers, about an inch apart. "And the rest of the darkness is just as small. But you're tenacious, that much is true. You don't want to go, and you make a lot of noise while you're here, so people notice. But you're this fucking small."

The Mexican cop finally stopped talking and got in on the driver's side. "We good to go?"

The skinny cop didn't answer at first, just kept looking at Bonda with an expression somewhere between fascination and disgust. Then he turned away.

"Yeah. Good to go."

The car pulled a U-turn and headed back down the hill to Hyperion, which would take them to Sunset, then Wilcox, and finally to Hollywood Station.

Tully Jarsdel rolled down the passenger window and took in the cool January breeze. They went around a curve, and he caught a brief view of the city. His city. There was the Vista Theatre and Children's Hospital and, far off, the spire of the Capitol Records building.

I'm here, and I'll make it right, he'd told Brahma. Yes, it had been a foolish promise, the kind you make without knowing what the terms really are.

But still, he'd made it. And now he made it again. And for a little while, at least, he felt some peace.

READING GROUP GUIDE

1. When Dustin Sparks—a special effects professional—discovers the victim's body, he notices that it resembles some of his work in horror films. Do you think graphic violence in movies can affect how we perceive reality? Why or why not?

2. Jarsdel found his career as a history professor unendurable and left his field to join the police force. What do you think inspired his career change? Do you think he made the correct decision?

3. Describe the relationship between Jarsdel and his parents. Why is there so much tension between them? Do you think it's fair for his parents to be resentful of his career choice?

4. What do you think of Jarsdel and Morales's dynamic? Do you think they work well together? If you were a detective, who would you choose as your partner? Why?

5.   In what ways does Jarsdel's academic background influence his police work? Is his background always helpful, or does it get in the way of the investigation?

6.   Aleena and Jarsdel debate the existence of true evil—Aleena claims that people do bad things to each other because of their circumstances, and Jarsdel believes that sometimes a person's 'badness' is inherent. Which side do you agree with? Are all people capable of evil?

7.   What do you make of someone like Jeff Dinan? Do you think he's a good person?

8.   Would working a disturbing case like this make you question your notions of good and evil? Do you think it's possible to investigate violent crimes without becoming jaded?

9.   What kinds of things do you associate with modern-day Hollywood? Do you agree with Stevens that the magic of old Hollywood has been lost?

10.   Think about someone like the Dog Catcher, who doesn't physically hurt people but still acts maliciously and with the intent to harm. Why does he do the things he does? Is he a bad person? Is he as bad as someone like Stevens?

11.   What do all of Stevens's victims have in common? Why does he target them?

12.   At the end of the book Jarsdel is conflicted about his place in the Hollywood Homicide, though he ultimately decides to keep his job. Why do you think he decides to stay? Did he make the right decision?

13. We are taught to not repeat the mistakes of the past, but Stevens replicates a killing device from ancient Greece. Discuss the consequences of venerating history, rather than using it as a warning. What are the dangers of trying to bring the past to life? Are there any benefits to it?

A CONVERSATION
WITH THE AUTHOR

The setting in this story is crucial to the development of the plot. What is it about Hollywood that made you choose to feature it so prominently in the book?

Hollywood is where I grew up, and it's strange—I was always conscious of its otherworldliness, even when I was very young. It's wild when you're raised in a place where it's the adults who are always playing make-believe. I don't just mean professional actors, who actually comprise a very small percentage of the population. I'm talking about the poor guy they got playing Doc Brown running around Universal Studios, or the costumed characters in front of the Chinese Theater. Countless others. Writers and directors and producers, set designers and FX crews, they dedicate their lives to telling stories. Stories are what built that town. And it's true—every now and then you do have that giddy experience of watching a film and then running into one of the actors at the grocery store. I can't describe what a thrill that is when you're a little boy obsessed with movies. So I always felt like it was a special, magical place—much like growing up in a circus, I imagine.

But you see the frayed edges too, and you see what happens when people run out of money or realize they've gotten too old, that what they came all the way out there for probably isn't going to work out.

The slowly dawning horror that they're going to have to admit that everyone who told them they were crazy for going to Hollywood was *right*. It's uniquely painful. Insult to injury. If you want to become a doctor and for whatever reason it just doesn't come together, nobody calls you an idiot. But you try and fail in the entertainment industry, and it's "What were you thinking? What made *you* think you were so special?"

Ever had one of those dreams that suddenly slides into a nightmare, without warning? Hollywood's just like that sometimes, and I thought it was the perfect place to set a story about desire, regret, and death.

The story is chock-full of details about forensics, human anatomy, police procedures, history, and philosophy. What was your research process like?

Researching for a debut novel is very tough, because you don't have any credibility. Most of the people you call up aren't going to get back to you, and I hit a lot of dead ends. I devoured every book on the subject I could find, including textbooks written for homicide investigators. I really wanted the story to feel authentic, and Det. Rick Jackson was gracious enough to look over the finished manuscript, telling me what I could fudge on and what I couldn't.

Most of the hands-on research I did was in the Contra Costa Sheriff's Citizens Academy, which is a kind of crash course in each branch of the department, from investigations to aerial pursuits to forensics. They conduct it for free as a way of showing interested civilians what police work is like. I actually plan on retaking it so I can stay current. It's terrific fun, but it's sobering too, like the day we learned vehicle stops. One of the deputies was playing the guy I'm supposed to pull over, and he comes stumbling out of the car, acting drunk, waving his hands around. They've given me a gun loaded with Siminutions, which are kind of like paintballs, but you fire them from a standard weapon, and you get the report and everything, the gun cycling like it normally would if you were using live ammo. I tell the guy to calm down, and he doesn't. We're playacting, and I feel a little silly, ordering him around. It's like a bad improv scene, me spouting all these stock cop lines I learned from TV. But then suddenly he whips out a black cell phone and thrusts it in my direction. And I shoot him, and the projectile hits him in the chest and he goes down. A few seconds pass before the deputy gets up and the next student takes my place, but I'm a little shaken by the whole thing. We were in broad daylight in the middle of a sheriffs' training facility—a controlled, safe situation, and I shot him. I thought, what if this had been real? What if this had happened at night, on the side of a deserted highway? I would've just killed a man for pointing a phone at me, and I'd have to live with that decision forever. I knew right then I wasn't cut out to make those kinds of decisions, that crime writing was as close to the real thing as I wanted to get. And it gave me a whole new respect for the law enforcement pros who face that situation on a regular basis.

With his background in academia, Jarsdel isn't a conventional detective. When you were creating his character, why did you choose to make him a historian?

The first reason had to do with practicality. I wanted him to be intelligent but not street-smart. And if he wasn't street-smart, he still had to have something that would make him special or set him apart. A scientific expertise might have worked, but as much as I love science I can't write about it with much authority. History on the other hand is my favorite subject to teach, and I felt at home creating a character who'd been an adjunct classics professor. It informs his worldview, his philosophy. It's also a convenient way to have him call forward an obscure bit of knowledge, hopefully without the audience asking why he would know that. And when I give some background on LA, maybe it seems like it's coming from him instead of me, which can make that kind of stuff feel a little less expository.

The second reason is because I deliberately asked myself, before I put a single word down on paper, what I could contribute to the genre of detective fiction. I knew I couldn't pull off a tough, alpha-wolf detective. It's been done too well, and by writers who really know that voice and can generate it authentically. Michael Connelly had worked for years as crime reporter before he published *The Black Echo*. When he writes Harry Bosch, you feel the weight of that character, can tell it's been earned from soaking up that world. I needed a way to make my perspective as an outsider work for me, not against me. I felt Jarsdel could offer a mystery lover a fresh perspective on the genre, allowing both me *and* the reader a way into the material that hadn't been tried before.

The Dog Catcher subplot is a surprisingly disturbing one—what made you include it in the narrative?

I enjoy stories that have a secondary mystery for the detective to solve. It offers a break from the main thread and allows you to discover things about the character, so I knew it was something I wanted to do in my own book. What was most important to me was that the sub-plot be relevant to Jarsdel's journey. The crime had to be repugnant to him on every level—spiteful, cruel, selfish, absolutely wicked. Because I knew he wasn't going to end up with Aleena at the end of the story, I had to give him a victory, something he could exit with and still have his head up high.

I love dogs, just adore them. I remember the incredible pain I felt when we lost our dog a few years back to bone cancer. One day she was fine, then it was downhill so fast, almost as if the diagnosis itself made her sicker.

Storytelling has to begin with what's compelling to the writer. If it doesn't move the writer, it's definitely not going to move the reader. Add to that my general disposition, which is unfortunately a *what if* personality. I torment myself with *what if* scenarios about things going wrong in my life—ruining my career, disgracing my family, ending up in prison. And since you can't prove a negative, no one can definitively tell me my fears are completely groundless, right? It's awful, but at least with writing, I can turn that mechanism loose.

I take an incident like my dog dying, and I think how much worse it would have been if it'd been caused by a malicious act instead of a disease. Then I compound that, think how much worse *that* would be if it occurred during a special, happy event, like a wedding. What would the fallout be? Would the marriage survive after getting started with a tragedy? I live with those kinds of *what if* questions, and they drive the darker sides of my fiction.

A plot like this one twists and turns, keeping the readers on their toes. How did you go about writing this story? Was it difficult to keep track of the plot points, or did everything fall into place?

My original story was much more of a straight line and not as dynamic. Both my agent and editor suggested places to weave in red herrings and kick up the pacing, which resulted in a substantially stronger plot. It was a long process, with several drafts. When you fix something, it often causes a continuity problem elsewhere, and you might spend whole workdays just tweaking timeline issues. It was a learn-as-you-go situation, and there were certainly many ways I could've worked smarter. With the second book in the series, I used a more efficient system where I'd keep track of plot points using scene numbers and a character manifest—similar to how you'd write out a beat sheet for a screenplay.

What books are you reading these days?

I'm on the second of Anthony Horowitz's *Daniel Hawthorne* series. It's a bold concept, with Horowitz writing in first-person as himself, and he's been asked by this brilliant but socially awkward detective to shadow him and document his cases. It's a new take on the Watson-Holmes paradigm, with very funny, fourth-wall-breaking details about Horowitz's life as a novelist and screenwriter. And he's a master of the genre, so the mysteries themselves are extremely satisfying.

In nonfiction, I just finished *Caesar's Last Breath*, by Sam Keane. It's all about the gases that make up our air—their discovery, their uses and misuses by humankind. You get the history of anesthesia, dynamite, the steam engine. Keane's one of the best contemporary science writers, and the book is pure pleasure.

I'd say the standout for me this year—the one that got inside my head and wouldn't let go—was *The Radium Girls*, by Kate Moore. It's the definitive account of the workers—young women and teenaged girls—hired to paint luminous radium dials in the '20s. The companies tell them the material's harmless, and the stuff is all over them every day—in their hair, in their mouths from pointing the brushes. It's heartbreaking, absolutely ghastly what happened to them. But then you learn the things they achieved for labor rights, how they changed the country, and you can't believe you haven't heard about these people before. It's the kind of book that makes you wonder why certain stories are included in the academic canon and others aren't, and who gets to decide what's significant. It's a knockout read on every level, and Moore's prose is just gorgeous.

ACKNOWLEDGMENTS

I couldn't have written *One Day You'll Burn* without the help of the Los Angeles Police Department, in particular two detectives from Robbery-Homicide Division. The first, Mitzi Roberts, graciously corresponded with me during the research phase of the book, providing invaluable technical assistance. The second, Rick Jackson, retired to a town in the East Bay only a few miles from where I live. If I were a sports writer, that'd about be the equivalent of Nolan Ryan moving in next door. After a mutual friend introduced us, Detective Jackson agreed to talk to me, ultimately answering any questions I had about what it was like being a murder cop. Here's this legend, a guy who's put away some of the most brutal killers in the state's history, a guy who appears as himself in half a dozen Michael Connelly books, and he's talking shop with me over lunch. I soon discover he's also one of the kindest, most giving people I've ever met and that we also share a passion for old movies. A great gift of writing is getting to meet your heroes and, every now and then, earning the privilege of becoming their friend.

The Contra Costa Sheriff's Department, including Sheriff David O. Livingston and the extraordinary team behind his Citizens' Academy, were instrumental in helping me gain a fuller understanding of police procedure. Jonathan Gray, MD, proved himself not only a remarkably generous physician but also a most patient brother-in-law for his willingness in answering my inexhaustible stream of grisly hypothetical questions. Any error in this manuscript, whether in regard to law enforcement or medicine or anything else, is entirely my own.

I'm forever indebted to Eve Attermann of William Morris Endeavor. There are authors, unknown authors, and unpublished unknown authors. I was firmly among the last category, unless you count my theater reviews, which had appeared in the sort of free local papers you get at the car wash. Ms. Attermann took a big chance on me, spending a year helping shape my manuscript before submitting it to publishers. The book wouldn't have gone anywhere without her.

I can't imagine there are many editors out there like Anna Michels, whose coruscating literary intellect is equally matched by imagination and love for story. She immediately understood the material and the world I was trying to create and exactly where to push for changes. Draft after draft, each clunky bit of syntax or lapse in logic or facile story point fell away, and what remained was the book I'd always wanted to write. What an impossibly big gift that is, and one for which she'll always have my deepest gratitude.

The book's copy editor, Sabrina Baskey, did far more than root out typos and formatting problems—fact-checking the entire manuscript and catching exactly the kinds of errors that would've driven me crazy later on. She even looked at maps of LA to make sure I had my characters walking in the right direction.

I'd like to give special thanks to the extraordinary folks at Sourcebooks responsible for the production and release of *One Day You'll Burn*. These include Beth Deveny, Kaitlyn Kennedy, and Kirsten Wenum. That beautiful cover is the work of art director Adrienne Krogh and artist J Dennis.

My dear wife, Anna, who stuck with me through all the years "House Magician" appeared on my nametag, deserves something in addition to my appreciation. Canonization, perhaps? And since this is going in the back of a crime novel, I can't get too mushy, but to Tenzel and Ahalya, just know that everything has more meaning now that you're here.

Enormous thanks also go to Dr. Carol Conner, Dr. Paul Puri, Haley Heidemann, Jessica Moss, Thomas Cooney, Lysley Tenorio, Dan Richland, Terry Johnson, Vince D'Assis, Ivy Summers, Ellen Evans, Annie Potts, Jeff Victor, Dr. Tim Plax, and Dr. Pat Kearney. Sune Rose-Wagner and Sharin Foo of the Raveonettes provided much of the soundtrack as I wrote this book. In many ways, "Ode to LA" gave me that initial spark, that essential little impulse that made me want to tell a story about the city I love. If you haven't heard it, I recommend you turn down the lights, get comfortable—preferably with three fingers of good scotch at your side—and put it on. You'll see what I mean.

Finally, to Stephen King—we've never met, but my life changed when I picked up *Firestarter* the summer I turned ten. For showing me what books could do and for taking me on all those wondrous adventures, thank you.

ABOUT THE AUTHOR

Joseph Schneider lives with his wife and two children in California. His professional affiliations include The Magic Castle and the Imperial Society of Teachers of Dancing. *One Day You'll Burn* is his debut novel.